COBRA
OUTLAW
COBRA REBELLION, BOOK TWO

TIMOTHY ZAHN

COBRA OUTLAW

Copyright © 2015 by Timothy Zahn

A Baen Books Original

Baen Publishing Enterprises
P.O. Box 1403
Riverdale, NY 10471
www.baen.com

ISBN: 978-1-4767-8143-3

Cover art by Dave Seeley
Cover art model by John Douglass

First Baen mass market paperback printing, May 2016

Library of Congress Control Number: 2014043648

Distributed by Simon & Schuster
1230 Avenue of the Americas
New York, NY 10020

Pages by Joy Freeman (www.pagesbyjoy.com)
Printed in the United States of America

MEAN THINGS COME IN SMALL PACKAGES

They were much smaller than the monster Merrick had fought back in Ukuthi's makeshift arena on Qasama, more compact in both length and girth. They also seemed less armored, and with smaller scales. But they had the same wide, half-open mouths and the same razor-sharp teeth.

And they were moving to the kill.

Merrick's first instinct was to swivel up onto his right leg and fire a blast from his anti-armor laser down each of those gaping mouths. Smaller and less armored or not, he'd nearly been killed by the jormungand Ukuthi had sent after him. Trying to play thorn-mace games against these things would be suicidally stupid.

An instant later, though, the inevitable consequences of such a move flooded in on him. He wouldn't be able to leave Kjoic alive and free, not after such a revelation.

Anya had warned him earlier that he might have to kill the Troft, and Merrick had pretended that he was ready and willing to do so. But he wasn't. Certainly not now; probably not ever.

Besides which, Kjoic still represented their best chance of getting access to the local Drim records, which meant that personal ethics and pragmatism were in alignment on this one. Merrick couldn't afford to let Kjoic die, either by the jormungands or by his own hand. There had to be some other way to get out of this.

He was still trying to come up with a plan when Kjoic opened fire.

COBRA
OUTLAW

CHAPTER ONE

It had been a long day, and a very long night, and the last thing Lorne Moreau Broom had expected to be doing at this hour was watching the sun rise over DeVegas province.

But as he'd long ago learned, life didn't always work out the way you expected.

It was a beautiful sunrise, too. Even seen through weary, half-lidded eyes. Often the early-morning sky in this part of Aventine's expansion region was obscured by low layers of stratus clouds or lingering banks of nighttime fog. But today there were only a few high wisps of red and pink cirrus to catch the growing light. It was as if the sun itself was curious to see the extent of the devastation that DeVegas province had absorbed in a single day.

A single, horrible, unbelievable day.

A private factory commandeered by a colonel of the Dominion of Man and his Marines. Three Cobras dead in a battle deliberately instigated by that same colonel. The rest of the province's Cobras effectively enslaved under threat of instant death.

And Lorne's father Paul spirited away for a terrible and utterly pointless interrogation that could lead to his death.

But the sunrise *was* beautiful.

Lorne rubbed at his eyes, his thoughts skidding like a bug on ice. Just because his brain refused sleep, he thought bitterly, didn't mean it was actually functional.

But it had better get functional. *He* had better get functional. And fast.

He gave the rising sun one last look. Then, mindful of the possibility that even a thick sheet of falling water might not completely shield him from the Dominion's infrared detectors, he backed away and slipped into one of the narrow crevices that scarred the rock behind Braided Falls.

The mayor of Bitter Creek, Mary McDougal, had described the open area behind the falls as little more than an extra-deep indentation in the rock. Badj Werle, one of Lorne's fellow Cobras, had over the years occasionally mentioned a small cave he and other teens had found back in the day.

Maybe Badj had been hedging the truth. Maybe McDougal truly thought that was all that was here.

Or maybe during the month that Aventine had been under Troft occupation the DeVegas Cobras had turned a teenagers' private hangout into a full-blown hidden fortress.

Lorne's mother Jin was still asleep on the cot he'd set up for her earlier from a stack tucked away in a side chamber. But it was a restless sleep, Lorne saw as he keyed in his optical enhancers' infrared setting.

Her shoulders and legs were moving beneath the blankets, and as he also keyed in his telescopics he could see that her lips and throat were twitching as well. Another nightmare, probably, like the one that had accompanied the moaning and muttering that had startled Lorne awake half an hour ago.

Still, even nightmare-wracked sleep qualified as sleep. If she didn't twitch herself awake, he decided, it would be best to let her be. Keying back the telescopics but leaving the infrareds on, he headed quietly toward the small kitchenette setup at the back of the cave.

Not quietly enough. He'd gone barely five meters when Jin abruptly jerked and sat bolt upright, her eyes wide, her hands curled into fingertip laser firing positions.

"It's okay, Mom," Lorne said quickly. "It's okay."

For a few seconds she held the pose, her eyes tracking around the cave, her brain apparently still struggling to extricate itself from her latest nightmare. Her face cleared, then tightened again as the real-life memories rolled over the fading dream images. Her hands opened, and her upper body sagged with weariness. "I'm sorry," she murmured.

"It's okay," Lorne said again. "Are you hungry? Can I get you something?"

"No," Jin said. "Thank you." She ran her hands briefly through her hair. "Did I wake you?"

"Not a problem," Lorne said. "I wanted to get up and check the perimeter anyway."

She exhaled a tired sigh. "Check the perimeter. It sounds so military."

"I suppose," Lorne said. In fact, that hadn't even occurred to him until she said it. Had he really been under military rule long enough for him to become accustomed to that way of thinking and talking? Apparently so. "I'm afraid military procedure is the order of the day right now."

"I know," Jin said. "But it shouldn't be. Not now. Not here." She looked toward the front wall of the cave. "Why is this happening, Lorne? We're five useless worlds in the middle of nowhere. What can the Dominion possibly want that's worth this much trouble?"

"I wish I knew," Lorne said. "Don't worry, we'll figure it out. And then we'll find a way out of it."

"Maybe," she murmured. "But not before . . ." She left the sentence unfinished.

Lorne felt his stomach tighten. Not before Commodore Santores and Captain Lij Tulu used their damned MindsEye brain sifter on his father. "Dad'll be all right," he said as soothingly as he could. "Santores said the thing was safe as long as they didn't rush the procedure."

"I know what he *said*," Jin countered. "You think he wouldn't lie through his teeth to get what he wanted?"

Lorne scowled. Of *course* Santores would lie. The Dominion wanted to find Qasama. Wanted it desperately. Santores would say whatever he thought necessary to get him the planet's location. "I know," he said. "But remember that Santores still has to work with Chintawa, and Chintawa's so far tried to keep our family on the ground and out of Dominion hands."

"He was trying up until yesterday," Jin pointed out grimly. "Who knows what he's thinking and doing today?"

"I don't think he'd abandon us just because of some tricked-out fake riot," Lorne said. "But you're right.

We need to know what's going on if we're going to come up with a plan."

"How?" Jin asked. "We can't use comms or radios. If we want to talk to anyone, we'll have to go there in person."

"Going downriver into Archway worked last night," Lorne reminded her. "We might be able to get away with it again."

"I wouldn't count on it," Jin warned. "Colonel Reivaro may be an arrogant bastard, but he's not stupid. If he hasn't already figured out the back door you used, he will soon."

"Probably," Lorne conceded. "We'll just have to find another way to—"

"Company," Jin interrupted, throwing off her blankets and jabbing a finger toward the small display at the front of the cave.

"On it," Lorne said, keying in his telescopics again as he jogged across the uneven floor.

The telescopics were a waste of time, he quickly discovered. The display was really nothing more than an extra-large peephole, a handful of fiber-optic lines that had been worked through a small gap in the wall. Enlarging the low-resolution image did nothing to genuinely enhance it.

Not that there was much to see regardless. The other end of the optics was pointed through the only real gap in the flowing water, a spot about six meters down from the top where jutting rock formations funneled and twisted the water to either side, creating the downstream interweaving that had given the falls their name. A meter and a half below the gap was a narrow ledge running behind the water that had lured daring teenagers throughout the years, and which now offered access to the hidden cave.

But while the gap might provide a view downriver, the flowing whitewater on either side of it severely restricted that view. About all anyone could see from the ledge—or from inside via the optics—was the river itself plus five to ten meters of bank on either side.

Which meant that all Lorne could really see was that an aircar had come into view and was settling to the ground near one of the eddy pools thirty meters downriver from the base of the falls.

He leaned close to the image, trying to sort through the visual confusion created by the shifting pattern of light and shadow thrown by the rising sun. As near as he could tell, the vehicle was a typical Aventinian two-seater. The door opened and a figure climbed out, then reached back in and retrieved a small bag, a stool, and a long, slender pole. He set the stool on the ground beside the eddy pool, sat down, and flicked the pole toward the water.

"I think it's Jake Sedgley," Lorne said, turning to face his mother. "He flies out here twice a week to fish. He's loud and opinionated, but mostly harmless."

"Opinionated enough not to have any friends?" Jin asked as she again pointed to the display.

Lorne turned back. Sure enough, another aircar had appeared, this one arrowing out of the sky like an avenging hawk straight toward Sedgley.

And this aircar was definitely *not* Aventinian.

"Watch him," Lorne ordered, hurrying across to the cave entrance. There was a large, wedge-shaped block of stone that had been standing just inside the cave when Lorne arrived yesterday, sized and shaped to fit snugly into the tunnel and disguise it as just another of the cliff face's many shallow crevices. He got a grip on the plug and eased it into position, hearing the faint whine as his servos took the stone's two-hundred-plus-kilogram weight. He made sure the plug completely filled the gap, then headed back toward his mother. "What's happening?" he called softly.

"We've got two men talking to your fisherman," Jin said. "Their faces are covered, but I think they're Dominion Marines."

"Oh, they're Marines, all right," Lorne said sourly as he came up beside her. The burgundy-black outfits were highly distinctive, as were the close-fitting helmets both men were wearing. "Interesting that they're wearing their helmets in broad daylight. I assumed that was mostly for night-vision capability."

"Maybe your midnight visit rattled Reivaro more than you thought," Jin suggested. "Does Sedgley always gesture that wildly?"

"He does tend to get expressive when he's making a point," Lorne said, frowning. She was right, though. The man's arms and hands were doing an awful lot of waving. Even for Sedgley.

"He seems pretty worked up," Jin murmured. "I wonder if he knows we're here."

"No idea," Lorne said. "Mayor McDougal said the Cobras used this cave during the Troft occupation, but I don't know how many civilians were involved with them."

With a particularly expressive flourish Sedgley plopped himself back down onto his stool. Pulling a knife from a belt sheath, he jammed the tip into the ground beside him. Then, with a final glare at the two Marines standing over him, he returned his attention to his fishing.

Lorne frowned. "Did you see that?"

"See what?" his mother asked. "Looks like they're leaving."

The Marines were leaving, all right, walking behind Sedgley and heading for their aircar. "I meant what Sedgley did with his knife," Lorne said, watching the Marines closely for any signs of last-minute trouble. "People don't stick their knives into the ground like that around here. Not a good knife, anyway. Definitely not right beside a river. Too many stones just under the dirt."

"So he was making a point," Jin said slowly. "But was that point to them, or to us?"

"Good question," Lorne agreed as he watched the Marines' aircar head into the sky. "Assuming it was to us, what could it mean?"

"Go to ground, maybe?" Jin suggested. "Or *stay* gone to ground?"

"Or stab them right where they live," Lorne countered. "That's the problem. It could mean pretty much—"

"Wait a second," Jin said. "What's he doing now?"

Lorne frowned at the display. Sedgley had pulled the knife from the ground and wiped the dirt off against his leg. He looked in the direction the Marines had gone, balancing the knife on his finger and idly seesawing it back and forth. The movement slowed to a halt, the knife tip ending up pointing downward at an angle.

Pointing directly at the spot where his fishing line disappeared into the water.

Sedgley held the pose a couple of seconds, then

began seesawing the knife again. He paused one more time, the knife again pointing at the fishing line. Then he flipped the knife back over and returned it to its sheath. Readjusting himself on his stool, he threw one more look at the sky and settled back to his fishing.

"He wants you in the river," Jin murmured.

"So it would seem," Lorne agreed. "Keep an eye on him while I get the scuba gear."

The climb down the cliff behind Braided Falls was as tricky as it had been the night before, even given the advantage of doing it in broad daylight this time instead of in total midnight darkness. The water in the river, once he reached it, was also every bit as cold as he'd expected.

But it was worth it when he finally worked his way to the eddy pool where Sedgley's baited hook was drifting in the low current and saw the small plastic sphere attached to the lead sinker.

He thought about opening the sphere right there and checking out the contents, on the off chance that the message required him to make direct contact with the fisherman. But as much as he hated the thought of having to turn around and make this underwater trek again, he was even less interested in taking the risk that whoever was at the other end of this particular communications had neglected to make his communiqué waterproof.

And so he carefully detached the sphere from the sinker, gave two gentle tugs on the line to let Sedgley know the package had been picked up, and headed back upstream.

Without his Cobra servos, he would never have made it against the current or up the cliff. Even with them he felt like an overheated aircar by the time he finally dragged himself through the crevice and into the cave.

"What happened?" his mother asked as she maneuvered the stone plug back into place.

"You were right," Lorne said, pulling the ball from inside his scuba suit and lobbing it over to her. "Can you figure out how to get it open? I need to get a towel."

Jin was sitting on the edge of her cot, peering at an unfolded piece of paper, when he rejoined her, dressed in dry clothes and only shivering a little. "What does it say?" he asked.

"I don't know," she said, handing him the paper. "You tell me."

Frowning, Lorne read the message. It was very short. *Croaker's, one hour after Anvil-rise. Kicker.*

"I'd like to hope it was more understandable before those drops of water got to it," Jin said.

"I don't think the water did much one way or the other," Lorne said, frowning a little more. "Okay. *Kicker* is easy. That's Brandeis Pierce, one of the Cobras."

"You know him?"

"A little," Lorne said. "Not as well as I do Badj or Dill. He's only been in DeVegas a few months, and most of that time he's been stationed at Smith's Forge. I don't know why they chose him for the contact."

"Maybe *because* you don't know him well," Jin suggested. "Reivaro may be keeping a close eye on the people you're closest to."

"I suppose that makes sense," Lorne conceded. "*Croakers*, I'm guessing, is a spot along the Pashington River near the Deuel Center where the spring frogs drive us all crazy."

"You sure?" Jin asked. "That apostrophe makes it look more like a business or bar or something."

"Which I'm sure was deliberate," Lorne said. "The Crogers are a huge family over in Willaway. If Reivaro intercepted the note and assumed a hasty misspelling, he could search forever without finding which *Crogers* it was talking about."

"Okay," Jin said, still sounding doubtful. "Far-fetched, but I played sillier word games when I was young. Which leads us to Anvil-rise. I assume he's talking about the constellation?"

"That's certainly the obvious reference," Lorne said, gazing at the note. "This time of year, it hits the horizon about three in the morning. Question is, was *obvious* what Kicker was going for?"

"You know of some other anvil in Archway or the Deuel Center?" Jin asked. "Especially an anvil that gets raised from an underground storage compartment or something?"

"Nothing that I—wait a second," Lorne interrupted himself as a sudden bizarre thought occurred to him. "Did you ever hear of a show called *Anne Villager*?"

"I don't think so."

"It's a paranormal psychological thriller drama mish-mash," Lorne said. "Locally produced in Archway. So cheesy that no one admits to watching it, but pretty much everyone does. Anyway, there's a line in the opening about Anne's murder, and how she rose for vengeance at the stroke of midnight."

"And . . . ?"

"Don't you see?" Lorne said, starting to feel foolish for even bringing it up. "Anne—Vil—rising?"

For a long, painful moment his mother was silent.

Then, she tilted her head thoughtfully. "And you say no one admits to watching it?"

"No one older than twelve, anyway," Lorne said. "What do you think?"

Jin gave a little shrug. "I think it's worth trying. As you said, we can't just sit here wondering what's happening out there. So an hour after midnight?"

"Right," Lorne said, trying to stifle his own misgivings. Leaving the cave would be a risk, all right. A big one. But it had to be tried.

Besides, even if the Marines caught him, he was sure that he hadn't seen enough of Warrior's navigational readings on the trip to Qasama for them to pull the planet's location from his mind. He was almost positive.

"For now, we should get some rest," Jin broke into his thoughts. "And probably some food."

"Right." Lorne looked around the cave. "And we might want to straighten up a little, too. I'd hate for any new allies we pick up to think we keep a messy hideout."

CHAPTER TWO

"I understand your concerns, Colonel Reivaro," Governor-General Chintawa said, his voice heavy with the seriousness of the situation, and—Paul Broom suspected—more than a little fatigue. Sunrise, in Paul's opinion, was way too early for this sort of confrontation, and from the circles under Chintawa's eyes it looked like he was of much the same mind. "But you also have to understand ours," Chintawa continued. "Incidents involving the Broom family always seem to create repercussions far beyond the family's political, economic, or social standing."

Reivaro snorted. "Please," he said contemptuously. "Let's dispense with the dramatics, shall we?"

Paul had seldom felt less like smiling than he did right now. Even so, he felt a bitter-edged smile tweak at his lips. After the deliberately choreographed slaughter at Archway that had led to Paul's arrest, Reivaro was the last person who should be complaining about dramatics.

13

Still, he could understand the colonel's frustration. From the moment the Marines had ushered Paul into their aircar, it had been clear that Reivaro had expected them to escort him to Capitalia, transfer him to a Dominion landing shuttle, and take him directly to the orbiting warship *Algonquin*, where Captain Lij Tulu was no doubt eagerly waiting to put their new prisoner under the MindsEye brain sifter.

Only it hadn't worked out that way. The party had reached the Dome only to discover that Governor-General Chintawa had ordered the Dominion landing shuttles locked down, with Cobra guards on hand to ensure the order was obeyed.

There'd been some brief and heated discussions, along with some unsubtle reminders about what Marine combat-suit firepower could do to Cobras. But it was clear that neither side wanted a repeat of the Archway confrontation, and so Paul had instead been put into one of the Dome's holding cells—under Cobra *and* Dominion guard—while the whole thing was sorted out.

Apparently, Chintawa wasn't ready to give him up. At least, not without a fight.

Now, with the sun peeking over the eastern horizon, the two sides had apparently finished their preliminary sparring and were ready to go head-to-head with their respective big guns.

It was an impressive lineup. On Reivaro's side were Commodore Santores and Captain Lij Tulu, seated at one end of the long assembly table, both officers looking far more alert and well-rested than anyone had any business looking at this hour. On Chintawa's side were Eion Yates, DeVegas province's premier industrialist and one of its major economic and political powerhouses, along with Cobra Commandant Yoshio Ishikuma, the commander of Paul's son Lorne's district. The thick red insignia neckband visible above Ishikuma's collar was a heart-rending reminder of yesterday's slaughter and its aftermath.

Seated beside Ishikuma, to Paul's mild surprise—

"Dramatics aren't the issue here, Colonel," Nissa Gendreves spoke up, her voice coldly professional. Like the two senior Dominion officers, she looked far more awake than she ought to. "The issue is that your charge against Cobra Broom is completely bogus. Our charge isn't."

For a moment Reivaro seemed taken aback. Apparently, he'd expected more polite sparring or at least a thicker layer of diplomacy.

But he recovered quickly. "And you know this from your vast experience with both political and criminal matters?" he inquired, just as frostily.

He had a point. Barely three months ago Gendreves had been a lowly intern, one of the governor-general's assistants, with no more power, knowledge, or experience than anyone else in a similar position. But the Troft invasion, along with having been in the wrong place at the wrong time, had abruptly catapulted her into a position power and visibility.

She'd taken that unexpected power seriously. So seriously that when Paul and Jin talked Governor Uy of Caelian into sending the prototype Cobra factory code-named Isis to Qasama instead of keeping it on Caelian she'd charged the whole bunch of them with treason.

Given the unarguable success of Uy's decision in ending the brief war with the invading Trofts, the whole issue should have quietly faded away. Unfortunately, there was a sizeable faction of the Cobra Worlds' governors and syndics who had never liked having Cobras around, and the war had done nothing to change their minds. They'd seized on Gendreves and her crusade against the Brooms, using her as a lever with which to push their own agenda.

Clearly, the last thing any of that group wanted was for Paul to be whisked up to one of the Dominion ships where he would no longer be a visible symbol for their cause. Just as clearly, none of them was interested in standing publicly against Santores and the Dominion. Hence, they'd tossed Gendreves to the wolves.

Or more likely, Paul thought cynically, they'd simply encouraged her to volunteer.

Still, maybe they were smarter than he gave them credit for. Even Chintawa was showing signs of intimidation in the presence of his high-ranking visitors. Gendreves wasn't. Maybe she was here for the simple reason that she really *was* the right person for the job. "I know it from a careful reading of Cobra Worlds law and my own observations," she countered.

"Of course," Reivaro said. "Unfortunately for you, the law you've been reading is obsolete. Dominion law takes precedence." He raised his eyebrows. "And by Dominion law Cobra Broom's actions on Caelian do not constitute treason."

Gendreves gave a little snort. "With all due respect, Colonel, that's ridiculous. Cobra Broom gave highly secret technology to—"

"Secret technology that's a century old," Reivaro interrupted. "No, Ms. Gendreves. Cobra Broom's alleged treason all those weeks ago is moot. What we're dealing with now is his involvement in yesterday's near-riot in Archway."

"There wasn't any near-riot," Yates spoke up, "since we're talking about law and observations. I was there. I saw it. Furthermore, what *did* happen was instigated by your own men."

"My men reacted to an overt threat that arose from the legal and proper performance of their duties," Reivaro countered. "It's unarguable that Cobra Broom was heavily involved in that incident. What's less clear is his involvement in other, more covert actions."

"If you're referring to the damage to my plant," Yates said bitterly, "that one's also roosting squarely on your porch railing. I warned your people—my *techs* warned your people—"

"We'll get to acts of sabotage later," Reivaro cut him off. "I'm referring to the sudden departure of Cobra Broom's daughter Jody from Aventine five days ago." He sent a dark look at Paul. "And the fact that she has now disappeared."

With an effort, Paul kept his face expressionless. Jody wasn't exactly missing—she'd simply slipped off Aventine and gone to the Hoibie homeworld in an attempt to stay out of Santores's hands.

Or at least that was what Santores had told Jin. Was the Dominion suddenly changing its story?

"Cobra Broom?" Reivaro prompted.

Paul held his gaze a moment, then let his eyes sweep across the table. Gendreves, looking hard and determined. Yates, looking impatient. Chintawa, looking tense and unhappy. Santores—

Santores, looking at everyone except Paul. Looking very intently.

And abruptly, Paul understood. This farce of a hearing wasn't about him at all. Something Jody had done had stirred up the Dominion hornets' nest, and Santores had staged this confrontation in hopes of finding out whether Chintawa and Ishikuma—and possibly Paul himself—were also involved. "Whatever Jody did, she did on her own," he said. "Neither the governor-general or anyone else outside our family knew anything about it. Or, I dare say, knows anything about it now."

Santores shifted his gaze to Paul, and for a moment the two men locked eyes. Then, Santores inclined his head. "So it would seem," he said. "In that case, I see no point in continuing."

"Unless you'd like to tell us what my daughter has done to annoy you," Paul offered. "I'm sure everyone here would be interested in hearing about it."

"Perhaps later," Santores said. "Governor-General Chintawa, I hereby exercise my right and duty under the Dominion of Man Statutes of Martial Law to take custody of Cobra Paul Broom."

"You have no such authority," Gendreves insisted before Chintawa could respond. "No declaration of martial law has been made."

"You're mistaken, Ms. Gendreves," Santores said. "Colonel Reivaro declared that state in Archway in response to the incident."

"An incident he himself provoked."

"In the performance of his duties."

Gendreves took a deep breath. "Commodore Santores—"

"Please," Paul said. "You can see his mind is made up. Do we really want a second Archway?"

Gendreves threw a furious glare at him. "No one asked you—"

"Enough," Chintawa said.

Gendreves sputtered into silence. Chintawa eyed Paul for a moment, then looked at the Cobras standing guard at the door. His eyes flicked almost unwillingly to Ishikuma and the loyalty collar around the commandant's neck. "Cobra Broom is correct," he said. "None of us wants that."

Gendreves opened her mouth to speak. Chintawa gave her another look, and she closed it again.

"Thank you, Governor-General." Santores gestured to the Marines behind Paul. "Take him to my landing shuttle."

One of the Marines took Paul's arm. Paul shrugged off the other's hand and remained seated. "I'd like some assurance that you'll tell me about my daughter on the way."

The Marine grabbed Paul's arm again, this time in a much tighter grip. Santores made a small gesture, and he reluctantly released his hold. "I'll tell you what I know," the commodore said. "I'm afraid it isn't much." He inclined his head microscopically. "My word on that."

"Thank you." Paul stood up. "Governor-General; Commandant Ishikuma; Mr. Yates." Deliberately, he forced himself to look at Gendreves. "Ms. Gendreves."

Ten minutes later, the Dominion shuttle lifted from the Dome's private landing terrace and headed into the sky. Two minutes after that, Santores stepped into the small, windowless compartment where Paul and his guards had been crammed, dismissed the Marines, and sat down facing his prisoner. "I appreciate you not making a fuss back there in the Dome," the commodore said. "Though of course I know why you did it."

"Do you?"

"You didn't want Chintawa or Gendreves forcing me to put all of Aventine under martial law," Santores said. "Which is fine. I don't want that, either." He smiled faintly. "Despite what you may think, we're all on the same side here."

"I'd like to believe that," Paul said. "Tell me about Jody."

"As I said, we don't know very much," Santores said, settling back into his seat. "One of the *Dorian*'s courier ships arrived at Aventine earlier this morning. Aboard was a report from Captain Moreau that he'd arrived at the Hoibe'ryi'sarai homeworld, only to discover that your daughter hadn't yet arrived. Neither had the Troft merchant ship we assume ghosted her off Aventine. Needless to say, this caused him some concern." He cocked his head. "Unless, of course, that world was never her intended destination."

"Hoibie," Paul said.

Santores frowned. "What?"

"It's Hoibie, not Hoibe'ryi'sarai," Paul told him. "Using the full demesne name makes you sound like a tourist."

"Ah," Santores said. "You seem remarkably unconcerned about the fate of your daughter."

Paul shrugged as casually as he could. "Jody went through a war," he reminded Santores. "She can take care of herself."

"Especially if her destination was actually Caelian?"

"What makes you think she's on Caelian?"

"No, no, that's not how this works," Santores admonished him. "You're the prisoner. You don't ask the questions. You answer them."

"My mistake," Paul said, forcing down a knot of sudden anger. Jin had warned him that Santores liked to poke at his opponents, hoping to make them angry enough to forget to think. "What makes you think she's on Caelian?"

"Various reasons," Santores said. "Not the least of which is that she has friends there."

"Quite a few of them, in fact," Paul agreed. "What have they done now?"

"What makes you think they've done anything?" Santores countered.

"You said *various* reasons," Paul reminded him. "Various implies more than one."

Santores studied him a moment, then gave a little shrug. "I suppose at this point there's no harm in telling you. One of Captain Lij Tulu's officers, Commander Tamu, took the courier ship *Squire* to Caelian four days ago for the purpose of putting Governor Uy under arrest." He smiled faintly. "A bone I intended to throw to Ms. Gendreves in hopes of getting her to forget about you and your family."

"And something unpleasant happened?"

"We don't know," Santores said. "Commander Tamu should have returned two days ago. As of this morning, he hadn't."

"Which means something unpleasant did indeed happen," Paul said. "Not exactly a surprise. Did you really expect to just waltz into Stronghold, pack Uy aboard a Dominion ship, and fly away free and clear?"

"Commander Tamu was fully prepared for trouble."

"Obviously not as prepared as he thought."

"I doubt that," Santores said grimly. "Don't forget Archway."

Paul ground his teeth together. "None of us will ever forget Archway," he said darkly. "So you think Jody is involved in Tamu's disappearance?"

"That's one possibility," Santores said. "We'll find out soon enough." His lips compressed briefly. "One way or the other."

Paul braced himself. "The MindsEye?"

"Yes," Santores said, eyeing Paul closely. "It's a bit ironic that our original goal for your interrogation may soon turn out to be unnecessary. The *Dorian's* courier also brought information that Captain Moreau had made contact with a Commander Ukuthi from the Balin'ekha'spmi—" He smiled. "Excuse me. From the Balin demesne. Ukuthi has given Captain Moreau what he claims are Qasama's coordinates."

Paul felt his eyes widen. After all his family had gone through to keep Qasama's location hidden; and now some Troft had just *given* that secret away?

Which would mean that all of this—Jody's hasty departure, Lorne's stalling, the Archway massacre—had been for nothing.

He forced the thought away. There was nothing that direction except anger and despair. "Congratulations," he said. "So now all you want is to dredge out whatever information I've got on Jody?"

"Not at all," Santores assured him. "And don't despair for your Qasaman friends yet."

"Meaning?"

"Meaning I don't believe this Troft and his alleged information," Santores said. "Neither does Captain

Moreau. He thinks the coordinates may be a midway point where Ukuthi will issue a new course and probably make fresh conditions."

"Or it's a trap," Paul murmured.

"I see fighting a war has given you a touch of warrior's paranoia," Santores said grimly. "Not necessarily a bad thing."

"Unless it so colors your outlook that it makes life meaningless."

"Part of the price warriors have chosen to pay," Santores countered, his voice going hard. "For decades you Cobras have fancied yourselves soldiers without ever having to face the true cost of that role. It's time that you learned about reality."

Paul's mind flashed back to the hell he and his family had just been through. "That's not fair," he said stiffly.

The lines in Santores's face softened, just a bit. "For some of you, perhaps," he said grudgingly. "Not for all. Certainly not for the Cobras in Capitalia."

"They were ordered not to fight."

"Those in DeVegas province and elsewhere in the Cobra Worlds disobeyed that order," Santores pointed out. "The ones in Capitalia could have, too." He waved a hand. "But that's not the point. The point is that we still need Qasama, and I'm not expecting Captain Moreau to get it from this Ukuthi character."

"Hence, me?"

"Hence, you," Santores confirmed. "One way or the other, we *are* going to get Qasama's location. If you have any as-yet unspoken information, this would be a good time to speak it."

"You already have everything I know."

"Perhaps. We'll soon find out."

With a conscious effort, Paul relaxed his muscles. "It seems to me that if you're going to dig into my brain, the least I deserve is a little information," he said, keeping his voice calm. "Specifically, what exactly do you need Qasama for? Granted, they're outstanding warriors, but the kind of space battle you're obviously trained for is well outside their area of expertise."

"True," Santores said. "I'm afraid that for the moment their significance will have to remain a secret."

"I see," Paul said. But people talked, he knew, and sometimes people chatted to each other about matters outsiders weren't meant to hear.

And Cobras had enhanced hearing.

Would he be able to eavesdrop on the conversations around him during the MindsEye treatment? He had no idea.

But he was going to find out.

"Fine," he said. "Can you at least tell me what you're planning to do about Captain Moreau?"

"First, we're refueling the *Hermes* and sending it to the *Dorian*'s coordinates," Santores said. "If we're lucky, they'll find the *Dorian* alive and well. If we're even luckier, they'll also find Qasama there."

"If not?"

"Then we'll see what *is* there and weigh our options." Santores's lips compressed. "One other thing you should consider. If Ukuthi is playing games with *us*, I don't doubt he's also willing and able to play games with the Qasamans. If that's the case, any delay in getting the planet's location may very well facilitate their destruction."

"Maybe," Paul said, determined not to be lulled by the man's apparent sincerity any more than he had been by the earlier verbal elbowing. "Let me point out in return that the Balins already had a run at the Qasamans, and lost badly. I can't see them being eager for a rematch."

"Unless someone new is in charge," Santores pointed out. "Demesne-lord changes happen, probably more often than you realize. Regardless, I trust you see now that this whole thing has moved well beyond the struggles and defiance of a single Aventinian family. The faster you recognize that we need to work together, the better our chances of living through this."

"Or you could leave my family alone and focus on all these other more important matters."

"Trust me, we're capable of doing both at the same time," Santores assured him. "Just as Colonel Reivaro is capable of getting our new armor factories retooled and operating at the same time he's setting up a network of informants among the DeVegas civilians. Once that network is in place, it should allow him to easily neutralize any further operations your wife and son might be planning."

A shiver ran up Paul's back. "You'd have done better to try *asking* for cooperation before demanding it."

"We *did* ask," Santores snapped. "The result was your daughter running away, your wife sabotaging a vital industrial facility, and your son attacking two Marines."

Abruptly, he stood up. "We're through with asking, Cobra Broom," he said. "The Dominion of Man is at war. Now, so are you. It's time for you to decide whose side you're on."

"Because you won't be asking about that, either?"

"No, we won't be asking," Santores said softly. "But we *will* be watching. Very, very closely."

CHAPTER THREE

Most of the officers and crewers Captain Barrington Moreau had worked with during his career in the Dominion Fleet had been true professionals, the sort of men who could maintain their calm and proficiency through the hell and death of combat. Ironically, perhaps, for many of these men it was the hours of safety and relative inactivity leading up to a battle that were harder than the battle itself. Tension, sleeplessness, and frayed nerves grated across individual psyches and interpersonal relationships, and Barrington had lost track of the number of arguments and brawls he'd had to avoid, live through, or break up over the years.

It was an emotional strain that Barrington himself was thankfully unaffected by. An hour or two before combat, perhaps, his mind and adrenal glands would start their pre-battle ramp-up, but until then he had no trouble putting the uncertainties and stress out of his mind.

The *Dorian* was two days out from the Hoibie home-world, with four more projected until they reached

Commander Ukuthi's coordinates, and Barrington was soundly and peacefully asleep, when he received the urgent summons to the ship's Command Nexus/Coordination Hub.

He tapped into the data stream while he dressed, and was up to speed by the time he reached CoNCH.

Up to speed on *what*, though, was still not entirely clear.

The ship's first officer, Commander Ling Garrett, was standing beside the command chair on CoNCH's upper level when Barrington arrived. "Status?" Barrington asked as he sat down.

"We're doing our third pass through the data," Garrett said. "Probability is up to eighty-seven percent that we clipped the edge of a flicker-mine net."

Barrington scowled as he twitched his eye, bringing up the result of the latest data scrub on his corneal projector. Flicker nets were the Troft weapon of choice for bringing ships out of hyperspace: fields of low-level but carefully tuned energy ripples that could stretch up to two million kilometers on an edge and could yank a ship out of hyperspace and scramble its drive sequencing. Until the drive was recalibrated, the victim would be trapped in space-normal, potentially easy prey for the spider ships that typically patrolled such nets.

"It *could* have been a spontaneous decalibration," Garrett said into his musings. "That does still happen."

"Not usually to three of the rotators at the same time," Barrington pointed out. "Do we know which Trofts live around here?"

"According to Chintawa's maps, this whole region is unclaimed territory," Garrett said. "That's presumably why Ukuthi sent us this along this route in the first place."

"Presumably," Barrington echoed the caveat, twitching his eyelid again to access the navigational section of the data stream. Despite his suspicions about Ukuthi's intentions and motivations, he'd given orders to stay on the Troft's course, and the readout indicated that the *Dorian* had indeed maintained that heading.

Which meant that if the flicker net had been set as a trap, the perpetrators had made a pretty sloppy job of it. Misaligning it so badly that the *Dorian* merely clipped the edge did nothing but alert them to the net's presence without even slowing their progress.

Unless the *Dorian* wasn't their target.

"Course check," he called toward the helm. "Vector from Aventine to Ukuthi's coordinates. Does it pass through the flicker net region?"

"Checking, Captain," the helmsman said. "Tentatively confirmed, sir."

"Tentatively?" Barrington echoed.

"We don't actually *know* how the net is laid out," Garrett pointed out. "That impact could have been against any of the edges."

He was right, of course. And the net's positioning would make all the difference as to whether or not a ship coming from the Cobra Worlds capital would be captured, inconvenienced, or missed completely.

But the fact that the projected course came anywhere near the net was both telling and ominous. "Let's find out which, then, shall we?" he said. "Helm: bring us around one-eighty. Make break-out thirty light-seconds this side of our contact with the net. Full stealth mode."

"Break-out thirty light-seconds from net, aye," the helmsman acknowledged. "Stealth mode, aye."

Garrett cleared his throat. "A comment, Commander?" Barrington asked quietly.

"It's occurred to me, sir, that if we stay here long enough to map out the net we're going to be late to our rendezvous," Garrett pointed out. "If the net has nothing to do with us, Ukuthi may decide we're not coming and leave. If that happens, and if the coordinates he gave us *aren't* Qasama, this whole exercise will have been for nothing."

"True enough," Barrington said. "And I completely agree. This net almost certainly has nothing to do with us."

Garrett frowned. "But then—?"

"But I think it has everything to do with the rest of the task force," Barrington continued. "Specifically, with whomever Commodore Santores decides to send to Ukuthi's rendezvous to meet us."

"If he sends anyone at all."

"Oh, he'll send someone," Barrington said grimly. "Even if it's just the *Hermes* with fresh orders. On the other hand, if he suspects we're walking into a trap, he could send the *Algonquin* to back us up, or even decide to come himself with the *Megalith*. If he does either, whoever's pulling the strings on this will have succeeded in completely splitting up the task force."

"One each at Aventine, the net, and with Ukuthi," Garrett said, frowning a little harder. "Does that make Ukuthi—? No. He wouldn't be involved, would he?"

"Not with that particular trap," Barrington said. "If he was, he would have given us a course that didn't take us anywhere near the net." He pursed his lips.

"Which isn't to say that he doesn't have schemes of his own in progress."

"Or we may be misreading this one," Garrett said, nodding toward the helm display. He snorted gently. "Though it could be highly entertaining to see what would happen if Commodore Santores is suspicious enough to bring the *Megalith and* the *Algonquin.*"

"Indeed," Barrington agreed, smiling tightly. "And if snagging *two* war cruisers would amuse them, think how much more their little faces would light up if they got three."

"So we're staying?"

"One thing at a time," Barrington said. "Let's map the net first, and figure out where we go from there."

"Yes, sir," Garrett said. He didn't sound happy with the decision, but he knew better than to continue arguing once his commander had made up his mind. "With your permission, I'd like to go to the sensor nexus and supervise the data collection."

"Good idea," Barrington said. "When the mapping is complete, report to the conference room."

"Yes, sir." Garrett hesitated. "Thank you, sir."

Barrington nodded acknowledgement. "Dismissed."

He watched Garrett stride across CoNCH, a sour taste in his mouth. *Thank you, sir.* Not thanks for Barrington's reading of the situation, or his tactical logic, or even for allowing Garrett to supervise the net mapping. *Thank you, sir,* for planning a meeting with the rest of the senior officers, lest they and their patrons someday bring accusations that the captain and first officer had kept the rest of the command structure out of the data stream on such a critical decision.

It was insane, of course. The captain of a Dominion

warship was supposed to have absolute authority over his vessel and crew, with no obligation to the rest of his officers except to listen to their suggestions and thoughts, and accept any such suggestions only when he chose to do so.

Officially, that was how it still worked. But such theory was no longer aligned with reality. The slow but steady rise of patrons and supporters over the years had created an equally slow but steady rise in the influence of politics into the upper levels of the military. Politics, not skill, now dominated the highest levels of military decision-making. Not just on Asgard, but even aboard ships of the line.

And it was a state of affairs that Barrington couldn't ignore. His own patron was reasonably powerful, but Barrington had no interest in matching him against the combined weight of the *Dorian*'s second, third, and tactical officers' patrons. Especially since his patron would be standing alone in any such contest, given Garrett's own lack of any patron at all.

Garrett.

It was a puzzle that Barrington had often wondered about during the long months of the task force's journey to the Cobra Worlds. There were still plenty of officers who'd risen through the ranks on pure merit, without anyone in the Dome or elsewhere outside the Fleet greasing the wheels for them. But in Barrington's experiences most such men were considerably older than Garrett, or considerably lower in rank. Certainly he'd never met anyone Garrett's age who was first officer of a war cruiser. Whatever the man's accomplishments had been before his assignment to the *Dorian* and this mission, they must have been spectacular.

Someday, Barrington told himself firmly, he would have to find a way to get a look at Garrett's full record. Not the truncated and suspiciously edited summary that had been in the *Dorian*'s personnel records when Barrington was given command a month before this long journey began, but the full version. Until then, he would just have to trust that Asgard knew what they were doing.

In the meantime...

He scowled at the displays. In the meantime, someone out there was playing games. Time to figure out what that game was, and who exactly was playing it.

Engineering Officer Kusari was intrigued by the development. Weapons Officer Filho was suspicious, but equally intrigued.

Tactical Officer Castenello was not only not intrigued, but openly contemptuous.

"With all due respect, Captain, this is ridiculous," he said, twitching his eyelid to close down the sensor report Garrett had loaded into the data stream. "There's no evidence whatsoever that this flicker net has anything to do with us. Or with Aventine or Qasama, for that matter."

"It's on the vector between Aventine and the coordinates Ukuthi gave us for Qasama," Kusari pointed out.

"Which means nothing at all," Castenello said scornfully. "Unless we were somehow able to confirm those coordinates while I was off-watch?"

Filho stirred. "Your tone borders on the unacceptable," he rumbled.

"My tone is precisely gauged to my words," Castenello countered. "Did you even *read* the report?

Eight spider ships, none of them bigger than scout class—they couldn't even take the *Hermes*, let alone the *Megalith* or *Algonquin*. If this is a trap for one of our ships, it's an incredibly inept one."

"Then what's *your* reading?" Garrett asked.

"They're pirates," Castenello said flatly. "Pure and simple. They're sitting on the Aventine-to-wherever vector in hopes of snagging a Troft merchant ship. That's the only thing that makes sense." He paused just a fraction of a second. "Sir."

Barrington felt the tension level in the room jump another couple of levels. None of *Dorian*'s senior officers particularly liked Castenello—actually, Barrington doubted anyone aboard really liked the man. But Castenello had a powerful patron, a senior member of the Dominion Central Committee itself, and the tactical officer had long since concluded that he could be as grating and unpleasant to the universe around him as he wanted. Provided he did his job with reasonable competency, no one in the Fleet could touch him.

But that didn't mean the man's blind spots shouldn't be pointed out to him. And Barrington *was* still the *Dorian*'s captain. "Interesting theory," he said. "May I point out in turn that, just as we don't know Ukuthi's coordinates are Qasama, we also don't know that those eight spider ships are the only forces guarding the net. That's merely the number we can see from this distance."

"Exactly," Garrett seconded. "Who's to say some Troft warship isn't running the same stealth mode we are?"

"Possibly near or behind one of the net generators," Filho agreed. "There's not a lot we can see through the energy glare."

"Or someone could be lurking out here like we are," Kusari said. "If he sticks to low-power mode we'd never spot him without bringing up our active sensors."

"And why would a hypothetical warship bother stealthing *or* lurking?" Castenello countered. "We're out in the middle of nowhere. As far as any lurking warship knows, the only ships that could possibly spot it would already be trapped in the net. Why waste energy with stealth mode when there's no reason to do so?"

He turned to Barrington. "My recommendation, Captain, is that we get back to the task of locating Qasama and completing the mission that Asgard and the Dome gave us. Time and lives are on the line, and the longer we sit here waiting for nothing to happen, the more of both are going to be lost." He looked around the table. "Or are there other recommendations?"

A small ripple of discomfort ran around the table. And on the surface, at least, even Barrington had to admit that Castenello's recommendation made sense. The visible Troft ships were small, compact things, and even a courier ship like *Hermes* had the firepower to hold them off until it could recalibrate its drive and escape. If the net instead caught one of the Dominion war cruisers, the resulting battle would be over within minutes.

But there was still something about this whole thing that was nagging at him. And Barrington had long since learned to trust his gut instincts. "Ukuthi didn't strike me as the type that panics easily," he said. "I don't think he'll cut and run if we're a day or two late."

"And if he does?" Castenello demanded. "Captain, we *need* Qasama."

"No; we *want* Qasama," Barrington corrected him. "We don't *need* it. Don't forget that we didn't even know Qasama existed until we arrived and started going through Aventine's records. If we can't find them, we can still go back to the Dome's original plan."

"My patron was never in favor of that plan," Castenello warned. "Nor were many others. Deliberately setting up the Cobra Worlds to lure in the Trofts is more cold-blooded even than normal Dome politics."

"And doing it to the Qasamans instead is better?" Barrington asked.

"Of course it's better," Castenello said contemptuously. "We sent out the Cobra Worlds colonists. The Qasamans got wherever they got on their own. The Aventinians are our people. The Qasamans aren't."

"They're still human," Garrett murmured.

"It's *us* versus *them*," Castenello retorted. "At its heart, that's really what politics is all about." He gestured to Barrington. "The point is that if you have the chance to switch the bait from Aventine to Qasama, but don't make that switch, the Dome will not be happy."

"The Dominion is either in the middle of a war, or on the brink of one," Barrington said. "The Dome isn't *supposed* to be happy."

"Don't be flippant, Captain," Castenello said stiffly. "I'm simply pointing out that we have obligations."

"I agree," Barrington agreed. "And one of the foremost of those obligations is to protect the other members of our task force. If this trap is meant for one of our ships, we need to stand ready to give aid."

"Fine," Castenello said. "If we want to assist the task force, let's just destroy the net and move on. Even if the Trofts have the necessary equipment at hand it would take them several days to rebuild it. If, more likely, they have to go back to one of their other worlds for replacement parts, they'd be out of the picture for weeks."

Kusari stirred in his seat. "Except that destroying or driving them away now will lose us the chance to see exactly who they are. *And* whether the net was aimed at us or is simply some pirate's merchant trap."

"And how do you suggest we distinguish between those options?" Castenello asked with strained patience. "A marauder spider ship looks pretty much the same as a military one."

"We'll know from their reaction when the *Hermes* starts firing back," Barrington told him. "A pirate isn't going to stick around for a real fight. A military force will."

"*And* the volume of fire *Hermes* sends back at the spiders should also draw out whoever they've got lurking in the glare," Kusari added.

"Exactly," Barrington said.

Castenello looked back and forth between them. "I'd argue the point further, Captain, but it's clear you've made up your mind," he growled. "With your permission, I'll return to my station and start drawing up combat contingencies."

"An excellent idea," Barrington said. "And with that, we're finished here."

Garrett nodded and stood up. "Gentlemen: you're dismissed to your posts," he said in the proper formal tone.

The others stood in turn and filed out. Garrett nodded a silent farewell to Barrington and started to follow.

"A word, Commander," Barrington called after him.

Garrett stopped a meter from the door, allowing it to close in front of him. "Yes, sir?" he asked, turning back around.

"Your take on the situation?" Barrington invited.

"Militarily? Or politically?"

"Either. Both."

Garrett gave a microscopic shrug. "It largely depends on what happens over the next few days. If it turns out the net *was* set for one of our ships, and our presence is the difference between victory and defeat, you'll be a big enough hero that not even Castenello's patron will be able to touch you." He pursed his lips. "Conversely, if he's right and the trap is just some pirates hoping to snag a merchant—*and* if we delay here long enough to miss out on Ukuthi's offer—he'll hang you out to dry. I doubt even Asgard and your patron together will be able to save you."

Barrington nodded. That had been his assessment, as well. "It's still the right thing to do."

"I agree, sir." Garrett hesitated. "For whatever it's worth, Captain, I don't think Commander Castenello's arguments are entirely based on tactical considerations. I think he's deliberately setting you up for a fall."

"Interesting thought," Barrington said. He'd already figured out that one, too. "Though if I were you I'd keep it to myself. It's a political minefield out there, and all you're wearing are carpet slippers."

"Indeed," Garrett said with a faint smile. "I really need to invest in some armored wading boots."

"I've often found them to be handy," Barrington agreed. "Still, I imagine there's a great deal of satisfaction in knowing that you've made it to your current position on your own, without the conniving or smoothing of hidden political forces."

Garrett shrugged again. "I'm told those forces aren't all that hidden if you know where to look."

"And can stomach what you see," Barrington told him. "War's an ugly enough business without injecting politics into it. Especially since in politics the flowing blood is mostly invisible. It can be a bit creepy."

"I'll remember that, sir," Garrett said. "If that's all, Captain, I'm still on duty in CoNCH."

"Dismissed, Commander," Barrington said. "No, wait. On second thought, I think I'd rather you go assist Commander Castenello with his tactical work. I'll take the rest of your watch."

Garrett's forehead furrowed slightly. But his nod was firm enough. "Yes, sir," he said. "Anything in particular you want me to keep an eye on?"

"Keep an eye on?" Barrington repeated, allowing some puzzlement into his voice. "You're not there to keep an eye on anything, Commander. You're merely to assist with the work, and to make sure all possible scenarios have been considered and prepared for."

"Understood, sir," Garrett said. With another farewell nod, he turned and left the room.

Not entirely based on tactical considerations. Barrington snorted under his breath. "You *think*, Commander?" he murmured into the silence.

But that was all right. Castenello might dream about taking down a Dominion ship's captain as a prize for his patron, but he was likely to find such prey harder to swallow than he realized. Barrington might not especially like political games, but he *did* know how to play them.

In the meantime, there was a puzzle here to be solved. And he and the *Dorian* were going to solve it.

CHAPTER FOUR

Merrick Moreau had been a Troft slave for only a little over three weeks. Most of that time had been spent aboard the transport that had brought him and Anya Winghunter from Qasama to Muninn, which had meant he hadn't had to do any genuine slave-type labor. Still, even without the work, and with only that brief exposure, he'd easily come to the obvious fact that being a slave was a terrible thing.

What *hadn't* been so obvious, which Merrick had only learned over the past few hours, was that being an *ex*-slave was nearly as bad.

Of course, maybe that conclusion only applied to self-freed slaves. Officially freed slaves might be given food and water for the road, or at least a polite word of dismissal.

Officially freed slaves certainly wouldn't have their former masters scouring the deep Muninn forest in search of them.

The Trofts were definitely out there. Merrick knew

it as he gazed out into the starlit gloom of the night. His trick with the crashed hang glider hadn't fooled them. They knew he was still alive, and they were going to get him back. Alive, or otherwise.

But if they were nearby, they were keeping quiet about it. Merrick's enhanced hearing was alive with strange noises, but there was nothing he could identify with Trofts or Troft vehicles. His enhanced vision, both infrared and telescopic, showed nothing but small- to medium-sized animals and birds going busily about their lives.

There were larger predators in the forest, Merrick knew, creatures of muscle, claws, and teeth that even Cobra weapons and programmed reflexes would be hard-pressed to deal with. Luckily, like the Trofts, so far they seemed to be keeping their distance.

There was a rustling in the leaves to his left. Reflexively, Merrick tensed, his hands curling into fingertip-laser firing positions.

But it was just Anya, shifting position in her sleep.

Merrick exhaled a silent sigh. Not that she was supposed to be asleep. Not now. Certainly not here. She was supposed to be leading them to a secret hideout where she'd said they would find her parents, who'd allegedly been hiding out ever since their failed revolt against Muninn's Troft overlords.

But he and Anya had stopped to rest, and Anya had fallen asleep, and Merrick had decided that a ten-minute nap couldn't hurt anything.

Especially since this whole scenario was still flying a whole forest of red flags in the back of his mind.

The idea of a hidden refuge and possible allies was certainly an alluring one. It was exactly what he and Anya needed if they were to catch their breath, regroup, and figure out their next step. They'd been sent here by Commander Ukuthi of the Balin'ekha'spmi demesne in hopes of finding out what the Trofts of the Drim'hco'plai demesne were up to in their private slave preserve. But so far the two humans hadn't made much progress.

The problem was that the abortive revolt her parents were supposedly on the run from had happened twelve years ago. Twelve *years*. Merrick couldn't figure out why Anya assumed the hideout even existed anymore, let alone that anyone was still using it.

In fact, the more Merrick thought about it, the more dangerously ridiculous the assumption became. If *he'd* been in charge of that long-ago revolt, he would have instantly abandoned any known shelter the minute the Trofts quashed the rebellion. After all, a victor's first step in that situation was usually to root out any surviving pockets of resistance, and part of that rooting would be to drag the location of every bolt-hole from the survivors. If the Trofts knew about Anya's refuge, even if that knowledge was over a decade old, simply strolling into it would not be a smart thing to do.

Yet Anya, who seemed clear-headed enough in other areas, seemed to have missed that piece of logic completely. More than that, she seemed convinced that her parents would still be waiting when they arrived.

Could it be simply a matter of her *wanting* her parents to be there? She'd implied that they'd run off after the revolt failed, leaving their twelve-year-old daughter and the other villagers holding the bag. She'd also admitted that she still harbored some not unreasonable resentment over the fact that she'd ended up as a slave under Commander Ukuthi's control.

But even the hottest angers tended to cool with time. After twelve years, maybe Anya was ready to offer her parents the chance to mend fences.

Or else she was looking for them in order to exact some sort of revenge. Merrick had known Anya barely a month, and he couldn't begin to guess all of what was going on behind those clear blue eyes.

He needed time to think, and he really hadn't had any. Maybe it wouldn't be such a bad idea to let Anya sleep as long as she wanted and in the process buy himself a little more time to ponder.

And to maybe come up with a Plan B if and when Anya's Plan A didn't pan out.

There was a quiet rustling in the undergrowth to Merrick's right. Carefully, he turned his head to look.

This particular animal hadn't yet shown up on his brief tour of Muninn's wildlife. But it was a good meter and a half long, it had the short neck, wide jaws, and long teeth of a predator, and it was moving stealthily in their direction.

If it had been broad daylight, Merrick would simply have fired a double burst from his fingertip lasers into the creature's half-open mouth and been done with it. Unfortunately, with Troft aircars presumably still flitting around up there, a flash of even muted artificial light would be dangerous.

Something a little more subtle was called for. Watching the animal's infrared signature closely, Merrick fired off a short burst from his sonic.

The IR pattern changed, and for a couple of seconds the creature seemed to stagger. Then the pattern returned to its original form, the animal regained its balance, and with only a brief hesitation it resumed its stalking approach.

Merrick grimaced. Unfortunately, that was more or less what he'd expected to happen. Cobras had two sets of implanted sonics: one designed to shatter glass and other resonant breakables, as well as interfering with listening devices; the other tuned to stun or disorient Trofts. The former would be of no use against an animal, and he'd now confirmed that the latter wasn't hitting any of the predator's vulnerable frequencies.

Merrick's gear also included a current-based stunner, which would almost certainly put the predator down for the count. Unfortunately, the stunner worked off Merrick's arcthrower, which would flash even more brightly than the fingertip lasers.

All of which, even more unfortunately, only left Merrick one option.

Reaching into his jacket, he pulled out the control bar he'd taken from his hang glider and got a grip on one end. The animal paused, as if evaluating this new move on the part of its prey, then continued inching forward. Merrick waited until it was just within reach, then leaned over and tapped the tip of the bar lightly against the top of its snout.

The animal snorted, twitching against what its brain probably registered as an annoying insect. Merrick tapped it again, and this time the predator snapped its head up and grabbed the end of the rod.

And with the animal's jaws partially open, Merrick swiveled around on his hip, pressed his left heel against the gap between the upper and lower teeth, and fired his antiarmor laser down its throat.

He'd been concerned that, even with the blast mostly contained, enough of the light might leak out to create a danger. Fortunately, the sharply back-angled teeth had put his heel well inside the jawline when he fired, and the only visible flicker was off the tongue and roof of the mouth. The creature collapsed and lay still.

"Is it dead?"

Merrick looked over at Anya. She hadn't moved, but her eyes were open. The variegated IR pattern of her face was still changing—clearly, she hadn't been awake very long. "If it isn't, it will be soon," he said. "How are you doing?"

"Well enough," she said, reaching up and briefly rubbing her eyes. She lowered her hands, and Merrick saw that her IR image had again changed with the newly altered blood flow. "Why did you let me sleep?"

"You seemed to need it," Merrick told her. "I don't think I've ever seen someone conk out so soundly lying on leaves and half-buried roots. Though after sleeping on a mat on the Sollas subcity concrete, I suppose even tree roots are an improvement."

"As you say, I was tired." She hunched her shoulders and pulled herself up into a sitting position. "Shall we go?"

"In a minute," Merrick said. "I need to ask you a couple of things first."

"Questions can wait until we're safely in the refuge."

"The questions are *about* the refuge," Merrick told her.

Her IR pattern changed subtly. "Ask, then."

"Let's start with your parents," Merrick suggested. "Tell me about their rebellion twelve years ago."

Another shift in the pattern. "What do you want to know?"

"What exactly happened?" Merrick asked. "I assume they didn't just pick up rocks and charge into battle."

"They *did* use rocks, where it was appropriate," Anya said. "Not held, but catapulted. They also used arrows, blowgun darts, and weapons dropped by winghunters upon the masters' positions." The IR pattern changed again. "But in the end, it all came to nothing."

Not surprising, if they were attacking laser-armed Trofts with bows and arrows. Sometimes, Merrick mused, there was a fine line between raw courage and ill-considered stupidity. "What kind of weapons did the winghunters drop?" he asked. "Homemade explosives? More arrows?"

"The winghunters dropped powder of freshly harvested bersark," Anya said. "It was hoped it would confuse or otherwise disable them."

Merrick winced. Unprocessed bersark, he'd been told, was a highly poisonous substance. Chemical warfare at its finest. "And if the bersark didn't get them, crazed kilerands would?" he suggested.

"That was another hope," Anya said, nodding. "Though kilerands normally eat bersark accidentally, when it's mixed in with their other foods. There was no promise that they would eat the powder that was dropped."

"Though even if they did, you'd still need the Trofts to make loud noises," Merrick pointed out. "That's what draws them, right? Loud noises?"

"There was no fear of that," Anya said bitterly. "The masters continually make loud noises. They shout when they want us to work. They shout when they want us to cower." Her throat worked. "They shout when they want us to die."

"I gather the bersark approach didn't work any better than the rest of it?"

Anya shook her head. "It was my parents' best hope. The masters had spent much of their rule in their own areas, isolated from the forest villages, and the rebels hoped they hadn't learned the nature of all our plants and animals. But they knew bersark well enough to know how to avoid it or counteract its effects."

"So the rebellion failed," Merrick said. "And your parents fled to this hideout? The one we're currently headed for?"

"Yes," Anya said. "It was secure, unknown to the masters."

"*Was,*" Merrick said, leaning heavily on the word. "That's the operative word here. *Was*. What makes you think the Trofts didn't have every local bolt-hole and hiding place identified and raided two hours after the last rebel surrendered?"

The blood flow in Anya's face again changed. "I don't understand."

"They would have interrogated their prisoners, Anya," Merrick said patiently. Was she really that naïve? "I know your people are brave, but a good interrogator can—"

"There were no prisoners," Anya said. "The masters killed them all."

Merrick frowned. "What are you talking about? There are *always* prisoners."

"Not here," Anya said, her face suddenly blazing with heat. "Not us. We do not surrender."

Merrick stared at her, a sudden chill running through him. He'd read about warrior cultures, mostly on Earth but some on other Dominion worlds, where surrender in battle was simply not an option. But neither the Cobra Worlds nor the Qasamans had any such military conviction.

It seemed unbelievable. Still, maybe he'd already seen a hint of that philosophy in action. Yesterday, high up on the cliff, Anya had been prepared to sacrifice her life to keep Merrick's secret from the Trofts. Maybe that readiness to die had been part of her culture, a part he'd never even suspected.

And as the new reality sank in, the conversation in Gangari on the previous day suddenly took on new meaning. *[The dark memory of years past, you still have it?]* one of the Trofts had asked.

[The dark memory, we still have it,] the man Anya had named as Henson Hillclimber had answered.

At the time, Merrick had assumed the alien and the human had been talking about the same thing. Now, he realized they hadn't.

The Troft's *dark memory* had been the insurrection itself. Henson's *dark memory* had been the shame of Anya's parents surviving the rebellion instead of dying with the other fighters.

"I'm sorry, I didn't understand," Merrick said in a low voice. "So they've been hiding out here all these years?"

"I don't know what they've been doing," Anya said, a little stiffly. "Whether hiding or continuing the fight. But if they're still alive, they'll be here. There's nowhere else for them to go."

"Ah," Merrick said. It seemed a rather dogmatic

statement, given that they were sitting in the middle of hundreds of square kilometers of forest. But there was clearly a lot he still didn't know about Muninn and its people, and he didn't feel like arguing from ignorance twice in the same conversation. "Just the same, it might be better if I went ahead and checked things out."

Anya gave a short, rather hollow laugh. "And you think you can find it without my help? A hidden sanctuary which the masters have undoubtedly searched for years to discover?"

"I thought you said they didn't know it was out here."

"They know there was a rebellion," Anya said. "They will surely be on the watch for future trouble."

And the forest was the obvious place for disaffected elements to meet and plan, away from prying eyes. The Trofts would have to be blind *and* stupid to miss that one. "All the more reason for me to go first," Merrick said. "Make sure there aren't any hidden watchers or search equipment."

"We go together," Anya said firmly. She shot a furtive look at the predator Merrick had killed and pushed herself to her feet. "Stay close, and be as quiet as you can."

Ten minutes later, they were there.

Though it took Merrick another minute to realize that. The clump of rock nestled among the bushes and matted grass looked no different than a hundred similar rocks they'd already passed on their nighttime trek. It was only when Anya turned to him and raised her eyebrows questioningly that he realized she was waiting for the threat assessment he'd promised.

Slowly, carefully, he gave the area a visual sweep.

There were several animals within range of his infrareds, but none of them seemed interested in the two humans who'd strayed into their territory. There was no hint of any Troft presence, either by sight or by sound. Either the aliens were still concentrating on the river ravine where Anya had dumped Merrick's hang glider or else they'd left their aircars back at base and were conducting their search on foot.

Abruptly, Anya clutched his arm. "Over there," she whispered urgently. "In the reedgrass."

"It's okay," Merrick soothed. "It's just a razorarm. Like the one we saw our first day on Muninn."

"I remember," Anya said tensely. "I also remember the battles you had with the same creatures in the Games on Qasama."

"Those were from a different group," Merrick reminded her. "They hadn't seen humans before and didn't know we were dangerous enough to avoid. This bunch has, and they do."

"That's an assumption," Anya shot back. "And a dangerous one. Why would the masters bring predators who avoid humans in order to discourage us from traveling through the forest?"

"We don't *know* that's why they brought them," Merrick countered. "We were just guessing."

"It was your own idea."

"And I was just guessing," Merrick said, starting to feel a little annoyed. How many times did he have to foul up before Anya gave up this belief that he always knew what he was doing? Especially here on Muninn? "I might easily have been wrong, or only partially right. Besides, there's also that wrecked Troft ship to consider. If the razorarm came from that, there's no telling where they were originally headed, or for what purpose."

"Perhaps," Anya said reluctantly, still staring in the razorarm's direction. "We must still be cautious."

"We are," Merrick assured her. "You can't see it in the darkness, but the razorarm's spines are still tucked against its forelegs, and it's standing straight up instead of crouching to spring. It knows we're here, but it's making no attempt to even get any closer, much less try for a snack. How does this door work?"

"You must lift the stone," Anya said. She didn't sound totally convinced, but she sounded marginally less nervous. "Normally it would require two or three men with bersarkis patches for extra strength to lift. But you should be able to move it alone."

"Probably," Merrick said, wincing. Yesterday, in Gangari, he'd been treated to a demonstration of what the refined poison bersarkis could do to people. It hadn't been pretty. "I thought it was only good for healing and driving teenagers into killing rages."

"It can also give added strength," Anya said. If she was offended by his reference to the Game testing yesterday, she gave no sign. "Its precise properties depend on the specific refining process used."

"Handy," Merrick said with a grunt. "Any way to tell which particular formulation is which? Color, texture, odor, an ingredients label—anything?"

"There are chemical tests," Anya said. "I know of no other way to distinguish one from another without trying it." She risked a look away from the razorarm. "But you have abilities far beyond ours. Perhaps you will be able to tell one from another simply by looking."

"We'll see if we get a chance to find out," Merrick

said, heading through the last line of trees to the boulder.

Confident words and analysis aside, he made sure to watch the razorarm as he walked.

But the predator did nothing but back up a couple of silent steps in response to Merrick's approach. It had a healthy respect for humans, all right. "Any special place I need to grab this thing?" he asked over his shoulder.

"There are knobs that are slightly smoother than the rest of the stone," she said. "Those are what the men usually use."

"Got it," Merrick said, nodding as he spotted the handholds. Crouching down, he locked his fingers around the two most convenient ones and eased back and up.

The boulder was heavy enough, and he could see why it normally took three juiced-up Muninnites to handle it. But it wasn't nearly as heavy as it ought to have been, which implied that someone had hollowed out part of it. He lifted it high above the surrounding grass, mindful of the clues that oddly damaged plant life could offer to searchers, and set it down on a thick mat of leaves that had collected beside a dead tree.

Beneath the boulder, as advertised, was a wood-lined shaft leading downward. Leaning gingerly forward, he peered into it.

The shaft went straight down about eight meters, with a ladder connected to the side to facilitate movement up and down. At the bottom it appeared to connect to horizontal tunnels or wide spots heading off in opposite directions. It was a bit difficult to tell from above, but Merrick's rangefinder put the size of the tunnels as a bit shorter than average human height, and not much wider. His infrareds showed no indication that there was any life bigger than a mole down there.

Still, the vital areas could be hidden behind baffles or heat sinks. The only way to find out would be to go down and take a look.

And it was for damn sure that he, a total stranger to anyone who might be down there, wasn't going to be first in line.

He straightened up and gestured Anya forward. "Here we are," he said. "After you."

The hideout consisted of two rooms, one at the end of each of the two short horizontal tunnels he'd seen from above. Both rooms were deserted.

"But they *were* here," Anya insisted plaintively as she walked back and forth between the two rooms, her feet slapping softly on the dirt floor, her voice echoing slightly from the rough-cut wooden boards forming the roof and partial wall shoring. "They *were*."

"It's been twelve years," Merrick reminded her, peering into one of the three bins against the wall of one of the rooms. The bin had been completely emptied, without any scraps or crumbs to indicate what might have stored there. "There are any number of reasons why they might have left."

"But..." Anya trailed off.

"If it's any consolation, it doesn't look like the Trofts got them," Merrick said, waving at the bins and the similarly empty shelves along one wall. "At least, not here. They wouldn't have bothered cleaning out everything. Or replacing the boulder up top, for that matter."

Anya didn't reply. Her gaze continued to move around the room, then past the vertical shaft to the other one, as if she thought that if she kept at it long enough her parents would eventually appear.

"Is there anywhere else you can think of that they might have gone?" Merrick asked into the silence. "One of the villages, maybe? Not Gangari, of course, but one of the others?"

"No," Anya said. She took a deep breath, her head and shoulders bowed slightly, her gaze on the floor in front of her. "Not to one of the villages. Not anywhere."

So much for that line of questioning. The absence of any life here seemed to have thrown Anya for a complete loop. "Okay," Merrick said after another moment of uncomfortable silence. "So we're all alone in this. That's fine—we were alone before we got here, and we did okay. Any thoughts as to what we should do now?"

Anya took another deep breath. "No," she said simply. "I'm sorry."

"Don't worry about it," Merrick assured her, trying to think. His Cobra training had included a unit on wilderness survival, and the Qasamans had given him some abbreviated instruction on infiltration, combat tactics, and evading enemy surveillance. In and among all of that, he ought to be able to come up with a plan.

Except that his brain was too exhausted to focus. But that was okay. Sleep could also be a plan. "First thing we need is rest," he told Anya. "The floor looks even less comfortable than the ground up top, but down here we won't have to worry about Trofts and predators. We'll crash for a few hours, then reassess the situation when our minds are clearer."

"We cannot stay here," Anya said. "There is no food. Or supplies, or weapons."

"That's why we're only going to stay long enough for some sleep," Merrick said, frowning as he looked around. There was no food, all right. But there were also no bunks, air supply or filtration gear, or bathroom facilities.

This wasn't any kind of hidden rebel headquarters, at least not the kind Anya had implied. It was no more than a way station, a quick bolthole for emergencies.

Had Anya known that from the start, and deliberately misled him? Or had she herself misunderstood?

Or had someone specifically and deliberately lied to her?

In which case, this might be a trap.

Merrick tensed, but a second later relaxed again. They'd been in the cavern for at least three minutes, and had been in the vicinity of the entrance for two or three more. If it was a trap, it should have been sprung long ago.

"If you wish sleep, then we shall sleep," Anya said, her voice dull with fatigue and a black disappointment. "It makes little difference to me."

"Come on, don't be that way," Merrick chided. "Anyway, just the fact you're talking like that is a classic sign of fatigue. Tell you what: you see if there are any sections of the floor that are—I don't know; maybe a little less hard than the rest. I'll go grab enough leaves to at least make a couple of half-decent pillows. I'll also put the rock back over the entrance in case the Trofts wander this direction."

"All right." Anya hesitated. "I'm sorry, Merrick Moreau. I've failed us."

"Oh, come on—we've hardly even started," Merrick said. "And don't forget, we wouldn't have gotten even this far if you hadn't taught me how to hang glide and then dropped my glider into the ravine. Under the circumstances, I think we're doing just fine. Some sleep, and then we'll figure out our next step. I'll get the leaves and be right back."

He headed up the ladder, feeling a grim set to his jaw. In fact, he'd already figured out what their next move would be. The wrecked Troft ship, the one whose crash site they'd spotted from the mountain, wasn't more than a few hours' journey away. He'd planned to visit it sometime anyway; first, to confirm that it was the source of the stray razorarms they'd run into; and second, to see if there were any clues as to what had caused the crash.

But for the moment that plan was going to remain his secret. He didn't think Anya was playing games with him, but with their lives firmly on the betting table he had no intention of taking unnecessary chances. Once they'd rested, and the sun had risen and warmed the forest enough to make them harder to spot on Troft infrareds, would be soon enough to share it with her.

CHAPTER FIVE

They were just one day out from Caelian, with four more to go until they reached Qasama.

And to Jody Moreau Broom's surprise and annoyance, she discovered she was getting cold feet.

It was discomfiting. It was also embarrassing, shameful, and annoying. She'd prepped her original proposal carefully, and delivered it to Moffren Omnathi with just the right mixture of passion and cold logic. Omnathi had listened gravely to her arguments, as a Shahni of Qasama should, and had then declared himself convinced. Jody Moreau Broom, daughter of Cobras, would be granted the privilege of becoming a Cobra herself.

Jody had convinced him. She'd also convinced herself. Now, less than a day after her triumph, she was wondering if she'd really and truly thought this through.

And she was three-quarters convinced that she hadn't. It was no light thing, after all, to become a Cobra.

To become a Cobra. To step willingly into the hideously complex Isis machine hidden somewhere on Qasama. To lie still while the computerized lasers, transorptors, and laminators implanted sonics, servos, layered bone-strengtheners, weapons, audio and visual enhancers, and a pre-programmed reflex nanocomputer into her body.

To let herself be turned into a machine of war.

She'd thought it was what she wanted to do. She knew it was something she *needed* to do. Her brother Merrick was lost in the vastness of the Troft Assemblage, snatched and taken somewhere unknown for purposes equally unknown. Jody's mother, father, and other brother Lorne were back on Aventine, trapped under the unblinking gaze of Commodore Rubo Santores and the three-ship Dominion Fleet task force that had appeared over Aventine, unexpected and unwanted, less than two weeks ago. If the Dominion's heavy-handed attempt to arrest Caelian's Governor Uy was at all representative of Santores's intentions toward the Cobra Worlds as a whole, Jody's family would have their hands full back home. She was the only one of the family with any hope of following up the tenuous lead that might or might not lead to her missing brother.

And the only chance she had against Trofts, the Dominion, and whatever else was out there was the secret edge she would have as a Cobra.

It was logical, reasonable, and practically inevitable. Jody's mother Jin had been the first female Cobra in Aventinian history. It was only right and proper that her daughter should be the second.

So why did the very thought of it make Jody shudder with what felt disconcertingly like claustrophobia?

Was it the fear of the procedure itself? Unlikely.

She'd had a couple of casual conversations with Ghush-tre, an Ifrit-ranked Qasaman Cobra and one of the four Cobras who'd accompanied Omnathi to Caelian, and Ghushtre had indicated that the operation was uncomfortable but largely painless.

Was it concern that she wouldn't be able to handle that kind of power? Again, unlikely. She'd spent some time during the war wearing one of the Qasaman Djinn combat suits, and while their capabilities were slightly different from Cobra equipment she'd adapted easily enough to its use.

The drugs, then? Normal Cobra training on Aventine took weeks. The Qasamans, digging into their pharmacopeia of mental-enhancement drugs, had been able to cut that learning curve down to seven days. Any chemical that could wield such power over human biochemistry carried equally potent risks, but the Qasamans had a long history with such things and she was confident that those risks would be cut to the barest possible minimum.

Was it the fact that her life would be cut short? Not necessarily in combat, but because of the anemia, arthritis, and other side effects that a hundred years of Cobra fine-tuning had been unable to eliminate? That was certainly a sobering prospect, but at twenty-one years of age, the thought of living only another fifty or sixty carried more intellectual significance than it did emotional weight.

It was as she puzzled her way down the list for the umpteenth time that the answer finally came.

It was the fact that, once she underwent the proce-dure, she could never, ever go back. Cobra gear, once implanted, was there to stay until the day she died.

Jody had always been the sort who liked to keep her options open. She could still remember the time her grandmother had quoted an old saying to her—*as you've made your bed, so shall you lie in it*—and thinking airily to herself that if she didn't like the way she'd made her bed, she'd just make it again.

Later, as she'd grown older, she'd realized the proverb was a warning that there were some decisions and actions that simply couldn't be undone. She'd accepted that in principle, but had nevertheless clung to the belief that such decisions were rare, and that a sufficiently clever person could avoid them completely.

Except that no amount of cleverness could sidestep this one. Once she entered the Isis machine, she could never go back. Ever.

And that wasn't just scary. That was terrifying.

"You okay?"

Jody jerked a little, twisting toward the voice. Somehow, while she'd been cogitating, Kemp had slipped unnoticed into the small lounge and stretched out on one of the couches. "Didn't your mother ever teach you not to sneak up on people?" Jody growled.

"Nope," Kemp said blandly. "Sneaking up on things is a time-honored tradition on Caelian."

"Lest they sneak up on you?"

"Something like that," Kemp said. "Besides, this one hardly counted. The way you were staring a hole through that wall, a screech tiger could probably have sneaked up on you. Mulling over the secrets of life, were we?"

"Something like that," Jody said, studying the man's face. Kemp—she still wasn't sure whether that was his first or his last name—had grown up on Caelian, a world whose hellish ecology had forced both the Cobras and non-Cobra colonists to achieve levels of human endurance and ingenuity that Jody wouldn't have thought possible even a year ago.

But that endurance came with a price. Even here, aboard a nice, safe Dominion courier ship like the *Squire*, Kemp's face carried the same alertness and wariness that she'd seen back on the planet.

She had never seen him truly relax. She wasn't even sure he *could* relax. "When did you decide you wanted to be a Cobra?" she asked abruptly.

His eyebrows raised slightly. "You seem to think I had a choice."

"I'm serious."

"So am I," he said. "You've been on Caelian. You know what it's like. We need as many Cobras as we can get, and not everyone is up to the job. Those who are—" He shrugged. "It's pretty much assumed that we'll step up."

"And now?" Jody asked.

"And now what?"

"Now that the Qasaman combat suits might be able to keep the citizens safe without you," she said. "What happens once they've got enough for everyone? Are you going to be out of a job?"

"Trust me—we're not going away anytime soon," Kemp assured her. "Those suits may keep off the spores and solve that part of the problem, and if they can keep it up long-term that'll be great. But there are still a hell of a lot of predators prowling around, and we may or may not be able to train the civilians to deal with those." He snorted. "Plus we now have the Dominion in the mix. If they seriously think they're going to come in and take over, they face a very rude awakening."

"I hope so," Jody said, wincing. She'd seen only a little of what Dominion Marine combat suits could do, but that taste had been enough to show that in a straight-up fight the Cobras were going to be dangerously outgunned.

Which wasn't really a surprise. Cobra gear had been designed a hundred years ago to allow soldiers to infiltrate Troft-held human worlds, which meant it had to strike a balance between power and undetectability. The Marines' equipment, in contrast, had no need for stealth and could pack in as much death as the designers wanted.

Still, firepower alone wasn't always the deciding factor. Jody had seen a pair of Qasaman Cobras take on those Marines and win. If the Dominion came to Caelian in force, she had no doubt that the Cobras would give a solid account of themselves. "Speaking of Marines, any word from the two inside the gunbays?" she asked.

"Not since this morning," Kemp said. "They're still refusing to come out until Shahni Omnathi guarantees to grant them full prisoner-of-war status."

"Yes, I heard about that," Jody said, grimacing. The request had sounded innocuous enough to her until Ghushtre pointed out that granting such status could be tantamount to accepting the notion that a state of war existed between Qasama and the Dominion. Since the Dominion hadn't declared war, that would imply that the Qasamans had done so. Omnathi had no intention of letting his world be maneuvered into that position, and Jody didn't blame him a bit.

Though at this point such semantic nuances might already be moot. Back on Caelian, during the joint Caelian-Qasaman assault on the *Squire*, Governor Uy's makeshift gunboat had taken out some of the Marines with the help of Qasaman Djinn targeting capabilities. Uy and Omnathi were probably taking the position that the killings came under the heading of defensive action, since the Marines *had* been firing on the Qasamans and Caelians at the time.

On the other hand, since Jody and two of the Qasamans had been caught and imprisoned while trying to infiltrate a Dominion military vessel, it could be argued that the rescue mission was indeed military in nature. On the *other* other hand, since the Cobra Worlds were theoretically part of the Dominion, Jody wasn't sure Lieutenant Commander Tamu had had the authority to detain them inside his ship in the first place without a warrant or at least just cause.

It was already a tangled mess, and that didn't even begin to address the political ramifications of the incident. Jody wished the diplomats luck with that one. "So we're just going to leave them in there?"

"Unless you've got a magic can opener that'll get us through the door without getting shot at," Kemp said.

"What about Ghushtre's idea about pumping sleep gas in through the ventilation port?"

"Two problems," Kemp said. "One, even with them asleep we'd still have to cut through the doors, and that armor's damn thick, every bit as thick as what's around the CoNCH control room. Two, they *do* have weapons in there, or at least so claims the one who's still talking to us. They might also have booby-trapped the doors."

Jody swallowed. "Oh."

"Exactly," Kemp said. "So for the moment, everyone's more or less agreed that we'll just let them run through whatever food and water they have in there and let them come out on their own after—"

He broke off, his face and body stiffening. Before Jody could ask what was wrong, he launched himself from the couch, hit the door jamb with the heel of his left hand to change direction and disappeared at full sprint down the corridor.

Jody had barely made it out of her own chair when a sudden voice split the silence. "Alert! All Cobras to the portside gunbay."

Jody mouthed a silent curse, then concentrated her full attention on her running.

Apparently, the Marine in the portside gunbay had found his own magic can opener.

Two Cobras were waiting just around a bend in the corridor from the gunbay when Jody arrived: Kemp and Nisti, one of the four Qasaman Cobras. Kemp glanced at Jody as she came into view, waved a warning hand for her to keep back. She nodded as she trotted up beside him. "Any idea what's going on?" she whispered.

"Everyone stay back," a tense voice called from around the bend. "You hear me? Your Cobra's down, and I've got a hostage."

"Please," a strangled, pleading voice added. "Please—do as he says."

The voice was so stressed that it took another second for Jody to realize it was Rashida Vil.

And that sudden realization sent a chill through her. Rashida was one of the Qasamans, originally brought along as a pilot and translator, before being forced by the Troft invasion to become a warrior as well. The young woman had risen to the challenge, showing strength and determination that Rashida herself probably hadn't realized she had. If she was *this* frightened, the danger must be worse than Jody had guessed.

"Just calm down," Kemp called back. "There's no need for anyone else to be hurt."

"But he's *blind*," Rashida wailed. "The Marine threw some sort of device—"

"Shut it," the Marine cut her off.

"Shut it yourself," Smitty's strained voice snarled. "What the hell *was* that? What did you throw at me?"

"Oh, stop whining," the Marine said contemptuously. "It was just a flash grenade. Your eyes will be fine in a few hours. I just want to talk."

"You could have talked from inside," Kemp called around the bend. "Or you and I could go talk in the lounge. I'm sure that would be more comfortable."

"This'll do for now," the Marine said. "But I *would* like to get all of you together. Especially Shahni Omnathi."

"And why do you think he would have any interest in talking to you?"

"Maybe he doesn't," the Marine said. "But this woman here is pretty scared, and I can't let her go until I've said my piece to the Shahni."

"Let's start with me," Kemp suggested. "Tell me what you want, and I'll decide whether it's worth bothering His Excellency about." He shot Jody a look. "For the sake of the woman, of course."

And accompanying the look was a smile. A grim smile, but a smile nonetheless.

Jody frowned. Smitty was blinded, Rashida was a hostage, and the Marine was loose on the ship. What in the Worlds did Kemp have to smile about?

And then, belatedly, she got it.

Because Smitty *wasn't* blinded. The grenade may have dazzled his eyes, but Cobra optical enhancements were totally independent systems, their sensors implanted in the skin around the eye sockets. Clearly, Smitty's overacting was for the Marine's benefit, playing his supposed helplessness for all it was worth in hopes of convincing his opponent that the only threats were waiting around the corridor instead of lying right at his feet.

And with that, Rashida's terror-stricken voice also snapped into perspective. Picking up on Smitty's cue, she was playing the helpless, terrified female hostage who couldn't possibly be a threat.

"Sorry, but what I have to say is for Qasaman ears," the Marine said. "Commodore Santores has a proposal to present the Qasamans. That's why Commander Tamu wanted Shahni Omnathi to come to Aventine, so that he and the commodore could discuss the matter directly."

"I thought Tamu came to Caelian to bring Governor Uy to the Dome so they could put him on trial for treason."

"I don't know any of those details," the Marine said. His tone was one of casual dismissal, as if the incident had simply been a misunderstanding instead of a violent clash that had ended in multiple deaths. "All I know is that there was a lot of discussion among the officers on the way here about how we could get in contact with Qasama. When Commander

Tamu found out Shahni Omnathi was here, naturally he jumped at the chance to invite him to Aventine."

"I remember it being more a demand than a request," Kemp said grimly.

"Yeah, Tamu can be a jerk sometimes," the Marine said. "But that's not the point. Commodore Santores isn't here, which means it falls to me to make his pitch."

"Like I said, go ahead," Kemp said. "But you start by talking to *me*. No, strike that—you start by letting your hostages go."

The Marine snorted. "You'll forgive me if I don't exactly trust your word. Not after what you did during a supposedly peaceful prisoner exchange."

"Our people shouldn't have been prisoners in the first place," Nisti put in harshly.

"They came aboard with malicious intent," the Marine countered. "Would *you* have just let men like that wander freely around your territory?"

"As our guest said, we've distanced ourselves from the point," Omnathi's voice came from the corridor on the far side of the standoff. Hopefully, he was standing out of range in the mirror-image corridor curve to where Jody and Kemp were currently skulking. "You say you have a proposal. Speak. I will listen."

"Thank you for your willingness, Shahni Omnathi," the Marine said. "Here's the basics. Commodore Santores wants to arrange an alliance between the Dominion and Qasama. To that end..."

He continued on; and as he did so, Jody stepped closer to Kemp. "Kemp?"

"Don't worry, Kazi's watching the other gunbay," he murmured. "If this is a diversion, the guy in there won't get very far."

Jody frowned at the curve of the corridor, listening with half an ear to the Marine's speech. Something was wrong here. "*Has* he tried anything?"

Kemp shook his head. "I haven't heard any noise. Trust me, there *would* be noise."

Jody clenched her teeth. There would be noise, all right. Noise, violence, and probably some death, too.

Yet none of that had happened. And if diversion wasn't the purpose of this standoff, what was? "Why was Rashida here?" she asked. "Isn't she supposed to be in CoNCH?"

"No, she's on a half-hour check schedule," Kemp said. "She was probably just keeping Smitty company. She does that a lot when he's on watch duty."

"So if the Marine has a view onto the corridor he'd know that," Jody said, trying to think. Given that practically everyone else aboard was either a Djinni or a Cobra, it certainly made sense for him to grab Rashida. "But if this isn't a diversion—"

"Oh, hell," Kemp said, very quietly.

Jody tensed. Had he heard something from the other side of the ship, some noise that her normal human hearing hadn't picked up? "What is it?" she whispered.

"Rashida and Smitty," Kemp said. "Our primary and secondary pilots. He's got both of them."

"It gains him nothing," Nisti said. "Ifrit Ghushtre and Shahni Omnathi have also made themselves proficient in the vessel's operation. And he will certainly not be permitted to come within firing range of either of them."

"Maybe he doesn't have to," Jody said slowly, staring at the curve of the corridor. If Rashida and Smitty were in the corridor, and Omnathi was at the far side listening to the Marine's pitch... "Where's Ifrit Ghushtre? Is he with Shahni Omnathi?"

"Yes." Nisti did a sudden double-take. "Son of a *snake*."

"Exactly," Jody said, her stomach tightening. "There's no one in CoNCH who knows what any of the controls and readouts mean."

"But how does that gain him anything?" Kemp asked, sounding bewildered. "We're watching CoNCH. Neither Marine can get in."

"Maybe they don't have to," Jody said, pulling up a mental image of the *Squire*'s layout. "Did anyone ever find an auxiliary control room? A mini-CoNCH, or something like that?"

"No," Kemp said. "Maybe a ship this small doesn't have one."

"Or maybe those backups are in the gunbays," Jody said.

"The *gunbays*?" Kemp's eyes widened. "You're kidding."

"Why not?" Jody said. "They're secure and well-armored, and they're far enough from the main CoNCH that a hit on one of them might leave the other one intact."

"Yes, but—" Kemp waved a helpless hand. "People *shoot* at gunbays. Don't they?"

"Probably," Jody said. "But the only way this makes any sense is if the other Marine is doing something in his bay while this one is holding our attention here."

"I agree with you, Cobra Kemp, that the notion borders on the ridiculous," Nisti said grimly. "I also agree with Jody Moreau that the possibility cannot be ignored."

Kemp glared at the corridor wall. "So what do we do?"

Jody tuned back into the Marine's monologue. He'd left the subject of treaties and was speaking about the wonders of the Dominion of Man and the privileges of being part of it. "We need to end this," she said. "I'm guessing Smitty and Rashida have worked out a plan to take him down and are waiting for an opening."

"Only they don't know we're running a time limit," Kemp said.

"They must be alerted," Nisti agreed. "Is there a code you can use to signal them?"

"Nothing that wouldn't be ambiguous and confusing," Kemp said, his forehead wrinkling. "We'd do better for one of us to circle around to where Shahni Omnathi and Ghushtre are and tell one of them to head back to CoNCH and find out what's going on."

"They will not leave," Kazi said grimly. "Shahni Omnathi, because his sudden departure from the conversation would alert the soldier that we were aware of his deception. Ifrit Ghushtre, because his task is to protect His Excellency. He will not leave without him."

"Even for something like this?" Kemp pressed. "Even if we can guarantee the Shahni's safety?"

"He will not leave," Kazi repeated.

"Wait a second," Jody said as a new thought suddenly struck her. "We don't need either of them to leave if we can get Rashida out of there."

Kemp shook his head. "The Marine isn't going to give up his hostage."

"No," Jody agreed. "Not unless he can trade up to something better."

Kemp's eyes widened. "Out of the question."

"We have no choice," Jody said flatly. "I'm practically the only person aboard who he wouldn't see as a threat. Especially since I'm a woman and we've seen that the Dominion doesn't think much of women. If I pitch it as one emotional female trying to protect an even more emotional female, he may go for it."

"No," Kemp insisted. "Aside from anything else, your mother will kill me if she ever finds out I let you do it."

"If you don't let me go she may never have the chance," Jody shot back. "The other Marine could be setting a self-destruct right now. Or overloading the drive, or who knows what."

"She's right," Nisti said. His voice was tight, but there was an edge of respect mixed into his tone. "Do not fear, Kemp. She is a Moreau. She will win through."

Kemp bared his teeth, then gave a reluctant nod. "You've just arrived, and I'm too slow to stop you from going in there. Got it?"

Jody nodded, feeling her pulse pounding at the base of her neck as she took a few silent steps backward. It was the only way, but that didn't mean she had to like it. Bracing her feet against the deck, she flexed her shoulders once to relax them and then launched herself toward the corridor curve.

Kemp hit his cue perfectly. "Jody, keep back—Jody, *stop*!" he said, raising his voice as she raced past him.

"Rashida?" she called, ignoring Kemp's order and dodging his token attempt to grab her arm as she ran around the curve into the gunbay area.

The scene was pretty much as she'd envisioned it. The Marine was standing beside the gunbay door, his back to the wall, his legs spread out in a solid shoulder-width stance. Rashida stood in front of him, her back to him, her body pinned against his chest by his left forearm across her throat. Smitty was on his knees across the corridor from them, his fingers pressed to his eyes, his face screwed up in pain at his blindness. The Marine's right hand was tucked away behind Rashida's back where Jody couldn't see whether he had a weapon there or not.

Though at this point a hand weapon would be pretty redundant. The Marine was wearing a Dominion combat suit, complete with the epaulets whose multiple auto-targeting lasers Jody had seen demonstrated back on Caelian. Those lasers could take out Rashida, Smitty, and Jody herself if the Marine chose: quickly, efficiently, and without the man himself having to move a muscle.

She was two steps in from the curve before the Marine seemed to recover from his surprise at his unexpected company. "Halt!" he snapped.

"Please," Jody said, trying for a tone of dignified pleading as she obediently came to a stop. "Please. Can't you see she's terrified?"

"As long as your Cobras keep their distance she's got nothing to worry about," the Marine said, his eyes flicking back and forth between Jody and Smitty.

"She's a Qasaman," Jody said, enunciating her words carefully. "More than that, she's a Qasaman woman. They're not used to this kind of thing."

"I thought they just went through a war."

"Not the women," Jody said, watching his face carefully. If she could get him to hook onto the Dominion cultural ethos that saw women as having limited capabilities and subservient societal roles, maybe she could make this work. "If you let her go, I'll take her place."

"Yeah, right," the Marine scoffed. "I'm supposed to believe this was your idea? That the Cobras are just offering the great Jody Moreau Broom up as a sacrificial lamb?"

"What sacrifice?" Jody countered. "You said there wouldn't be any trouble as long as no one attacked you."

"Don't play cute," the Marine growled. "I know damn well that you're planning a—"

And in the middle of his sentence Rashida grabbed the arm pressed against her throat, jabbed her right heel down on the Marine's foot, bent her left knee to bring her left heel up against the wall between his thighs, then straightened the knee and sent them both toppling forward. Before the Marine could move his free foot to try to break their fall, an invisible wall seemed to slam across Jody's body, blurring her vision and tilting the universe violently around her. Rashida and the Marine continued their face-first fall—

They were a fraction of a second from impact when a faint flash of current arced from the stunner in Smitty's right little finger to the top of the Marine's head. Rashida landed hard on the deck, the Marine slamming down on top of her.

And as they hit the deck, a small handgun went skittering across the deck from the unconscious Marine's hand.

"Clear!" Smitty barked, scrambling to his feet. Grabbing the Marine's arm, he flipped his unconscious form off Rashida and dropped to one knee beside her. "Rashida?" he asked anxiously, reaching a hand to her cheek.

"I'm all right," Rashida said, sounding a little winded as she pushed herself up, glancing over as Kemp and Nisti charged around the corner. "He's heavier than he looks."

"Probably the combat gear," Smitty grunted, shifting his hand to her upper arm. "Let's get you to sick bay and make sure he didn't crack any of your ribs."

"I don't think he did," Rashida said again, wincing a bit as he helped her to her feet. "We also need to go there to have your eyes looked at."

"Afraid that'll have to wait," Kemp said as he and Nisti knelt beside the unconscious Marine and began carefully removing the tunic with its lethal epaulets. "We think this was a diversion to keep us occupied so the Marine in the other gunbay could do something in there, possibly messing with one of our flight systems. Rashida, you need to get to CoNCH right away and see what's going on."

"Understood," Omnathi said. "Djinni Nisti, escort her to CoNCH."

"Yes, Your Excellency." Scooping up the handgun and tucking it into his belt, Nisti took Rashida's other arm, and the three of them disappeared around the corridor curve.

"Okay, he's disarmed," Kemp announced, and Jody turned around again to see him carefully folding up the Marine's tunic. "What would you like me to do with him, Your Excellency?"

"I'm told there is a compartment aboard with reversed locks where Jody Moreau was kept prisoner while on Caelian," Omnathi said, regarding the Marine thoughtfully. "Will that serve?"

"It should, Your Excellency," Kemp confirmed,

getting a grip under the Marine's arms and hauling him upright. "Jody, come show me where it is, will you?"

It took two minutes for Jody to lead Kemp to the makeshift prison where she'd spent two glorious days before the Qasamans had broken in and freed her. Kemp spent another ten minutes going through the cabin and removing everything the Marine could conceivably use as a weapon or for escape once he woke up. Only then was he willing to leave the unconscious man alone.

They reached CoNCH to find Rashida and Smitty at the control consoles, Omnathi standing silent watch behind them. "Prisoner is secured, Your Excellency," Kemp murmured as they came up behind the older man.

Omnathi nodded acknowledgment. "Cobra Smith?" he prompted.

"I think we got it in time, Your Excellency," Smitty said. "Rashida's double-checking, but I think we stopped him."

"What was he doing?" Jody asked.

"Trying to change our course back to Aventine and then lock down the helm," Smitty said grimly. "He got most of the first part keyed in, but luckily he hadn't gotten to the second yet. Rashida's got us back on our original course, and I *think* we've got him locked out. At least for now."

"Do we know where the control cables come into CoNCH?" Kemp asked. "If we can cut them, that should end it for good."

"It should," Smitty agreed. "Except that we don't know if they even come in here."

"They shouldn't," Omnathi said. "A system meant

for use in the event of disaster in CoNCH should have entirely separate control lines."

"Yes, of course they should," Kemp said, sounding disgusted with himself. "Sorry—wasn't thinking."

"Luckily, I don't think he knows a lot more about the nav system than we do," Smitty said. "I'm guessing you'd normally man each gunbay with a gunner and a spotter who doubles as your emergency control tech. It looks like Tamu only had time to get the gunners in place."

"The one we caught was certainly a Marine," Jody said. "Let's just hope the man in the other gunbay isn't a control tech."

"He isn't," Omnathi assured her. "If so, he would have made this move much earlier. Most likely immediately after we came aboard, when we ourselves had only limited knowledge of the vessel. Since it has apparently taken this long for him to read and understand the operational manual, it is clear he's also a warrior."

"Yes, that makes sense," Jody said, feeling her face warming. Like Kemp, she hadn't thought her comment all the way through before opening her mouth.

Still, Omnathi was probably used to that. He was roughly the same age as Jody's mother Jin, but his physical condition was that of a man a decade or two older than that. A lifetime of mind-enhancing drugs had made him one of Qasama's best strategists, but that brilliance had come at a severe cost.

Ghushtre had promised that the drugs Jody would be taking to speed up her Cobra training were of a much milder variety. Still, they *were* from the same chemical class as the ones that had taken their toll on Omnathi.

Firmly, Jody put it out of her mind. There were more than enough things to worry about right now without dragging in future ones.

"Is the threat now neutralized?" Omnathi asked. "Rashida Vil?"

"A moment." Rashida made a final handful of keystrokes and then peered at one of the displays. "Yes, Your Excellency."

"Good," Omnathi said. "Now perhaps you will explain to me how it is you're still alive."

Rashida stiffened. "I don't understand, Your Excellency."

"The Marine had a weapon held against your back," Omnathi said. "You attacked him, yet he did not fire. Explain."

"I cannot," Rashida said. "Perhaps the confusion of Cobra Smith's sonic blast put it from his mind."

"Such an attack should have been even more likely to prompt a counterattack." Omnathi shifted his eyes to Jody. "Jody Moreau? Have *you* an explanation?"

"I don't know, either," Jody said. "But it's likely that the Dominion of Man trains its soldiers to defend its women. In the quickness and confusion of the moment, that instinct of protection may have overridden other considerations."

"Sounds good to me," Kemp seconded. "You were taking a hell of a risk, though, Smitty. Even without the sonic he could have fried all three of you before he even hit the deck."

"You want to argue, argue with Rashida," Smitty said. "It was her plan and timing."

Jody frowned. "*Her* plan?"

"Well, it's not like I could say anything, not with

Dogbreath staring right at me," Smitty pointed out. "Rashida came up with the plan and mouthed it to me in between all those weepings and wailings."

"Except for the stun-lightning at the end," Rashida said. "I hadn't thought of that."

"Right, that one was mine," Smitty confirmed. "She'd already pointed out that once he was lying flat on the deck with the top of his epaulets toward me I'd be out of range of his lasers. But she *would* still be in range, and I wanted to make sure he didn't take a grudge shot."

"He *is* still alive, isn't he?" Rashida asked hesitantly. "I asked Smitty to keep him alive if possible."

"Yes, he's fine," Kemp said. "Stunner head shots can be risky, but he survived it. Though if it was a choice between you and him, I'd have let him croak, too."

"Thank you," Rashida murmured.

"And with the vessel again under our control," Omnathi said, "you and Cobra Smith will go to the sick bay to be examined."

"Yes, Your Excellency," Rashida said, giving the sign of respect as she stood up.

"Yes, Your Excellency," Smitty echoed, also standing up and fumbling briefly before he could get a grip on the back of his chair.

Omnathi gestured. "Jody Moreau, you will accompany them."

"Yes, Your Excellency," Jody said. "A thought first, though, if I may. Now that we have access to the portside gunbay, we may be able to locate the control cables coming from there and maybe track them to wherever they end up. That might give us a clue to where the ones from the starboard bay come in, and cut them at that end."

"Good idea," Kemp said, nodding. "With your permission, Your Excellency, I'll get started on that."

"Agreed, Cobra Kemp," Omnathi said. "We shall begin the investigation immediately. Well done, Jody Moreau."

"Thank you, Your Excellency." Jody touched Smitty's arm as he and Rashida passed her. "Which of you needs me the most?"

"I do," Smitty said. "Rashida is breathing okay again, so she was probably just winded. You can take my other arm and make sure she doesn't steer my shins into anything. I never noticed what lousy peripheral vision these optical enhancements have."

"You got it," Jody assured him. "Okay, Rashida: in step. Left, right, left..."

CHAPTER SIX

After a boyhood filled with the excitement and drama of adventure tales, Paul found the MindsEye room to be something of a disappointment.

He'd expected it to be dark and gloomy, with subdued lights blinking ominously from black consoles; or else pure white, gleaming with chrome and clean ceramic, the lair of a pathologically germophobic mad scientist. But it was neither. It was simply a normal-looking compartment off the *Algonquin*'s sick bay recovery room, its walls and ceiling the same soothing blue as the room where the ship's chief medical officer had given him a quick exam and certified him fit for the procedure.

"Let me explain how this is going to work," Captain Lij Tulu said, standing between and half a step behind a pair of combat-suited Marines as the med techs strapped Paul into a heavily padded chair at the center point of three wall-to-ceiling pillars. "We'll start by mapping your entire brain on a cellular and electro-biological level. Once we have our baseline, we'll ask you some questions to identify and mark the sections of memory we're most interested in. After that, we'll start sifting through those regions and look for the specific memories we need."

He smiled, a snake's smile. "If we're lucky, we'll find the visual image of that navigational display and get Qasama's coordinates on the first pass. If not, we'll keep at it until we've looked at everything."

"You're wasting your time," Paul said, trying to filter the dread out of his voice. Commodore Santores had assured him that the MindsEye was perfectly safe as long as it was handled properly. He'd also added his personal guarantee that Lij Tulu would take every precaution to protect him.

All of which made perfect sense, of course. Santores desperately wanted Qasama's location, and the commodore would hardly risk damaging one of the only two people on Aventine who might hold that information.

There was just one small flaw in everybody's logic. As far as Paul could tell, no one had ever tried the MindsEye on a Cobra before.

The device had never been used on someone with a layer of tough ceramic laminae on the skull bones. It had never been tried on someone with a network of optronic equipment jacked into the brain from the ears and eye sockets.

It *especially* hadn't been tried on someone with a nanocomputer implanted under his brain. A nanocomputer whose designers had very much *not* wanted their toy attacked, neutralized, reprogrammed, removed, or in any other way messed with.

They'd not wanted it so much, in fact, that they'd put in some nasty safeguards to make sure none of that happened.

"Last chance to be reasonable," Lij Tulu said as the techs finished and stepped away from the chair. "Tell me where Qasama is and you'll be sleeping in your own bed tonight."

"I don't know where it is," Paul said, looking him straight in the eye.

"Maybe," Lij Tulu said with a shrug. "Maybe not." He gestured to the man seated at the main control board. "Let's find out together."

Paul closed his eyes, feeling a wan smile tweaking at the corners of his lips. Some *very* nasty safeguards . . . and Paul himself had no idea what those safeguards were. Or what it took to trigger them.

That, too, was something they would all find out together.

The Deuel Center had started life as a Cobra way station some twenty years earlier, a place for storing supplies and equipment where local scavengers couldn't get at them. But as the DeVegas province population grew and other stations were established, the center had been abandoned. It had been subsequently bought by a local naturalist, renamed for her late husband, and set up as a nature observation post for local biology and ecology students.

It was rarely used outside of daylight hours, which made it ideal for a late-night rendezvous. More importantly, from Lorne's point of view, the fact that it had been closed and unoccupied for the past few hours meant that the day's residual heat had long since dissipated, which meant that anyone skulking inside would stand out like a torch on Lorne's infrareds.

But the place was as dark on IR as it was in the enhanced starlight of his light-amplifiers. If Colonel Reivaro had learned about Lorne's clandestine meeting, he was at least smart enough to pass over the obvious ambush locale.

Lying among the reeds near the river's edge, Lorne took a moment to check his nanocomputer's clock circuit. It was three minutes to one.

He eased a little closer to the rippling water, keeping one eye on the sky and the other on the riverbank. Spine leopards also liked to establish way stations along rivers, and while most of them preferred to hunt in the daytime, it wasn't at all unheard of for one of them to awaken with an appetite and go on the prowl for a snack. It would be highly embarrassing if one of the predators nailed him before Reivaro even had a chance at his shot.

One o'clock came and went. Kicker was now officially late, assuming Lorne had interpreted the message correctly. Still, there were plenty of innocuous reasons why the other Cobra might have been delayed. Lorne would give him another half hour before moving on to other options.

It was seventeen minutes after one when the diffuse glow of distant headlights appeared among the trees to the north. Lorne notched up his audios, and a moment later picked up the faint sound of an approaching car. He did a quick estimate of the vehicle's intercept time, then sent a slow, careful look around. An approaching vehicle was the classic diversion, and he had no intention of getting caught that easily.

No trap had been sprung by the time the vehicle emerged from the scattered thickets about two hundred fifty meters away. It was hard to identify through the glare of the headlights, but it looked and sounded like a pretty standard Cobra patrol car. It continued on for another fifty meters or so, then rolled to a stop. A figure climbed out, even harder to make out in the headlight shadows than the vehicle itself. The figure took a few steps toward the river.

And there was a flash of light behind the headlights as a flicker of laser fire shot toward the riverbank.

Lorne tensed, pressing himself closer to the ground. The laser fired again, paused, then fired a third time. Probably a Cobra, but Dominion Marines used lasers, too. Easing his head up a few centimeters, Lorne searched the target area, trying to figure out what the shooter was firing at.

Nothing. Notching up his opticals' light-amp level, he let his eyes continue on, sweeping the entire riverbank. His gaze reached the section directly across the river—

He froze. Crouched beside a gnarled tree on the far bank was a second figure, whose approach Lorne had missed entirely. Feeling his heartbeat suddenly speed up, he keyed in his telescopics.

It wasn't Kicker. But it *was* another familiar face: Dushan Matavuli, one of the biggest ranchers in this part of the province. More importantly, a man who'd actively helped Lorne's fellow Cobras, especially his friends Dillon de Portola and Badger Werle, during their guerrilla war against the occupying Trofts.

And then, as Lorne tried to pierce the gloom around the other man, Matavuli lifted a hand and beckoned.

Lorne wrinkled his nose as he glanced at the river. *Nice night for a swim*, he thought sourly. On the surface, it was hardly an outlandish request—after all, he'd sneaked into Archway last night via the Caluma River, and then sneaked his mother out the same way. And just this morning he'd gone for a similar dip in order to retrieve Kicker's message.

But that had all taken place in the Caluma, which was well-traveled, well-monitored, and relatively free of predators. This was the Pashington, which meandered through the sparsely populated ranching areas of DeVegas province and was none of the three.

Still, if it was the only way, it was the only way. Getting up into a crouch, Lorne started to slip off his jacket—

And dropped instantly back to the ground, one leg collapsing beneath him to angle him into a sideways dive as his nanocomputer took over his servo network, triggering a pre-programmed evasive maneuver. Something big was coming over the river in a fast, shallow arc, heading straight toward him.

He was two meters from where he'd started, rolling up into a defensive crouch with fingertip lasers ready, when the object hit the riverbank halfway up the slope with a muffled thud. Lorne peered at it, automatically holding his breath in case it was some sort of gas bomb.

It wasn't a bomb, or any other kind of weapon. It was, instead, the grabber hook off a vehicle-mounted winch. Even as his brain caught up with that identification, there was a stuttering *whoosh* as the attached cable splashed into the river water.

He was still trying to figure out what was going

on when the cable rose a few centimeters from the water, clearly being pulled from the other end, and dragged the grabber across the ground until it hooked on the curve of a thick tree root poking up among the reeds. A final tug locked the grabber firmly into the root, and the cable stiffened as it was pulled taut.

And as Lorne peered across the river again he saw Matavuli gesture him to cross.

"You've got to be kidding," Lorne muttered, looking at the cable. He looked back at Matavuli, who was now pointing to the taut cable with one hand and tapping the back of his own head with the other.

Was he suggesting...?

Ridiculous. The Cobra gear had been designed for combat, with the pre-programmed reflexes necessary for combat survival. The techs who'd put it all together surely hadn't bothered with crazy daredevils' tightrope-walking capability.

But Matavuli was still jabbing his finger at the cable and pointing to the general area on his head where Cobra nanocomputers were located. And the option, apparently, was a midnight swim.

The laser fire to the north was still going on, but it had slowed markedly from its earlier volume. If that was Kicker's diversion, it seemed to be coming to a halt. If Lorne was going to do this, he needed to do it now.

Clenching his teeth, wondering distantly just what kind of nasties might be lurking under the rippling river surface, he rose to his feet, stepped onto the cable, and started walking.

And to his astonishment, kept right on going.

Lorne had long since become used to having his nanocomputer take command of his body at moments of danger, and he also knew a whole list of techniques for setting it up to execute specific maneuvers. Even so, everything he'd ever done had been a variant of some technique or group of techniques he'd been taught back at the academy. To discover that his equipment still had secrets he'd never suspected was more than a little disconcerting.

But this was definitely real. Lorne and his brother Merrick had tried the tightrope thing a few times when they were children, and Lorne had never made it more than two steps before flailing his way to a helpless tumble from the line, which had fortunately been set only thirty centimeters above the ground. Now, though, he was striding almost casually across the river, his outstretched arms waggling up and down of their own accord as his nanocomputer guided his steps and his balance.

Thirty seconds later, he was across.

Somewhere during Lorne's journey Matavuli had disappeared, backing away into the brush. But Lorne didn't need him to show the way. Dropping back into a crouch on the soft ground of the bank, he followed the cable through the reeds and bushes.

At the end of the line, as expected, he found Brandeis "Kicker" Pierce with the cable now lying loose on the ground in front of him. Also in front of him were a pair of deep indentations where he'd dug his heels into the ground while he belayed the line.

Wrapped around his throat was the red neckband that Colonel Reivaro had ordered placed on all the DeVegas Cobras.

"Broom," Pierce murmured, throwing a quick look at the sky. "I see you got our message. Any problems getting here?"

"None that I noticed," Lorne said, frowning. There was a slight tingling at his ears, the sound created by the Cobra microphone-blocking sonic. "And if Reivaro tracked me, he really should have sprung his trap by now." He nodded toward the neckband. "Do those things transmit, too?"

"We don't know," Pierce said. "But better safe than sorry. Especially given what happens when we displease our new masters."

Lorne winced. From the quick run-down he'd received from Yates during the rescue of his mother he knew there was a small explosive charge in each of the neckbands. Nothing too big; but then, it didn't take much force to shatter someone's windpipe or shred a nearby artery or vein. "Yes, I heard," he said. "What can I do?"

"I don't know," Pierce countered. "What *can* you do? Not about this," he added, wagging a finger at the neckband. "Digger's already looked at it, and he can't figure out how to get the damn things off. Not without blowing the occupant's head off, anyway."

"Let's not be too hasty," Lorne said, moving closer and keying a bit more power to his light-amps. The neckbands definitely *seemed* foolproof: no obvious latches or fasteners, no surface features that might give a clue as to the mechanism beneath the outer layer, no mottling or other hints showing up on infrared.

Still, there might be a side-door trick Reivaro hadn't thought of. "How much room is there between your neck and the collar?" he asked.

Experimentally, Pierce slipped a finger behind the neckband. "A centimeter," he said. "Maybe one and a half. But there's nothing back there that'll help—Digger's already looked."

"That's okay," Lorne assured him, looking around. "Is Matavuli still here?"

"He's gone back to the car," Pierce said, nodding up the slope of the bank. "Filling out a report on the river-water quality, in case someone in a uniform wanders by and asks. You need him back here?"

"No, you can deliver the message for me," Lorne said. "Here's what I need for him to do."

Pierce listened in silence as Lorne laid out the plan. "Going to be tricky," he warned when Lorne had finished. "Matavuli's got no real reason to go to Capitalia, and if Reivaro's got any brains, he'll be watching for odd travel moves."

"Not a problem," Lorne assured him. "As one of the biggest ranchers in the province, Matavuli has to be concerned about the disruption in Cobra patrols that Reivaro's restrictions are likely to cause. There *have* been disruptions, haven't there?"

"Oh, believe it, baby," Pierce assured him. "Between the guards he's slapped on Yates Fabrications—did you hear they'd gotten it up and running again?"

"No, I hadn't," Lorne said. He'd hoped his mother's sabotage would slow down Reivaro's plan for at least a few days. Clearly, Santores was serious about putting Aventine's industry base under his control. "What are they making?"

"Some kind of armor plate, just like Reivaro said," Pierce said. "Heavy stuff, too, a lot heavier than the fabricators are used to. No telling how long they'll hold up before this wrecks them. Yates's spitting nails—Reivaro's had to confine him to his house."

"With more Cobras siphoned off for guard duty, no doubt."

"Well, he's sure not going to waste his Marines on that," Pierce said. "They're all busy watching his headquarters and his hindquarters. If you didn't accomplish anything else with that raid last night, you at least put the fear of God into him."

"Good," Lorne said. "The more effort he puts into watching his own back, the less he'll have for watching everything else's. You think Matavuli will be willing to go?"

"If I can convince him he can make the trip plausible," Pierce said. "Reivaro spent a lot of today ramping up the threats and warnings. Yates's factory was just the first—they've already confiscated a couple of homes and at least one ranch for operational bases and troop quartering. Matavuli's got a family and a crew of ranch hands to support, and the Troft invasion pushed him pretty close to the line. He can't afford to take another hit."

"He should be fine, provided he goes to the Dome first," Lorne said. "The other trip can be slipped in afterward, with an equally reasonable rationale. There won't be anything suspicious for Reivaro or anyone else to point to."

"Assuming Reivaro needs anything more than his own fevered imagination," Pierce growled. "But this sounds like our best shot. Assuming it works, how and when do I contact you?"

Lorne pursed his lips. One day for travel each direction, just to be on the safe side, plus another three or four for the necessary work... "You still stationed at Smith's Forge?"

"Officially, yes, but Reivaro's signed me for a couple of shifts a week on Archway patrol," Pierce said. "Don't know if that'll hold up, but for now that's my schedule."

"Where are you supposed to be the day after tomorrow?"

"That'll be one of my Smith's Forge shifts," Pierce said. "How about Whistling Waller's Tavern? It's at the south end of town, right up against the fence."

"I've heard of it," Lorne said. "Hopefully, Matavuli will be able to get you a preliminary report before we meet."

"Unless Reivaro decides to shift everyone and everything around again," Pierce said acidly. "He's like a sociopathic kid with a new set of toy soldiers."

"Yes, that sounds like him," Lorne said carefully, a bit taken aback by the anger simmering beneath Pierce's professional calm.

And belatedly, it occurred to him that while he and his mother had been holed up in the cave all day, resting and thinking, Pierce and the other Cobras had been facing Reivaro and his Marines, taking and obeying orders, with the collars wrapped around their necks a constant reminder that they were a single infraction away from instant death.

Lorne might be on the run, but in many ways he had it easier than anyone else in the province.

"So that's it?" Pierce asked.

"That's it," Lorne confirmed. "I take it I head back the same way I came?"

"Unless you'd rather swim it this time." Pierce

shook his head. "I can't believe there's still stuff tucked away in the nanocomputer that we didn't know about. They might at least have mentioned the wire-walking thing to us."

"That assumes they knew about it themselves," Lorne pointed out. "Who's to say they did?"

Pierce grunted. "Which begs the question of what *else* might be in there nobody knows about. But never mind that now." Reaching down, he picked up the cable and then set his heels back in the impressions in the ground. "Be sure to unhook the grabber and toss it back once you're over. Those things don't come cheap, and Matavuli will skin me alive if I lose it."

"Understood," Lorne said. "Good luck."

"Thanks," Pierce said. "Watch yourself, okay? You *and* your mother."

Lorne winced. Safe in their cave, while the others faced death. "I will," he said.

"I mean it," Pierce said, a sudden new intensity in his voice. "We've been hit hard, and we're riding low in the water. We'll come back; but right now, what we need is a symbol of defiance. You and your mother are that symbol." He smiled humorlessly. "It doesn't hurt that you're both legends, either. So stay hidden. And stay free."

They would indeed stay free, Lorne promised silently as he retraced his steps across the slender cable to the other side of the river. But they wouldn't stay hidden. Not by a long shot.

So Colonel Reivaro didn't like rogue Cobras showing up in his headquarters and threatening him? Good. Lorne didn't like what the Marines were doing to his town and province, either. That made them even.

Reivaro seemed to think fear was a good way to dominate the people of Aventine. Time to see how well he liked it when the push came from the other direction.

CHAPTER SEVEN

Merrick had set his nanocomputer clock circuit to wake him after five hours. But the stress of the day, plus the hard floor of the hideout, made sleep elusive and unrestful. Four and a half hours after he and Anya had settled down, after already having been awake for a good half hour, he finally gave up.

Anya took the short night in stride. She also seemed to have accepted that her failure to lead them someplace useful wasn't really her fault. Or if she hadn't, at least she made no further apologies or self-deprecating comments about it.

The sky to the east had begun turning to blue, Merrick saw as he lifted the boulder and climbed back into the cool, fresh air, though the sun had yet to rise high enough to be visible over the mountains. He made a quick check for Trofts and predators, and finding neither he and Anya headed off once again into the forest.

As he had the night before, Merrick made sure

to watch and listen carefully for roving patrols. Once again, the aliens were conspicuous by their absence. Either they were still way the hell off elsewhere in the forest, far enough that their aircars weren't audible, or else they'd concluded he really *was* dead and all gone back to their bases.

Merrick wished he could believe that. It would make life so much easier if he and Anya could move around more or less freely.

Unfortunately, he didn't believe it for a minute. He'd taken down a Troft aircar with one of his fingertip lasers, and even though he'd tried to make it look like the shot had come from his hang glider's control bar instead, there was no way around the fact that advanced weapons weren't something Muninn's human slaves should have access to. Even if the Trofts believed he was dead, they would certainly keep up the search until they had at least recovered his body.

Maybe they weren't patrolling the skies nearby because they were concentrating all their recovery efforts on the distant ravine. But no matter how impenetrable the area's vegetation, sooner or later they would realize he hadn't died there and would expand the search. When that happened, Merrick knew, he'd better have a plan ready.

The crash site that Merrick and Anya had seen two nights earlier from halfway up the mountain behind Anya's village hadn't been very revealing. It had been little more than a burned-edge gash through the trees, with the doomed vehicle itself out of sight. About all Merrick had been able to glean from the view was that it had been a large aircraft or small spacecraft, and further deduction had suggested it had been one of the freighters bringing in razorarms from Qasama. *Why* the Trofts wanted razorarms here, particularly razorarms that had learned that humans weren't to be messed with, was still a mystery.

The crash was several days old, and Merrick wasn't sure what exactly he thought he might find there. But he needed some answers, and he and Anya needed someplace to go. The crash site seemed like a reasonable place to start.

Merrick usually had a pretty good sense of direction. But navigating the Muninn forest proved trickier than he'd expected, with the terrain and occasional impassable clumps of trees and bushes forcing him to veer off course or sometimes turning him around completely. Fortunately, Anya had a better feel for the forest than he did and was always able to get them back on track.

Still, between the travel and the ever-present need for vigilance, progress was slow. The distance to the crash site was less than fifteen kilometers, but it wasn't until early afternoon that they finally arrived.

At first glance, the ship looked to be in surprisingly good shape. It was about a hundred meters long, a fairly typical size for a Troft medium freighter. The style, too, was familiar: Merrick had seen other such ships hunting for razorarms back on Qasama. He and Anya had happened to arrive near the bow, and aside from some serious dents and cracks where the ship had plowed through the trees, it looked mostly undamaged.

But that first look was deceptive. As they worked their way across the scorched ground alongside the wreck, Merrick saw that the aft hull plates were blackened with heat stress, and there were considerably more cracks in the sides than even at the bow.

Anya spotted that, too. "Why is the back part more damaged than the front?" she murmured.

"I don't know," Merrick said. "Let's take a look."

The scorched ground and burned grass turned out to be much easier to traverse than the main part of the forest had been, though the ashes sometimes hid shards of broken tree or jutting roots that could trip up an unwary traveler. As they worked their way aft, Merrick began to pick up the stench of burned plastic, hydraulic and coolant fluids, and a dozen other odors that he couldn't identify. Whatever had happened back there, it had clearly left a serious mess behind.

It wasn't until they reached the rear of the ship that they found out just how big a mess it was.

"By the heavens and the land beneath," Anya murmured, her voice nearly unrecognizable.

"Yeah," Merrick agreed grimly, staring at the gaping, ragged-edged hole in the ship's starboard stern. Beyond the hole, the compartment's blackened walls were bent and cracked.

"What kind of weapon could have done such damage?" Anya asked, peering into the opening.

"Oh, there are plenty that could do that," Merrick said grimly. "I saw some of them on Qasama. But I don't think it was an attack. See how the edges of the hole angle outward? That implies the explosion came from inside, not outside."

"Then it was an accident?"

"Probably," Merrick said. "Let's see if we can get inside—I think I see some gaps we can squeeze through."

It *had* probably been an accident, Merrick reminded himself as he led the way carefully through the wrecked engine room. That was certainly the most likely explanation.

But he couldn't help remembering that those two Trofts on the mountainside had seemed awfully interested in seeing what Merrick and Anya knew about the wreck.

An internal explosion could have been an accident. It could also have been sabotage.

The engine room's doors were warped and jammed shut. But as he'd already noted, there were several cracks in the wall where seams had burst under the shock and pressure. They were narrow, but a couple of them proved to be passable. Merrick and Anya eased their way through, being careful not to slice clothing or flesh on the jagged edges, and headed inside.

Merrick had expected to find similar damage further in. To his mild surprise, the rest of the ship, even the sections just beyond the engine room bulkhead, seemed largely undamaged. The damage that *was* there looked more like a result of the crash than from the explosion. Apparently, the engine room had done a good job of containing the blast.

Just ahead of the engine room was the cargo section, which had been partitioned off into smaller cage-size compartments by sturdy open-mesh barriers. Definitely a livestock setup, almost certainly for the razorarms they'd encountered a few times in the forest. All the cages were empty, their doors hanging open.

"No corpses," Anya murmured, looking around. "They must all have escaped alive."

"At least temporarily," Merrick pointed out. "After

a crash like that, there could have been a lot of walking wounded."

"They may have been injured," Anya agreed. "But none were bleeding."

Merrick frowned, keying up his light-amps and infrared. There was nothing he could see in the pens that would support such a conclusion. "How do you figure that?"

"No blood flies," Anya said, gesturing. "If there were blood, blood flies would gather to feed."

Merrick winced. He hadn't heard of blood flies before, but they didn't sound pleasant. In fact, they sounded like something that would fit right into the Caelian ecological structure. "Unless they don't like razorarms," he reminded her. "They may only have a taste for local blood."

Anya shook her head. "It's not the blood itself they like, but the tiny creatures that gather and grow on the blood."

"Tiny—? Oh; bacteria," Merrick said, nodding. And it was reasonable to expect that *some* variety of Muninn's bacteria would find razorarm blood an acceptable meal and breeding ground. "That's good, actually. If the razorarms all made it out okay, the crew probably did, too. That means no bodies."

"I've seen bodies before," Anya said calmly. "Many of them. They don't disturb me."

Merrick felt his throat tighten. He'd seen bodies, too, far more than he liked. And they *did* still disturb him. "The living areas will be further forward," he said. "We'll take a look there, then go on up to the control section."

The living areas were a mess. Chairs and tables that should have been stowed or secured were scattered around, and the decks were littered with small items that should similarly have been put away before landing. "The crash definitely seems to have taken them by surprise," Merrick commented as they peered through the galley door. "Don't seem to be any foodstuffs mixed in, though, so I'd guess no one was eating when the engine blew."

"Does that mean they must have been nearly to the ground?" Anya asked. "All would have jobs to do at that time, would they not?"

"I don't know," Merrick said. "I really haven't the faintest idea how a ship like this works."

"But I thought you had penetrated to the control areas of the ship that brought us here," Anya objected. "Didn't you see how they operated?"

"Different situation," Merrick said. "I only saw one small monitor station. Anyway, we were still just cruising at the time. I assume everyone has a job for landing, but I don't know..." He paused as an odd thought struck him.

"What is it?" Anya asked, craning her neck to see further into the galley. "What do you see?"

"Nothing here," Merrick said. "I was just thinking about the engine room. If someone was on duty back there, he would probably have been vaporized by the explosion. That means a lot of blood, probably pretty evenly spread across the walls." He gestured aft. "So just how fast do these blood flies of yours chow down, anyway?"

"Not so fast that they would have finished and been gone in only these few days," Anya said slowly.

"So no one was on duty back there," Merrick concluded, a knot starting to form in the pit of his stomach.

He really *didn't* know anything about spaceships; but at the same time, he couldn't remember seeing a single drama set in space where *someone* wasn't in the engine room, especially during liftoff and landing.

Of course, those dramas had dealt with human ships, not the Troft equivalents. On top of that, they *had* been fiction.

But it still seemed odd. "Or else he was on his way back—"

He tensed, looking around him. Somehow, while he'd been contemplating the mystery of the missing engineer, Anya had managed to slip away. "Anya?" he called, turning around.

She was nowhere to be seen. "Anya!"

"Here," her voice came from around the next corner ahead. "I thought I heard—"

Her voice cut off in mid-sentence. Swearing under his breath, Merrick charged down the corridor, hands curling into fingertip-laser positions. He rounded the corner—

And came to a sudden halt. Anya was standing in the middle of the corridor two meters ahead, her back to him, her shoulders stiff. "What is it?" Merrick asked, coming up beside her.

She lifted a hand to point in front of her. "Look."

At a half-dozen places down the corridor were clusters of softly buzzing insects, some motionless on the deck, the rest swarming lazily around them or going back and forth between the various clusters. Merrick frowned.

And then, the hairs on the back of his neck stiffened. "Are those . . . ?"

Anya nodded. "Blood flies," she said quietly. "How many masters, do you think, were aboard?"

Merrick looked down the corridor. Six clusters of flies. Six patches of blood.

Six dead Trofts?

Only it made no sense. This was a *corridor*, for heaven's sake. Not the bridge; not engineering; not sick bay; not the mess room. The patches weren't even clustered up against a wall, where the unfortunates might have been thrown by the impact of the crash.

Why in the Worlds would they all have been here? More importantly, why would they all have died here?

"Do we continue on?" Anya murmured.

Merrick took a careful breath. Six dead Trofts... "We go on," he said. "There might be other... evidence... further forward."

He was very careful, as he led the way past the flies, not to step on the spots where they were feeding.

They found no more clusters of flies as they moved through the corridors. But a few of the flies were still in evidence, flittering lazily about or pausing here and there on the deck. Merrick and Anya kept going; and finally, at the very front of the ship, they reached the control room.

To find one final cluster of blood flies, this group gathered around the pilot's seat.

"So there was a seventh master aboard?" Anya asked, gazing at the circling insects.

"Looks like it," Merrick said. "Remember the flies we passed on the way here? I think they were working on a blood trail." He pointed aft. "Whatever happened back there, I'm thinking the pilot was still alive. He'd mostly bled out, but he had enough strength and presence of mind left to crawl up here and bring the ship down with a minimum of damage."

"And then he died," Anya murmured. "And then the other masters took away the bodies?"

"I assume so," Merrick said. "It's not like you could crash a ship like this without someone noticing. There would have been Trofts on the scene as soon as they could scramble their aircars, probably within an hour. They'd have searched the ship, retrieved the bodies—" He scowled at a conspicuously empty pair of slots on the control board. "And pulled the data records," he finished. "Which means this little side trip was a complete waste of time. We still don't know why the Trofts are bringing razorarms to Muninn, and it doesn't look like there's anything left in here that's going to tell us."

"Yet perhaps the ship could be of other use," Anya said thoughtfully. "As you say, the masters have been here. Are they likely to return?"

Merrick shrugged. "Eventually, I assume they'll either try to move the wreck to one of their bases or, if that's not possible, to at least strip it of everything useful."

"But this won't be for some time yet?"

"No idea. Probably not." Merrick frowned suddenly. "Are you suggesting what I *think* you're suggesting?"

"We need a place to stay for a time," Anya pointed out. "Will this not do?"

Merrick looked around, chewing the inside of his cheek. If the Trofts had finished their preliminary investigation—and they'd certainly had enough time to do that—then there was no real reason for them to come back to the wreck anytime soon. There would be food and shelter, and if they stuck to the center areas, the sheer mass of metal would even absorb and dissipate their heat signatures.

But if the Trofts *did* decide to pay a surprise visit, their comfy little shelter would instantly turn into a death trap. "I don't know, Anya," he said hesitantly. "It might be safe for a day or two. But—"

He broke off, frowning in concentration. There'd been a sound just then, coming from the starboard side of the control room. A sound that had sounded like stealthy predator claws scraping softly against metal...

He looked at Anya. Her eyes were darting around the room, her throat tight. So she'd heard it too. Merrick keyed up his audios, turning his head slowly back and forth, waiting for the noise to repeat.

It did so, and this time he had it. There was a small, narrow door in the wall to the right of the main control console. An equipment access hatch, most likely. That was a good sign—if the space was mostly filled with machinery or electronics, whatever had found a way in was probably pretty small.

Which wasn't to say it might not also be dangerous. Motioning Anya to stay back, Merrick crossed the room and crouched beside the door. Now, close up, he could see that it was slightly out of true, its frame possibly warped in the crash.

Experimentally, he gave a gentle pull on the door's handle. The door didn't budge, but the handle itself seemed securely attached.

There was no doubt Merrick could get the door open. The question was how close he wanted to be to the compartment, and whatever was inside it, when he did.

Fortunately, there was a simple solution.

Sitting down in front of the door, he got a grip on the handle with his right hand and set his left foot against the wall beside the latch. A good tug with servo-enhanced muscles, combined with a simultaneous shove off the wall, should open the door and at the same time scoot him a meter or two back from whatever might come leaping out. Hopefully, that would buy him enough time and distance to let him either kill or stun it.

Or so went the theory. Unfortunately, the only way to find out for sure was to do it. Taking a deep breath, he braced himself, then yanked and kicked. The door popped open as Merrick's rear lifted briefly from the floor and then thudded down again on the deck—

And inside the compartment, twitching violently backward in surprise, was a Troft.

Not much of a Troft, really, Merrick saw as his brain reset its anticipations from possible deadly predator to probable deadlier enemy. The Troft was shorter and scrawnier than most of those Merrick and Anya had run into since leaving Qasama, with a wide-eyed and borderline terrified expression on his chicken-beaked face. His upper-arm radiator membranes were fully stretched out with fear or surprise or some other strong emotion. The compartment where he was half-lying, half-crouching was larger than Merrick had expected, but there wasn't a lot of room to spare for its current occupant. Gripped in the Troft's hand was what looked like a small knife.

And then, even as Merrick reflexively put targeting locks on the knife and the center of the Troft's forehead, the membranes closed down, the alien's whole body sagging with relief.

The posture lasted maybe two seconds. Then, just as suddenly, the Troft seemed to straighten up, or at least go as straight as his position in the cramped space would allow. [Slaves, you are,] he intoned in cattertalk.

Or tried to intone, anyway. His voice came out sounding more like that of a nervous youngling on his first trip away from home. [Assistance, I require it,] he continued, his voice sounding a little more weighty this time. [Assistance, you will provide it.]

He held out his hand, and Merrick saw now that what he'd thought was a knife was in fact only a small file. However the Troft had gotten himself stuck in there, he'd apparently been trying to grind away enough of the misaligned door to get it open.

[The order, I obey it,] Merrick said automatically, pushing himself off the deck.

And winced even before he heard Anya's quiet but sharp intake of breath. Merrick's accent, both his Anglic and his cattertalk, weren't quite right for Muninn's humans or for the Drim'hco'plai demesne Trofts who owned the planet. Anya had pointed that out even before they'd left Qasama, and they'd agreed that Merrick should pose as a mute.

Now, after a day of talking with Anya without having to worry about that, Merrick had completely forgotten the role he was supposed to be playing. But it was too late now.

Fortunately, the Troft didn't seem to notice. Possibly he had more important things to worry about.

His own current physical condition, for starters. As Merrick took the alien's outstretched hand he realized that what he'd taken to be scrawniness was instead dehydration and malnutrition.

Had he been trapped in that narrow space since

the ship crashed? It seemed incredible, but given the shape of the door Merrick couldn't see any other possibility.

Especially now that he was close enough to see— and smell—the sanitary collection system at the back of the compartment that had been improvised from a storage pouch and tool belt.

The compartment opening was narrow, but not too narrow to be a problem. Merrick got him out easily, and at Anya's silent prompting took a couple of respectful steps back while the alien rubbed, kneaded, and massaged his cramped arms and legs back into usefulness, all the while muttering phrases under his breath that Merrick's cattertalk lessons had never covered.

Finally, after a couple of minutes of work and curses, he straightened up, flapping his radiator membranes once and then resettling them against his arms. He was still short and a little emaciated, but he was once again a Troft, master of Muninn and all it contained.

And Merrick and Anya were once again slaves.

[Water, you will bring it to me,] he ordered. [Food, you will bring it to me.]

[The order, we obey it,] Anya spoke up before Merrick could respond.

Which was fine with him. She knew proper slave behavior far better than he did, and there was no reason to give the Troft another crack at Merrick's foreign accent if they could avoid it. She was welcome to take the lead from now on.

[Food and water, my companion will bring it,] she added.

Merrick gave her a little bow of his head and a mental salute for quick thinking. Perfect—setting her up as the dominant one of the pair would explain why she was doing all the talking. They'd passed the ship's galley on the way forward; hopefully, whoever had taken away the bodies hadn't also cleaned out the food stores. He bowed to the Troft and started to turn—

[The food and water, the female will bring it,] the Troft said. [The male, he will stay with me.]

Merrick froze in mid-turn, an uncomfortable feeling creeping up his back. He turned back to the Troft, to find the alien staring straight at him. For a half second their eyes met, before Merrick remembered his place and quickly lowered his gaze.

[The delay, why is there one?] the Troft demanded.

[The order, I obey it,] Anya said, and left the compartment.

Merrick kept his eyes on the deck, feeling sweat gathering on his forehead. *Now* what?

[Your eyes, you will raise them to me,] the Troft ordered.

Bracing himself, wondering distantly if a slave could be ordered to show disrespect to his masters, Merrick lifted his gaze to the Troft. The alien was still watching him. [Your name, you will give it to me.]

Merrick swallowed. [My name, Merrick Hopekeeper it is,] he said.

[My name, Kjoic it is,] the Troft responded. [Master Kjoic, that is how you will address me.]

[The order, I obey it, Master Kjoic,] Merrick said, frowning to himself. As far as he could remember, Kjoic was the first Troft who'd actually introduced himself since Commander Ukuthi sent him and Anya on this mission. Was Kjoic a more liberal breed of slave master? Or was he simply new to the position?

Merrick had never learned how to estimate Troft ages from their appearance. Now, he wished he had. Knowing Kjoic's age might have offered some clue to his odd behavior.

[The food, I will eat it,] Kjoic continued. [The journey to your home, we will then begin it.]

Merrick's stomach tightened. In retrospect, it was the obvious course of action for a rescued castaway trying to return to his people.

Except that Gangari was the absolute last place on the planet he and Anya could afford to go. After the violence of yesterday's escape, the whole village would be crawling with Trofts hunting for a clue as to the fugitives' whereabouts.

[The order, I obey it,] Merrick said, thinking furiously. [The hour, it is become late. The journey, it cannot be completed before nightfall.]

Kjoic's radiator membranes fluttered. [The journey, it cannot be undertaken at night?]

[Night predators, they also journey through the forest,] Merrick said.

[The reasoning, it is valid,] Kjoic said. [The journey, we will wait until morning to begin it.]

Merrick bowed his head. So he'd at least bought them a few hours. Though what they would do with that extra time he couldn't guess. [The order, I obey it,] he said.

[An order, I have not given one,] Kjoic said mildly. [Your words, they thus mean little.]

Merrick clenched his teeth. Who in hell *was* this guy? [Respect, the words are marks of it,] he explained. [The words, required of all slaves they are.]

[The words, they still mean little,] Kjoic said, sounding a little cross. [Your village, what is its name?]

Merrick froze. What was he supposed to say *now*?
[My village—]

[Svipall, our village is named,] Anya's voice interrupted.

Merrick looked behind him. Anya had returned, a bag of meal bars and a large bottle of water in her hands. [A full day, the journey will require it,] she added as she walked over to him.

[The journey, we will begin it in the morning,] Kjoic said, taking the bag and bottle. [The meal, I will eat it. A protective barrier against night predators, you will construct one.]

[The order, we obey it,] Anya said, bowing.

Apparently, Kjoic had no problem with a proper slave response to a proper order. That, or he was too hungry to split hairs. He was digging into the meal bar bag as Merrick and Anya left the compartment.

Merrick waited until they were two corridors away before speaking. "Nice timing," he murmured. "I had no idea what to tell him. Is Svipall a real village, or was that just to stall him off until we can ditch him?"

"It is real," Anya said grimly. "It is a village south of Bragi, the home of Ville Dreamsinger."

"Oh," Merrick said, nodding. Ville was a slave who'd been sold to one of the other Troft demesnes, and who'd been recalled when the Drim'hco'plai decided to bring them all back to Muninn. Ville had traveled from the slave ship's landing site with Anya and Merrick and the rest of the Gangari group. "Is that a problem? I seem to remember your villagers being reasonably civil toward him when we arrived."

"The feelings between Gangari and Bragi aren't the difficulty," Anya said. "The difficulty is that when I left, the masters had a small presence in Svipall. It may be that they still do."

Merrick winced. "Great."

"I am sorry," Anya said. "The presence was not large, and I had forgotten about it until after I spoke."

"Yeah," Merrick muttered. "Well...we've got a day to figure out something."

"And a night," Anya said pointedly.

"And a night," Merrick agreed. In fact, the simplest approach might very well be to wait until Kjoic was asleep and then slip away. Whatever predators might be wandering through the Muninn darkness would be a damn sight easier to deal with than having a Troft as a traveling companion.

In the meantime, Kjoic had ordered them to secure the wrecked aft part of the ship against those predators. For the moment, at least, Merrick needed to be a good, obedient little slave.

There was no possible way to block or otherwise secure the gaping hole in the outer hull. It was too large for anything Merrick had seen during their passage through the ship, and removing interior walls or furniture to fill in the empty space would be impossible to do without revealing Merrick's Cobra weaponry and strength. Fortunately, the cracks in the inner wall, while numerous, were much easier to close. It took an hour of scrounging and another hour to figure out how to wedge everything in place, but in the end they managed to close off every opening they could find that would admit anything larger than a mouse.

Kjoic arrived on the scene just as they were finishing work on the last crack. He'd changed his clothing, Merrick noticed, and added a wide belt with a set of small tools attached. After a couple of hours with a water bottle, the alien's skin already looked a little more filled out. He must have been seriously dehydrated. [Excellence, the work has it,] the Troft declared.

[Your approval, we are grateful for it,] Anya said, bowing.

[Predators, we are safe from them.] Kjoic paused. [Safety, we nearly have it.]

Merrick frowned. *Nearly*?

As if in answer to the unspoken question, the Troft stepped to the opening Merrick and Anya had used earlier, into which Merrick had wedged a pair of bunks from the ship's crew quarters. [This opening, predators may yet force their way through it,] he continued, pulling a small tool from one of the pouches on his belt. He slid a switch, and abruptly the corridor lit up with the acrid blue fire of a cutting torch. A few quick touches to the spots where the bunk frame pressed against the blackened frame—[Security, we now have it,] Kjoic said with satisfaction as he closed down the torch. [Entrance, predators may now not achieve it.]

Merrick suppressed a grimace. Predators would have a job getting in, all right. Unfortunately, he and Anya would now have an equally tricky job getting *out*.

[The night, we approach it,] Kjoic said, holding a finger briefly near the cutting end of the torch and then putting the tool away. [Food, I have had it. Food, you may now also have it.]

Anya bowed. [Gratitude, we offer it.]

[The galley, it is forward,] Kjoic said, gesturing. [Food, you may take whatever of it you wish. Your work, I will stay here and examine it more closely.]

Once again, Merrick made sure to wait until they were out of earshot before speaking. "Well, *that* tears it," he growled.

"You can no longer open the path?" Anya murmured.

"Oh, I can open it just fine," Merrick told her sourly. "The problem will be cutting the welds without leaving evidence that could come back to haunt us. Especially since he knows what he's doing when it comes to welding. There's a good chance he'll recognize the difference between a flame weld like he did and a laser cut like I would do."

"They are that different?"

"They are to someone who knows what to look for," Merrick said. "Did you notice how he put his finger near the torch head before he put it away? Experienced welders do that to make sure it's cool enough to not damage the pouch. My Great-Uncle Corwin taught me that one—he fiddles a lot with metals and ceramics, and ruined a couple of perfectly good torch holders before a professional welder clued him in."

Merrick jerked a thumb over his shoulder. "More to the point, Kjoic didn't look at the torch as he did it. The move was pure habit."

Anya was silent for another few steps. "What then is your new plan?"

"Same as the old one: getting out of here while he sleeps," Merrick said. "I just don't know anymore how we're going to do it."

Anya touched his arm. "You'll think of a way."

"Sure," Merrick said, wishing he felt that confident. "In the meantime, we've been ordered to eat. That's the first Troft order I've heard yet that I'm in full agreement with."

CHAPTER EIGHT

It was odd, Paul thought, how darkness of heart, lightness of head, dimness of vision, and silence of hearing could all exist in such harmony together. Perhaps someday he would write a paper on the subject.

Though the vision wasn't really all dimness. There were flashes of light, probably one every minute or two. He wasn't sure about that—his nanocomputer's clock circuit didn't seem to be working properly at the moment.

Occasionally, the flashes gave way to more complete visions: memories mostly, though usually they went by so quickly that he couldn't figure out what they were memories of. But mostly it was just light, like there was a viewscreen just a degree or two out of his line of sight that was playing one of those memories.

The silence wasn't all silent, either. There were voices muttering or rumbling in the background, counting out numbers or letters, occasionally making some comment he couldn't understand. Sometimes he thought about keying his audio enhancers, but usually those moments of real conversation were so short that by the time he'd made up his mind to listen in, it was too late.

But at least the voices proved he wasn't alone. That was good, because it certainly *felt* alone.

The darkness of heart he couldn't quite figure out. Something must be wrong, but he couldn't for the life of him remember what it was.

"Captain," a distant voice said.

Paul frowned inside himself. *That* was a voice he recognized, though he couldn't place it. But the *Captain* part—that had to be Captain Lij Tulu. That particular name had cropped up many times throughout the dimness and darkness.

"Commodore," a second voice—Lij Tulu's?—said. Unlike the usual voices hovering at the edges of Paul's hearing, there was some actual emotion in Lij Tulu's. Surprise, maybe. Would surprise be the right reaction for hearing the commodore speak to him?

"I'm sorry, sir—I wasn't informed you were aboard," Lij Tulu continued.

"That's because I specifically left orders that my arrival not be reported to you," the commodore said.

"Indeed," Lij Tulu said. A new emotion had overtaken the surprise, and Paul took a moment to try to puzzle it out. Annoyance? Resentment?

Fear?

"Continuity is important to the MindsEye process," the commodore said. "I didn't want you to interrupt your work for a formal welcome."

"I see," Lij Tulu said. Some of the emotion was gone, Paul noticed.

But only some of it. Whether it was annoyance,

resentment, or fear, there was still an echo of it lurking in his voice.

Belatedly, Paul realized that he should have keyed up his audios. But following quickly on that thought came the realization that he was already hearing the conversation just fine. Apparently, the commodore wasn't bothering to keep his voice down the way the others usually did.

"I wish you'd called first, though," Lij Tulu continued. He wasn't keeping his voice down, either. "I could have saved you the trip across. I'm afraid we haven't yet located the proper memories. But it's still early in the process. I'm sure we'll locate them eventually."

"Hopefully before Captain Moreau brings back the coordinates himself?"

"I don't believe for a minute this Ukuthi character really means to give him that information," Lij Tulu said stiffly. "Trust me, Commodore—I'll have it long before any Troft gives it up."

"And Cobra Broom is handling it well?"

"His vitals are well within acceptable range," Lij Tulu said. "He should come through without damage."

"Good," the commodore said. "And the memories you *have* found?"

"We're stockpiling them, as per standard procedure," Lij Tulu said. "If there's nothing else, Commodore, we're quite busy here."

"As a matter of fact, Captain, there *is* something else we need to discuss," the commodore said. "Can he hear us?"

"No, sir. The only way into his auditory center is via the MindsEye path, and we closed that down right after his final briefing and instructions."

That was interesting, Paul thought. Did that mean his audio enhancers didn't, in fact, feed into his brain's hearing center? He'd always assumed that they did, but Lij Tulu seemed to be contradicting that.

"Why, does this concern his family?" Lij Tulu continued.

"It could," the commodore said, his tone going grim. "The *Falcon's* returned from Caelian. It seems that the *Squire* has disappeared."

"Disappeared? You mean left the planet?"

"That's the most likely explanation," the commodore said. "Except that the Caelians won't talk about it. Everyone Commander Ferrero could get hold of insisted he talk to someone else. It was like a damn Roselle circle down there."

"What about Governor Uy?"

"Allegedly unavailable," the commodore said. "Supposedly still recovering from the injuries he sustained during the Troft invasion."

"If that's not just an excuse, it follows that he can't have gotten very far," Lij Tulu pointed out. "Where and how extensively did Ferrero search?"

"He didn't," the commodore said. "He stayed in low orbit the entire time."

"He didn't *land*?" Lij Tulu demanded, sounding scandalized. "How exactly did he plan to do his job without getting his boots dirty?"

"He decided to exercise the better part of valor," the commodore said. "Because the *Squire* might have left, it might have been moved...or it might have been destroyed."

There was a sound that Paul tentatively concluded was a derisive snort. "I hardly think *that* could be the case."

"You may have to retrain your thought processes," the commodore said, his voice hardening. "Ferrero thinks he spotted signs of heavy laser scoring on the landing field ground south of Stronghold."

"He *thinks* he spotted laser scoring? A first-year midshipman can identify that kind of damage."

"Not on Caelian, he can't," the commodore said. "The damn flora grows so fast that it could mat over a full-bore battleground within a couple of days. I've got my tactical people looking over his recordings, but I'm not optimistic they'll be able to pull anything solid."

"It still doesn't make any sense," Lij Tulu said. "Aventine hasn't got weapons capable of taking out the *Squire*. And if *they* don't, Caelian damn well doesn't."

"That assumes that the Cobra Worlds' listed assets are in a one-to-one correspondence with their real assets," the commodore pointed out. "We don't really know *what* Caelian's got. Especially not after having taken down a couple of Troft warships. It's possible they were able to salvage and restore some of the weaponry."

"Or maybe Troft weaponry got there via a more direct route," Lij Tulu said.

"That possibility hadn't escaped me," the commodore agreed. "Captain Moreau's interaction with that Balin'ekha'spmi commander, Ukuthi, shows that at least one Troft demesne is poking around the edges of all this. If one, why not two or three?"

"Or it could all be coming from just Ukuthi," Lij Tulu pointed out. "He already seems the type to play the ends against each other. Playing Moreau for a fool while stirring the Caelian pot would fit right in with that kind of duplicity."

"Which is why I'm not sending the *Falcon* back

there," the commodore said. "If and when we meet the Caelians again, we'll be going in with the *Algonquin* or the *Megalith*. Just in case the Trofts are indeed on the playing field."

"I agree, sir," Lij Tulu said. "Just give the word— we're on ninety-minute standby."

"Easy, Captain," the commodore said. "I said *if and when*. We're not going to rush this. We're certainly not going to Caelian until you finish your examination of Cobra Broom. No, I think we can afford to let Uy sit in silence a few more days. Give him time to think about the consequences of whatever it is he's doing."

"Hopefully, he won't take advantage of the lull to prepare more heavy weapons," Lij Tulu warned. "Assuming he actually has any, of course."

"I'm certain he'll be making all the preparations he can," the commodore said. "But all that will accomplish will be to make the psychological slap that much harder when we sweep those defenses away."

"Yes, sir." To Paul's mind, Lij Tulu didn't sound completely convinced. But it was possible his ears were playing tricks on him. Or whatever it was—ears or something else—that was picking up this conversation.

"Meanwhile, the *Hermes* is on its way to rendezvous with the *Dorian*," the commodore continued. "We'll see if Ukuthi's coordinates are worth anything. If not, he and the Balin demesne may need a psychological slap of their own."

"The *Algonquin* stands ready for that, as well, sir." Lij Tulu paused. "If I may ask a question, Commodore?"

"Certainly."

"Why exactly did you come across to see me, sir? This could all have been handled via comm."

"Up to now, yes, it could have," the commodore agreed. "We now get to two points that couldn't. Two points, Captain, which you're to keep strictly to yourself for the present. Point one: if we haven't located Qasama within the next thirty days, I intend to revert to the original plan."

"To use Aventine as bait?"

"Not quite," the commodore said. "Instead of Aventine, we'll be setting the dummy base on Caelian."

There was a soft hissing noise. "I don't think Governor Uy will think much of that idea."

"I'm certain he won't," the commodore agreed. "And if he reacts as badly as I'm expecting . . . well, let's just hope he's willing to see reason. Your engineers are already slated to create the necessary installations. I came here to tell you that, with Colonel Reivaro tied up with the Aventinian Cobras, it'll be your Marines who'll be tasked with suppressing any Caelian opposition."

"After more talking, I presume?"

"Not this time," the commodore said grimly. "The thirty days I'm allowing for the Qasama discovery represents all of the time the plan authorizes for diplomacy and persuasion. *All* of it. If we use up those days and come up empty, the next visit to Caelian will be the start of the building process."

"Understood, sir," Lij Tulu said. "Though I presume it can't look that way?"

"Correct," the commodore said. "Your Marines will need to create the same sort of situation Santores engineered in Archway. Whatever ultimately happens out here, we'll need to be able to present the Dome with unequivocal proof that we acted in strict accordance with Dominion law."

"Don't worry, sir," Lij Tulu said. "I know how to handle it."

"Good," the commodore said. "Then to my final point. I promised Governor-General Chintawa that I would protect Cobra Broom as best I could against any MindsEye side effects. With the *Dorian* gone, the time-line ticking down, and Caelian having suddenly become a giant question mark, I can no longer afford to keep that promise. Whatever you need to do in order to dig out Broom's memories..." He left the sentence unfinished.

"Understood, sir," Lij Tulu said. "If Qasama's coordinates are in there, we'll find them."

"Good," the commodore said. "Carry on, Captain."

"Yes, sir," Lij Tulu said. "Thank you, Commodore."

The conversation had been important, Paul decided as the silence again flowed over him. But *how* it was important, and what the full implications of it might be, he found himself unable to pin down.

But he would continue to mull at it, and sooner or later he would figure it out.

And, really, he had plenty of time.

"Corwin? Corwin!"

Corwin Moreau froze at his basement workbench, his chest tightening as he looked across the basement toward the stairway leading up into the main part of the house. He knew his wife's tones of voice better than he did his own. And the tension he could hear there... "Down here, Thena!" he called back. Carefully, he laid the piece of experimental ceramic he'd been working on back into its mold.

And then, reaching beneath the workbench, he slid the hidden handgun from its holster.

"Stay there," Thena called. "We're coming to you."

We. Taking a deep breath, Corwin thumbed off the gun's safety. For the past four days, ever since the Archway massacre, he'd been expecting just such a late-evening visitation. The only question had been whether the intruders would be Chintawa's people or Dominion Marines.

Either way, he intended to be ready.

The footsteps above him tracked across to the stairway and became footsteps on the stairs. Keeping the gun out of sight beneath the workbench, he lined up the muzzle on the base of the stairway.

Thena appeared first, her legs recognizable from the slacks he knew she was wearing this evening. There was a single person behind her, the shoes indicating that the visitor was probably a man, following about three steps back.

And both the shoes and the trousers looked to be normal civilian weave and cut instead of the Aventinian or Dominion uniform that Corwin had been expecting. Had Chintawa decided to play this low-key?

They continued down the stairs, Thena finally reaching a level where Corwin could see her face. Her expression held the same tension he'd heard in her voice when she first called to him, but he could see nothing of the fear or outrage that an official visitation should have prompted. And indeed, as the man descended further, Corwin could see that the rest of his outfit was also civilian, a nice but relatively inexpensive suit.

His face, as it came into view, was one Corwin had never seen before.

"Corwin, this is Dushan Matavuli," Thena said,

stepping aside at the foot of the steps to allow the visitor to approach the workbench. "He's a rancher from DeVegas province."

Corwin caught his breath. DeVegas. "Welcome to the Island, Mr. Matavuli," he said cautiously. "What can I do for you?"

"You're secure down here?" Matavuli asked, looking around. "I mean, *really* secure?"

"I was once a governor," Corwin reminded him. "It's a job that makes paranoids of even the most innocent of men. Trust me—I have all the bells and whistles to ensure that private conversations in this house remain private."

"I hope you're right." Matavuli took a deep breath. "I have a message, and a request, from your great-nephew Lorne."

Long practice enabled Corwin to keep his face expressionless. As soon as he'd heard that Matavuli was from DeVegas, he'd hoped he was bringing word from either Jin or Lorne.

But that didn't mean he was ready to take anything his visitor said at face value. Up to now, Commodore Santores's people hadn't shown much interest in subtlety or subterfuge. But there was a first time for everything. "I'm listening," he said.

"First, the message," Matavuli said. "He said he's looking forward to eating drogfowl cacciatore with all of you. Don't ask me what that means, 'cause I haven't the foggiest."

Corwin looked at Thena, watching some of the tension fading from her face, as he knew she was seeing the same change in his own face. The last time the family had been together, on the eve of the Troft invasions of Qasama and the Cobra Worlds, they'd had drogfowl cacciatore.

Not only that, but the menu had been mentioned in the mysterious message they'd received from the Trofts after Merrick's disappearance. Whoever Matavuli was and however he knew Lorne, Corwin knew now that his great nephew trusted the man.

Which wasn't exactly the same as Matavuli being trustworthy. Corwin had played enough politics in his day to know that smiles and endorsements didn't necessarily mean a dagger wasn't hidden away somewhere. "Don't worry, we know the context," he assured their visitor. "What's the request?"

Matavuli's face screwed up in a scowl. "Well, that's a little more complicated. You have time to talk?"

"The night is young," Corwin assured him. With only a slight hesitation, he slid the handgun back into its concealed holster. "There's a couch and a couple of chairs over there behind the kiln," he added, pointing with his other hand. "Make yourself comfortable while I get us something to drink."

"Better make it a stiff one," Matavuli warned over his shoulder as he headed toward the conversation nook. "I got a feeling you're going to need it."

After Kjoic's ordeal trapped in the cramped access compartment, Merrick had expected the Troft to make an early night of it. And in fact, the sun had barely set behind the forest when Kjoic headed off to the main bunk area. On the way he told Merrick and Anya that they would leave for Svipall as soon as it was light, and advised them to get some rest.

It was the second Troft order that Merrick was

more than willing to accept. The arduous day's travel, combined with the equally strenuous day before and the short night's sleep in the middle, had left his own eyelids as heavy as Kjoic's, if not more so. He and Anya found a pair of bunks in what appeared to be an off-duty sleeping area in the rear of the ship and settled down.

But before allowing himself to fall asleep, Merrick set his nanocomputer to wake him in three hours. First light, he knew, was about ten hours away, and he intended for the two of them to be long gone before Kjoic discovered his new slaves were missing.

He awoke three hours later to the silent alarm going off in his head, feeling more tired than when he'd first closed his eyes. For a few minutes he lay motionless, listening. They were close enough to the wrecked engine room for his enhanced hearing to pick up some of the forest noises filtering in through the broken hull, but he could hear nothing from the forward part of the ship.

Time to go.

He slipped out of bed as quietly as he could, leaving Anya still asleep in her own bunk. There was no point waking her until he had their escape route ready.

With the interior of the ship in near-total darkness, the soft starlight seeping in through the gaps in the hull and bulkheads was almost bright by comparison. More importantly, it was bright enough that with his light-amps at full power Merrick could keep an eye on the treacherous footing along the way.

His first stop, he decided, would be the wide crack he and Anya had entered by, the opening Kjoic had welded the bed frames into. If any of the welds had come loose, he might be able to get them out without having to use his lasers. He crossed the debris-strewn floor toward the bulkhead—

[Sleep, it eludes you?]

Merrick froze. The voice had come from almost directly in front of him, no more than a couple of meters back from the crack he was aiming for. [Sleep, it indeed eludes me,] he confirmed, trying to keep his voice calm. [Startlement, you have given it to me.]

[Startlement, it was not my intent,] Kjoic assured him.

Merrick bowed his head toward the Troft, thinking furiously. He knew from Anya's coaching that slaves were supposed to watch out for the masters' best interests. But were they permitted to take the initiative in such things, or simply wait for orders?

He didn't know. But if he didn't risk it, he might not ever find out what Kjoic was doing here. Or, more importantly, if and when he was planning to leave. [Sleep, does it also elude you?] he asked. [Refreshment, may I bring it to you?]

[Sleep, it does not elude me,] Kjoic said. [Our safety, I sought to confirm it.] He pointed at the gap with the welded bunks. [The barrier, it is holding.]

[Such news, it is welcome,] Merrick said, a sour taste in his mouth. So much for sneaking out. [My service, do you require it?]

[Your service, I do not require it,] Kjoic said, his voice suddenly distant. [Knowledge, speak it to me. Murder for profit, do humans engage in it?]

Merrick blinked. Where the hell had *that* come from? [Your question, I don't understand it,] he stalled.

[Killings, they occurred here,] Kjoic said, his radiator

membranes fluttering. [Profit, the captain sought it. Loyalty, the crew demanded instead.]

Merrick shook his head. [Forgiveness, I beg it. Understanding, I do not have it.]

Kjoic gestured toward the sky. [An unknown ship, it spoke to the captain upon our arrival,] he said. [Great profit, it promised in return for our cargo.]

An eerie feeling crept up Merrick's back. So someone else out there wanted to get hold of Qasaman razorarms?

Was that someone another string to Commander Ukuthi's bow, sent here either as backup or replacement for Merrick and Anya? Or were there other players in this game? [Obedience to the original contract, the others wished to maintain it?] he asked.

[Understanding, you have it,] Kjoic said, his membranes fluttering. [Defiance, they demonstrated. Combat, the captain began.]

Merrick winced. A sudden, violent free-for-all battle would certainly explain the blood residue in the corridor. [Your life, they yet spared it?]

Kjoic gave the Troft clacking-jaw equivalent of a bitter laugh. [My life, *I* yet spared it,] he said. [Cowardice, I demonstrated it. My comrades, I abandoned them. A sanctuary, I sought it.]

[A sanctuary, you found it,] Merrick said as he finally got it. He'd vaguely assumed that Kjoic had been in the access compartment trying to fix something when the ship crashed, though he'd recognized that the theory didn't made much sense. Kjoic hiding from a running battle made a lot more sense. [Death, the others all succumbed to it?] he asked.

[The truth, I do not know it,] Kjoic said. [Movement,

I could hear it after the crash. Voices, I could hear them. Survival, I know not if any achieved it.]

Merrick nodded. The movement and voices could have been survivors of the bloodbath, or they could have been the local Trofts' rescue team. [Yet call out, you did not?]

Kjoic clacked his jaw again. [A fool, I am not one, Merrick Hopekeeper,] he bit out. [Life, I did not wish to give it up.]

Merrick winced. [Forgiveness, I beg it,] he said. Of course Kjoic hadn't called for help. He'd had no idea who was out there, or whether or not they would want to leave witnesses behind. [Reason, I did not employ it.]

[Forgiveness, I grant it,] Kjoic said. [A slave, you are merely one.]

[Gratitude, I offer it,] Merrick said mechanically, his thoughts racing.

Because if some of the other crewmen had survived, one of them might know something about the mysterious ship lurking around out there trying to buy Qasaman razorarms.

And if the ship was from Commander Ukuthi, he and Anya were suddenly no longer alone in Ukuthi's crazy scheme. With allies would come a whole list of options and possibilities. Especially if those allies came packaged inside their own warship.

Of course, they might have turned tail and run once their offer to Kjoic's captain fell through. The attempted mutiny and subsequent crash would have drawn far more attention than they probably wanted.

Still, they might not have run far. If Merrick could get word to them, they might still have a chance of pulling this off.

But only if he could question the survivors, or else retrieve the data records the rescue team had pulled.

And for both of those, he needed Kjoic alive and well.

And even as he reached that conclusion, the last piece fell into place. Instead of demanding that Merrick and Anya bring them to the local Troft HQ—[Our village, that is the reason you wish to go to it,] he said. [A story, the survivors will have told one. That story, you wish to learn it.]

[Wisdom, you have it,] Kjoic said, his radiator membranes fluttering again. [Logic, you also have it. The rulers, I cannot yet approach them. Information, I must first obtain it.]

[Understanding, I have it,] Merrick said, feeling his own pulse speeding up. And of course, none of the humans in Svipall were likely to have the information Kjoic wanted.

But if the Troft base Anya remembered was still there, it might be possible for them to break in and find the relevant records. Which was, in fact, the same thing Merrick needed to do.

Which meant that from now on he and Kjoic were going to have to work together.

[Intelligence, you have it,] Kjoic said, and with his enhanced vision Merrick saw that the Troft was gazing intently at him. [Surprise, I have it.]

Merrick felt his throat tighten. Only they would have to work together as master and slave.

And he had better not forget that.

[Kindness, you show it,] he said, ducking his head humbly. [Ideas, I sometimes have them. Worthless, they most often are.]

[Ideas, do not disparage them,] Kjoic said severely. [Worthless, they may be. Worthless, they may *not* be.] He waved a hand. [Travel, we undertake it at first light. Your sleep, return to it.]

[The order, I obey it.] Merrick hesitated. [Your sleep, you also need it.]

[My sleep, I return to it soon,] Kjoic promised.

Anya was lying quietly in her bunk when Merrick returned, her eyes intent on him. "Is all ready?" she whispered.

"I couldn't get to the opening," Merrick whispered back as he lay down on the bunk beside her. "But it doesn't matter. We're not leaving. Not yet."

Anya stirred. "I don't understand."

Quietly, Merrick gave her a summary of his conversation with Kjoic. "I know it's dangerous," he said. "But for the moment, our goals are running parallel. So for the moment, anyway, I think it's best we stick together."

For a long moment she was silent. "Perhaps you do not fully understand the situation," she said. "We cannot simply walk into Svipall. The people there do not know us."

"Which is good," Merrick said. "If they don't recognize us, they can't turn us in to the Trofts."

"But how can we claim the village as our own if they do not recognize us?"

Merrick winced. He hadn't thought about that part. "I see what you mean. I guess we'll have to play it a bit more circumspect."

"What does that mean?"

"It means I need to think about it," Merrick conceded. "If worse comes to worst, though, we can make up an excuse to pick a different village. Maybe we'll run into a nest of something nasty along the way and have to divert."

"Some predators, you mean?"

"Exactly," Merrick said. "I'm sure we can find *something* big and toothy enough to scare away a couple of timid slaves. Or we could even invent some superstition that prevents us from going into Svipall on this particular day."

"*Invent* a superstition?" Anya seemed stunned. "Merrick, the masters have been here for many generations. They know everything about us."

"The Drim Trofts might," Merrick said. "But Kjoic won't. He's not a local—his accent alone shows that much. Besides that, I think he's probably young, and he certainly hasn't had much experience with slaves."

"Why do you conclude that?"

"Because he knows the basic rules, but none of it comes naturally," Merrick said. "It's like he's reading off a script that he knows pretty well, but has never actually performed. I think any slips we make—by which I mean any slips *I* make—will probably go unnoticed."

"And if you're wrong?" Anya countered. "If he realizes who we really are?"

"He won't," Merrick said. "If we're careful—"

"If he learns the truth, you will have to kill him," Anya whispered harshly. "Are you prepared to do that?"

Merrick felt his stomach tighten. It was a valid question. A darkly unpleasant question.

Still, it wasn't like he hadn't killed Trofts before. He had. Far too many of them.

But those killings had all been in battle, where

he'd been fighting for his life and the lives of his comrades around him. Taking out Kjoic, especially without warning, would be little more than murder.

No. Not *little more than*. It would *be* murder.

Anya was still waiting. "Don't worry," he said. "I'll do whatever's necessary to keep us safe."

Which, he realized, was not exactly an answer to her question. But it was the best he could do. "Anyway, we need to get some sleep. We've got a busy day ahead."

And really, there was a good chance that if Kjoic learned the truth he would try to kill or capture them.

If he did, whatever happened afterward wouldn't be murder. Not really.

CHAPTER NINE

"He's back," Jin announced from the front of the cave.

"Who, Matavuli?" Lorne's voice wafted from the rear. "That was quick."

"No, it's your fisherman," Jin said. "Jake Sedgley."

"Okay, that's good too," Lorne said. "Hopefully, he's brought word from Matavuli. Or Uncle Corwin. Or both."

"Maybe," Jin said, wincing as she looked back at her son, sitting at the table in front of the cave's collection of blasting caps, detonators, and all the rest of the ingredients necessary for building concussion, fragmentation, fireblast, and smoke grenades.

Her tension-fogged brain still wasn't completely clear on how Lorne had ended up with that particular job. She could remember comparing notes with him last night, and reaching the conclusion that the Qasamans had given him fractionally more explosives training than they'd given her.

But she also remembered that on a purely practical

level the difference wasn't all that significant. In fact, the disparity really just boiled down to the difference between miniscule and ridiculously miniscule. Neither of them had any serious expertise or experience with things that go boom, and both were promising candidates for accidental self-mutilation.

Which meant that the main reason Lorne had taken this task upon himself was that he'd gotten to the Cobras' stash of explosives first. And had then flatly forbidden his mother to interfere.

Jin should have argued the point. She could do so now, in fact. Lorne was younger, smarter, and far more capable than she was of taking this fight back to the Dominion. If she blew her hands off, it wouldn't be nearly as devastating to the people of the Cobra Worlds as it would be if he did.

Besides, she had so much less to live for.

She turned back to the fiber-optic display. *Stop that*, she ordered herself. Paul would be all right. He'd defeated way stations' worth of spine leopards during his tour of duty in Aventine's expansion regions. He'd made it through a war and back. He'd survived getting half his leg blown away. Whatever evil the Dominion had built into their MindsEye machine, he would get through that, too.

"Any sign of our new lords and masters?" Lorne asked.

"The Dominion?" Jin asked. "Not yet." There was a sudden dark movement at the top of the display—"Wait a second," she corrected. "We've got another incoming."

"Figures," Lorne muttered, coming up beside her. Jin felt a small flicker of relief—at least while he was here watching Sedgley settling down to fish he couldn't also be back there juggling blasting caps. "I just hope he and Matavuli have been clever. Getting caught with a note on him would *not* be a good thing."

"Even a coded note," Jin agreed, frowning. There was something about this whole thing tickling at the back of her mind...

"And there they go," Lorne said as the newly arrived aircar settled to the riverbank beside Sedgley's vehicle. Two uniformed Marines got out and crossed to where Sedgley was sitting on his stool. "And there *he* goes," he added as Sedgley jabbed the end of his pole between the stool's legs and supports and stood up, facing the incoming Marines with his fists on his hips. "I'd give a month's salary to listen in on this one."

"He'll be lucky if he doesn't get hauled away to detention," Jin said.

Lorne shrugged. "There's that."

But if the Marines had come to arrest Sedgley, they were taking their time about it. For nearly half a minute they just stood there, watching Sedgley's increasingly animated gesturing without any visible reaction. Even without their helmets, the vagueness of the display would have made it impossible to tell whether they were responding to any of Sedgley's diatribe or merely listening to it.

And then, all at once, one of the Marines stepped past Sedgley and picked up the pole.

Sedgley made a grab for it. The other Marine was ready for the move and caught his arm as he turned, hauling him back out of range. Sedgley tried pulling away, but the Marine deftly transferred his grip to a wrist lock. After that, Sedgley had no option but to just stand there, clearly seething but unable to do anything without getting his wrist broken.

The first Marine looked carefully over the pole, then began slowly reeling in the line, studying every centimeter as it slid into the spool. The hook and sinker came out of the water and were reeled in, and the Marine shifted his grip on the pole and took them carefully in hand. Jin held her breath...

And with a contemptuous gesture, he thrust the pole back into Sedgley's hand. The second Marine released the fisherman's other arm, and together the Marines returned to their aircar. A moment later it lifted and headed south, toward Archway.

Lorne huffed out a breath. "Well," he said. "That went better than I was expecting. Keep an eye out while I go get the scuba gear."

"Wait a minute," Jin said, frowning again as she watched the aircar fade away into the distance.

"No, it's okay," Lorne said over his shoulder as he headed across the cave. "They checked his pole and line, but not his stool, tackle box, or creel. I'm betting the message is in one of those."

"That's not what I meant," Jin said, trying to think. Thinking was much easier since the Qasamans cut that tumor out of her head. But there was something here that still eluded her.

And then, suddenly, she had it. "The Dominion aircar," she said. "It didn't come from the same direction it did the last time."

Lorne turned back, frowning. "Maybe it was on patrol," he said slowly.

"Or maybe there was another reason."

"Okay, let's think it through," Lorne said. "What direction *did* it come from?"

"Basically, from straight above us," Jin told him, replaying the memory. "Like it had been following the river."

"Maybe like it had been lying in wait for him?" Lorne asked, coming back to her side. "There are lots of trees about half a klick upstream of the falls. Plenty of room for an aircar to hunker down out of sight." He shook his head. "No, wait, that doesn't make sense. If they wanted to watch him, all they'd have to do is go to high altitude—Marine aircars are bound to have higher ceilings than our civilian versions. They could just hover and watch."

"So they weren't just watching," Jin said slowly. "Could they have been up there dropping someone off?"

For a moment Lorne was silent. Then, he took a deep breath. "Oh, hell," he murmured.

Jin's throat tightened as the full implications of her suggestion seemed to slam into her. If the Marines had dropped off a commando team to hit the cave—"That doesn't mean they've found us," she said quickly. "Not necessarily. It could be a duck blind sort of thing."

"A what?"

"Something I read a long time ago," Jin said. "If birds see a person go into a duck blind, they'll be nervous. But if *two* people go in, then one leaves, they relax, thinking they're alone again."

"So Reivaro sends an aircar and a couple of Marines to poke Sedgley with a stick," Lorne said slowly. "Figuring that we're someplace where we can see the confrontation. While we're busy watching Sedgley, someone else gets into position to watch and see if we contact him after the aircar leaves."

"That's what I'm thinking," Jin said. "So what do we do?"

Lorne gazed thoughtfully at the display. "Well, obviously, I can't go out until we're sure it's clear," he said. "I was just thinking...there's really no cover right up at the edge of the falls. Nothing that would hide a couple of Marines, anyway. You could put them under a camouflage blanket, I suppose, but getting into position without being spotted would be tricky."

"Unless they thought we'd be so busy watching Sedgley that we wouldn't notice them."

"I'd like to think Reivaro has more respect for us by now than *that*," Lorne said. "But if you *really* want to watch Sedgley without coming out into the open, your best bet is right there." He gestured toward the display. "The ledge."

"Assuming they know it's there."

"Easy enough to map the cliff face through the water," Lorne pointed out. "The aircar that came by two days ago probably had the equipment to do that."

Jin thought it over. On one level, it was insane. On another, it was not only likely but practically inevitable. "How would they get there? I haven't seen what the terrain looks like up top. Can the cliff even be climbed?"

"There are one or two of places where it can be done," Lorne said. "It's easier starting from the bottom than from the top, though neither is exactly a stroll on the terrace. The top-down approach is the trickiest—we lose one or two daredevil kids a year out here that way. But getting to the ledge from either direction gives

Reivaro the same problem as just planting someone on top: the approaches are mostly outside the water and way too visible." He rubbed his chin thoughtfully. "But what he *could* do is have an aircar drop the watchers into the river somewhere upstream and have them work their way underwater to the falls."

"Securely anchored, I assume?"

"*Very* securely anchored," Lorne confirmed grimly. "The river runs a lot faster above the falls before it widens out down below. It'd probably wind up being a sort of sideways rappelling maneuver."

Jin felt her stomach tighten. "And once they got to the ledge, the only place they could see through the water...?"

"Would be right here," Lorne finished for her, again pointing at the display. "Right in front of the fibers."

There was a moment of silence. "Well, at least we'll know when they get here," Jin said. "I hope they keep their eyes outward. How visible are the other ends of the optics?"

"Hopefully, not very," Lorne said. "I didn't really look all that closely."

"Nothing we can do about it now, I suppose."

"Nope," Lorne agreed. "If we can't get out to go for a swim, we can't go out to fiddle with camouflage, either. Looks like there's nothing we can do until we figure out whether we're being duck-blinded or giving Reivaro more credit for cleverness than he deserves."

"I suppose," Jin said. "By the way, just for the record, I don't know if the bird thing is actually true."

"Doesn't matter—the principle's still valid," Lorne said. "Anyway, I kind of like the term *duck-blinded*. We should use it more in conversation."

He hunched his shoulders once, then turned and headed toward the rear of the cave. "Guess I'll get back to work," he said. "Keep an eye out, will you? Let me know when they show up."

They showed up exactly twelve minutes and forty-three seconds later: two shadows that passed across the display, one of them disappearing for another fifty-two seconds as the man apparently continued on to the far end of the ledge and then rejoined his companion. The shadows settled down on opposite sides of the gap, a slice of their shoulders and arms just visible at the edges of the display.

"Well, that tears it," Lorne growled as he stood beside Jin, arms folded across his chest. "Damn. I was supposed to meet Pierce tonight at Smith's Forge."

"That's pretty far from here, isn't it?" Jin asked, trying to visualize the map of the area. She probably knew more about the expansion regions than most Capitalians, given that her son was stationed here. But there were a lot of details and distances, not to mention a fair number of small towns, that were still a bit hazy in her mind.

"About fifty kilometers," Lorne said. "Not too bad. I could run it if I had to."

"A bit obvious if they're watching from aircars."

"Which is why running would be a last resort," Lorne agreed. "Plan A was to go downstream in the scuba gear, then head cross-country to Matavuli's ranch and borrow one of his cars or bikes. He usually has a vehicle or two stashed in one of the storage barns near the Pashington River near where we met two nights ago."

Jin gazed past the two newcomers at the fisherman

down the river. "I wonder if Sedgley's brought new instructions."

"I was wondering that, too," Lorne said sourly. "But whether he did or didn't, there's nothing I can do until they give up and leave."

"Which probably won't be until Sedgley leaves," Jin murmured, her thoughts suddenly racing in an unpleasant direction. She hadn't had a really good look at the area behind the falls after Lorne's rescue of her from Archway three nights ago. But what she *had* seen, if she was remembering it correctly, was that there was a slight curve to the cliff face at the height of the ledge, plus a couple of stone outcroppings that blocked the view from one side of the falls to the other.

Which meant that if Lorne was careful, he might be able to pull out the plug that sealed the cave's entrance, slip down the side of the cliff, and get into the river without the two watchers spotting him.

If he was careful. *If* he was feeling desperate or reckless.

And *if* Reivaro hadn't sent more Marines than just the two they could see flanking the display.

She looked sideways at her son. Lorne was gazing at the display, a hard look on his face. He was serious about all this, she knew. Serious enough that he might decide to be desperate *and* reckless.

There was a good chance he'd already thought of that angle. If he hadn't, the last thing Jin wanted to do was suggest it to him.

"Sedgley won't be fishing all day," she pointed out. "Once he's gone, you should have enough time to find any note he's left and still make it to your meeting."

"Unless, as you say, the meeting's been changed,"

Lorne said. "Besides, if I were those Marines, I'd stick around long after Sedgley himself takes off on the chance that one of us will would come out of hiding to look for a message. No, one way or other, I figure the meeting's pretty much off."

"Maybe that's a good thing," Jin said. "If Reivaro's suspicious enough to be watching Pierce, maybe watching him do nothing tonight will convince him that he's not worth the effort and manpower to tail."

"Maybe," Lorne said. But he didn't sound convinced.

"Besides, you can use the extra time to work on your bombs," Jin added. "Maybe now you can go a little slower and more carefully."

"They're just smoke and concussion grenades," Lorne reminded her. "I'm not looking to escalate this any farther than it already is."

"Concussion grenades that can take out a combat-suited Dominion Marine?" Jin asked mildly.

"Of course," Lorne said, starting to sound irritated. "Not much point to them if they can't—"

"Grenades that you're working on in your shirt sleeves?" she continued. "In proximity to your aged, feeble mother, who's also in her shirt sleeves?"

"You're not *that* feeble," Lorne said. But the irritation vanished as he saw her point. "Fine. I'll be extra careful."

"Thank you," Jin said. The two watchers, she noted, still shifted occasionally in their places, but otherwise seemed to be settling in for the long haul. "Just try to relax," she added. "I know it's hard, but there's really nothing you can do."

"Not for now," Lorne said. "But sooner or later they'll have to leave." He huffed out a breath. "I'll be back there—" he gave her a lopsided smile "—working slowly and carefully. Let me know the instant anything changes."

Barrington was at Castenello's station, listening to the tac officer run through the various contingency plans, when the two Troft warships arrived at the flicker mine net.

Fortunately, they didn't seem to have noticed the *Dorian*, skulking along in stealth mode nine million kilometers away.

Unfortunately, they also didn't seem to have come just to see the sights.

"The pattern of shuttle dispersement would indicate they're extending the net," Commander Garrett told the senior officers Barrington had hastily summoned to the conference room. "From the directions they're taking the new generators, it looks like they're adding segments in all four directions."

"If there was any doubt they're gearing up for some big-game hunting, I think we can safely put those doubts to rest," Barrington said grimly. "Have we been able to glean anything about their capabilities?"

"Not really, sir," Castenello said. "They're too far out for us to get anything meaningful from the passives. However, from their sizes and acceleration profiles— plus the number of small craft they obviously have on board—they appear comparable to the larger ships of the Drim'hco'plai task force we tangled with over the Hoibe'ryi'sarai homeworld four days ago."

"In fact," Garrett interjected, "it's entirely possible they're the exact same ships."

Barrington suppressed a grimace. Those Drim'hco'plai

ships had been half as big as the *Dorian*, and nearly as well armed. And there were two of them here, plus whatever firepower the original spider ships had aboard.

Back at the Hoibe'ryi'sarai homeworld, for whatever reason, the Drim'hco'plai ships had withdrawn after that first brief engagement, apparently unwilling to make a toe-to-toe fight of it. Whether they would be operating under the same orders or restraint out here was anyone's guess.

Worse, there was no guarantee that these two were it. Out here in deep space, far from any planetary masses, hyperspace was smooth and easily navigable, and microjumps were both safe and common. As the *Dorian* could do a quick jump and be in the midst of the net region within seconds, so too could any other Troft warships lurking in the area. Moreover, as long as the incoming ship avoided hitting the net itself, it could jump out just as quickly and easily. Battles in deep space tended to become free-for-alls, with every bit of chaos and risk that the term implied.

"The point here, Captain," Castenello said into Barrington's thoughts, "is that we're seriously overmatched. We need to think about our exit strategy."

"What about the *Hermes*?" Kusari spoke up. "You think *we're* outmatched, what happens to them if they come charging in and hit the net?"

"If we leave, they won't have a chance," Filho added the obvious.

"You think they'll have much more of a chance if we stay?" Castenello countered. "I don't." He looked at Barrington. "I know it sounds harsh, Captain. But such are the realities of war. The *Dorian* is vital to our mission. The *Hermes* is, ultimately, expendable."

Garrett stirred in his seat. "You're assuming Commodore Santores will indeed send *Hermes* back to rendezvous with us," he said. "But as I recall, there were suggestions on the table that he might instead send the *Algonquin* or even come himself with the *Megalith*. If he does either, they would be as outmatched as we would be on our own." He gestured. "But if it were the *Algonquin* and the *Dorian* together...?"

"The commodore isn't going to send another cruiser," Castenello scoffed. "Not when he has no idea what kind of game Ukuthi is playing."

"Actually, that's *exactly* what he might do," Kusari murmured. "He wasn't promoted to flag rank just because he could smile nicely at appropriations meetings."

"And if there's even a small chance he can draw the heat off the Cobra Worlds and onto Qasama, I believe he'll jump at it," Garrett seconded.

Castenello shook his head. "He wouldn't risk the *Megalith* that way," he insisted. "Not without a more reliable collection of facts to go on."

"It doesn't really matter," Barrington said as Kusari drew a breath to reply. "We really have no choice for the moment but to stay put."

Castenello's eyes widened, then narrowed. "Meaning?"

"Meaning that while both of those warships are on this side of the net, we can't risk bringing up the drive," Barrington said. "They could be on us long before we could bring the weapons to power."

"You assume they would already have the necessary microjumps programmed into their helms," Castenello countered. "If they're not expecting company, but are just here to assist with the net extension, we might catch them flat-footed."

"I'd hate to bank on that," Filho warned. "Especially since the spider ships routinely seem to be running preprogrammed jumps."

"Exactly," Barrington said. "Unfortunately, that also leaves out the possibility of sending the *Iris* out to Ukuthi's coordinates and seeing if he might like to join the party."

"So we just sit here?" Castenello demanded.

"We just sit here," Barrington confirmed. "But only until the net catches someone. Assuming that someone is coming from Aventine, they'll drop out on the other side of the net."

"Ah," Garrett said, nodding understanding. "At which point the warships head across to engage, leaving us free to do *our* microjump into the impending battle."

"They'll still see us powering up," Castenello pointed out. "And they'll already have *their* weapons powered up, so it's not like we'll catch them completely off-guard. So what exactly is the point of waiting around?"

"The point is that either the *Hermes* or the *Megalith* is heading into a trap, and that we'll be here to assist," Barrington said. "Other than that, what's the point of *any* military?"

Castenello's lip twisted. But he remained silent.

"Very well, then," Barrington said, looking around the table. "Systems will remain in stealth mode, but with a ninety-second reactivation code. I'll want a set of microjumps calculated and ready to execute, with options of dropping us into firing range of either of the two warships. I'll be recording a set of warnings, which will be translated and likewise ready to transmit within that same ninety-second time frame. Commodore Santores's envoy, whether it's the *Hermes* or the *Megalith*, could be here as early as tomorrow, so we'll be at BatPrep Three for the next twelve hours, then go to BatPrep Two, with BatPrep One again on a ninety-second timing. Questions?"

Castenello opened his mouth, but closed it again without speaking. "Good," Barrington said briskly. "Then I believe we all have our work before us. Dismissed, and good luck."

CHAPTER TEN

Back on Aventine, especially in Capitalia where Merrick had grown up, it had been more or less accepted that being "on time" really meant being within fifteen minutes of the agreed-upon hour. Though there were certainly people who tried to be punctual, for the majority a more casual approach seemed to be the order of the day.

Qasama had been exactly the opposite. There, the people seemed to make a point of being punctual, right down to the minute. The military were even more obsessive about such things than the civilians, with the timing and coordination of their attacks scheduled sometimes within half a second.

Kjoic would have gotten along swimmingly on Qasama.

"Not exactly what I'd consider first *light*," Merrick murmured to Anya as they finished checking the emergency travel packs Kjoic had found in a compartment near one of the airlocks. "I mean, really—you can still see stars in the western sky."

"But they have all vanished from the eastern sky," Anya pointed out. "Is that not what *first light* means?"

"I suppose," Merrick grumbled. "I just hope the nastier nocturnals have started settling down for the day. I'd hate to trip over one of them while it was still hungry."

Anya frowned. "I thought you did not need sunlight to see."

"I don't," Merrick said. "But Kjoic doesn't know that. I'd rather he not find out."

She flushed. "Oh, of course," she said in a subdued voice. "I'm sorry."

With an effort, Merrick dialed back his grouchiness. It wasn't Anya's fault, after all, that he'd slept poorly and not nearly long enough. "Sorry," he apologized. "Just nervous, I guess. Going on an intimate little road trip with a Troft wasn't exactly what I'd planned for today."

Anya reached over and squeezed his hand. "We will be all right," she soothed. "You have learned much about slave behavior. And as you said, he is inexperienced in such matters."

[Slaves, they will approach me,] Kjoic's voice came down the corridor from the rear of the ship. [Your presence, I require it.]

[The order, we obey it,] Anya called back. She squeezed Merrick's hand again, then picked up her pack and slung it over her shoulder. Merrick scooped up the other two packs and followed.

Kjoic was waiting beside the gap in the bulkhead, which he'd used his cutting torch to reopen while the others were checking the packs. Laying across his hands was a heavy-duty military laser handgun, which he was peering at as if trying to figure out which was the business end. [Information, I require it,] he said, extending the weapon toward Merrick. [Firing, is it capable of it?]

Merrick froze. A Troft, offering a slave a *weapon*? What in the Worlds did Kjoic think he was doing?

For that matter, never mind what Kjoic was supposed to do—what was *Merrick* supposed to do?

He had no idea what proper protocol was for this situation. And judging from Anya's suddenly taut silence, neither did she.

[That knowledge, I do not have it,] he improvised, making no move toward the weapon. [Such devices, slaves are not permitted to touch them. Information on its function, I do not have it.]

[Knowledge, I must have it,] Kjoic insisted, still holding out the laser. [Danger, we may encounter it. The weapon, I must learn if it is functional. Shots, I must then number them.] He thrust the laser closer to Merrick. [The weapon, I insist you examine it.]

Merrick clenched his teeth. Whatever the protocol or prohibitions might be concerning weapons, he'd now been given a direct order. [The order, I obey it,] he said with a sigh. Stepping forward, he gingerly picked up the laser.

He'd seen many such Troft weapons during the Qasaman invasion, though he'd never spent any real time examining them. Still, the thing seemed straightforward enough: trigger, safety, power pack, sights, load indicator, fire selector.

The question was whether a slave like Merrick should actually know what any of those were or what they did.

It was a risk either way. Still, Merrick's cover was that he'd been one of Ukuthi's slaves, and that he'd been with the invasion force on Qasama. Such a slave would see armed Trofts around him every day. Besides that, even a local who'd never been above the atmosphere had probably seen the local Trofts carrying guns, possibly even using them.

[Knowledge, do you have it?] Kjoic pressed.

[Some knowledge, I have it.] Merrick turned the laser around and offered it, butt-first, to Kjoic, wondering briefly what the Troft would have done if he'd instead pointed the weapon at him. [An indicator, this appears to be one,] he continued, pointing at the load indicator. [Full, the status bar indicates it.]

[Shots, how many does it contain?] Kjoic asked, taking the laser and studying the indicator.

[That knowledge, I do not have it,] Merrick said, wondering if Kjoic was really that uninformed. Obviously, the number of shots would depend on the power level of those shots, with the life of the pack further dependent on whether the selector was set for semi or full auto. Did Kjoic really not know that?

Maybe he was simply more accustomed to less complicated civilian guns. The Cobra Worlds had a whole range of different weapon types; presumably the Trofts did, too. [Forgiveness, I beg it,] he added.

[Forgiveness, I grant it.] Kjoic took the laser and carefully slid it into the belt holster he'd already fastened around his waist. [That knowledge, it is of no immediate consequence. Protection against predators, we now have it.] He gestured to the packs on Merrick's shoulders. [Supplies, we have sufficient?]

[Supplies, we have sufficient,] Merrick confirmed.

Kjoic turned to the opening, his radiator membranes fluttering. [The journey, let us begin it.]

They worked their way out of the wrecked ship, picking carefully through the debris field surrounding it. Somewhere along the way, Anya managed to deftly take the lead, moving in front of Kjoic and leaving Merrick to bring up the rear.

It was the ideal marching order, of course, given that Anya was the one who knew where they were going and Merrick's Cobra gear could protect the group best from a rearguard position. But Kjoic had no way of knowing either of those facts, and Merrick spent the first half hour waiting tensely for the Troft to decide that he wanted the male slave breaking trail instead.

Fortunately, he seemed alternately fascinated and intimidated by the forest around him, all of which left little attention to spare for mundane things like giving orders to his new slaves. Either his lack of expertise was once again showing or else he just assumed the locals knew best how to handle this part and had decided to let them sort it out as they chose.

The crash site was about two kilometers south of the road Merrick and Anya and the others had taken when they'd first been dropped off on Muninn. Merrick had assumed that Anya would take them back up to that narrow strip of pavement, at least until they had to veer off again to head to Svipall. But instead of retracing their way north, she led them due east, paralleling the road but keeping to the wild. Clearly, her plan was to stay beneath the forest canopy and as far away from the search parties to the north as possible.

Under the circumstances, it was probably their best strategy. But it also came with some risky drawbacks.

This section of the forest seemed darker and older to Merrick, with a sense of tension and animosity quivering through it. A part of the planet where humans never ventured, perhaps, and where Trofts maintained their distance high above the treetops.

But despite Merrick's feelings of foreboding, the first three hours passed more or less uneventfully. There were a few incidents when small- and medium-sized animals came close, but all of them seemed more curious than hungry and were easily driven off with the thorn maces that Anya had torn from the trees and equipped them all with. Kjoic, in particular, seemed to take a perverse delight in swinging at the creatures with his club, and by the fifth such encounter wasn't even bothering to draw his laser before wading into the brief battles.

Merrick let him have his excitement, as an obedient slave should. Still, he was careful to put a targeting lock on every predator that moved within a dozen meters of the party. Much as he didn't want to reveal his hidden weaponry to Kjoic, he was even less inclined to let any of them get killed to protect the secret.

They were four hours into the march, and Kjoic was clearly starting to get fatigued, when the Troft finally called a break.

[Svipall, how much farther is it?] he asked as they sat on a pair of dead logs, munching meal bars from their packs.

[The journey, it is a long one,] Anya said. [One day beyond this one, the journey will require it.]

[The journey, it is long indeed,] Kjoic said, his radiator membranes fluttering. [This information, you should have given it to me. A shelter, we will need it. A shelter, I could have searched the ship for it.]

[A shelter, I searched for one,] Anya told him. [A shelter, there was not one.]

[A shelter, you would not have recognized it,] Kjoic countered. [A search, I should have made it.]

[A shelter, we can build it,] Merrick put in, trying to defuse the confrontation. This was going to be difficult enough without getting the Troft angry at them. [A shelter, we built one our first night returned to Muninn.]

Kjoic's membranes stretched out a little farther. [A return, you speak of it,] he said. [A journey, what kind was it?]

Merrick winced. Stupid, *stupid*. But it was way too late to call back the words. [Slaves of a distant master, we were they,] he admitted. [Our world, we were returned to it five days ago. The reason, I don't know it,] he added, to forestall the next question.

[Svipall, you have not visited it in many days?] Kjoic asked.

[Svipall, we have not forgotten its location,] Anya assured him.

[My question, that is not it,] Kjoic said. [Svipall, could it no longer exist?]

Merrick looked at Anya. Now that Kjoic mentioned it, that was a damn good question. With the Games presumably siphoning young people from the various villages, not to mention whatever the Trofts were up to here, there was no guarantee that anything from Anya's childhood was still the way it had been before she was taken off-world.

Anya's throat worked. [Svipall, we have not visited it in many days,] she conceded. [The village, I am yet certain it still exists.]

For a long moment Kjoic was silent. Then, slowly,

his membranes reseated themselves against his upper arms. [The dangers of the night, you can defend me against them?]

Merrick pursed his lips, noting the irony. The Troft—the *armed* Troft, no less—was asking *them* for protection? [Protection, we will provide it,] he assured the alien.

[Protection, to the best of our abilities we will provide it,] Anya corrected, flashing a look at Merrick.

[Your abilities, I will rely on them.] Abruptly, Kjoic stood up. [The journey, we will continue it.]

For the next few hours the party continued to make good time. There were a few brushes with predators, some of which stopped being merely curious and turned nasty. But between the thorn maces and an occasional and reasonably well-placed shot or two from Kjoic's laser, they managed to escape without injury. Whatever the Troft's inexperience with military weapons might have been, he hit the learning curve with a will, coming up to speed faster than Merrick expected. Clearly, it was this specific model of gun that had confused him, not laser weapons in general.

It was three hours until sundown, and they'd reached a more open area of the forest, when it all went to hell.

For Merrick, it started with a tight feeling in his gut, a sense of dread he could neither identify nor explain. He found himself walking closer behind Kjoic, his eyes sweeping the woods around him, using his infrareds to try to pierce the larger clumps of bushes and low foliage around them. So far there was nothing they hadn't seen and successfully tangled with before, but the sense of imminent danger remained.

More ominously, Anya—who was far more attuned to this planet than he was—was evidently feeling it, too. She had slowed her pace, her eyes moving back and forth more frequently than before, her pair of thorn maces no longer hanging loosely at her sides but angled up in white-knuckled grips. Not just ready for trouble, but expecting it.

Whether Kjoic noticed the change in mood wasn't clear. He made no comments as he slowed to match Anya's new pace, never questioning the reason for it. Possibly he was once again getting tired and merely glad for a small breather.

Merrick was wondering if he dared risk the distraction of asking Anya what she was seeing, hearing, or smelling when she came to an abrupt stop. "Do you smell it?" she asked tensely.

Merrick inhaled carefully, trying to sort out the forest aromas.

And then, there was no need to answer. Two giant jormungand snakes slithered into view from the tall grass twenty meters away, heading directly toward them.

They were much smaller than the monster Merrick had fought back in Ukuthi's makeshift arena on Qasama, more compact in both length and girth. They also seemed less armored, and with smaller scales. But they had the same wide, half-open mouths and the same razor-sharp teeth.

And they were moving to the kill.

Merrick's first instinct was to swivel up onto his right leg and fire a blast from his anti-armor laser down each of those gaping mouths. Smaller and less armored or not, he'd nearly been killed by the jormungand

Ukuthi had sent after him. Trying to play thorn-mace games against these things would be suicidally stupid.

An instant later, though, the inevitable consequences of such a move flooded in on him. He wouldn't be able to leave Kjoic alive and free, not after such a revelation.

Anya had warned him earlier that he might have to kill the Troft, and Merrick had pretended that he was ready and willing to do so. But he wasn't. Certainly not now; probably not ever.

Besides which, Kjoic still represented their best chance of getting access to the local Drim records, which meant that personal ethics and pragmatism were in alignment on this one. Merrick couldn't afford to let Kjoic die, either by the jormungands or by his own hand. There had to be some other way to get out of this.

He was still trying to come up with a plan when Kjoic opened fire.

Not with the single shots the Troft had used earlier against the other predators, either. These were full-bore, multi-shot bursts that raked each of the giant snakes in turn, blowing off little puffs of green smoke and filling the air with a well-remembered stink.

But as Merrick had discovered during his earlier battle, the ablative material making up the scales rendered such attacks useless. "The mouths!" Merrick snapped, reflexively giving the warning in Anglic. "Shoot into the mouths!"

[The attacks, into their mouths send them!] Anya said in cattertalk.

For a second Merrick thought Kjoic either hadn't heard the instruction or else his brain was so frozen

by fear that he couldn't act on it. His shots continued
to rake the jormungands' backs as the snakes continued their advance. They opened their mouths all the
way—Merrick once again shifted his weight onto his
right leg and started to bring up his left—

And then, almost at the last second, Kjoic finally
shifted his aim and fired a long burst down each gullet.

The jormungand on Qasama had never given Merrick
a chance at a clear shot down its throat. This pair were
either too eager or too inexperienced for such caution,
and it cost them their lives. They jerked violently as
the laser fire burned through their guts, one creature
dropping dead on the spot, the other managing to crawl
another half meter before likewise succumbing.

[Strange creatures, these are they,] Kjoic said, his
radiator membranes fluttering like crazy with reaction.
[Such dangers—]

[Escape, we must make it,] Anya cut him off, her
voice trembling. [Safety, we must reach it.]

Merrick frowned. But the jormungands were *dead*.

And then, abruptly, it hit him like a punch in the
gut. Yes, *these* jormungands were dead. These two
small, eager, *inexperienced* jormungands.

And where there were babies—

He was opening his mouth to second Anya's urgent
plea when the full-sized jormungand burst from between
two of the distant trees and charged toward them.

There was no time for warnings. No time for running. Back in the Qasaman arena, on relatively flat
ground and open terrain, Merrick had been easily
able to move fast enough to stay ahead of the giant
snake. Here, on the jormungand's home territory, faced
with a forest's worth of bushes, grasses, and tangled

vines, he and the others didn't have a hope in hell of outrunning it.

And he'd already discovered that even the full force of his Cobra weaponry could barely make a dent against the full-grown version of these nightmares.

Which left only one chance.

[The trees, we must climb them,] he snapped, dropping his thorn maces and grabbing Anya's and Kjoic's arms. A quick glance over his shoulder spotted two likely trees a few meters apart; half urging and half dragging, he pulled the other two backwards toward them. Kjoic resisted the pull for about a second before he apparently realized that his laser was going to be of no use, then caught up with Merrick's pace, holstering the weapon as they ran.

The jormungand had closed to about twenty meters by the time they reached the trees. [Up!] Merrick ordered, for once not bothering with proper cattertalk grammar as he grabbed Kjoic around his torso and shoved him up into the lower branches of the nearest tree. [Climb!]

Kjoic needed no further urging, scrambling up the branches as fast as he could. Merrick caught Anya around her waist, a small part of his mind crossing its fingers that Kjoic was too busy with his own escape to notice anything else, and threw her three meters straight up into the branches of the other tree. Half a second and a quick leap later, he was up there beside her.

Even at that, he nearly didn't make it. He was halfway to his target branch when the jormungand's front end rose from the grass and its teeth snapped together bare centimeters below his feet.

Merrick wasn't sure how much farther up the snake could reach. He had no intention of finding out the hard way. Urging Anya on ahead of him, he kept climbing.

The jormungand snapped once more at them— reaching nearly another meter higher up the tree, Merrick noted with a shiver—and then subsided. It slithered over to Kjoic's tree, apparently decided the Troft was too high to waste a lunge on, and settled back to the ground.

To wait.

"What do we do?" Anya asked tautly.

Merrick gazed down at the jormungand. Its head was swaying back and forth as it gazed upward first at Kjoic, then at Anya and Merrick, then back at Kjoic. It was making no attempt to leave, nor was it showing any signs that it would be doing so in the near future.

"Merrick? What do we do?"

"I don't know," Merrick admitted, staring down at the jormungand. Back on Qasama, he'd won his first jormungand fight through luck and a healthy application of high explosives. Here, that option wasn't available, and even with Kjoic's laser tossed into the mix, there was no way they could take the thing down. Not without an even larger slice of luck than he'd had the last time. Certainly not without revealing his true identity.

So what was left?

Without the others to slow him down, Merrick could probably outrun or outmaneuver the creature, and possibly lure it away. But it had a very settled look about it, and there was a fair chance it would ignore one escaping quarry in favor of maintaining its siege on two other potential meals.

Alternatively, sometimes animals could be driven away with sufficient injury or pain, as the party had done with the other predators they'd encountered during their journey. But even in Merrick's limited experience, jormungands seemed either too stupid or too arrogant to know when they were going to lose. Possibly because that rarely happened.

Which left him only one other maneuver to try.

He craned his neck to look around the bole of the tree he and Anya were clinging to. Kjoic's arms were visible, wrapped securely around his own tree's trunk, but his head and torso were hidden from view. "I'm going to try something," Merrick murmured to Anya. "I'll be back as soon as I can. Cover for me if Kjoic asks a question, okay?"

"What if he asks a question that he wishes you to answer?"

"Tell him I climbed higher hoping to find something," Merrick said, craning his neck to look upward. The tree was tall enough, he decided, to make that story believable. "You can say I'm looking for an insect nest, something like hornets, whose venom I can use to drive the jormungand away. You know the local plants and animals—make up whatever sounds reasonable."

"I will try." She squeezed his arm. "Be careful."

"You, too." Balancing on a pair of branches, he turned his back to the tree, put a targeting lock on the next big tree over to give his nanocomputer the distance, and jumped.

The nanocomputer did its usual magic, arcing him to a precise landing on the two branches he'd been aiming for. He worked his way around the trunk, targeted the next tree over, and jumped again. He moved one more tree away, then froze in place, keying in his infrareds and audios. Hopefully, somewhere nearby would be what he was looking for.

There it was, two more trees over: the infrared signatures of eight fafirs, a kind of hairy mix-up of wolf and ape that Merrick and Anya and their group had tangled with their first day on Muninn. The predators were clinging to various low branches, either resting from a kill or waiting for something killable to wander by.

Raising his hands, Merrick target-locked three of them and fired his lasers.

The dead fafirs hit the ground. Merrick did likewise, dropping into a crouch and letting his knee servos absorb the impact. Keeping a wary eye on the rest of the pack overhead, he collected the carcasses and headed back toward Anya and Kjoic.

The jormungand was right where Merrick had left it, lying midway between the two trees, alternating its attention between them. Merrick moved to just within its view and then dropped two of the three corpses he was carrying onto the ground.

The dull double thud got the snake's attention. It turned its head toward Merrick, and for a few seconds they locked eyes. Then, making sure he was ready to jump any direction necessary, Merrick heaved the remaining carcass toward the jormungand, landing it about five meters in front of the snake.

The jormungand looked down at the fafir, then back up at Merrick, then at the fafir again. Then, moving warily, it slithered forward. Still watching Merrick, it snapped its mouth open and closed, devouring the fafir in two massive bites.

Merrick waited until the snake was again looking at him. Then, he picked up the other two fafirs and started backing slowly away. The jormungand responded by moving toward him, but slower than its earlier attack speed. Merrick matched the pace, and after about ten steps dropped the second fafir. He backed up another five steps and stopped.

Again, the jormungand came to a halt at the fresh kill, eyeing Merrick as if wondering what this new game was. Merrick waited, and after another moment the snake once again accepted the proffered meal, this time taking three bites to devour it. Merrick again began backing up, and after a few more steps threw a quick look over his shoulder toward the fafirs' tree.

Most of the remaining predators had fled after his attack, but two were still crouched on their branches, both eyeing Merrick and the approaching jormungand. Merrick target-locked them, then turned back to the jormungand.

It was still coming toward him, but once again had slowed its pace, as if deliberately matching Merrick's. Merrick continued backing up until he was only seven or eight meters from the tree. Then, raising his arm over his head, he aimed his little finger behind him and fired his fingertip laser three times.

His arm moved as he fired, his nanocomputer using the target lock, kinesthetic memory, and his servos to adjust the aim. A moment later, there was a muffled double thud as the fafirs fell to the ground. Merrick dropped his final carcass on the ground and continued backing up toward the tree. He watched the jormungand eat the fafir, then leaped upward into the tree.

As he made his way back toward the spot where

Anya and Kjoic were waiting, he got a glimpse through the branches as the jormungand settled down and started eating the last two fafirs.

Anya was peering anxiously in Merrick's direction as he made the final leap back to her side. "The jormungand is gone," she murmured. "What did you do?"

"I gave it a choice," Merrick murmured back. "The chance to trade an easy meal for an even easier one." He looked around the bole of the tree. [The danger, it is momentarily past,] he called. [Our journey, we must continue it at once. Climb down, you must do it.]

[Climb down, I will attempt it,] Kjoic said.

Merrick frowned. The Troft's voice had gone oddly tense. [A problem, is there one?] he asked.

[A problem there is none,] Kjoic said, still in that strained voice. There was a rustle of leaves—[Descent, I am making it.]

Merrick looked at Anya. "Any ideas?"

She shook her head. "I saw two small flashes of light a few minutes after you left."

"He fired his laser?"

"I believe so," Anya said. "But I do not know what the shots were for."

"I guess we'll find out," Merrick said. Kjoic, he noted was making good progress toward the ground. "Come on."

Kjoic was leaning against the tree trunk, his radiator membranes fluttering, when Merrick and Anya reached him. [A small accident, there has been one,] the Troft conceded now. He looked down. [Careless, I have been it.]

Merrick winced. Just below Kjoic's right knee was a long, angry red welt, with a second welt above the ankle. From the placement and alignment, it was clear that the Troft had burned both sections of his back-jointed leg with a single near-miss shot. [The accident, how did it happen?] he asked.

[An animal, it approached me,] Kjoic said. His voice still sounded pained, but now a layer of embarrassed disgust had been added to the mix. [Two shots, I fired them at it. The animal, I missed it.]

But he hadn't missed his own leg. Maybe he wasn't as accustomed to laser weapons as Merrick had thought. [Walking, can you do it?]

[Walking, it will be difficult,] Kjoic said. [But walking, I will do it.]

[The distance, it will not be great,] Anya assured him. [The shelter, we must soon begin building it.]

[Distance from the large snake, I request much of it,] Kjoic said.

[Agreement, you have it,] Merrick said. [Anya, she will lead us.]

[Assistance, you will provide it,] Kjoic said, beckoning to Merrick. [Support, you will give it to me.]

[The order, I obey it,] Merrick said, stepping to his side.

Even with Merrick's help, it was slow going. Kjoic's injury apparently went deeper than its outward appearance indicated, giving him a pronounced limp and weakness in the leg. Several times along the way Merrick was tempted to simply pick up the Troft and carry him, which would have made the trip both easier and faster.

But while Trofts weren't massive creatures, they weren't exactly lightweights, either. Carrying Kjoic for more than a couple of minutes at a time would risk exposing Merrick's secret.

Fortunately, Anya found a good site for their shelter after only twenty minutes. Leaving Kjoic in the center of a small hollow, she and Merrick raided a nearby stand of the familiar fuzzy bamboo-like spikes for the necessary building material. Kjoic was skittish the whole time, insisting that one of them stay within his view in case he needed to be protected from more predators.

Fortunately, no such threats materialized. Unfortunately, the resulting slow-down in the collection process meant it was already full dark before the shelter was finished. Kjoic had eaten his evening meal bar while the others were working, and by the time Anya fastened the final spike in place the Troft was fast asleep.

And Merrick and Anya finally had a chance for a private talk.

"But it is dangerous," Anya insisted. "More dangerous than it even was before."

"Then we'll just have to be more careful," Merrick told her, sending a quick look at the shelter a dozen meters away. Kjoic looked to be fast asleep, but he could presumably wake at any moment and Merrick didn't want him wondering why his new slaves had left the shelter go off whispering between themselves. "We make sure we don't get into a situation where he has to climb or run."

"I do not know the behavior of *your* world's predators," Anya said stiffly. "But ours are not always thoughtful enough to give warning of their attacks."

"Sure they are," Merrick said, fighting hard not to snap at her. The long day and jormungand encounter had taken their toll, and he was tired and grouchy. "You smelled the jormungand as we were getting close, didn't you? There you go."

"Do you expect me to smell *all* the animals?" she growled back. Clearly, the day had been hard on her, too.

"No, *you* just focus on sniffing out jormungands and getting us to Svipall," Merrick said. "I'll keep track of everything else."

"And once we arrive?" she demanded. "Have you a story that will gain us entry? Or have you new faces for us to wear that will fool the masters searching for us?"

"Let's just concentrate on getting to Svipall in one piece, okay?" Merrick said. "We'll figure out the rest once we get there."

"Merrick Moreau—"

"And don't forget, we're a party of three now," Merrick said, cutting off whatever objection she'd been about to raise. "They're looking for two renegade humans, not an injured Troft and his personal slaves. Especially not an injured Troft who's also trying not to draw attention to himself."

"Until he learns the fate of the rest of the crew," Anya reminded him. "Once he does, he will very much be demanding attention."

"And with luck, we'll be gone long before then," Merrick soothed. "We just have to make sure to pull *our* information from whatever files Kjoic is able to access before he pulls *his*."

Anya exhaled a long, shuddering sigh. "And then what, Merrick Moreau? Even if we are successful, then what? We are here; Commander Ukuthi is not. How do we get the information to him?"

"I don't know," Merrick admitted. "If Ukuthi had been able to send a whole team like he'd wanted... look, all I can say that if whatever the Drims are doing is hurting your people, I'll do whatever I can to stop it. Okay?"

"We are slaves," she said stiffly. "That is by definition a hurtful thing."

"Yeah, I suppose," Merrick conceded. "Like I said, I'll do what I can. Next question: with Kjoic's leg the way it is, can we still reach Svipall tomorrow?"

"That will depend on whether the master can keep to a good speed and not tire too quickly," Anya said. "If he can, I believe we can reach the village by nightfall." She paused. "And then," she added, "as you said, it will be time for you to figure out the rest."

"Thanks, I got that," Merrick said sourly. "And speaking of rest, we'd better get some. I'll take the spot by the door, just in case; you'll have to crawl over Kjoic. Try not to wake him up. First light, I assume?"

"First light," Anya confirmed. "You will wake us?"

Merrick nodded, keying in his nanocomputer's alarm. "Sleep well, Anya."

"Yes." She hesitated. "You too, Merrick Hopekeeper."

Merrick felt his stomach tighten. *Hopekeeper.* It was the Muninn-style name she'd given him a few days ago when first introducing him to the rest of their party. At the time, he'd thought the title rather grand and decidedly complimentary.

Now, with everything that had happened since then, the name seemed merely ironic and mocking.

Ten minutes later, they were settled down for what remained of the night: two slaves, and an injured master who was as much on the run as they were. The perfect end, Merrick decided, to the perfect day.

Still, there was always tomorrow. And tomorrow would surely be better.

CHAPTER ELEVEN

Sedgley fished for about four hours before packing up his gear and turning his aircar back toward Archway. Lorne had hoped the Marines lurking behind the falls would linger no more than another hour and then do likewise.

Instead, they stayed perched on the ledge for the entire day, into the evening, and—as best as Lorne could tell—through the entire night. If they did take a few hours off, they were certainly back in position before sunrise the next day.

"This is ridiculous," Lorne fumed to his mother as he checked the display for the umpteenth time. "Reivaro's *got* to have better things for these clowns to do than sitting on a ledge watching water run downhill."

"Could it be someone else?" Jin suggested. "Not Marines, but maybe some locals the Dominion hired to play neighborhood watch?"

"And who were willing to rappel sideways down the

falls and sit on a ledge for a day?" Lorne countered. "I don't know anyone who hates the Cobras and loves the Dominion that much."

"Then if not some*one*, how about some*thing*?" Jin offered. "Remotes or robot sentries?"

"I haven't seen the Marines using anything like that," Lorne said. "Besides, remotes are risky—too many ways to confuse them or hijack their control or data signals."

"Then Reivaro *must* be convinced we're somewhere in the area," Jin said.

"Sure seems that way," Lorne agreed. "The question is what we do about it. If I go out there and take them out, he'll know for sure where we are."

"Assuming you *can* take them out."

"There's that," Lorne conceded. He'd successfully taken out a pair of Dominion Marines once before, but that had required a specific location and careful setup, neither of which he had here. "But if we just sit here, they win by default."

"True, but if Reivaro *doesn't* know about this place, we also don't want to risk exposing it," Jin said firmly. "It's too good a base, and not just for us."

"Agreed," Lorne said. "On top of which, it's not really our secret to give away." He scratched his cheek thoughtfully. "So our best approach would probably be to get out of here without them seeing us, set up a camp or temporary base somewhere within view of Sedgley's fishing hole, and let Reivaro find that one. Once he does, and after he figures he's driven us away, he should move his search elsewhere."

"Sounds like a good plan," Jin agreed. "Any idea how we do that?"

"Not a clue."

For a moment they eyed each other in silence. "So what now?" Jin asked at last.

"Well . . ." Lorne's eyes flicked over her shoulder. "I suppose I could make a few more bombs."

Jin's eyes narrowed, just enough to plainly show what she thought of that idea. "I thought you finished the ones you needed last night."

"I did," Lorne said. "But there's plenty of material, and it's not like I've got anything better to do. Call me if anything happens." He headed toward the rear of the cave—

"Hold it," Jin said. "They're on the move."

Lorne turned back around. One of the two shadows that had been bracketing the display was gone. The other was in motion, moving across the view and also disappearing. "Well, *that's* new," he commented. "Have you ever seen them both move at the same time?"

"Not while I was watching," Jin said. "One might leave for a few minutes, but the other would always stay until he got back. You suppose Sedgley's on his way?"

"Could be," Lorne said, checking his clock circuit. "He doesn't go fishing every day. Though when he does, he's usually earlier than this."

"Well, *something's* got them riled up," Jin said. "The way they were moving didn't look like they were just finding new places to sit. You suppose more Cobras might have decided to come here?"

"I hope not," Lorne said. "If those collars have locators—and Reivaro would be a fool not to have included some way to keep track of them—then they'll blow the hideout right there." He muttered a curse under his breath. "I wish whoever designed this display had given it some swivel capability. It would be awfully nice to know what was going on down below."

"Maybe there's another way," Jin said, looking at the stone blocking the entrance. "If we took out a few of the optical fibers and then pulled the block back a couple of centimeters, could we thread the fibers through the gap far enough to take a look?"

Lorne huffed out a breath. "Risky," he warned. "If our friends didn't leave but just moved over, we're likely to poke one in the back of the neck."

"I know," Jin said. "But the alternative is to wait until something happens right in front of us."

"Assuming it's something we can also figure out," Lorne conceded. "So far we're not doing so good on that one. Okay, but we can leave the peephole alone—I saw a spare fiber cable in one of the cabinets. Keep an eye on things while I go find a stiff wire or something to fasten it to."

He found the fiber cable right where he remembered seeing it. A bit more searching got him an eyepiece and a two-meter telescoping probe. He cobbled it all together, making sure to work in a right-angle bend at the front end of the cable, and took the whole thing back to the front of the cave.

His mother was standing beside the plug, her ear pressed against the stone wall. "Anything?" Lorne asked.

"Nothing I can positively identify," Jin said. "The waterfall's just too noisy. But I *did* seem to hear a voice a couple of minutes ago."

"But not since then?"

"No," Jin said. "Which doesn't prove a thing, of course. How do you want to do this?"

"I'll move the stone; you slip the probe through and take a look," Lorne said.

"You sure you wouldn't rather see what's out there?"

"If the coast is clear, I can take my turn then," Lorne said. "If not, I want to be ready to get the stone back in place the second you reel in the probe." And, he didn't add, if the Marines *were* laying a trap for them out there, he wanted to be in position to shove his mother out of their line of fire and do whatever damage he could before they took him down.

"Okay," Jin said, turning the probe over in her hands and getting a feel for it. If she'd figured out the unspoken part of Lorne's plan, she didn't say anything about it. "Ready."

Lorne nodded and got a grip on the plug's handholds. Taking its weight with his servos, he eased it up and backwards. Jin was ready, easing the probe forward through the gap as soon as it was big enough. Lorne froze, holding the stone in midair, the roar of the waterfall turning to thunder as he notched up his audios. Even with all the noise, there was a chance the Marines would give some forewarning as they moved in for the kill...

"Lorne, you said teens like to climb up the side of the waterfall?" Jin asked.

Lorne frowned. What in the Worlds was she bringing *that* up for? "The crazier ones, yes," he said. "Why?"

"Because we've got a new batch of them," she said, moving her eye away from the cable. "Take a look."

Still frowning, Lorne set down the rock and took the cable from her. A quick look to both sides confirmed that the Marines or whoever had been there had indeed withdrawn from view. Rotating the angled end of the probe again, he looked downward.

His mother was right. Two ground cars were parked at the foot of the falls, just outside the major spray zone, and a half dozen teens were gathered around them gesturing and, presumably, cheering wildly as three of their number climbed the cliff. Already the leader had covered a quarter of the distance between the ground and the ledge, and the other two weren't more than a couple of meters behind him.

And Lorne suddenly had his chance.

"Here," he said, thrusting the probe and cable back into his mother's hands. "I need to get suited up."

"What if they see you?" Jin called after him as he sprinted toward the scuba storage cabinet.

"If I'm fast enough, they won't," Lorne called back as he stripped off his jacket and tunic. "Pack me some grenades, will you?"

He was suited up in three minutes flat. Loading his clothing into a waterproof bag, he returned to the door. "How are they doing?" he asked as he rejoined his mother.

"The leader's almost to the ledge," she said, pulling in the probe and taking hold of the stone's handgrips. "I'm still not seeing signs of the Marines."

"Not surprised," Lorne said, checking the mouthpiece on his air tank. "They can't afford to let anyone see them up here—the minute they do, this particular catbird seat is useless to them. They're probably hanging on their lines just above the lip of the falls, under cover of water and hoping like hell their anchors hold."

"I hope so," Jin said, her face and voice tense. "Are you sure you want to do this? You've already missed your rendezvous—there's no guarantee you'll be able to connect with Pierce now."

"Not going to try," Lorne told her. "Got a new plan. No time to explain, but don't wait up. Where are my grenades?"

"Here." His mother gestured to a backpack at her feet. "I gave you five concussions and three smoke— that's all I could fit in."

"Great—thanks," Lorne said. "Seal up behind me, will you?"

"I will." She paused, and Lorne could tell that she desperately wanted to talk about whatever his new plan was. But she also knew the window of opportunity was brief, and that there was no time. "Be careful."

"You, too, Mom."

A few seconds later he was on the ledge, getting his mouthpiece in place as he felt the stone plug being pushed into position at his back. He turned around, crouching down to get a grip on the edge where he could lower himself down the cliff face.

And as he did so, the lead teen burst triumphantly into view, grinning broadly as he shook the water from his hair.

Lorne froze. If the boy didn't pause to rest on the ledge, but instead continued on upward, he might still get out of this unobserved. The teen paused, one foot on the ledge, rubbing his palm vigorously on his thigh as if erasing an itch. His eyes were directed upward, toward the rest of his climb. The rubbing hand came to a halt—

And to Lorne's astonishment, the fingers curled briefly into a fist with the thumb sticking rigidly out along his leg.

The teen held the pose for no more than half a

second. Then, still without looking toward Lorne, he continued his upward climb, disappearing into the mist.

Lorne didn't hesitate. He found his foothold and started down his considerably more treacherous route. Clearly, the teen had known Lorne and his mother were hiding here, and had apparently also known or at least suspected that there were watchers who needed to be chased away.

But there was no guarantee that the rest of the teens were also in on it. The faster Lorne made himself scarce, the better.

Five minutes later, he lowered himself into the churning water. Settling to the very bottom, he started his leisurely drift downriver.

Once again, he spent the whole trip wondering if the Dominion might have come up with a way to pick out his heat signature from the cold, flowing background. Once again, it appeared that they hadn't. A particularly distinct set of smoothed stones marked his destination; climbing out under the protection of a small copse of thorn trees, he shucked off his scuba suit and changed into his spare clothing. He strapped on his backpack, gave the area a careful scan, and headed out.

Matavuli's ranch was one of the largest in the province, covering an area of nearly twenty square kilometers. There was a strip about two kilometers wide between the river and the edge of his land, but this particular section of it was heavily forested and Lorne made it across without any signs he'd been detected.

The ranch's northeast vehicle garage was about a hundred meters in from the perimeter fence. Here, with no convenient tree cover available, Lorne took the entire distance in a dead run. He reached the garage, pulled open the door, and slipped inside.

There he paused, keying his opticals and audios to check for trouble or unexpected company. From the direction of a feed truck to his left came the sound of cloth on skin—

"About time," a voice boomed.

Hastily, Lorne dialed back his audios. "Sorry," he said as Matavuli straightened up from the truck's open engine compartment.

"'Sorry' don't feed the bulldog," Matavuli growled. "You have any idea how many times I've torn down and rebuilt this engine since you missed your meeting with Pierce? No, of course you don't. What happen, you get pinned down?"

"Basically," Lorne said as he crossed to the truck and peered into the engine compartment. It was half disassembled, all right. "Reivaro apparently decided Sedgley couldn't possibly be as innocent or curmudgeonly as he looked and posted a couple of watchers."

"Right on your front porch, I assume," Matavuli said, nodding. "Yeah, that's kind of what I figured. Nick got 'em chased away all right?"

"Nick? Oh—the climber," Lorne said. "Yes, they disappeared back up the falls. At least, I assume that's where they went. So you're the one who sent them?"

Matavuli grimaced. "Not so much sent as allowed to go," he said sourly. "Nick's been wanting to try that climb ever since he saw one of his more damn-fool classmates do it last year."

"Well, for whatever it's worth, he was doing fine when I left," Lorne offered, finally understanding why the teen had looked only vaguely familiar. With most of his Cobra duties centered around Archway and the areas to the north, he hadn't actually seen any of Matavuli's children in years. Nick, the eldest, had obviously done a lot of sprouting during that time.

"Yeah, and skydivers whose chutes fail are fine at the halfway point, too," Matavuli countered. "I'll be happy when he's back here. Not before. Oh, and the others in the group don't know why they're there, so I hope you didn't show yourself to them."

"I didn't," Lorne said. "But I definitely did need Nick's help. Thanks for letting him go."

"Yeah, you're welcome," Matavuli said. "So what do you need? Besides one of these." He waved at the garage's collection of vehicles.

"For starters, information," Lorne said. "Specifically, what exactly is happening in Archway?"

"Don't really know," Matavuli said. "Seems quiet at the moment. Though with the Dominion sitting on all the communication streams they could have dismantled the whole downtown and shipped it to Caelian and we wouldn't know it." He snapped his fingers. "Oh wait—yes, there was something. Yates Fabrications has shut down. Just temporarily, they say, but of course they *would* say that."

"Sabotage?"

"Or else hammering out all those armor plates wrecked the machines," Matavuli said. "Just like Yates said it would."

"Yes," Lorne murmured, frowning. "So they really are making armor? I assumed that was just Reivaro's excuse for taking over the place and goading us into a confrontation."

"No, they're really doing it," Matavuli. "Or so I assume. Don't forget everything I hear from Archway these days is at least third-hand, so take it with as much salt as you want."

"I'll keep that in mind," Lorne said. "Do any of these third-hand reports mention how closely Reivaro is watching people coming in and out of the city?"

"No, but even if you get in you're not going to get very far," Matavuli warned. "They've got your face, you know, from the official records."

"I figured they would," Lorne said. "I was mostly interested in whether or not they've set up identity checkpoints at the gates."

"I'm sure they'd like to," Matavuli said. "Right now I doubt Reivaro's got the manpower." He gestured at Lorne's face. "But there are plenty of Marines wandering around. All it'll take is one of them spotting you."

"That's why I'm going to hunt up a patch of poison gorse on my way in," Lorne said, wondering distantly if he really ought to be telling Matavuli all this. True, Werle and de Portola had vouched for the man, and Lorne had heard from other sources that Matavuli and his family had been staunch supporters of the resistance effort during the Troft occupation. Still, just because the Trofts had never gotten anything out of him didn't mean the Dominion wouldn't.

Matavuli gave a low whistle. "Nasty stuff," he said. "Face and hands?"

"Probably just face," Lorne said. "It should leave enough red puffiness to confuse their facial-recognition algorithms."

"I hope so, for your sake," Matavuli said dryly. "A

prison cell's bad enough without your skin trying to itch its way off your body."

"And I won't exactly be looking for trouble, either," Lorne said. "Even in Archway I imagine Reivaro's men are spread pretty thin."

"Should be," Matavuli agreed. "Though with Yates's plant shut down he might have shifted some guards from there to the gates."

"I wouldn't if I were him," Lorne said. "If it *is* just a temporary stoppage he won't want to risk more permanent sabotage while they're not paying attention. Either way, I'll just have to risk it. Okay if I borrow one of your bikes?"

"Sure, if you can hotwire it," Matavuli said. "I don't want Reivaro coming after me for giving it to you."

"Good point," Lorne agreed, wincing. He hadn't thought of that angle. "Unfortunately, I don't know how to do that."

"Kids," Matavuli said reproachfully. "Fine; I'll show you." He looked around and pointed to a beat-up Road Racer motorbike that had seen quite a few better days. "Come on—the Racer will be the easiest. So you're heading to Archway? I thought you and Pierce were going to wait for your uncle."

"I figured I'd wait someplace where I might be useful," Lorne said as he wove his way through the garage to the Racer, resisting the urge to point out that Cobras usually didn't need to borrow vehicles without the owner's permission. "But thanks for the reminder. Did Uncle Corwin think he could do it?"

"He said no promises, but that he'd enjoy the challenge," Matavuli said as he collected his tools. "Personally, I think it's a hell of a long shot."

"Long shots are all we've got right now," Lorne said. "Speaking of which, I also need to find a place for a little target practice. Any suggestions?"

"I thought you Cobras already came with all that targeting stuff."

"This is a little different," Lorne told him. "I need to learn how to throw bombs with some semblance of accuracy."

"Fun," Matavuli said with a grunt as he came up to Lorne's side. "That what's in the backpack?"

"Don't worry—they're safe enough," Lorne assured him. "The problem is that throwing things isn't part of the standard Cobra repertoire."

"You mean like walking a tightrope?"

Lorne frowned at him. "Are you saying we *do* have target-throwing ability?"

"Not saying you do; not saying you don't." Matavuli gestured toward Lorne's head with a screwdriver. "But that programming's a hundred years old, right? Who knows what might be in there that everyone's forgotten?"

Lorne pursed his lips. Matavuli had a point. Aside from a few tweaks that had been added to the opticals, arcthrower, and audios, the nanocomputer programming was the same as it had been for his great-grandfather Jonny Moreau and the rest of the First Cobras.

And even then, the only adjustments the Cobra Worlds had made had been additions. As far as he knew, none of the original programming had been deleted. There could be whole blocks of hidden data and techniques that no one knew about, simply because no one had needed to use it.

If Lorne could unlock those hidden techniques,

maybe he could find something that would help even the odds.

"Okay; pay attention," Matavuli said, pointing to a curved plate on the top of the Runner's engine cluster. "Under here is the starter..."

It took Matavuli five minutes to hotwire the bike. It took Lorne, under the rancher's watchful eye, closer to twenty.

But by the time he was done he had the technique down cold.

"Good," Matavuli said, wiping his hands on a rag and gesturing toward one of the other vehicles, a two-seater. "Now get in the crawler."

"Why?"

"You wanted target practice, right?" Matavuli reminded him, crossing to the main doors and shoving them all the way open. He gestured. "Oh, and you can leave the bombs here."

"I'd rather take them with me," Lorne said. He slipped off the backpack as he got into the crawler and set it on his lap. "Don't want someone else finding them. So where are we going?"

"Trust me," Matavuli said, smiling tightly as he got behind the wheel. "I've got just the place."

The place turned out to be an irrigation ditch.

"You're kidding," Lorne said, eyeing the ditch as he and Matavuli climbed out of the crawler. It was about three meters wide, two deep, and eighty meters long, mostly straight but with a couple of small bends in it.

"What kidding?" Matavuli countered. "It's deep enough to make you invisible except from straight overhead, and it's long enough to give you some distance to play with. Best of all, it's dry right now."

"Yeah, that's a nice plus," Lorne agreed, frowning as they walked toward it. "Getting in and out could be a trick."

"Not really—there's a ledge midway down that runs the whole western edge." Matavuli eyed his backpack. "You weren't planning on using actual bombs for this, were you?"

"Not at all," Lorne assured him. "I was hoping to dig up some stones or something."

"Not many big stones around here." Matavuli dug into his hip kit and came up with three large box-end wrenches. "These do?"

"Perfect," Lorne said, taking them. They were a bit lighter than his bombs, but close enough for practice. "Isn't two meters kind of deep for irrigation?"

"One: string grass grows deep roots," Matavuli said. "Ergo, the deeper the ditch, the better they get watered and the more the sheep and cattle get to eat. Two: you know as well as I do that the rains can be iffy in the summer. That means that in a pinch we can also use the ditch as a water-storage tank."

"Sounds to me like excuses," Lorne murmured.

"Exactly," Matavuli said, nodding. "All of which I'm ready to trot out if the Dominion asks the same question. Because...?" He raised his eyebrows expectantly.

Lorne smiled as he finally got it. "Because what the ditch *really* is is a slit trench."

"Bingo," Matavuli confirmed. "A bunch of us dug these back when the DeVegas Cobras were irritating the hell out of the Trofts and we figured that sooner or later they'd give up on that whole minimal-damage war philosophy and start full-range bombings. I had plans to do five or six more in other parts of the ranch, but the invasion ended before I got to them."

"Sorry it was wasted effort," Lorne said.

Matavuli gave him a sideways look. "You're sorry the Trofts got kicked out too soon? Seriously? Anyway, it's nice to finally get some use out of the thing. Watch your step."

Lorne had assumed that the ledge Matavuli had mentioned would be a carved section of the wall, like a normal stairway step. It turned out to be considerably more sophisticated: a meter-wide metal shelf sticking out from the wall, overhanging a third of the trench's floor area. "Shrapnel protection?" he hazarded as he hopped down to the shelf and then to the floor.

"Of course not," Matavuli scoffed as he followed more slowly. "Mineral enhancement. String grass grows better if it's got extra trace metals. The water leaches zinc, manganese, and iron off the plate."

"You've got an answer for everything, don't you?" Lorne commented, slipping off his backpack and setting it down on the ledge.

"That's how you stay alive," Matavuli said, joining him on the trench floor. "Okay. See that tree root sticking out of the wall about fifty meters away? See if you can hit it." He held out one of the wrenches. "What do you do first?"

Lorne took the wrench. "Well, for a lot of our maneuvers we start with a targeting lock to give the nanocomputer the distance. So..." He peered down the trench at the root and did the lock. "And now I suppose I just throw." Cocking his arm over his shoulder, he threw the wrench.

It thudded to the ground ten meters short of its goal.

Grimacing, Lorne tried again. The second shot landed about two meters closer. "Any thoughts?" he asked.

"Yeah, I'm thinking I should have brought more wrenches," Matavuli commented as he handed Lorne the last wrench.

"Cute," Lorne growled, glowering at the distant root. He'd given the nanocomputer the distance; it could presumably figure the object's weight from the heft of his arm servos. What else could it need?

"Maybe you have to do more like a forty-five degree arc," Matavuli suggested. "You've been throwing closer to thirty."

"Or I need to tell it the angle I want to throw at," Lorne said, looking up at the sky. Open sky, with nothing for his opticals to lock onto, so it couldn't be another targeting lock. Kinesthetic feedback from his arm servos, maybe?

Hefting the last wrench, he target-locked the root and then pantomimed a slow-motion throw, arcing the wrench through the same thirty-degree angle he'd already tried twice. Bringing his arm back again, he threw.

Again, no good. "I've still got a couple of screwdrivers, if you want to try one of them instead," Matavuli offered.

"We'll save them for later," Lorne growled. He jogged down the trench, retrieved the wrenches, and returned.

Matavuli was trying out some odd posturings, moving his arms around like a confused living statue. "Try this," he suggested, holding up his left hand and pointing like a hunter marking a flock of game birds. "Point your left arm at the throwing angle you want while you throw the wrench with your right."

Lorne tried it. It didn't work. "Anything else?"

"Hey, *you're* the Cobra," Matavuli said. "Fancy moves are your business, not mine."

"So they are," Lorne said, a thought suddenly striking him. The targeting lock's primary purpose was to let the nanocomputer aim Lorne's lasers and arcthrower. It also worked to give range for the wall-bounce, but only when the lock was followed by a jump instead of weapons fire. He'd already tried a lock and a throw, without success.

But the jump was normally just a straight-on leap, with no further data needed. As he and Matavuli had already noted, to calculate a throw the computer needed not just the distance but also the desired initial angle. And it needed the angle *first*, because different types of throws required different angles.

Or if not first, then perhaps simultaneously?

He lifted his left arm to a forty-five-degree angle in the direction of the root, holding the pose while he put a targeting lock on the root. Again cocking his arm over his shoulder, he started to throw.

And to his surprise and relief, he felt the familiar disconnect as his nanocomputer and servos took over from his muscles, shifting his arm's position and speed and sending the wrench flying down the trench to bounce squarely off the root.

"Whoa!" Matavuli said. "I hope that wasn't just a lucky shot."

"Let's find out," Lorne said. Lowering his arm to

a thirty-degree angle, he again target-locked the root and threw a wrench.

The servos had to work harder this time, whipping his arm faster as dictated by the physics of a shallower throw. Again, the wrench nailed the root dead-center. For his final throw, Lorne aimed high, seventy or eighty degrees from horizontal, and watched in satisfaction as the wrench flew its high parabolic arc and again hit the root.

"I think you've got it," Matavuli said. "Congratulations."

"Thank you," Lorne said, a shiver running through his sense of satisfaction. So easy... and yet no one had ever suggested the programming was even there. "I think we're done here. Let me go get the wrenches and—"

"Hold it," Matavuli said, grabbing his arm. "I hear an aircar."

Lorne keyed up his audios. It was an aircar, all right, approaching from the east. "Sound like one of the Dominion's."

"No kidding," Matavuli growled, hopping up on the ledge and climbing back to the surface. "Get under the ledge—come on, *move* it. And don't forget your backpack."

CHAPTER TWELVE

Ten seconds later Lorne was lying on the ground, wedged between the floor, the ledge, and the trench wall, his backpack in similar concealment at his head. The aircar reached them, and from the sound he guessed it was making a leisurely circle around Matavuli. Then, it came closer, and a careful look past the edge of the ledge showed it settling to the ground on the eastern side of the trench, opposite the point where Matavuli had climbed out. The engines spun down, and he heard the sound as two doors opened. There was the faint crunching of footsteps on string grass—"Morning," a helmet-filtered voice called. "Dushan Matavuli, right?"

"You've got my face on file," Matavuli called back. "You want something, or are you just going around crushing people's grass?"

"We thought we saw something fall onto your ranch," the Marine said. "Wanted to check and make sure everything was all right."

Lorne winced. They must have spotted that last, high-arc throw.

The big question was whether they'd seen it clearly enough to tell that it was a wrench. If so, he and Matavuli were in deep trouble. If not, maybe they could be bluffed back out of here.

"Probably a hawk," Matavuli said. Evidently, he was going to give option two a try. "They dive at rats and ground squirrels all the time."

"Really," the Marine said. "A hawk."

"Or a peregrine or a swallowtail shrike," Matavuli said impatiently. "There are a lot of vermin in grass fields. Vermin attract predators. Do I have to draw you a flow chart?"

"No, we're familiar with vermin," the Marine said acidly. "Mind telling us what you're doing out here?"

"It's my ranch," Matavuli said irritably. "I have to go places on it."

"Your nearest cattle are over half a klick away," the Marine countered. "What are you doing *here*?"

"One of my workers lost some tools yesterday," Matavuli said. "I'm looking for them."

"Someone else lost them, but *you're* the one looking for them?"

"Yeah, because I've got *him* cleaning the half-track's treads," Matavuli said. "Trust me; I'd rather hunt lost tools."

Lorne clenched his teeth. It was a nice story, with a nice snappy punch line to it.

The problem was that it could also be easily checked out . . . and once the Marines caught Matavuli in a lie, Reivaro could have him hauled in for further questioning or imprisonment. Or worse.

"Considering the stuff you probably drive through, I can't blame you," the Marine said, a little too casually. "What did you lose, some wrenches?"

"Three of them, yeah," Matavuli said. "Why, you got some spares?"

"They're over there," the Marine said. "Forty-eight meters, down in that—what is this thing, anyway?"

Matavuli launched into the irrigation and water storage story he'd spun for Lorne earlier. But Lorne wasn't listening. Something in the Marine's voice told him that they didn't believe a word and were simply feeding the rancher extra rope in hopes that he would eventually hang himself.

And if they concluded Matavuli's presence by the trench was somehow significant and decided to search it . . .

Carefully, making sure his arm didn't show around the edge of the ledge, Lorne reached up to the backpack lying above his head and eased it open. This was going to be tricky, not to mention dangerous. But he could see no other option. Right now he was below the Marines, where their epaulet lasers couldn't easily target him. But the minute they jumped into the trench, it would all be over. Not only would Lorne be in their sights, but being squeezed in beneath the shelf gave him exactly zero maneuverability.

Matavuli was talking about the province's variable weather systems and their effect on rainfall by the time Lorne had pulled out one of the homemade concussion grenades. He'd included a timer, but had designed them so that the main activation mechanism would be the impact of intense laser fire. If he could get the grenade close enough to the Marines, their combat suits' auto-defense systems should do the rest.

No battle plan survives contact with the enemy, his Qasaman commanders had often warned him. Briefly, Lorne wondered if the saying also applied to battle theory versus battle reality.

Matavuli was running through the metallic-element-leaching bit when the listeners apparently decided they'd had enough. "Okay, fine, shut up," one of the Marines cut him off. "We're going to need you to come with us."

Wedged beneath the ledge, there was no way for Lorne to use his new pinpoint throwing skills. He would just have to throw naturally and hope for the best. Leaning out from the shelf as far as he dared, he lobbed the grenade upward toward a spot midway between the two Marines, then ducked back, pressing his face and chest against the side of the trench.

The grenade was more powerful than he'd expected, the concussion ricocheting around the trench and slamming into his back. For a brief moment his whole body seemed to spin as the shockwave temporarily scrambled his sense of balance. Then the dizziness passed, and he rolled back out from under the ledge.

The two Marines were no longer visible at the edge of the trench. But he could see a pair of motionless feet. Grabbing his backpack, he leaped up to the surface.

The Marines were stretched motionless on the ground, angled backward from the direction of the blast. Lorne glanced at the other side of the trench, noting to his relief that Matavuli was getting shakily to his hands and knees, then stepped up to the first Marine and sent an arcthrower blast into the inner control edge of his left epaulet. A second blast went into the right epaulet. He moved to the other Marine, giving the arcthrower capacitor a few seconds to recharge, then similarly burned out the control edges of the second man's epaulets.

Then, just to make sure, he used his fingertip lasers to cut all four epaulets off the combat suits.

Matavuli was standing on his side of the trench by the time the job was finished, looking a little unsteady but on his way to recovery. "You okay?" Lorne asked, stuffing the epaulets into his jacket.

"Think so," Matavuli said. "Those damn things are loud, aren't they?"

"They are that," Lorne said, giving the sky a quick check. "I don't suppose there's any chance that they haven't already been missed."

"Probably not, and if you're smart you'll get the hell out of here," Matavuli said. "I mean that—*go*. You can come back for the Racer later after they give up the search."

Lorne grimaced. Except that part of that search would probably include hauling in Matavuli and his entire family. Especially if the unconscious Marines and their aircar were still here.

Which meant Lorne's first job would be to get rid of both. "Thanks, but I'm going with Plan B," he said. Grabbing the two Marines around their waists, tucking one of the men under each arm, he trotted toward the aircar.

"Whoa, whoa," Matavuli called after him. "Where do you think you're going?"

"Away," Lorne said, dumping the Marines unceremoniously in the back and climbing into the driver's seat. "Give me a thirty-second head start and then call it in to Archway. Tell them I was hiding in that group of leafbarks over there, that you didn't know I was even in the area until I tossed some kind of bomb at them. I came out, stole their aircar, and took off, and you just now recovered enough from the blast to call for help."

"You know there's not a chance in hell they'll believe that."

"Probably not, but it's the best I can do," Lorne said. "Good luck."

He closed the door and turned his attention to the controls. They were laid out differently from the Aventinian equivalents, but there wasn't anything too far out of the ordinary.

Except, of course, for the weapon, sensor, and pursuit panels. They looked complicated and nasty, and Lorne intended to leave them strictly alone. Keying in the grav lifts, he headed into the sky.

He'd been in the air no more than twenty seconds when the radio crackled on. "Unit Seven, report," a stiff voice came over the speaker. "I say again: Unit Seven, report."

For a moment Lorne was tempted to see how long he could string the dispatcher along. But it didn't seem worth the effort. "Unit Seven is temporarily out of service," he called toward the mike. "Can I take a message?"

There wasn't even a brief hesitation. Clearly, the dispatcher had already figured out there was a problem. "Identify yourself," he ordered.

"This is Cobra Lorne Broom," Lorne said. "I'd like to speak to Colonel Reivaro."

There was a short pause—"This is Reivaro," the colonel's voice came on. "Broom?"

"Yes," Lorne confirmed. "And before you scramble anyone to shoot me down, be advised your two Marines are sleeping it off in back. Their lives may not be valuable to you, but I imagine they are to them."

"They're valuable to me, too," Reivaro growled. "What do you want?"

"You can start by unplugging my father from your mind-sifting machine and letting him go," Lorne said. "After that, you can lift martial law, get those damn dog collars off our Cobras, and negotiate with our people for what you want instead of demanding it like a collection of petty tyrants."

"And then go home and fight our war by ourselves, I suppose?" Reivaro asked, heavily sarcastic.

"That would be nice," Lorne agreed.

"No, that would be stupid," Reivaro said. "And not just on our part. Or do you really think that the only Troft demesnes who might not like having humans on Assemblage borders are the ones you and Qasama have already defeated?"

"Probably not," Lorne conceded. "But we have a few allies of our own out here. Anyone who comes after us will need to add that into their calculations."

Reivaro snorted. "You mean the allies who sat by and watched while you were invaded?" he countered pointedly. "The ones who made sure you were winning before they so much as lifted a finger?"

Unfortunately, the man had a point. "We've proved ourselves now," Lorne said. "They'll be with us from the start next time."

"You don't even believe that yourself," Reivaro

scoffed. "The way Troft demesne-lords shift partners and alliances, you can't even keep track of them, let alone build anything solid on them. Like it or not, Broom, we're all we've got out here. You, the Dominion, and Qasama. Humanity."

Ahead, the Archway skyline had appeared on the horizon. "Then we should learn to work together like allies instead of playing conqueror and slaves, shouldn't we?"

"We're at war, Broom," Reivaro said. "The way you survive a war is by letting the people who know what they're doing give the orders. You may think a couple of weeks fighting a Troft occupation gives you credentials in that area. It doesn't."

"Maybe not," Lorne pointed out, thinking furiously. His original plan—actually, his original plan plus its five variants—had long since gone by the wayside. Now, he was riding a spine leopard with no obvious way to get off. "On the other hand, you don't know how things are done at this end of the Troft Assemblage. It could be very different from how they work at your end."

"Possibly," Reivaro conceded. "But in my experience, and in the experience of the Dominion of Man, Trofts are Trofts. They play by certain rules, and if you don't know how to play their version of the game you're in for a lot of hurt."

"We've already been there," Lorne said. Sneaking into Archway was out. So was trying to fly somewhere else; if Reivaro didn't already have a tracer and three more aircars on him, the man was way too incompetent to hold his job.

Which left only one option. If he couldn't sneak into the city, he would just have to bull his way in.

"Oh, please," Reivaro said contemptuously. "You don't even know your own history. Your great-grandfather, Jonny Moreau, personally went through a thousand times more hell during the first Troft invasion than everyone on the Cobra Worlds combined. If all you can do is spout platitudes and stupidity, you might as well shut your mouth and stop embarrassing yourself."

"That's okay—I was done anyway," Lorne said. "Just remember when you start handing out reprisals that I left these two alive and well. As I also did with the last two you sent after me."

"You skated right to the edge then, and I'm guessing you probably did here, too," Reivaro said. "You remember in turn that luck like that doesn't last forever. Sooner or later, you're going to slip up and kill someone . . . and when you do, the charges against you won't just be assault and sedition. They'll be straight-up murder."

"I'll keep that in mind," Lorne said. "But don't try to count these two on my score if you shoot me down."

It was as good an exit line as any, he decided. Glancing around the control panel, he found the radio switch and shut it off.

Hopefully, the Marines would continue to hold back for a while, at least until Reivaro decided there was no other way to stop him. In the meantime . . .

In the meantime, a look at the ground below indicated that the wind was coming from the northwest. Turning the wheel, Lorne sent the aircar in a lazy arc, circling the distant city until he could turn back toward it with the wind directly at his back.

Halfway through the maneuver, he spotted two more Dominion aircars, one pacing him from above, the other from behind. Hopefully, they had orders to hang back until and unless the hijacker did something that might constitute a threat or an attempt to escape.

Hopefully, by the time Lorne put his new plan into motion, it would be too late for them to stop him.

With Aventine's expansion regions still so sparsely populated, there was no reason in theory for Archway or any other city to build itself to any significant height. In practice, though, the continued threat of spine leopards throughout the territory meant that towns of any serious size had to be fenced or walled for protection. Given that fact, economic and political realities often meant it was easier to build upward inside a town wall than to try to persuade the local government to spend the money to remake and extend the wall.

So while much of Archway was still relatively flat, two or three stories at the most, there were four clumps of taller buildings, one near the center, the others nestled up to the fence, where the buildings rose to six, seven, or eight stories.

One of the clusters, the southwest group, was close enough to Lorne's apartment that he was quite familiar with it. More importantly, he knew one of the buildings intimately, not just the businesses housed there but also the internal layout of two of its floors. Information he would bet strongly Colonel Reivaro and his Marines *didn't* have.

Still, knowledge was one thing. Using that knowledge successfully was something else entirely.

The city loomed dead ahead. Lorne eased back on both his altitude and his speed, aiming for the six-story building in the center of the southwest cluster.

Just beyond it along his approach angle was another six-story building, the two separated by a relatively narrow street.

It was a perfect spot for a wall-bounce, the Cobra method for getting from the top of a building to street level in a hurry. Briefly, he wondered if Reivaro knew about the trick, then put it out of his mind. Whether the colonel knew about it or not, the twist Lorne was planning would hopefully throw him off the scent enough for Lorne to make his escape.

Almost there. Lorne dropped the aircar's altitude a little more, leveling off about two meters higher than his target building's roof. The autopilot control . . . there it was. A final tweak of the aircar's vector, and he keyed in the autopilot. Opening his backpack, he pulled out one of the smoke grenades and set its timer for one second. He put the grenade in his lap, then he sealed the pack again and slipped his arms into the straps.

Almost as an afterthought, he dug out the Marine laser epaulets from his coat and dropped them onto the floor. Reivaro would certainly bump up his hoped-for charges if Lorne was caught with them, and anyway the things might have built-in trackers.

The building swept toward him. Taking hold of the door release with one hand and the grenade with the other, he started his mental countdown.

And as the aircar passed the center of the roof he popped the door and leaped out, his legs pumping frantically as he fell. He hit the roof, stumbling for a fraction of a second before his legs synched with his forward momentum. Pushing his servos even harder, he put on a burst of speed and charged toward the edge of the roof. Above him, his borrowed aircar continued on across the city; a quick look over his shoulder showed that the other two Marine aircars had abandoned their distant pursuit and were moving in for the kill or capture.

Lorne turned his attention forward, twitching a target lock onto the building across the street. Ten steps to go. He waited until he'd covered three of them, then triggered his smoke grenade and dropped it beside him. Two more steps, and he heard the muffled *chuff* as the grenade went off, releasing a thick stream of smoke.

And as he reached the edge of the roof and jumped, the wind-borne cloud enveloped him, blocking him from view of the Marines flying overhead.

His feet hit the wall of the other building about half a story down, his knees bending to absorb the impact, his nanocomputer waiting until his head and torso had rotated a few degrees downward before straightening his knees and sending him flipping back toward the wall of the building he'd just taken off from. Normally, the programmed technique would send him bouncing back and forth between the buildings, slowing his speed of descent with each impact, until it finally landed him on the ground at a speed his knees and servos could handle without injury.

But that wasn't how today's script was going to play. Today, if Lorne had positioned himself and his leap correctly, his second impact wouldn't be against a solid wall, but in the center of a large, floor-to-ceiling conference room window.

He had indeed done it right. As he shoved off the first impact and started his midair flip he saw his target window behind and beneath him. A quick burst of fingertip-laser fire around the rim to soften the metal frame—

With a thud, he hit the window feet-first, breaking it loose from its frame and knocking it inward. The shatter-resistant glass bounced against some obstruction, nearly catapulting him back out again, and his nanocomputer again had to take over to reestablish his balance and bring him to a crouching halt on the angled plate. Carefully, still in his crouch, he turned around.

And froze.

He'd miscalculated. The window he'd thought was an import company's often-empty conference room had, instead, dropped him into the company's main office.

And it was anything but empty. Five men and six women were seated at their desks or else frozen in mid-step, staring at the intruder in wide-eyed silence. Two of the men were doing their staring partially through the window now propped lopsidedly against the edges of their desks.

They still hadn't moved as Lorne straightened from his crouch, his heart thudding, a sinking feeling in the pit of his stomach. "Hello," he said into the silence. "Sorry about this."

And then, someone murmured the magic word.

"Broom."

Lorne swallowed, his mind flooding with bitter memories of Capitalia in the first few hours of the Troft occupation. During that period of chaos and fear, the aliens had demanded that the city's Cobras and governmental officials be turned over to them, and the majority of the citizens had been only too willing to comply.

That attitude and utter lack of resistance had been in marked contrast with the stories Lorne had heard about DeVegas province's fight against the invaders. Lorne had taken those stories to heart, assuming that the people here would stand with equal solidarity against the Dominion's current efforts at intimidation.

But now, as he stared into the faces surrounding him, he belatedly realized something that hadn't occurred to him before.

Archway wasn't composed of ranchers like Matavuli, or the foresters and farmers of small towns like Bitter Creek. Archway was a *city*—smaller than Capitalia, but just as urban. And while the outer protective fence was a constant reminder of the threats lurking out there, most of the city's inhabitants had probably never even seen a spine leopard, let alone had to rely on a Cobra for protection against them.

These men and women had no reason to stick their necks out for a man on the run. In fact, they had every reason in the Worlds not to.

And then, a smallish man in shirtsleeves and loosened jacket collar and a complete lack of hair leveled a finger at Lorne. "Get off the window," he ordered briskly. "Come on, get *off*."

Lorne took a pair or steps to the side, stepping off the glass and onto the floor. It still wasn't too late to make a run for it, he knew. If he could persuade them to hold off calling it in for at least a couple of minutes. "My name—"

"We know who you are," the bald man cut him off. "Fred, Ambrose—get that window propped back up. Tommy, Jake—shove one of those desks over to hold it up. You—Broom—get over here."

Lorne had to quickly dodge out of the way as the other four men broke their own paralysis and hurried to the window and one of the nearby desks. "Come on, Broom, shake a leg," the bald man ordered. He grabbed a briefcase from beside one of the nearby desks, opened it, and dumped the contents onto the desktop. "They saw you with that backpack, right?"

"Probably," Lorne said, completely confused now.

"Whatever's in there goes in here," the man ordered, pointing at the empty briefcase. "Fred, you're about his size. Can he borrow your coat?"

"He can have it," one of the men moving the window said over his shoulder, grunting as he and the other man levered the window back up against the opening. "Georgette's been at me to get a new one anyway."

"Thanks," the bald man said, heading for a coat rack in the corner. "Ladies, get your coats and bags, if you please. As soon as they're done with the window, we're all going for a walk."

By the time Lorne had the bombs transferred to the briefcase, the bald man was back with a brown mid-length coat. "Try this on," he said. "I'm Gary, by the way."

"Lorne," Lorne said automatically. "Look, I appreciate all you're doing, but you have to understand that Colonel Reivaro isn't going to be happy with you helping me."

"Colonel Reivaro can take a flying leap at himself," Gary said tartly, taking Lorne's empty backpack and tossing it under the desk. "Anyway, you're too late. We've already discussed this latest invasion and decided we're not going to cooperate with it any more than we did the last one. Ladies? Come on, Fred—you're holding up the group. You ready, Broom?"

"Yes," Lorne said, slipping on the coat. It was a shade too big, but he doubted anyone but a tailor would notice. "Where are we walking to?"

"Jonquil's," Gary said. "That's a bar down the block. Kath, go get the elevator, will you? You got a place to stay, Broom?"

"Actually, I was thinking about my own apartment," Lorne said. "The Dominion's bound to have already gone through everything, and I doubt they'd expect me to show up there again."

"Maybe," Gary said doubtfully. "Just make sure you check it out first. Hate to go to all this effort just to watch you get snatched again before midnight. Okay; let's go."

"Yes," Lorne murmured as they all trooped out of the office and to the elevator standing open down the hall. "Speaking of effort...I'm sorry, but I have to ask."

"Have to ask what? Why?" Gary started ticking off fingers. "One: you're one of us. Two: Reivaro and his uniformed goons aren't. Three—" He flashed Lorne a dark look. "One of you Cobras saved my sister's youngest son from a spiny two years ago when the idiot decided climbing the Smith's Forge fence would be a good way to challenge authority and silly adult rules. The spiny was no more than five meters out when the Cobra nailed it." He hissed out a sigh. "His name was Jankos."

Lorne felt his stomach tighten. Jankos had been one of the three Cobras who'd been gunned down by Reivaro's Marines in front of Yates Fabrications six days ago. "Yeah," he said heavily.

"We all have stories like that," Gary continued. "Everyone in DeVegas does. So this is for Jankos, and the others, and Archway." The corner of his lip twitched in a small smile. "Oh, and a little of it's for you."

"I'll take everything I can get at this point," Lorne said as they all crowded together into the elevator. "Thank you. All of you."

"Save your thanks until we see if this works," someone advised dryly.

"That's okay," someone else said. "If it doesn't, we'll at least all get to be cellmates together."

To Lorne's mild surprise, not to mention probably everyone else's, it worked.

The smoke from his grenade had dissipated by the time the group hit the street, the new clarity permitting a good view of the half dozen Dominion aircars circling the area like angry vultures. The group had made it half a block when the first ground vehicles roared up and skidded to a halt.

Only they skidded to a halt five blocks away.

"Ha," Gary said with grim humor. "Looks like Reivaro outsmarted himself this time. They figure you hit the ground running and are trying to contain you."

Lorne smiled tightly. "In one of the most densely populated parts of Archway."

"Yes, indeed," Gary agreed. "Nicely done."

"Thanks," Lorne said. Not that he'd considered that aspect when he threw this whole thing together, of course. All he'd really cared about was having a pair of buildings tall enough and close enough together to do a wall-bounce.

But, of course, in Archway tall buildings necessarily meant high population density. If Lorne couldn't take direct credit for this one, he could probably allow his subconscious the honor.

"Happy hunting," Gary said, throwing a mock salute at the distant Marines. "Here we are."

"Wait a second," Lorne said, slowing down. He hadn't recognized Jonquil's name when Gary said it earlier. But now that he saw where they were going—"This might not be a good idea. I've been here a few times, usually with other Cobras. They might recognize me."

"Don't worry about it," Gary said. "Quill's a good friend—he'll cover for us. That's why we're here instead of somewhere else."

"See, we were all out of the office when you came bounding through the window," Kath explained. "*You* propped that window back up, not us."

"We were as surprised as anyone when we got back and found our office like that," Fred added blandly. "Which'll be in, what, about an hour?"

"Maybe an hour and a half," Gary said judiciously. "We've got a lot of brainstorming to do about that new Balin proposal, and it's cheap-drinks hour. An hour and a half be enough?"

"I'm sure it will," Lorne said. "Thank you."

"Come on, come on," Ambrose chided. "I can smell the scotch from here."

Lorne had been in Jonquil's probably no more than twice in the past year—it was one of Badj Werle's favorite spots, but Cobra salaries didn't allow that kind of splurging very often. Still, he felt horribly conspicuous as Gary led the way through the smaller tables toward a back room set up for larger groups.

They were in the process of seating themselves when an older man in an apron embossed with the bar's name came bustling up. "Hey, Gary," he said in greeting. His eyes flicked across the group, pausing for just a fraction of a second on Lorne before continuing. "Another of your famous off-site business meetings?"

"Hey, as long as we discuss business, it's a business expense," Gary said. "You know Jankos's cousin Peter, right, Quill?"

"I've seen him around," Quill said, giving Lorne a long, cool look. "So, you folks ready for your third round yet?"

Lorne frowned. Their *third* round?

"Sounds great," Gary said calmly. "We all had our usuals for the first two rounds, right?"

"Yep," Quill confirmed. "I assume you're all running tabs?"

"As always," Gary said. "And make this third round on me."

"That's what people like to see in their boss," Quill said dryly. His eyes flicked one last time to Lorne, and this time his head inclined microscopically. "And the second round was on me. Have a good meeting, folks." He turned and headed back toward the bar.

"You two going to sit down?" Ambrose prompted.

"Sure." Gesturing Lorne to one of the two remaining chairs, Gary pulled out the other and sat down. "Like I said," he added in a quieter voice, "we're not Capitalia."

"So I see," Lorne said as he sat down. The group's third round . . . which meant that they must have been sitting here at least half an hour before Lorne burst through their office window. Assuming Quill was also able to fiddle his records, Reivaro would have to search long and hard for witnesses before he could prove otherwise.

And if Lorne did his job properly, the colonel wouldn't have time to do that. He would, in fact, have considerably more pressing problems on his hands than a possible nest of uncooperative civilians.

"Of course, if they start a complete door-to-door, you might still be in trouble," Gary continued as if their earlier conversation had never been interrupted. "Got any ideas about that?"

"Not really," Lorne said. Though now that he mentioned it, something *was* starting to come together in the back of his mind. "Though I'm guessing he doesn't have the manpower for that."

"Not unless he whistles up a whole raft of reinforcements from the Dominion ships," Gary agreed. "The Trofts did that, you know. We made such a screaming nuisance of ourselves they couldn't keep a lid on us alone."

"Easy, hero-boy," one of the women said dryly. "It was the Cobras and the ranchers who did most of that screaming, remember? The rest of us didn't do a whole lot except sit on the sidelines and cheer."

"Hey, cheering is part of it," Gary insisted. "Especially when we're also not turning people in to the Trofts. Am I right, Broom?"

"Absolutely," Lorne said. "It's a lot more than Capitalia could manage to do."

"There you go," Gary said to the woman. "Though I suppose you could make a case that comparing us to Capitalia is damning with faint praise."

"No damning or faintness intended," Lorne assured him. "The way I see it, in war or any other kind of catastrophe, you have to do whatever the universe drops onto your plate. If you get thrown onto the front lines, you fight. If all you get is a support role, you support."

"And sometimes that landing-on-your-plate thing happens literally," Fred commented dryly.

"Hopefully not very often," Lorne agreed.

"But seriously, a disguise would be good," Gary said. "Quill isn't the most politically astute person on the block, but he knew who you were the second he saw you. Most of Archway will, too."

"Not to mention any Dominion man who spots you," Kath warned. "They've downloaded the whole province ID listing, and they've got some kind of implant that lets them just twitch an eye and pull up who you are."

"Yes, I know," Lorne said. "What do you suggest?"

"False nose and beard," Fred said promptly. "That always seems to work on Anne Villager."

"And considering you don't seem to have shaved for a couple of days, you're already started on the beard," Gary said, peering critically at his face. "Don't know where you'd find a false nose, though."

"I'll think of something," Lorne assured him. "And I'd better get going." He started to stand up.

"Whoa, son, what's your hurry?" Gary admonished. "You need to stay put for a while, remember?"

"Besides, the third round's on the way," Kath added. "You don't drink, it just gets thrown away."

"I guess we can't have *that*," Lorne conceded. "Twenty minutes, no more."

"Twenty minutes," Gary promised. "Speaking of stuff getting dropped on your plate, who's up for some appetizers?"

Lorne's twenty minutes ended up getting stretched to an hour by the sudden appearance of a squad of Marines on the street outside.

Fortunately, they seemed to be searching mostly empty shops and apartments, and though one of them stepped into the bar, he left again after a quick word with Quill and an even quicker look at his notepad. Twenty minutes later, Quill came by the table to quietly inform Gary that the soldiers had left the neighborhood.

Still, there was no point in taking any more chances than necessary. Lorne gave it another twenty minutes, just to be sure, before heading out into the street.

He half expected a Dominion aircar to drop from the sky before he'd gone ten steps, with Reivaro and a squad of grinning Marines swarming out to make the arrest. But the sky was clear, the search having apparently moved elsewhere. Joining the crowds of pedestrians, he headed down the street.

He'd told his new drinking companions that he was heading to his apartment, which was four blocks east and two north from Jonquil's. But in the intervening time he'd had time to reconsider his options and to come up with a new plan.

It was a risky plan. Worse, it relied heavily on the assumption that the vast majority of Archway's citizens were as firmly behind the Cobras as Gary and his group. But he had little choice. With his face on the Marines' files, he wouldn't get very far unless he found a way to make that face unrecognizable.

And aside from Fred's suggestion of a false nose and beard, there was only one way he could think of to do that.

The Malagar Building was one of three four-story structures at the edge of the southwest cluster. The bottom floor was taken up by shops, restaurants, and a small walk-in medical clinic, with the second and third floors containing offices of various sorts.

The fourth floor, however...

He entered via one of the restaurants, coming in the main entrance then moving straight through to the kitchen and the back elevator. He saw several people along the way, but if any of them recognized him, they made no sign. He took the elevator to the third floor, got out, sent the elevator back to the first floor, then forced open the doors and climbed up the cables to the fourth floor. All told, it was a transparent ploy, possibly even edging toward childish, but the more he could muddy Reivaro's future investigations, the better.

The corridor he emerged onto was empty, but his audios could pick up the hum and muffled noises of activity. He walked toward the sound, turned a couple of corners.

And there it was, facing him from above a pair of double glass doors:

POLESTAR PRODUCTIONS
HOME OF TRIBECCA, GREENDALE, AND
ANNE VILLAGER

The woman seated at the desk beyond the doors glanced up, did a double-take, and grabbed for her comm. She spoke urgently for a moment, got a reply, and buzzed Lorne in.

She'd gone quiet and goggle-eyed by the time Lorne joined her in the reception area. "Hello," he said, shifting to his infrareds to try to read her emotions. She was nervous and stressed, but that was about all he could get.

Fortunately, the awkward silence didn't last long. "Hello," a middle-aged man said as he pushed open a side door and hurried across to the desk. "I'm James Hobwell, Greendale executive producer. This is a—" He broke off, harrumphed, and seemed to gather himself. "What can we do for you, Cob—young man?"

"That depends," Lorne said, studying his face. At least as nervous and stressed as the receptionist. "What I need could be dangerous. Colonel Reivaro won't like it if he finds out."

Hobwell glanced at the receptionist, then drew himself up. "I've had better men than him mad at me. Tell me what you need."

Lorne took a careful breath. He wasn't reading any duplicity in Hobwell's face, which was a good sign. But he also knew that promises made in a quiet place among friends could easily splinter when the going got rough.

Still, right now it was all he had.

Hobwell was still waiting. "What I need," Lorne said, "is to talk to one of your makeup artists."

CHAPTER THIRTEEN

During the three days the *Dorian* floated silently in the darkness nine million kilometers from the Trofts' flicker-mine net, Barrington had spent some of his idle minutes running calculations on the likely moment when his ship would find itself plunged into battle.

Two of the numbers were straightforward. It was easy to calculate how long it would have taken the *Hermes* to arrive at Aventine from the point where the *Dorian* had dropped it, and equally simple to figure the time it would then take for the trip from the Cobra Worlds' capital to the flicker net.

The other two numbers—how long it would take Commodore Santores to read Barrington's report, and how long it would take him to decide on a course of action—were far softer numbers. Still, Barrington had spent a fair amount of time interacting with the commodore on the voyage from Asgard, and he had a pretty good feel for how his superior thought and acted. The timing would also depend on other factors, such as whether the commodore had been on duty when the report came in, and whether other matters on Aventine might be competing for his attention. Ultimately, he ended up with a probable six-hour range.

One hour before the shortest and most optimistic of his calculated times, he raised the *Dorian's* readiness level from Battle Preparedness Two to BatPrep One.

Commodore Santores had apparently assigned a high priority to the *Dorian's* situation. Exactly ninety-two minutes later, the *Hermes* hit the Trofts' net and was yanked back into space-normal.

"It hit about fifteen percent off the center point," Commander Garrett reported. "As close to a dead-center hit as I've ever seen. If we're still looking for proof that the net was intended for us, this is as good as we're likely to get. Range reads out at a hair over nine-point-three million kilometers."

Barrington nodded, automatically converting the number to thirty-one light-seconds. Everything they were observing was therefore half a minute out of date. "Enemy response?"

"Both warships are moving in for the kill," Castenello called. "Two is closest; it's on the far side of the net and will be in laser range in six minutes. One is on our side and about four minutes behind it." He threw Barrington a dark look. "Unfortunately, One is the closer target."

Barrington stroked a finger thoughtfully on his lower lip. Unfortunate, because while One would be the easier of the two for the *Dorian* to tackle, it was also the smaller threat to the *Hermes*. If Barrington chose to engage One, *Hermes* would be alone as it faced off against Two.

There was, of course, a standard tactical response to this kind of situation. Barrington would normally bring the *Dorian* into the battle with a microjump that would take it into toe-to-toe range with Two and attempt to put Two out of action before One made it into range. If he succeeded, then it would be the *Dorian* and *Hermes* that would be double-teaming One instead of being on the receiving end of such firepower concentration.

The problem was that the geometry here made such a plan impossible. Two was on the far side of the net, where the *Dorian* couldn't reach it. And as Castenello had already pointed out, tackling One would still leave the *Hermes* on the short end of the odds against Two.

"Picking up fire!" Garrett snapped. "The *Hermes* has engaged."

Barrington cursed under his breath as he looked over at the tactical display. The images confirmed what logic had already told him: the *Hermes* was still well out of laser range of the approaching warship.

Which meant that Lieutenant Commander Vothra had just wasted energy and gained nothing.

Or had he?

Barrington twitched his eye, tapping into the tactical data stream, and keyed for a fine-tune filter. If he could get a view through the glare from One's engines and cut through the sensor haziness created by the net itself...

And there it was. "Fresh movement," he called. "Three spider ships engaging the *Hermes*—designate Three, Four, and Five."

"Acknowledged," Castenello called back. "The

Hermes has fired on Three; Four and Five ten seconds from laser range."

"The *Hermes* is engaging Five," Garrett put in. "Damage unclear."

"Two nearly within laser range of the *Hermes*," Castenello said. "Captain, we need some orders here."

"Thank you, Commander," Barrington said, clenching his teeth as he studied the data stream.

"Captain, are we going to engage?" Castenello pressed. "The *Hermes* is facing annihilation."

Barrington frowned, focusing on the beleaguered courier ship. Castenello was right. The *Hermes* was facing impossible odds. In fact, with a three-to-one advantage, the spider ships should already be blistering away the outer hull.

Only they weren't. In fact, it didn't look like they were even trying.

"Captain?" Castenello demanded.

Again, Barrington tapped into the data stream. All three of the spider ships were in range now, yet none of them had opened fire on the *Hermes*. They were taking the courier's fire without replying, as if their goal was merely to drain its missile tubes and overheat its lasers.

And if they were genuinely reluctant to damage their prize...

"Helm: new course," he ordered. "Take us into the net directly between—"

"Into the *net*?" Castenello interrupted. "Sir—"

"Directly between One and Two and as close to the *Hermes* as possible," Barrington continued. "Tactical Officer: approach, please."

"Yes, Sir," Castenello said between obviously

clenched teeth. Popping his straps, he stalked across CoNCH to Barrington's station. "Permission to speak candidly, Captain?" he asked, his voice stiff but quiet enough that only Barrington and Garrett could hear. At least he had that much tact.

"Of course," Barrington said.

"Sir, if you're trying to pick up the *Hermes* and get out, this isn't the way to do it," Castenello said. "We can drop into range without hitting the net—"

"Can we, Commander?" Barrington interrupted. "With us over thirty light-seconds out and the *Hermes* likely already into battle maneuvers? If we try to jump into retrieval range without knowing their exact position, we have a small but dangerous chance of ramming right into them."

"Those risks can be minimized, Sir."

"Or they can be eliminated," Barrington said. "Because the one place we *know* they aren't is in the plane of the net itself. They'll have drifted this direction and be making every effort not to cross the plane again." He raised his voice. "Helm, once you've calculated our jump, I also want whatever rotation is necessary to turn us with our flanks facing the warships."

"Captain, have you gone *insane*?" Castenello demanded, his eyes wide. "Running broadside tactics against ships that size will be suicide."

"*If* they wanted our destruction," Barrington said. "In this case, I don't think they do. I think they're hoping to take the *Hermes* intact. My guess is that the fleet commander is letting the spider ships probe for weaknesses or trying to come up with disabler codes."

"And if you're wrong?" Castenello shot back. "Let me remind the captain that we're thirty seconds behind what's happening out there. They may very well have already engaged the *Hermes*."

"Your concerns are noted, Commander," Barrington said. "Helm?"

"Vector plotted and laid in," the helmsman confirmed. He didn't sound any happier than Castenello, Barrington noted, but he had nowhere near the rank necessary to object. "Yaw turn programmed."

"Commander Filho?"

"Lasers, Pluto cones, and missiles ready," the weapons officer confirmed.

And with that, there was nothing left but to do it. "Commander Garrett, bring us to full power: *mark*," Barrington ordered. The *Dorian* had thirty-one seconds to bring its active sensors, laser capacitors, and ECM to power before the lightspeed-limited evidence of that activation propagated to the Troft warships. Ten more seconds after that, he decided, for the opposing captains to spot the Dominion warship and start turning their attention in this direction—"Make jump forty seconds from mark." He looked at Castenello. "Return to your station, Commander."

"Yes. Sir," Castenello ground out. Spinning around, he stalked back across CoNCH.

"I hope this works, sir," Garrett murmured. "If it doesn't, I expect he'll make it his goal in life to nail your hide to the hull."

"If it doesn't work, neither of us is likely to live to sit before an Asgard hearing," Barrington pointed out. "Confirm readiness."

"Capacitors eighty percent and flash-charging,"

Garrett said, his voice back to its normal professional crispness. "ECM ready. Pluto cones armed and conditionally aimed; active sensors on line and tied into lasers and launchers."

Barrington nodded. "Helm, as soon as we've delivered our first broadside, set course for a zero-zero with the *Hermes* and rotate to retrieval position. How fast can you recalibrate the drive?"

"The book says twelve minutes, Sir," the helm said. "Commander Kusari thinks we can do it in ten."

"Tell him he's got nine," Barrington said. The countdown timer hit zero—

In an almost-felt blink of an eye, the *Dorian* jumped into hyperspace, crossed the nine point three million kilometers, and slammed into the flicker net, bouncing out again into space-normal.

Right into a full-blaze firefight.

Barrington had used the half-minute time lag to his advantage. But that sort of information delay was a two-edged sword. Apparently, sometime in the past forty seconds, the Troft warships had changed their mind about taking the *Hermes* and its crew intact.

And the courier ship was fighting for its life.

"Laser broadsides: *fire*," Barrington snapped. There was the distant rumble of sequentially cascading capacitors as the lasers spat energy at the swarming spider ships. "Pluto cones: *fire*. Enemy damage?"

"Significant damage to Three and Four," Garrett reported. "Five is moving to put the *Hermes* between itself and us."

Though scrambling like a maniac to get out of the *Dorian*'s line of fire wasn't stopping it from continuing its attack on the *Hermes*, Barrington noted.

"Missiles: *fire*," he ordered. "Then signal the *Hermes* to prepare for pickup." He shifted his attention to the two incoming warships—

Just as the entire ship shuddered beneath him.

Someone out there had scored a direct hit.

"Damage report!" Barrington snapped, his eyes flicking over the tactical display as he searched for the source of the attack. The three spider ships were disabled or out of firing position. The two Troft warships were still just barely in laser range, and there was no indication that either had fired a missile.

"Debris," Garrett snapped back. "We were rammed. Looks like there was a fourth spider ship."

Barrington swore under his breath. With the limited sensor capabilities created by their distance and the net itself, there had always been the risk that they would miss something vital before they jumped in.

But to have come so close that the ship was effectively inside the *Dorian*'s point-defense system was something he could never have anticipated. "Get us to the *Hermes*," he ordered. "And get the drive back on line."

"That may be a problem, Sir," Garrett warned tautly. "The epicenter of the collision was at Twenty-One Gamma."

Barrington felt his breath catch in his throat. Starboard-aft, right over Reactor Two.

Where Commander Kusari was currently recalibrating the drive.

Twitching his eye, he tapped into the damage-control data stream.

It was worse than he'd expected. Fifteen men were down, though so far no deaths were being reported.

The impact had thrown Reactor Two into auto-scram, and it was in the process of running a self-check as it worked its way back up. Another three minutes, the computer estimated, and it would once again be at full power.

Under normal conditions, the *Dorian* could run perfectly well with only one operating reactor. Unfortunately, these were not normal conditions; and with a pair of Troft warships closing in on them, this was not a good time to be down to sixty percent of laser power.

They still had one ace in the hole. But just one, and it was risky, and Barrington had no intention of using it unless he absolutely had to. "Time to zero-zero?" he called.

"Three minutes twenty," Garrett said. "Troft warships—"

There was a slight shudder as some of the *Dorian*'s outer hull boiled off. "—have reached laser range," Garrett continued. "Hits on Four Epsilon and Eight Delta."

"Full laser volley on Two," Barrington ordered. "Follow with Pluto cones and missiles to both warships. ECM?"

"ECM reads active," Garrett said. "We won't know effectiveness until they start throwing missiles."

And if the evidence from the Hoibie homeworld confrontation was any indication, the ECM would be only partially effective. "Status on drive recalibration?"

Garrett didn't answer. "Commander?" Barrington demanded, turning to look at the other.

To find that his First Officer's face had gone pale. "Sir, Commander Kusari is down," he said, his voice under rigid control. "A ruptured hydraulic pipe. The pressure . . . both his legs, sir."

Barrington cursed, tapping into the data stream and keying for sick bay. Dr. Lancaster ought to have at least a preliminary report on Kusari's condition by now.

Only he didn't. Because Kusari was apparently not in sick bay. Frowning, Barrington did a search.

And felt his mouth drop open. Kusari was still in Reactor Two, overseeing the recalibration.

Garrett must have caught that fact the same time Barrington did. "Sir, Commander Kusari—"

"Yes, I know," Barrington cut him off. The med data stream now showed that Kusari had ordered temporary sheathing for his burned legs, plus injections of painkillers and stimulants, and was stretched out on a gurney at his station hammering at his board. Determined to get the *Dorian* out of here or else to die at his post.

Possibly to do both.

Barrington checked the timer. Four minutes to recalibration, if Kusari's original estimate was still valid. Six minutes if they had to go with the book's.

And with two enemy warships roaring into battle, those extra two minutes could mean the difference between survival and obliteration.

"Pluto cones away," Castenello reported. "Missiles targeted and ready."

With an effort, Barrington returned back to the tactical. Kusari was one of his senior officers, and after Garrett, was probably his most loyal supporter amid the politics that always seemed to be a subtext to the *Dorian*'s officer contingent's interactions.

But the engineering officer's fate was out of his hands. The *Dorian's* wasn't. "Stand by missiles," Barrington ordered, watching as the Pluto cones burst into their high-speed shrapnel loads. From Two came a burst of point-defense laser fire that flickered among the shrapnel, vaporizing the shrapnel—"Missiles: *fire*."

The missiles shot from their tubes and accelerated toward the Troft ships, their vectors partially obscured by the light show from the Pluto cone shrapnel and also cloaked by their own ECM. Barrington watched their trails, mentally crossing his fingers—

"Incoming!" Filho snapped.

Barrington wrenched his eyes from his own missiles' traces and looked to the *Dorian's* flank. Yet another spider ship had slipped into attack range, its approach ironically masked by the debris of one of the attackers the *Dorian* had shattered. The tactical was marking five incoming missile traces, probably the spider ship's entire load.

The point defenses were blazing away, throwing shrapnel, laser bursts, and ECM confusion at the attackers. But it was likely already too late. One of the missiles detonated...two...three...the last two were nearly past the defenses' effective range—

And abruptly, both missiles exploded.

It took Barrington a second to realize what had happened. Then, feeling a tight grin creasing his cheeks, he punched the radio control. "Thanks for the assist, *Hermes*," he said. "What's your status?"

"Not good," Lieutenant Commander Vothra's tense voice came back. "But that doesn't mean we can't give a decent showing of ourselves. Our missiles are gone, but we've still got one-quarter power for the lasers.

Targeting's gone, too—we'll need to stay tied into your sensors if we're going to do any good."

Barrington nodded. He'd wondered how they'd managed that double-tap. Apparently, Castenello had done a quick sensor-link, which had not only given the *Hermes* the targeting control Vothra needed, but had also given the *Dorian's* own fire control a wider parallax spacing.

Under some circumstances, Barrington would have been more than happy to utilize the tactical officer's link and the *Hermes's* remaining firepower. But today wasn't about victory, but survival. For all of them. "Belay that," he told Vothra. "We're coming up on a zero-zero; prepare to dock."

"Sir, with all due respect, you need us out here," Vothra said. "I appreciate the rescue, but it's not going to mean much if the *Dorian* gets hammered to pieces in the process."

"I have no intention of losing the *Dorian*," Barrington assured him. "And I'm only losing the *Hermes* if its commander is pig-headed enough to stay in the open while we jump. Prepare to dock, Commander— that's an order."

"Yes, Sir," Vothra said. "Rotating into position. We'll be ready by the time you get here."

Barrington checked the timer. Thirty seconds to retrieval; another minute at least after that for reca-libration.

And meantime, the *Dorian* was still being hammered by Troft lasers, its outer skin being systemati-cally boiled off.

He frowned, focusing on the damage schematic. The enemy warships were taking the *Dorian's* hull off, piece by piece, section by section, not starting at the sensor clusters like normal enemy tactics but simply starting at a convenient spot and burning the hull down to its inner skin.

They didn't want the *Dorian* intact. But they apparently didn't want it totally obliterated, either.

So what the hell *did* they want? Did they seriously think they could take it with the core intact?

He was startled out of his reverie by yet another dull thud from the depths of his ship.

But this thud was familiar, even comforting.

"The *Hermes* is secured," Garrett confirmed. "Casualties being transferred aboard."

Barrington scowled. Vothra hadn't mentioned casualties, but of course there must have been some. The *Hermes* could hardly have been hammered that hard without someone aboard getting hurt or dead.

But again, all of that was out of his hands. He glanced at the timer—one to three minutes remaining until they could escape—and then focused on the tactical. A double barrage might keep the Trofts back long enough, but expending that level of firepower would all but drain the *Dorian's* missile supply. That would bode ill for future combat.

Still, dying with missiles still in their tubes made even less sense. He opened his mouth to give the order—

"Recalibration complete," Garrett snapped. "Jumping—"

Abruptly, the CoNCH external displays went dark.

The *Dorian* had escaped.

Barrington checked the timer, then looked at Garrett. "I'll be damned," he said.

Garrett shrugged, his face sagging visibly with relief and draining tension. "Well, you *did* tell him you wanted it done in nine," he reminded Barrington.

"So I did," Barrington agreed, tapping into the data stream. Sick bay was filling up with casualties, he saw, some from the *Hermes*, most from the *Dorian*.

And now, finally, the check-in list included Commander Kusari.

"You have CoNCH," he told Garrett, unstrapping and standing up. "Get us back on Ukuthi's course. As much speed as we can handle."

"Yes, sir," Garrett said. "Sick bay?"

Barrington nodded. "Sick bay."

Dr. Lancaster had always been a thin, almost gaunt man. Today, Barrington noted, his gaunt face looked almost skeletal.

"I'm sorry, Captain," he said in a low voice. "There's nothing I can do for him. Not here; not in the time I have. Both legs will have to be amputated."

Barrington looked past the doctor's shoulder toward the open door of the recovery room. There were nineteen other men in there along with Commander Kusari, with thirty-eight others either currently undergoing emergency surgery or in the intensive-care ward.

Fifty-eight injured, many of them badly. Ten others already dead.

More on the way.

Including one of the *Dorian*'s senior officers.

Barrington had seen men die before, many times. Sometimes they'd died because of orders Barrington himself had given; sometimes because of orders other men had given; sometimes simply through the ill fortunes of war.

But this one was different. It *felt* different. The Trofts' tactics hadn't fallen into any of their usual patterns. They'd been up to something.

But what? What had they hoped to gain by grinding the *Dorian* down instead of simply blasting it to atoms? They had to know that there would be no military secrets to be looted—there were whole systems aboard designed to do nothing but vaporize every cubic millimeter of high-tech equipment well before any boarding party could get through the hatches.

So why had the Trofts risked so much, and been willing to absorb so much damage of their own? Was a dead Dominion warship hulk worth that much to them? Were they hoping to find exotic materials or study the interior layout so as to better focus future attacks?

But a carefully surgical destruction of the *Dorian* would have provided the same opportunity. Especially since taking the ship apart would have the extra advantage of not leaving anyone alive able to shoot back.

Were they hoping to bag a ship's worth of prisoners? Again, useless. Critical information was carefully doled out and compartmentalized so that the officers and crew of a given warship knew nothing beyond their own orders. Certainly nothing that would enable an interrogator to glean vital bits and pieces of Asgard's overall campaign strategy. Besides, enough prisoners had been taken in this war that they were typically repatriated after a few weeks. Neither side wanted to feed and house the other's soldiers any longer than they had to, and both apparently had political interests in getting their own people home.

Barrington had long since accepted the unpleasant fact that some of the men under his command would die. That was the way of warfare.

But he had never accepted the idea that they should die for nothing. At the very least, they shouldn't die without someone knowing what the enemy had hoped to gain from their deaths.

Somewhere, there was an answer, and come hell or high water, Barrington was going to find it. That was not negotiable.

And speaking of non-negotiables... "How long can you hold off the amputation?" he asked Lancaster.

The doctor's eyebrows rose up his wrinkled forehead. "Excuse me?"

"It's a simple question," Barrington growled. "How long before you have to amputate?"

Lancaster's mouth set itself in a firm line. "I know what you're thinking, Captain," he said, his tone a mix of compassion and firmness. "But I'm afraid it won't work. A proper stem-cell regeneration will take far too long. The damage is too great, and it's starting to spill into his lower abdomen. Even at its most accelerated, a safe and proper regeneration would require at least—"

"Yes, I know—four weeks," Barrington interrupted. "My question is whether you can keep him safely on support another two or three days."

The compressed line of Lancaster's mouth opened a bit as his eyes did the same. "Three *days*?" he echoed. "Captain, I can't possibly do a regeneration in that time."

"No, you can't," Barrington agreed. "But I know someone who can."

Lancaster shook his head. "Sir, with all due respect—"

"Data stream," Barrington again interrupted, pointing at the doctor's eye. "Cobra Paul Broom."

Reluctantly, Lancaster twitched his eye. Barrington watched as he read, noting how the doctor's frown deepened midway through. "Well?"

"I don't believe it," Lancaster said flatly. "Either the treatment and recovery time were grossly underestimated, or else the initial damage was grossly *over*estimated. There's no known medical way this report could be true."

"And if that turns out to be the case, you can go ahead and amputate," Barrington said. "But not now. Not yet. If there's even a chance of saving his legs, I want him to have it."

Lancaster hissed out a sigh. "I can hold off the operation for another few days. But there's a risk that he'll end up dying. I accept the order, but be advised that I intend to put on the record that I take this course of action under protest."

"So noted," Barrington said. "Now, I believe you have other patients to attend to."

He turned and started down the corridor. "And if the Qasamans refuse to help?" Lancaster called after him.

"They won't," Barrington said.

And they wouldn't, he promised himself darkly as he headed back toward CoNCH. One way or the other, the Qasamans would heal Kusari, along with anyone else Lancaster and his top-of-the-line Dominion medical expertise couldn't help. The Qasamans would help.

Or they would be sorry. Very, very sorry.

CHAPTER FOURTEEN

Kjoic had spent the night fitfully, the pain from his injured leg making him toss and turn and often waking him completely. The sudden movement within the cramped space of their shelter usually also startled Merrick awake, and he often lay that way for many minutes after Kjoic had once again fallen into his restless slumber.

Merrick had never done well with interrupted sleep cycles, and he knew he would pay for it in grogginess the next morning. But at least he was spared the frustration of the Troft demanding that his slave do something about his discomfort. Each time he woke, Kjoic merely shifted into a more comfortable position, or at least a less uncomfortable one, and settled down again.

Which was all to the best, because Merrick hadn't the foggiest idea how to relieve a Troft's pain anyway.

Through it all, Anya slept soundly. Or at least pretended to.

The grogginess Merrick had predicted was indeed fogging his brain by the time the eastern horizon began to brighten. Fortunately, it wasn't as bad as he'd expected. He must have gotten more rest during those nighttime catnaps than he'd realized.

Hopefully, it would be enough. The Muninn forest, with all its uncooperative flora and deadly fauna, was unlikely to go easy on him just because he was sleepy.

The day's march quickly turned into a copy of the previous afternoon's trek, except that it lasted all day instead of for only half an hour. Still, Kjoic showed some improvement. The previous afternoon, he'd been unable to limp unaided for more than a couple of minutes at a time before he needed to lean on Merrick's arm. Now, in contrast, he was able to push himself for ten or even fifteen minutes at a stretch, though by the end of that time he was staggering and his radiator membranes were stretched out as far as they would go. Usually Merrick would then help him for another five minutes, after which the party would need to take a short rest.

When they weren't walking, limping, or staggering, they seemed to be constantly facing off against predators. During the morning alone they had five run-ins; two against groups of fafirs, three against solitary hunters of a species Merrick didn't recognize. Fortunately, between Anya's acute sense of smell and Merrick's enhanced vision and hearing they spotted each of the threats with enough time to prepare, and all the attacks were driven off more or less easily. Kjoic only had to use his laser twice, and even then the shots probably weren't necessary.

But the stress and occasional sudden maneuvering

of combat took their own toll on the Troft's stamina. Gradually, his periods of unassisted walking became shorter, until by midafternoon he was back to the two- and three-minute stints he'd exhibited the previous day.

It was an hour before sunset when he finally gave up.

[The journey, I cannot continue it,] he said as he sank awkwardly onto a section of dead log. [The pain, it is too severe.]

[The village, it is not far,] Anya said as she and Merrick sat down near him. [Assistance, we may offer it to you.]

[The journey, I cannot continue it,] the Troft repeated, his radiator membranes fluttering with pain and fatigue. [A shelter for the night, you will build it.] He gave Merrick a sudden, sharp look. [An alternative, one occurs to me. A transport, can the village provide it?]

Out of the corner of his eye, Merrick saw Anya's eyes widen. [A transport, I do not know if the village has one,] he said cautiously. [The forest, the villagers do not lightly enter it.]

[The forest, they will enter it for a master,] Kjoic said with ominous certainty. [The village, you will go to it now.]

Merrick stared. Was the Troft actually suggesting—? [Your safety, we cannot sacrifice it,] he protested. [The master, we may not abandon him.]

[The master, you will not abandon him,] Kjoic growled. [The village, alone you will travel to it. The female, she will remain with the master.]

A shiver ran up Merrick's back. It was an opportunity he'd wished for a hundred times in the past two days: the chance for total freedom of action. Assuming he could find the village, he would be able to check things out without having to worry about giving away his capabilities to their new master.

But if the price of that freedom was to leave Anya alone with the Troft and the dangers of the Muninn night... [The forest, it is dangerous,] he pointed out the obvious. [The danger, it would be all around you. The risk, it would be great.]

[The risk, it would be small,] Kjoic disagreed. [The female, I have seen her battle.] He patted the laser at his side. [My weapon, I also have it.]

[Your words, I hear them,] Merrick said, carefully not pointing out that Kjoic had already shot himself once with that weapon. [But the dangers—]

[My words, you will obey them,] Kjoic cut him off. [The order, it is given. The village, you will travel to it.] He lifted his hand from his laser and pointed a finger at Anya. [A shelter, you will build one.]

Merrick frowned. If the Troft was expecting Merrick to bring back transport before nightfall, what need was there for a shelter?

[Caution, we must exercise it,] Kjoic said, as if anticipating Merrick's unspoken question. [Other preparations, we must make them. A transport, the village may not be able to provide one until morning.]

Merrick looked at Anya. She didn't look especially happy at the thought of spending the night alone with the Troft. But she clearly recognized the realities of a decision made and an order given.

As did Merrick. The patterns and habits of being a slave, he noted uneasily, were all too easy to slip into. [The order, we obey it, Master Kjoic,] he said. He levered himself up off the ground, remembering to make it look like his muscles were as tired and sore as they should be after a strenuous day. [This place, I will return to it soon.]

[A safe journey, may you have it,] Kjoic said.

[Your concern, I thank you for it.] Merrick looked again at Anya. [The materials for the shelter, may I help collect them before I leave?]

Kjoic squinted toward the sunlight filtering through the western trees. [The materials, you may collect some of them,] he said. [Your journey, it must begin soon.]

[The journey, it will begin soon,] Merrick promised. He raised his eyebrows. "I think we just passed a patch?" he said in Anglic, pointing toward a spot just off their path and about twenty meters back.

"Yes," Anya confirmed. "There will be more than enough there." She bowed to Kjoic. [The materials, we will bring them.]

The patch of bamboo spikes was right where Merrick remembered it, and was indeed as extensive as Anya had suggested. There would be more than enough for the shelter she would be building. "Any trick to getting to Svipall?" he murmured as they began collecting the spikes.

"No," she murmured back. "You must continue to the east until you reach a rapid-flowing river, perhaps six meters across. Follow it until you reach the village. The distance should only be three more kilometers. The village is on the northern bank of the river, with no need for you to cross it."

"Sounds good." Merrick peered off to the west. "*Could* we make it by dark if we start now?" he asked. "It's not particularly smart to split up this way."

"*We* could make it, yes," Anya said. "But not with

the master. Not with his injury." She touched Merrick's arm. "Do not worry about me. As the master says, I know how to fight."

"As long as he doesn't accidentally shoot you," Merrick muttered under his breath.

"The order has been given," she reminded him. "The order must be obeyed."

"I suppose," Merrick conceded. "Anything else I should know about Svipall?"

"I have never visited it," she admitted. "All I know is that it still exists, for I saw it when we were atop the mountain."

"Ah," Merrick said, wincing at the ridiculousness of his question. Of course she didn't know anything about Svipall, having been off-world for the past twelve years. Even if she'd visited the place before then, any memories she'd had would be long out of date by now. "Sorry—stupid question."

"Do not *say* that!" Anya snapped.

Merrick twitched back from the unexpected intensity. "Don't say what?"

"That you are stupid," she bit out. "You will not say such things about yourself. Ever."

"All right, all right," Merrick said, frowning. Where had *that* one come from? "I'll be back as soon as I can. With or without transport."

"You're not going to ask them for help, are you?" Anya asked, eyeing him closely. Her anger had disappeared from the surface, but he could sense it still simmering just out of sight. "You're a stranger, you still don't speak with the correct accent—"

"And I'm on the run," Merrick said patiently. "Yes, I know. And no, I'm not going to ask. If I find something that'll serve as transport, I'll just borrow it. Good enough?"

Her expression said that it most definitely *wasn't* good enough. But she merely sighed and nodded. "Be safe," she said.

"I will." Merrick hesitated, then gently touched her cheek. "You, too."

Ten minutes later, having gleaned enough spikes for Anya to build a two-man shelter, Merrick headed off alone into the forest.

Without Kjoic's injured leg to hold him back, he made good time. After the first few minutes he settled into a travel pattern that consisted of half a minute of loping run, a brief pause to look and listen for danger, then another half minute of running.

Thirty minutes later he reached the river Anya had told him about and changed course to follow it. From that point on, mindful of how predators tended to gather around sources of water, especially at sunrise and sunset, he added more frequent stop-and-listen pauses to his routine.

As it turned out, Anya had underestimated the distance to Svipall by several kilometers. Even at Merrick's enhanced pace, the sky was starting to darken when he finally arrived. He approached the village slowly and carefully, keeping to the trees, trying to get a feel for the place.

In some ways, it reminded him of Anya's home village of Gangari. The two settlements were about the same size, a kilometer or so across, and both were surrounded by open fields where the forest had been cut back and the land cultivated. The modest buildings with their peaked roofs and decorative carvings would have fit right in with Gangari's design, and the inhabitants he glimpsed between the buildings wore similar clothing, with the color palette running the same gamut of bright to muted.

But there were two major differences between the two villages. One of them was the large, gray, warehouse-like building pressed against Svipall's northern border, the side opposite from the river. The other was the three-meter-tall chain-link fence that completely surrounded the village, cutting it off from the cultivated area.

Merrick hadn't spent much time in Gangari, but he'd spotted a few storage areas in passing. The gray building didn't look like any of them. It was two stories tall, windowless, with no carvings or artistic features that he could see. One hundred percent utilitarian, and a brooding utilitarian on top of it.

The fence was similarly plain and functional, except that it was an odd sort of functionality. Merrick had tangled with several of Muninn's predators, and most of them had some version of claws or talons. A chain-link fence, certainly one with the loose mesh this one exhibited, would be only a minor obstacle for any clawed creature with even the most rudimentary climbing skills.

But the mesh *was* tight enough to be difficult for human fingers, and it would be impossible for human feet.

Which led to the intriguing conclusion that the fence wasn't there to keep the predators out but to keep the villagers in.

Activating his telescopics, adding in some light-amplification to compensate for the waning daylight, he began to systematically scan the village.

Unfortunately, from where he stood there wasn't much to see. There was a three- or four-meter-wide area between the fence and the nearest of the enclosed houses, but no one seemed to be using that area as a walkway. Probably never did, actually, if the undisturbed grass along the fence was any indication. Elsewhere in the village he could see people walking back and forth, but his glimpses were too brief for him to see anything about their expressions that might help him gauge their moods. If he ever made it back to Aventine, he told himself firmly, he would campaign for the next generation of Cobra opticals to be equipped with image-capture capabilities.

He shifted his attention back and forth between the gaps, frowning. There were plenty of bright-colored outfits over there, but so far he'd seen no sign of the copper-trimmed black clothing that the referees at Gangari's version of the Games had been wearing. Did that mean Svipall didn't go in for bloody combat among their children? Or were the referees just elsewhere in the village at the moment, out of Merrick's sight? Another pair of figures swept into view past one of the houses—

Merrick stiffened. The two figures striding across his view were combat-clad Trofts.

There weren't just two of them, either. the first pair was followed by a second, then a third, then a fourth. Eight warriors, marching in military formation through a human village.

Marching in the direction of the big gray building.

Merrick watched them go, following their progression through the gaps until the angles of the houses cut them off from his sight. There hadn't been much to see except that they'd maintained their pace, apparently not stopping for anything or anyone.

And if they weren't going to the gray building, they were going somewhere very close to it.

There hadn't been any serious Troft presence in Gangari, at least none that Merrick had spotted. The two aliens who'd dropped in via aircar had seemed almost casual about their visit, at least until Merrick and Anya showed up.

Could he and Anya be the reason the soldiers were in Svipall? Merrick hadn't spotted any sign of pursuit in the past couple of days, but it was certainly possible that someone had realized the fugitives would have to come out of the forest sometime, and had decided to focus the recapture effort on the towns and villages.

But that wouldn't explain the gray building.

Merrick chewed at his lip. Clearly, he'd gotten about all he was going to get from out here. If he wanted to know what was going on in Svipall, he was going to have to go in.

He lowered his eyes to the field stretched outside the fence. Gangari had a similar field surrounding it, mostly planted with the bersark plant that was the source of the bersarkis drug used in the Games. This field, too, was made up of the same plants.

But the Gangari field had also included a pathway composed of slightly different plants, some variant that looked like bersark but didn't carry the same dangerous poison. It was reasonable to assume that the residents of Svipall had done the same.

More importantly from Merrick's point of view, the two plants looked different under infrared. Activating that part of his opticals, hoping that the trick would still work in the rapidly fading light, he peered at the field.

The good news was that the field was indeed composed of both plants. The bad news was that if a path had ever existed, it was long gone. All that remained were scattered patches of the safe plant, with the connections between them overgrown by the bersark.

Merrick smiled tightly. Whether by design or accident, the neglect of the pathway had pretty much eliminated any chance that someone could enter the village from this direction. That meant the Trofts had no need to guard against any such intruders.

Unless the intruder happened to be a Cobra.

The first safe patch was four meters away and a meter square. Merrick made it easily, landing dead center. The next was both farther and smaller, five meters inward and half the size of the first. He made that one as well. Slowly, carefully, he zigzagged his way across the field until he ended up in one final safe zone barely a meter from the fence.

Given the inherent dangers of a bersark field, it was unlikely that anyone in Svipall would make a break for it in this direction, from which it followed that the Trofts probably hadn't bothered equipping the fence with either sensors or dangerous levels of current. Just the same, Merrick took a couple of extra minutes to study the mesh before concluding that it was in fact safe. Waiting until there was a break in the traffic beyond the row of houses, he made one final jump, rolling over the top of the fence and landing on the strip of grass beyond.

Again he waited, crouched low, his audios at full power as he listened tensely for any sign that his entrance had been spotted. Again, nothing. Taking a deep breath, noting the same exotic mixture of cooking aromas he remembered from Gangari, he straightened up and slipped along the side of the nearest house. He waited near the front until his audios indicated that there was no one walking nearby, and with only a little trepidation stepped past into the main part of the village.

Like Gangari, Svipall's houses were small but neat, with carvings and other decorative features on their walls and the edges of their roofs. They were packed fairly tightly together, with the limited open land around them mostly being used for food gardens. He wondered briefly why the passage he'd just walked through wasn't likewise being utilized, and it was only as he looked back that he realized with some embarrassment that he'd just walked carelessly through a triple row of what looked to be some kind of root vegetable.

Hopefully, he hadn't damaged any of the plants. If he had, it was too late now.

He peered down the narrow and meandering street that wound between the gardens. Between the houses to his left, he could see a bit of the distant gray building. None of the Trofts that had passed by this spot earlier were visible.

Still, that was the direction they'd gone. If he was going to find out what they were up to, he'd better get after them.

"An evening of hope to you."

Startled, Merrick turned. An old woman was sitting on a small porch attached to the house to his right, working silently on a piece of cloth with some kind of knitting needles. "And to you," he replied, hoping that was the proper response. It wasn't a greeting he'd heard anyone on Muninn use before.

Apparently, it wasn't. "What hope do *I* need?" the woman asked, peering oddly at him through the gathering gloom. "*You're* the one young enough to be taken." Her eyes narrowed. "What am I saying? You've already been brought in for the Games, haven't you?"

Merrick winced. Great—she'd pegged him as a stranger. Just great. "I was brought in, yes," he improvised. "As to hope, all people need that, do they not?"

She made a strange sort of grunting noise in the back of her throat. "Hope is no longer with us," she said with a sigh. "Death and madness will continue until none but the masters remain to tally."

Merrick felt a shiver run up his back. There was a futility in her voice that he'd never heard in Anya or even the other slaves on their transport ship. It was as if the woman had completely given up.

Maybe she had. Anya had been a slave for Commander Ukuthi, who had apparently treated her well enough that he'd trusted her to go on this mission with him. The other slaves on the transport had likewise been with foreign masters. Maybe a lifetime on Muninn had simply beaten this woman down to the point where there was nothing left but to wait for death.

Or maybe it was something about Svipall specifically. Something the Trofts were doing here.

Something involving that gray building.

"Perhaps hope will return," Merrick said. "I must leave now. May your evening be pleasant, and your night restful."

If it wasn't a standard farewell, it apparently wasn't ridiculous enough to spark unwanted curiosity. The old woman merely nodded and returned to her knitting, the infrared pattern of her face showing no extra surge of emotion that might indicate suspicion. Turning, Merrick headed off down the path between the houses toward the gray building.

No one was visible. That bothered him, especially considering that there'd been a fair amount of foot traffic going back and forth only a few minutes ago. He tried notching up his audios to try to get some clue as to where everyone was, but the sounds of his own footsteps was drowning out any noise anyone might be making, and he didn't want to risk drawing attention by suddenly stopping to listen. He reached the end of the staggered row of houses and eased his eye around the corner.

Part of the mystery, at least, was now solved. Between the houses and the gray building was a wide open area, into which a large crowd had gathered. It was hard to tell for sure from his angle, but it looked like they had formed themselves into a circle, several people deep, with an open area in the center.

It looked like a sports rally, or some other kind of preparation for a game. For *the* Games? Probably.

Only unlike any other game or sport Merrick had ever attended, the crowd here wasn't cheering or chanting or even talking among themselves. They were utterly silent, as if it were a wake or funeral instead of a game.

Maybe it was. *Death and madness*, the old woman had said.

Merrick had seen some of the madness in Gangari, when Henson Hillclimber had refereed combat between a pair of preteen boys. The fight had gone on way longer than it should have, thanks to the bersarkis drug that Hillclimber had administered to the fighters.

But even with that drug-induced frenzy, that Game had ended in only unconsciousness. Did the Games in Svipall operate under more lethal rules?

And then, without warning, the whole open area lit up.

Reflexively, Merrick ducked back behind the edge of the building. But there was no outcry or other evidence that he'd been spotted and targeted.

He stayed pressed against the side of the house for another few seconds. Then, gathering himself, he eased back to the corner and again looked around it.

Sure enough, the lights weren't part of an intruder alarm. They were, instead, coming from a set of four pole-mounted floodlights that he hadn't noticed, and which had turned the center of the open field into daylight brightness.

And now, with the spectators' faces much easier to see, Merrick realized that the old woman's hopelessness wasn't an isolated case. Every face he could see had the same resignation deeply etched into it.

Slowly, he scanned the faces, looking for one that might still have a spark of life in it. If he could find someone—anyone—who hadn't given up, maybe he could approach him and find out what the Trofts were doing in that big building.

And then, abruptly, he caught his breath. Standing on the edge of the crowd, their faces in profile but readily identifiable, were three of the slaves from their transport ship: Leif and Katla Streamjumper and their young daughter Gina. Three of the group that had accompanied him and Anya on their two-day walk to Gangari after the transport dropped them off on Muninn.

Gangari was where he and Anya had left them. So what were they doing in Svipall?

Best-case scenario was that the Trofts had taken the handful of people who could identify the fugitives on sight and scattered them around to some of the nearby villages. Worst-case scenario was that the Trofts had already guessed that Merrick would be showing up at Svipall.

There would probably come a time when Merrick would need to reveal himself and confront the Trofts. But that time wasn't tonight. Not if he could help it.

The fading daylight had turned nearly to dark by the time he returned to the spot where he'd jumped the fence. It was dark enough, in fact, that he quickly discovered that his infrared trick for distinguishing the plants from each other no longer worked.

Luckily, with a boost from his opticals' light-amp setting, he found that the spots where he'd landed on the way in were easily identifiable from the bent and broken plants. Launching himself over the fence, he hit the first safe area, regained his balance, and jumped for the second.

He was two jumps from the end of the field and the safety of the forest when a large aircar abruptly shot into view over the trees to the north.

Merrick dropped into a crouch, cursing his lack of vigilance. He'd been so focused on getting across the field that he hadn't kept his audios keyed for unexpected company. If that aircar was hunting him, he was in serious trouble.

But the Trofts inside seemed to have other plans for the evening. Instead of continuing toward him, the aircar came to a halt just outside the reflected glow from the Games area, which was by now about two hundred meters away from him. There it settled into a low hover, as if its occupants had merely come to watch the show.

Perhaps they had. A sports arena term he'd read once flicked to mind: *owner's box*.

Merrick apparently hadn't been spotted. His primary job now was to keep it that way.

If he stayed where he was, waiting for the Games to start and the aircar's occupants to be more distracted, he might have a better chance of hopping out of here undetected. On the other hand, the longer he crouched in the middle of an open field, the greater the chance that someone up there might do a random IR scan. Merrick eyed the aircar, feeling sweat gathering under his collar, trying to decide which option posed the smaller risk.

Only then did it suddenly dawn on him that while his neck was indeed sweating, his heartbeat was also increasing, his vision felt a little odd, and there was a new and disturbingly sour scent in the air.

He looked down. He'd landed in the middle of the safe zone . . . but when the aircar's sudden appearance had sent him into a crouch he'd reflexively put out a hand for balance.

And that hand had landed squarely on top of one of the bersark plants.

His first impulse was to jerk back from contact with the broken stem and leaves. A second later he realized that if the poison was a contact variety, it was far too late. If it was instead airborne and not contact . . . but it was too late for that, too. One way or the other, he'd been exposed, and there was nothing he could do about it.

Except get the hell out of here before whatever was going to happen happened.

But there was still the aircar hovering over Svipall. And it was getting louder. It must have seen him and—

He frowned. The aircar hadn't moved. Yet it was louder. Had it somehow revved up its grav lifts without rising any higher?

No, that wasn't it. Because the insects were also louder. So were the scratchy scurrying sounds of small animals in the forest beyond the bersark field, and the flapping of birds flying nearby.

He must have somehow notched up his audios. But a quick check showed that he hadn't. His hearing had suddenly just gotten better.

He looked back at the aircar. As his hearing had improved, he realized with mild interest, so had his sight. Even through the glare of the floodlights he could now make out the symbols on the vehicle's side, the cattertalk script marking it as the property of the Drim'hco'plai demesne.

The demesne that had enslaved Muninn for generations . . . and suddenly Merrick felt a righteous anger boil up inside him. How *dare* they do this to his fellow humans? He straightened to his feet, bent his knees for a mighty leap that would send him soaring across the sky to the aircar—

He staggered as a sudden wave of vertigo swept over him, knocking him off his feet and threatening to slam him face-first into the bersark. He caught himself in time, gripping the plants as he tried to stop the violent spinning in his head. The spinning slowed, and he started to stand up again.

And cursed as a bird slammed into his shoulder, again knocking him off balance. He winced at the impact, though a small, functioning part of his brain noted with some surprise that a collision that would definitely leave a bruise wasn't hurting. He got back to his feet again and glanced around, looking for his assailant.

It wasn't just a single bird. It was a whole flock of them: dark, streamlined shapes—ten, fifteen, maybe more—all of them curving around and swooping out of the sky.

Heading straight toward him.

The damn things were *attacking*.

And suddenly, something within him snapped.

He could target them, he knew: lock his opticals sequentially on the birds and blast them to feathers and charred meat. But that would be too easy. Too quick. The birds wanted him? Fine. He would make sure they learned pain before they died.

He dropped into a crouching stance, hands held up and flat like game paddles. The birds shot toward him—

He slapped away the first wave without any of them getting past his defenses, batting them away to both sides like leaves in the wind. The second wave did a little better, a couple of them getting through and slashing past him with wings and talons. He could feel the wetness of blood on his cheeks, but still there was no pain. The birds kept coming—

And then, suddenly, they were gone.

He looked around him, breathing hard. The birds were scattered across the field, unmoving, dead or stunned.

One battle against flying things had been won. Now, the second battle could begin.

He looked up at the aircar. Unbelievingly, it still hadn't moved. Hadn't it seen or heard the carnage of the battle?

Apparently not. And as it had with the birds, that arrogance would cost them. He bent his knees again for the magnificent leap that had been so rudely interrupted.

And spun around. Had that been a snapping of branches in the forest?

It had. Even in the dim light he had no trouble seeing the three human silhouettes skulking in the bushes.

Watching him.

Agents of the Trofts? Probably. Agents or slaves, it was really all the same.

One more distraction for him to deal with.

He spun around on one foot, then shoved off the ground with that same single leg, just to show he could do it. He landed just past the edge of the field, hitting the uneven forest ground a bit off-balance. No problem—his nanocomputer could handle the readjustment. The other humans had scurried backwards at his sudden arrival, but they couldn't scurry faster than a Cobra.

He smiled at the thought of a Cobra scurrying. His instructors back at the Sun Center would have been horrified at the very thought of such a word being used for the noble warriors they were molding. The Qasamans—

Actually, the Qasamans would probably be amused. That was one thing about the Qasamans: they might take themselves and their world deadly seriously, but at least they had a sense of humor lurking behind it all.

What the people of Muninn thought about scurrying he didn't know. Nor did he really care. All he knew was that the ones in front of him were doing a pretty good job of it as they tried desperately to get away from him.

As well they should. Merrick strode toward them like an avenging demigod—which, really, he was—wondering if he should bother with a target lock and deciding against it. His bare hands had been good enough for the birds. They would certainly be good enough for people, too. He raised his right hand . . .

And felt his feet stumble to a confused halt. His bare hands . . . his bare *hands* . . .

He looked around him, blinking and staggering with a fresh surge of vertigo. But this time, instead of coming off the dizziness with a sense of power and majesty, the spinning in his mind seemed to drag him over an unseen precipice into a dark pit.

"Quickly, now," a voice murmured in his ear.

Merrick came to with a start. He was walking—or, more correctly, staggering—through the forest, a pair of strong hands around each of his upper arms steadying him. He craned his neck to look back over his shoulder, only to discover to his shock that Svipall was no longer in sight. More than that, whereas it had been merely a heavy dusk before, now a total blackness was pressed all around him.

A blackness, and people. How many people, he couldn't tell. But there were definitely more than just the two who were holding his arms. At least two others, maybe more. Was it a parade? He chortled a sudden giggle at the thought.

"Quiet," someone growled. "You want to get us all caught?"

"Sure, why not?" Merrick said, feeling a ghost of his earlier confidence rippling through him. Let the Trofts come. He could take them. He could take all of them. He was a *Cobra*.

He frowned. Right—he was a Cobra; and with that thought came the belated realization that he had optical enhancements that could relieve some of the darkness around him. A bit of fumbling with the control, and suddenly the blackness lightened to a muted gray.

There were five of them, he saw now: two young men helping him along, a third young man bringing up the rear, and a middle-aged man and woman in front. Their outfits seemed to wrap tighter around them than the usual Muninn clothing, and were composed of mottled shades of brown, gray, and dark green. Rather like the camo gear he'd seen hunters wearing back on Aventine, he vaguely recalled. "Where are we going?" he asked.

"Shut up," one of the men holding him bit out. "Stupid, *stupid*. You ruined everything."

"No, no," Merrick admonished him. "Not stupid. Don't call me stupid. Anya doesn't like it when people call people stupid." He closed his eyes, an odd weariness washing over him.

And jerked as a pair of hands grabbed his shirt collar. "Anya?" a woman's voice demanded. "Who do you mean, Anya?"

Merrick opened his eyes. The woman who'd been

in front was suddenly staring into his face, her eyes barely thirty centimeters from his. "What?" he asked.

"Anya," she repeated, her tone urgent, her fingers gripping his collar tightly. "Who is this Anya? What other name is she called?"

Merrick had to think a moment. He'd know her as just *Anya* for so long... "Winghunter," he said. "She's called Anya Winghunter."

Something in the woman's face seemed to somehow go deeper. "Where is she?" she demanded. Her head twisted back and forth to both sides, as if Anya might be lurking somewhere in the woods around them. "Did you just leave her *alone* out here?"

"Of course not," Merrick said, wrinkling his nose. Anya was fine—couldn't this woman see that? "She's with the master. Master Kjoic."

The woman's grip tightened. "She's with a *master*?"

"Isn't everyone?" Merrick countered. For some reason the response struck him as wonderfully witty, and he laughed.

Or rather, he giggled. Again. A small, severe part of his mind informed him that giggling wasn't a very dignified way for a grown man to laugh. But he didn't care.

"Where is she?" the woman demanded again. "*Where is she?*"

"Take it easy," Merrick said, frowning into the wild eyes. This woman seriously needed to calm down. "She's right over there." He pointed straight ahead.

He frowned. His nanocomputer had a built-in-compass, which was inexplicably telling him he was facing north, not west. When had they all changed direction?

Didn't matter. Anya was to the west—that much he knew. "No—*that* direction," he amended, shifting his pointing finger toward his left.

"How far?" the woman asked.

"A few kilometers." Merrick considered. Did his nanocomputer keep track of things like that? Probably, but he couldn't remember how to access the data. No matter. "About eight of them, probably. She built a shelter, so they're all right."

"What did she make the shelter out of?" the middle-aged man asked. "Bambus?"

"I don't know the name of the stuff," Merrick said. "Green, fuzzy, pointy things. Big clusters of them."

"How big a patch was it?" the man asked.

"How should I know?" Merrick countered. "We didn't count the things. There were a lot of them, that's all I know."

"Was it near the river?" the woman asked.

"I don't think so," Merrick said, trying to think. The world was going hazy again. He keyed up his opticals, but it didn't seem to help. "There was a small stream nearby, not a river. I hopped it on the way out."

The man and woman looked at each other. "Could be the Dewer's Hollow bambus patch," the man suggested.

"Sounds like it," the woman agreed. "You'd better take him home while we sort all this out. I'll take a few men and go find her."

"No, *you'll* take him back and *I'll* go get her," the man said. "There's a master with her, remember?"

"And he's got a laser," Merrick said. "But don't worry—he's also got a bad leg." This time it wasn't a giggle, but a single, explosive guffaw. "Because—*he shot himself!*"

Again, the man and woman looked at each other. "Better take a couple extra," the woman advised.

The man nodded, gave Merrick a final look, then headed away at a brisk walk. "But don't hurt him," Merrick called after him. "Really—don't. He's our ticket into Svipall and that big gray box."

He didn't remember much about the rest of the trip. Mostly he remembered shuffling along in a sort of mental haze, a fogginess punctuated at intervals by sudden flashes of clarity.

Only sometimes the clarity...wasn't.

Sometimes he was completely lucid and able to think. Other times he came up out of the haze charged, revved, and ready to declare war on the local Trofts, their demesne, and the whole Trof'te Assemblage.

And other times he came out literally shaking with fear, self-loathing, and despair. Wondering what in the name of everything holy he was doing here.

It was while he was struggling through one of the maelstroms of depression that the haze rolled in one final time and then melted into a final and welcome darkness.

CHAPTER FIFTEEN

The Integrated Structural Implantation System—Isis, for short, because no one in their right mind would ever use a thirteen-syllable name if they didn't have to—had been a major factor in the Qasamans' victory over the invading Trofts. As such, it was a military secret of the highest order, and Jody found it completely understandable that not a single Qasaman aboard the *Squire* would breathe word one to her about where it was being hidden.

Still, from hints her parents had dropped before the trouble with the Dominion kicked in, she'd figured it had started out somewhere on the property of her mom's old friend and comrade-in-arms, Daulo Sammon.

She also had no doubt that Omnathi had moved it the second the last Troft ship left orbit. Something that immensely powerful would hardly be left even nominally in the hands of a single Qasaman family. Especially a village family that wasn't in any way connected to the more dominant city power structure.

It was therefore something of a shock when, after landing the *Squire* outside Azras, Omnathi directed her and the others into a waiting convoy of trucks and passenger vans and sent them trundling off into the forest.

It was an even bigger shock when they drove through the gate at the village of Milika. By the time the convoy came to a halt outside the Sammon family mine, she had already used up her quota of surprise for one day.

With Rashida, Smitty, and Kemp playing escort, she got into the waiting elevator car. The operator did something complicated with a group of levers and controls set into the car's wall, and with a shuddering clank, they headed down the rough-edged shaft.

"I do so enjoy first-class travel," Jody murmured. The car gave a sudden jerk, throwing her off balance. She grabbed for the wall and got Kemp's hand instead.

"Easy," he said soothingly, his strong hand and arm holding firm against the lurching of the car.

His strong, *servo-enhanced* arm, Jody remembered with a twinge of something that felt strangely like squeamishness. It was the same artificial strength she herself would have soon.

She glared at the bumpy wall passing by the small, wire-netted windows of the car. *Stop that*, she scolded herself. She'd already been through this angst trip once. Or maybe twice—emotional battles weren't something she typically kept track of. The point was that the decision had been made, seconded, and voted on, and she was going to do it.

Because if she didn't, Merrick might die. That was what she needed to focus on. Her brother was out there somewhere, and she was never going to be able to challenge the Trofts who'd taken him away without the edge that Isis could give her.

"And don't worry about this thing," Kemp added. He was still holding her hand, Jody noted, even though she was fully back on balance again. Not that she was complaining. "The car, I mean. It's sturdier than it feels."

The car lurched again, even more violently. "Could have fooled me," Jody said.

"Exactly," Smitty said. "It's classic wolf-in-sheep's-clothing camouflage."

"You look as harmless as possible in order to keep the bad guys from realizing there's something important or valuable down here," Kemp said.

"Yes, I know how the wolf thing works," Jody said, feeling her teeth trying to clatter together as the car picked up a new vibration. "Kind of defeats the purpose if we fall to our deaths, though."

"Not a chance," Smitty assured her. "This kind of window dressing is always very calculated." He nodded toward the elevator operator, who still hadn't said a single word to any of them. "Odds are that a small variation in that lever combination he threw at the beginning will just take us to one of the mining levels and no further. A place like this is perfect for hiding stuff." He gestured to the operator. "Am I right?"

The Qasaman gave him a long, cool look. Then, still without saying a word, he returned his attention to the controls.

"Not all on Qasama appreciate what you've done for us," Rashida murmured.

"That's okay," Smitty said. "A lot of people on Aventine don't appreciate us, either."

"They'll come around, Rashida," Kemp assured her. "There's a lot of history your people have to work through, and a lot of stuff *our* people have to live down. But we'll make it."

"Yet we may never be truly friends," Rashida warned.

"That's okay, too," Smitty said. "All we really need right now is to *not* be enemies."

"He's right," Kemp said. "And sometimes nations and worlds become friends because a few individuals take that first step."

"Hear, hear," Smitty said. He smiled at Rashida.

And an instant later lost the smile, and his balance, as the car abruptly jolted to a stop. Silently, the operator opened the door and pointed down the tunnel ahead of them.

"Thank you," Jody said. She didn't wait for a response, which was just as well.

The tunnel looked exactly like some of the similar ones they'd passed on the way down: dimly lit, slightly meandering, with rough walls, ceiling, and floor. With Kemp in the lead, the four of them worked their way along the passage. Smitty, Jody noted with some bemusement, had fallen back behind Rashida in rearguard position.

Even here, safe on Qasama, the habits and reflexes of life on Caelian were never far below the surface.

Isis had been set up just around a sharp turn in the corridor, fifty meters from the elevator, behind a false wall that had been patterned to look like the rest of the tunnel. Dr. Glas Croi, the Aventinian robotics genius who'd been Isis's prime developer, was waiting there, along with a handful of Qasaman techs. An air of expectation seemed to have settled over the whole group. "Ms. Broom," Croi said, offering his hand. "It's an honor to meet yet another distinguished member of the Broom-Moreau family."

"Thank you," Jody said, a twinge of guilt poking at her. Compared to the successes of pretty much everyone else in her family, her small successes hardly even registered. "I trust everything's ready?"

"It is." Croi cocked an eyebrow. "Are *you*?"

"I am," Jody said.

And to her mild surprise, she meant it. Not just on an intellectual level, but also on an emotional one. She was ready, willing, even cautiously eager to become a Cobra. Like her father, her brothers, and her mother before her.

They'd all taken this step, accepted the responsibility and consequences, and gone on to do great things. There was no way she was going to let them down.

"Good," Croi said, an odd hint of reluctance in his tone somewhat belying the cheerfulness of the word itself. Possibly it was the fact that Jody was a woman, and only the second of her gender to undergo the Cobra surgery. A fair percentage of the Cobra World authorities, and probably an even higher percentage of the Qasamans, probably believed it was utter foolishness to waste one of Isis's few remaining sets of Cobra equipment on a female.

Jody's mother had proved them wrong. Jody was determined to do likewise.

"Good luck," Kemp said, taking her hand. The touch lingered a second or two longer than it probably needed to. Still, it was comforting and encouraging, and Jody would never turn down an honest expression of either. "Our smiling faces will be the first thing you see when you come out of it," he added. "Take care."

Thirty minutes later, she was strapped down on an elaborately contoured table, facing a complex array of lasers, scalpels, 3-D printers, lamination machines, and three or four devices whose purpose she couldn't even guess at. "Last chance," Croi said, a bit gruffly. "Once we put you under and start the procedure, there's no going back."

"I understand," Jody said, forcing her voice to remain steady. She didn't care much for surgery, and even with the procedure fully automated, this whole thing promised to be a nightmare. "Let's get on with it."

"Right," Croi said. "Pleasant dreams."

And as the world and the shiny equipment faded into blackness, Jody's last thought was a bittersweet farewell to the life that she had now really and truly left behind.

"Cobra Broom? *Cobra Broom? Answer* me, damn it."

Slowly, resentfully, Paul clawed his way up from the quiet darkness. What in the Worlds was all the shouting about?

"This is Captain Lij Tulu," the voice said. It seemed a little louder this time. "I need you to lift your arm. Lift your right arm. Now."

Paul smiled to himself. Lift his arm, indeed. Didn't Lij Tulu remember that his arms were strapped down? He certainly *should* remember—he'd been there when the techs had done it.

"Open your eyes, Cobra Broom," a different voice put in. Unlike Lij Tulu's voice, which sounded angry, this one sounded worried. *Very* worried.

The darkness was continuing to brighten, and as all the random pieces of thought and memory began to come together Paul permitted himself another private smile. So the MindsEye had failed. They'd dug straight through his skull and back again, and had come up dry. Either he'd managed to keep Qasama's coordinates a secret or, more likely, those numbers had never been inside his brain to begin with.

No wonder they were all angry and worried. Commodore Santores wanted those numbers, and Lij Tulu had promised to get them. Lij Tulu and the whole team were in hot water now.

And if what Paul had seen at Archway was any indication of Dominion ruthlessness, he wouldn't want to be in Lij Tulu's boots right now.

"Open your eyes. Please."

Finally—a *please*. A small effort at civility, to be sure. But as Paul had discovered with his own children, even small efforts were worth rewarding.

He opened his eyes.

To his surprise, he wasn't strapped to the MindsEye chair anymore. Instead, he was on a partially reclined table, apparently somewhere in the main sick-bay complex. All the straps that had been holding him to the chair were gone, too.

Facing him were two men: Lij Tulu, and an older, white-haired man Paul couldn't remember seeing before. "About time," Lij Tulu growled. "Now lift your damn arm."

For a brief second Paul thought about lifting his arm, targeting Lij Tulu's left cheek, and giving a quick slash with his fingertip laser that would leave the captain a nice scar to remember him by.

But that would be unprofessional. Worse, it would be the sort of vicious payback that Colonel Reivaro might do. It seemed wrong, somehow, that the Dominion's backwoods descendants here on Aventine should be more civilized than the mother worlds, but such was clearly the case.

Lij Tulu hadn't said *please*. But again, as with children, the adults often had to lead by example. Obediently, he lifted his right arm.

Only he didn't. He lifted, or tried to lift, but the arm didn't move.

And he'd already seen that there were no straps. No straps, no weights, no one sitting on it. The arm simply refused to move.

He looked down at the arm, the last bits of blackness evaporating in the explosive burst of adrenaline that surged into his bloodstream. What had they done to him? What in God's name had they *done*?

"You can do it," the white-haired man said, his voice taut. "Come on. Use your muscles. Just your muscles."

Paul stared at him. Just his *muscles*? But he hadn't had to use just his muscles for years. Not since the Cobra servos had been implanted there.

And then, with another jolt of adrenaline, he got it.

"What did you do?" he croaked. His mouth and throat were dry, his voice that of a stranger.

A voice he also hadn't heard in quite this way since the activation of his audios. Like listening to a recording of your voice for the first time, he thought mechanically, without the added bone conduction that added a layer to the perceived sound that a recorder didn't get. Only this time, the difference was in the opposite direction.

His servos didn't work. His audios didn't work. And the only connection between those systems was—

"You bastards," he breathed. "What did you do to my nanocomputer?"

The white-haired man winced. Lij Tulu's face was a mask. "It seems to have shut down," the captain said, his voice under rigid control. "We don't know yet if it's permanent, or whether it's doing some kind of reboot."

"We were hoping you could tell us," White Hair put in.

"How should I know?" Paul shot back. "I'm not a tech. What if it's gone completely? What then?"

"In that case, I assume you'll have to learn how to live like a normal human being," Lij Tulu said. "Don't worry—billions of us manage it every day."

Paul could have strangled him. He could have leaped from the table, wrapped his hands around the man's throat, and choked the casual cruelty out of him.

Only he couldn't.

Lij Tulu was wrong. Paul could never be a normal human being. Not anymore. It wasn't just a matter of using his muscles—he and every other Cobra did that every day. The problem was that, without the nanocomputer compensating for the weight of the bone laminae and the natural resistance of the servos by echoing his muscles' every move, Paul might was well be wearing a suit of medieval Earth armor. A suit, moreover, whose joints had started to rust.

"Can't you do *anything*?" White Hair asked.

Paul looked down at his arm. The muscles were still there. All he had to do was use them. Setting his teeth, he concentrated.

It was, indeed, exactly as if the arm were encased in armor. The limb came up slowly, hesitantly, as if the muscle memory were as confused by all this as Paul's brain was. He tried moving the elbow, the wrist, and the fingers, reflexively listening for the faint whine of the servos.

But there was no whine, and the joints all moved with the same sluggishness.

Sluggishness, and a hint of pain. The arthritis that had plagued every Cobra since the very beginning was starting to present, and the stress created by the non-working servos could only make it worse.

"There you go," Lij Tulu said. "See? You *can* do it. A little practice, and you'll be up and running triathlons before you know it."

"I'll be sure to invite you to the race," Paul said. "I'd like to speak with Commodore Santores."

"Yes," Lij Tulu murmured, and for the first time a hint of uncertainty flicked across his face. "Unfortunately, the commodore is very busy right now."

"It's a busy time for all of us," Paul bit out. "I'd like to see him."

Lij Tulu shook his head. "Not possible."

Paul hesitated. But at this point, he really had little to lose. "Not even if I'm ready to give him Qasama's coordinates?"

For a brief instant, Lij Tulu's eyes went wide. But only for an instant. "Really," he said, smiling thinly. "Magic numbers that threats, appeals to patriotism, and even the MindsEye itself were unable to pry out of your brain. And *now* you're ready to give them to us?"

"Not *us*," Paul corrected him. "Commodore Santores. And *only* him."

"Again, why now?"

"Because the situation's changed," Paul said. He lifted his arm again. "I'm sure the commodore would want to know the details."

"What makes you think he doesn't?"

"Your expression," Paul said. He looked at White Hair. "Your accomplice's expression. The fact that Commodore Santores explicitly promised that no harm would come to me."

Lij Tulu's lip twitched. "Sometimes promises made in good faith prove impossible to keep," he said. "Especially in time of war."

"I'll be sure to remember that," Paul said. "Especially the war part."

Lij Tulu's eyes narrowed. "He's all yours, Doctor," he said, gesturing to White Hair. "See what you can do with him." He inclined his head to Paul. "Cobra Broom."

Turning, he strode from the room. To Paul, even his back looked worried.

"We'll make it better," Doctor White Hair promised. Unlike Lij Tulu, he didn't even try to hide his anxiety. "I promise—" He broke off, wincing, as the irony of his word belatedly registered.

"Promises, Doctor," Paul reminded him quietly. "Promises in time of war."

The doctor shivered. "Yes," he murmured. "Time of war."

"We are met at this table," Commander Castenello said, his words and tone the painfully formal pattern required by the present situation, "to make petition to Captain Barrington Moreau, commander of the

Dominion of Man War Cruiser *Dorian*, for his data, his reasoning, and his thoughts in regards to the military action initiated on 15 March 2507, Ship's Date, at fifteen-twenty-two hours, Ship's Time. In accordance with Standing Regulation Sixty-Two, Subsection Four, this Enquiry Board has been convened at the proper time and place."

Barrington suppressed a grimace. The *proper* time and place? Try the *minimum* time and place. Sixty-Two specified that this kind of internal inquisition had to wait until at least twenty-four hours after the ship had disengaged from the enemy and status reduced below BatPrep Two.

And so they all sat here together, the *Dorian's* senior officers, listening to Castenello run the specified phrasing, waiting to see what the captain's response would be.

Exactly twenty-four hours and ten minutes after their escape from the Troft net.

He looked around the table, listening to Castenello's droning with half an ear as he studied his officers' faces, wondering who the tactical officer's two secret allies were. Sixty-Two required that a minimum of three officers sign off on an Enquiry Board, officers whose names would remain secret from the captain himself. That meant that at least two of the eight men facing him were as concerned about his handling of the Trofts as Castenello was.

But which two? Commander Garrett was out of the reckoning; the first officer was Barrington's strongest ally. Lieutenant Kusari, still in his induced coma in sick bay, was also out. Lieutenant Commander Filho was a possibility—he certainly had ambition, and there was a school of thought in Asgard that the fast track to promotion was the discrediting of the officers higher up the chain of command. But given Filho's sterling performance with the *Dorian*'s weapons during the encounter he might hesitate to tarnish the incident by bringing his captain's decisions into question.

That left Chief Surgeon Lancaster, who didn't really count, and the fourth, fifth, and sixth officers, none of the latter, in Barrington's estimation, having particularly distinguished themselves during the long voyage or the subsequent encounters with the Trofts. The most likely scenario was that it was two or more of those lower officers who'd decided or been persuaded to back Castenello's play.

The tactical officer finished his prescribed recitation and stopped. "Let the record show that, with the exception of Commander Kusari and Chief Surgeon Lancaster, all members of the senior staff are present," Barrington replied with the prescribed response. "Commander Castenello, if you have specific comments or questions, speak them now."

"My comments are six, Captain Barrington," Castenello said. "First: you were warned by this group of officers in the days and hours before the engagement of the unfavorable odds entailed by the presence of two major Troft warships plus subsidiary war vessels. Second: you were reminded even as the action began of those odds and the dangers therein. Third: as expected, serious damage has been sustained by both the *Dorian* and the *Hermes*. Fourth: the intel collected from the engagement is no more than would have been collected should the *Dorian* have declined to engage and remained strictly an observer. Fifth: the total number of casualties sustained during the engagement are greater than would have been sustained by the *Hermes* alone should the *Dorian* have declined to engage. And sixth: the delay created by waiting for the *Hermes*'s appearance may very well have lost us our contact with Commander Ukuthi and any hope of finding Qasama."

He raised his eyebrows slightly. "My question is only one," he continued stiffly. "*Why*? Why did you risk so much for so little?"

Again, he stopped. Barrington let the silence linger another couple of seconds, keeping his face impassive. He waited until the fifth officer started to squirm—Barrington's usual indicator when he was forced to play these games—and then cleared his throat. "Let me answer your comments in order, Commander," he said. He frowned slightly, as if reconsidering. "On second thought, permit me to answer all of them together."

He drew himself up as far as he could while still remaining seated. "Because we are a warship of the Dominion of Man," he said, throwing in every gram of dignity and resolve that hundreds of years of blood and death had earned for the Service. "We do not hide from the enemy. We do not run from the enemy. And we absolutely do *not* abandon our fellow officers and men to the enemy."

He paused, counting off two more beats of silence. "Furthermore," he continued, "two of your comments are demonstrably inaccurate. You have, in fact, no idea whatsoever how much intel has been gained from the engagement. I know you have no idea because at this point *none* of us has. Once the data have been analyzed, you'll be free to make your own assessment and, if justified, restate your comment. Until that point, the comment is wrong."

"Perhaps," Castenello said, his voice studiously neutral. "May I ask which other comment you deem to be incorrect?"

"I don't *deem* anything," Barrington countered. "The fact is that we have *not* lost more men than the complete destruction of the *Hermes* would have entailed. So far we've lost only ten men, barely a third of the *Hermes* complement."

"Excuse me, Captain, but that's hardly the full story," Castenello said stiffly. "There are fifty-eight more men in sick bay, many of whom Dr. Lancaster believes will not survive the next few days. Certainly the death toll will ultimately reach and surpass the *Hermes*'s complement."

"If and when it does, you'll again be free to restate your comment," Barrington said. "Until then, the comment is wrong." He cocked his head. "As to Commander Ukuthi, you already know my answer to that one. Whatever conflicts and politics are going on out here, we're a wild card, and Ukuthi clearly wants that card in his demesne's hand. He's not going to give up on us that easily."

"Perhaps," Castenello said, not sounding at all convinced. "I suppose we'll find out."

"I suppose we will," Barrington agreed. "Have you anything else to say?"

Castenello seemed to measure the captain with his eyes. "Not at this point, sir," he said. "I simply note that the engagement and your decisions surrounding it warranted the calling of an Enquiry Board."

And Castenello wanted to be on the record as

having called that Board, Barrington noted cynically. "Your dedication to regulations is noted, Commander," he said, allowing just a hint of sarcasm into his tone. "If there are no further questions or comments...?"

He looked around the table. No one seemed inclined to jump in. "Then I declare this Board to be ended." He looked at Castenello. "Until such future time as it is deemed necessary for it to reconvene," he added.

Castenello's expression flickered, enough to show that Barrington's guess had been correct. The tactical officer had been hoping that the captain would slip up on the required protocol somewhere along the line. That wouldn't have been a fatal flaw by any means, but it would have provided a small bit of additional ammunition that Castenello could use should matters ever reach full court-martial status.

Which they never would, Barrington told himself firmly. No matter how good Castenello was at these political games, Barrington would be able to hold his own.

Assuming, of course, that he could persuade Commander Ukuthi to take the *Dorian* to Qasama. *And* that the Qasamans could be persuaded to cooperate.

Around the side of the table, Garrett cleared his throat. "Dismissed," he said.

There was a general shuffling as the assembled officers pushed back their chairs and filed silently out the door. Barrington watched them go, a hard knot forming in the pit of his stomach.

Qasama.

That was the gamble Commodore Santores was banking on to save the Cobra Worlds from the horrors that Asgard and the Dome in their infinite wisdom had devised for the innocent colonists there. On a smaller scale, it was the same gamble Barrington and Castenello were on opposite sides of. If the Qasamans were able to heal the majority of the injured crewmen, Barrington would come out of this incident with enough prestige and political position that Castenello would have no choice but to back off. If the Qasamans refused, there would almost certainly be a court-martial somewhere in Barrington's future.

The depressing part was that if Barrington won this round, all Castenello had to do was wait for the next questionable incident and try it again. Unless Castenello himself made a fatal mistake, Barrington would always be on defensive.

Still, there was a war on, and even those Committés who reveled in these political posturings tended to mute their enthusiasm during times of threat. If Castenello kept pushing, it was possible that he would overrun his bounds and run afoul of his own patron once the *Dorian* returned to the Dominion.

Qasama was the key. The world that could save Barrington's career and the lives of Barrington's men.

And all it would cost would be that world's complete destruction.

War is hell. It was an obvious statement, so obvious that Barrington couldn't even remember which Earth general had said it. What was less obvious was that the hell wasn't just for the vanquished, but for the victors as well.

That seemed wrong, somehow. Victory should mean something. But somehow, it was always the case. With a sigh, he pushed back his chair.

Only then did he suddenly notice that Garrett

hadn't left with the others. The first officer was still sitting quietly in his chair, waiting for Barrington to finish his musings. "Was there something else, Commander?" he asked.

"Nothing specific, sir," Garrett said. "I just wanted... he's up to something, Captain. I don't know what yet, but he's definitely up to something."

"You mean Commander Castenello?" Barrington shrugged. "Of course he is. He's up to whatever will get me out of my job. I thought all my officers knew that."

"I meant he has a plan, sir," Garrett said doggedly. "Are you sure there's nothing in the data we got from the engagement that he can use against you?"

"There wasn't as of an hour ago," Barrington said, twitching his eye to pull up the data stream. "And there still isn't."

"Unless the tactical department has something they haven't yet put up."

"I sincerely hope that's not the case," Barrington said darkly. "Withholding data from the captain is a serious offense. Castenello would hang himself if he tried that."

"Unless he can claim the data's still undergoing analysis."

"He can claim anything he wants," Barrington said. "He still needs to put it in the data stream as soon as the scrubbing's been completed."

"But he *doesn't* have to put up speculation and educated guesses," Garrett reminded him. "He's got a lot of wiggle room in there, and he knows how to use it."

"I appreciate the warning," Barrington said. "I'll

keep an eye on the data stream, see if I can figure out the hand he's trying to deal himself."

"Yes, sir," Garrett said. He started to push back his chair.

"What's your assessment of the engagement?" Barrington asked.

Garrett paused. "Sir?"

"The Trofts' tactics," Barrington said. "With the firepower they had available they could have blown the *Hermes* out of the sky inside of two minutes. But they didn't. Why?"

"I assume they were hoping to take it more or less intact," Garrett said, looking puzzled. "The Trofts at our end of the Assemblage have tried that any number of times."

"Exactly," Barrington agreed. "Which means they've surely learned by now that we've got every useful bit of data and tech doomsdayed. So what were they hoping to gain?"

"Prisoners, maybe," Garrett said slowly. "Or else the demesnes out here don't know about all our doomsdaying."

"Which is ridiculous," Barrington said. "Whoever launched the attack on Qasama and the Cobra Worlds has to be in close contact with the demesnes at our end. Otherwise, why attack a few minor outposts of humanity, especially right now? It's not like they were bothering anyone."

"Then it has to be prisoners," Garrett concluded. "Someone wants Dominion Fleet personnel. Probably hoping to learn more about what's going on back there."

Barrington pursed his lips. That made sense even if the attackers were connected to the demesnes currently at war with the Dominion. No matter how closely a group of demesnes cooperated with each other, they were all still continually on the lookout for ways to gain an advantage or a bit of extra position over everyone else, enemies and allies alike. "That's possible," he said. "But here's my problem. We hit the edge of the net while heading toward Ukuthi's rendezvous point. The *Hermes* was caught because it was also heading toward those coordinates. Right?"

"Unless they were trolling for a Troft merchant ship, as Commander Castenello suggested," Garrett pointed out. He frowned. "Except that they attacked the *Hermes* immediately, which they shouldn't have done if they'd been expecting a freighter."

"Right," Barrington agreed. "They should at least have opened communication with an unfamiliar and unexpected ship before opening fire."

"And the only logical place for them to have set up their trap was along the Aventine-to-Qasama vector," Garrett said. He flashed a sudden, tight smile. *"That's* why you aren't concerned about whether Ukuthi waits for us or not. You were right from the start: Qasama is either at the coordinates he gave us or somewhere beyond it on the *Hermes's* original vector."

"Exactly," Barrington said. "If it's the first, that makes Ukuthi an honest Troft, which means he may be someone we can do business with. If it's the second, it means he's a cheater but a poor and unimaginative one, which means whatever threat he represents can probably be easily neutralized." He scowled. "Unfortunately, it's occurred to me that there's a third option."

He stopped, watching Garrett's face. The young officer's expression changed from anticipation at what the captain was going to say, to surprise that the captain wasn't saying it, then to understanding and thoughtfulness as he realized the captain was expecting him to come up with the third option himself. "We hit the edge of the net because we were following the course Ukuthi gave us," he said slowly as he worked it through. "If we'd been a little off that course we would have missed it completely."

His eyes narrowed. "*Or* we would have been caught in it. Were the ambushers his allies, and Ukuthi was trying to get rid of us?"

"I don't think so," Barrington said. "Remember, the two big warships weren't there when we first showed up. If we'd hit the net with just the spider ships waiting, we'd have cut through them like a laser through fiberboard." He lifted a finger. "*But*. If we'd gone back to Aventine personally to report instead of sending the *Hermes*, we would have hit the net after the Troft warships were in position."

"So it was a test?" Garrett asked, sounding a bit confused. "Ukuthi was trying to see if we would follow his directions without deviation?"

"I don't know," Barrington admitted. "And that's my problem. Our appearance at the Hoibie homeworld had to have been a surprise to him. Given that, I can't see how Ukuthi could have had enough time to set up the net on the fly, not unless his couriers are a lot faster than anything we've seen elsewhere in the Assemblage. The only way I can make sense of this is if he knew someone else had set up the net, and that someone wasn't from his demesne or an allied one."

"The Drim ships," Garrett murmured thoughtfully. "They had him pretty well cornered and were just waiting for the Hoibies to give up and hand him over. You think someone bragged a little too much on an open mike?"

"It's certainly happened before," Barrington said. "Something along the lines of 'Don't be a fool, Commander—our allies have already set up a net to capture the next human ship to Qasama.' Or some such."

"'And once we've destroyed the Dominion ships, your demesne will be next,'" Garrett added the likely next line of Barrington's imagined conversation. "In that case—"

Abruptly, he snorted a laugh. "And Commander Castenello was even on the right track. Ukuthi was hoping we'd be grabbed by the net, blow away the spider ships, and in the process find out who the hell they are."

"Very good," Barrington said, nodding. "Or at least that's the conclusion I came to. So here's the crux. If the situation *is* indeed Option Three, what exactly does that make Ukuthi? Potential ally? Potential enemy? Extremely clever opportunist?"

"Probably all three," Garrett said. "The clever part, certainly. Using Cobra Merrick Broom's name as a hook for you shows that much."

"Especially since it might not be just a hook," Barrington pointed out. "The kind of deviousness we're ascribing to him is quite consistent with him capturing a Cobra and managing to persuade him to go off and spy for him."

"He sure persuaded *us* to do some of his dirty work for him," Garrett said sourly. "And cost us a lot of lives along the way."

"He'll be making up for that soon enough," Barrington promised ominously. "He'll be agreeing to take us to Qasama. And he'd *better* not try to weasel it."

"Yes, sir," Garrett said. "If there's nothing else, Captain, with your permission I'll return to my station."

"Go ahead," Barrington said. "No, wait."

"Yes, sir?"

Barrington hesitated. He really wasn't supposed to ask this.

What the hell. "Do you happen to know which other officers signed off on Castenello's Enquiry Board?"

Garrett's lip twitched. He knew the captain wasn't supposed to ask that, either. "Off the record, sir?"

"Very much so," Barrington assured him.

Garrett seemed to brace himself. "I don't know who the second was, sir. But I was the third."

Barrington felt his mouth drop open. "*You?*"

"Yes, sir," Garrett said. "I was sure you could stand up to his complaints and charges, and I thought it would be better to get it out in the open."

Instead of letting Castenello worm his doubts into the other officers behind Barrington's back? "I suppose that's reasonable," he said. "Thank you, Commander. Dismissed."

Garrett's lip twitched. "Yes, sir."

The door closed behind him, and Barrington permitted a quiet but heartfelt curse. Reasonable or not, logical or not, politically smart or not, it was clear that Garrett wasn't at all happy with his own decision to back the Enquiry Board. It had come out all right, but everyone—Garrett included—could see that it was simply Castenello's first shot in what was probably a long-term campaign.

And when that fresh hammer came down, whether Barrington managed to dodge it or not, Garrett would have to deal with the knowledge that he had helped set the whole thing in motion.

Most senior officers wouldn't care, but would simply join in the game, lining up where they chose, or where they presumed their patrons would want them. Not Garrett. Without a patron, he would instead line up as his rank, position, and military protocol demanded.

He'd made that choice here, for better or worse. And while they all waited for Castenello to play his hand, Garrett would carry a lingering, low-level sense of guilt.

And Barrington knew that anything that distracted a senior officer could be a bad thing in time of war. A *very* bad thing.

Damn Castenello anyway for engineering this mess.

And speaking of engineering...

Putting Castenello out of his mind, Barrington tapped into the data stream. There was no change in Kusari's condition, either better or worse. But there *was* a new note from Dr. Lancaster, urgently requesting that the captain authorize the proposed amputation of Kusari's legs.

Barrington pushed his chair back from the table. He would answer Lancaster's request, all right. He would go down to sick bay personally and tell the surgeon straight to his face to keep his damn cutting laser off his engineering officer's legs.

And after that he would call engineering and try to beg, borrow, or steal a little more speed out of the *Dorian*'s engines.

CHAPTER SIXTEEN

Three days.

That was how long Jin had been stuck in this stupid cave. Three days.

Three freaking *days*.

She glowered at the outside display, feeling helpless, useless, and frustrated. During the Troft invasion of Qasama, it had sometimes seemed like people never stopped or even slowed down, even for a minute. Everyone seemed to have a dozen tasks, with only enough time to accomplish half of them. Jin had often been run ragged, with barely enough time to eat or sleep.

Given the choice between that and this forced idleness, she would take being run ragged any day.

The most frustrating part was that she really shouldn't be in this situation. By every stretch of military logic, she should have been freed from the torture long ago. There was no reason why Reivaro's watchers should still be lurking outside her door, peering through the

waterfall at Sedgley as he sat yet again on his stool for
another day's worth of fishing. Nothing had happened
here in the past two days, not since the daredevil
climbers had gone up the edge of the waterfall, giving
Lorne the chance to slip out. Since then, no one had
approached Sedgley, not even any more of the Marines
who had arrived that first day to question and otherwise
harass the man. Surely even Reivaro could see that it
was a waste of effort to keep two of his troops out here
when they could instead be terrorizing the citizens of
Archway or something.

Especially given how boring a subject Sedgley really
was. Once he settled down with his line in the water
and his rear on his stool, he usually stayed pretty well
put, recasting his line now and then but otherwise
hardly moving.

The edges of the shadowy figures on the ledge also
seldom moved, Jin had also noted. It was like some
sort of bizarre long-distance staring contest.

All of which simply added to Jin's own boredom.
Motionless Sedgley; motionless Marines; nearly motionless landscape. In fact, aside from the river itself, the
only thing out there that *was* moving was a car coming down the narrow road that paralleled the river.

Jin frowned. Not an aircar, but an ordinary ground
vehicle, the kind the majority of Aventine's citizens
owned.

Yet every time the Dominion had dropped by for a
visit, the Marines had invariably arrived in an aircar.

Her first thought was that it was someone from
one of the large farms or ranches to the northwest
who for one reason or another didn't want to use
the main road a few kilometers east. But the driver

didn't seem to be in any real hurry to get wherever he was going.

And then, as the vehicle came alongside Sedgley, it coasted to a halt. There was another short pause, and a man stepped out. He walked over to Sedgley, who seemed to be ignoring him completely, and seemed to begin talking.

Jin frowned a little harder, wishing for the hundredth time the fiber optics could give better definition. The newcomer's face was still maddeningly vague, but there was something strangely familiar about him. Something about his height and hair color and the way he walked. His jacket, too, seemed like something she'd seen before.

And then, abruptly, it all clicked together.

That was Uncle Corwin out there.

Jin's first, horrified reaction was to wonder why in the Worlds he had come here to the cave. Her second, equally horrified reaction was to realize that his presence here was practically inevitable. Lorne had sent Matavuli to talk to him, and Matavuli would naturally have told him where his niece and her son had gone to ground. Assuming Lorne had been able to contact Matavuli when he escaped from the cave two days ago, he would certainly have warned the rancher about the Dominion watchers. But there would have been no reason for Corwin to check in with Matavuli before he himself left Capitalia.

In fact, with the Dominion in position to monitor all of the province's communications, there was every reason for the two of them *not* to try to make contact.

Matavuli might have tried to send people to watch the roads for Corwin's approach. But the group would have had to be small—the more people who knew

Corwin was coming, the bigger the chance that the news would leak. Besides which, given the direction Corwin had approached from, it looked like he'd deliberately avoided getting anywhere near Matavuli's ranch. Again, the kind of caution that under normal circumstances would have been perfectly reasonable.

And Jin now had a decision to make.

Up to now, she'd been working under the hope that the Dominion only *suspected* that she and Lorne were based somewhere in the neighborhood. Once the watchers behind the waterfall tagged Corwin, that hope would be gone.

And once Reivaro knew for certain that there was a base here, he would surely bring in whatever troops and resources he needed to find the cave.

Jin couldn't let that happen. The cave was the one secure place they had, the best rallying point she and Lorne could ever have for organizing serious opposition against the Dominion's aggression.

And the only one who had any chance at all of stopping that was Jin herself.

It might already be too late, she knew as she sprinted toward the rear of the cave. The watchers might already have identified Corwin, and if they had they might already have called in that information. Still, there was a fair chance the watchers wouldn't want to put sensitive news like that on radios or comms, even if they were pretty sure none of the Aventinians could tap into such transmissions. They might at least wait until after the two men by the river finished their chat and Corwin was on the move again.

The rest of the grenades Lorne had built were still lined up on the work table. Scooping up two of the concussion types, Jin returned to the front of the cave. Corwin and Sedgley were still where she'd left them, with Sedgley still squatting on his stool and Corwin still standing behind him, both of them gazing out at the river.

She stepped to the door plug, tucked the grenades under her arms and got a grip on the handholds. The two watchers were still more or less flanking the display, which put them about five meters to the left of the cave entrance. For a second she considered trying to target-lock them via the display, decided that the round-the-corner toss she would need to pull off would probably overstrain the nanocomputer's extrapolation ability. This one she would have to do entirely on her own.

She pulled out the plug, working hard to minimize any stone-on-stone grating, and set it aside. Getting the grenades in hand, she armed them, counted down four of the five-second timers—

Leaning out into the swirling mist behind the waterfall, she lobbed the grenades toward the watchers and ducked back inside.

The blasts were *loud.* Much louder than she'd expected, especially given the mass of stone between her and them. She waited five seconds, then slipped through the opening and sidled carefully along the ledge. If the watchers were wearing Dominion combat suits, they might be at least partially conscious, and she needed to be ready for any trouble they might still be able to create.

To her relief, the grenades seemed to have done their job. As Jin came around the bend in the rock she saw both Marines slumped motionless at the ends of tether lines disappearing up into the rushing water. Their heads were still mostly upright, which worried her until she realized that it was probably the neck pieces of their helmets that were keeping their heads from sagging. Rather like abandoned marionettes, she thought as she edged toward them. The blast from the grenades had left only minor marks on their combat suits, which eased her fear that Lorne might have been overenthusiastic in the amount of explosive he'd used when building the weapons.

Of course, now came the task of figuring out what to do with her new prisoners. Matavuli might know somewhere she might be able to stash them—from what Lorne had said, the rancher knew everything about this part of the province. She would have to find a way to get a message to him.

But first she would have to figure out a way to keep the Marines unconscious until they could be more permanently tucked away. Unfortunately, her generation of Cobra gear hadn't included Lorne's and Merrick's stunners, which meant she would probably have to go with some sort of drug-based sedation.

Still no movement. She moved closer to the hanging men and peered through their helmet faceplates.

And felt her breath freeze in her throat.

Not *like* abandoned marionettes, as she'd thought a moment ago. Not *like* at all.

They *were* marionettes.

The two Dominion Marines who had kept her trapped in that damn cave for three days straight were nothing more than dummies.

She was staring at the blank manikin faces when a motion through the water caught the edge of her eye. She spun around, bringing up her hands into laser-firing position.

But it was only Sedgley's aircar, hovering outside the falls at her level. Through the water-misted windshield she could see Sedgley and Corwin gazing tensely at her.

She swallowed a useless curse. What could she tell them?

But she had to tell them *something*, and fast. There might still be a chance of salvaging something from this, but the window of opportunity was already closing. Motioning them back to the river bank, she made her way along the ledge to the edge of the waterfall.

The climbers two days ago had taken over an hour to work their way up the cliff and nearly that long to get back down again. Jin, with Cobra servos and strengthened bones, did it in four quick jumps.

Sedgley and Corwin were standing outside the aircar when she joined them. "What the hell was *that*?" Sedgley growled, jabbing a finger up at the waterfall. "Is that what you Cobras call keeping a low profile?"

"Are you hurt?" Corwin added before she could answer.

"No, I'm not hurt," Jin said. "And it's called exigent circumstances," she added to Sedgley. "I saw Uncle Corwin arrive, and knew that if the Dominion spotted him they'd jump to exactly the right conclusion."

"So you popped a couple of grenades up their rears," Sedgley bit out. "Right. It's not like they haven't figured it out *now* or anything."

"Oh, they've figured it out, all right," Jin told him grimly. "Those watchers up there aren't watching anything. They're nothing but dummies."

The two men's eyes widened in unison. "They're *what*?" Sedgley demanded.

"You heard me," Jin said. "Which means Reivaro

has known about the cave all along. Or at least long enough."

"You mean you let them just dangle a couple of bags of—" Sedgley swallowed the word. "And you never figured it out until *now*?"

"They were probably real at the start," Corwin said, his eyes steady on Jin. "A couple of Marines dropped in, moved around enough to be convincing, and then somewhere along the line were swapped out for the replicas."

"So they know about the cave," Sedgley said bitterly. "And they know about you and your son. *And* they know about me. Terrific. So basically they know everything."

"Except maybe that *we* know that they know," Jin said. "And they may not know about—" She raised her eyebrows at Corwin, got the faintest hint of a confirming nod in return.

"Know what?" Sedgley asked, looking back and forth between them. "No, never mind. I probably don't want to know. So what now?"

Jin stared up at the waterfall. The Dominion had known about the cave. Not surprising, in retrospect, given the advanced sensor technology they undoubtedly had to work with.

Which meant that their strategy *hadn't* been to track and capture the fugitive Cobras as she and Lorne had thought. It had been merely to pin them down and keep them neutralized.

Only they weren't neutralized. She was out, and Lorne was out.

Reivaro would know she was out soon enough. The big question was, did he also know Lorne had gotten clear? "Do you know if Lorne made it to Archway?" she asked Sedgley.

The other snorted. "Oh, he made it, all right. Dropped out of a Marine aircar onto one of the buildings and disappeared. The Marines spent the rest of the day looking for him."

"But they didn't find him?"

"Not as far as I know. Of course," he added, "they don't exactly consult with us on things like that."

"I don't suppose they do," Jin agreed. "Okay, then. If Lorne's in Archway, I should be there, too."

"Yeah, good luck with that," Sedgley said. "Reivaro's got the place pretty solidly locked down."

"Lorne got in," Jin pointed out. "I can, too."

"How?" Corwin asked.

"My problem, not yours," Jin said. "*Your* job—" she jabbed a finger at Corwin "—is to go to Smith's Forge and meet a Cobra named Kicker at a place called Whistling Waller's." She shifted the pointing finger to Sedgley. "And *you*—"

"Whoa, whoa," Corwin protested. "Slow down. Matavuli just said for me to deliver the item to you and you'd send it down the line."

"I know," Jin said. "But you're going to have to do that for me. Whatever Lorne's got planned, he can't do it alone. I need to get in there and help him."

"But I don't even know where this Whistling Waller's place is."

"I do," Sedgley said. He hissed out an exasperated sigh. "Hell. I suppose I can't get in any deeper with Reivaro than I already am. I'll take you there. Unless you had something else in mind?" he added to Jin.

"No, actually, I was going to suggest you show him

the way." Jin gestured to Corwin. "And you'd better make it the whole package, too, not just the samples. We're going to have to move faster than I thought. I presume you *have* the whole package?"

"It's available, but it'll take a few hours to get it." Corwin looked at Sedgley. "Will that be a problem?"

"Not sure what you'd do about it if it was," Sedgley said sourly. "Doesn't matter—I think Pierce is on edge patrol until about six tomorrow evening anyway. Give him an hour to finish his reports and get changed, and he should be available around seven. We'll hang out somewhere safe and hit Whistling Waller's then."

"You have a place that qualifies as safe?" Corwin asked.

"I know a couple of spots," Sedgley said. "Question is, whose car do we take?"

"You'll take Uncle Corwin's," Jin said. "I'll take yours, if you don't mind. You've been going back and forth from Archway for a couple of days now—if they're scanning tags but not bothering to look too closely inside the vehicles they've already checked out, I may be able to slip in before they realize you're not the one driving."

"Don't know as I'd bank on that," Sedgley said doubtfully. "But I guess that's as good a place to start as any."

"Just be ready to run," Corwin warned. His mouth tightened. "Note I *didn't* say be ready to fight."

"Don't worry, I know what I'm up against," Jin assured him grimly.

"Okay." Corwin nodded toward the cave. "Do you need to get anything before you go?"

Jin felt her jaw tighten. Yes, there were things up there she could use. Lots of things. Changes of clothing, emergency rations, maybe a few more grenades.

But if the Dominion was on to her...

"Yes, but no," she told him. "It would be embarrassing to get caught with my arms full of supplies. Let's just go."

"Okay." Corwin stepped close for a quick hug. "Be careful," he murmured into her hair.

"You, too," she murmured back.

Ninety seconds later she was in the air, heading toward Archway. The days she'd seen Sedgley fly in he'd always seemed to travel at a leisurely pace, the speed of a man who wasn't in a hurry and knew the fish would be there whenever he arrived. She tried to match that style, knowing full well that it probably wouldn't help her much.

Still, if there was one thing she'd learned from fighting the Trofts on Qasama, it was that the side with the superior firepower and intel often fell into the self-built trap of casual complacency. If Reivaro thought he was fully on top of things, she and Lorne might still have a chance of surprising him.

And if Sedgley was secretly working for Reivaro? Well, she had that one covered, too.

Because despite what she'd just told them, she had no intention of going anywhere near Archway. That was Reivaro's stronghold, and as such was probably the best-protected place in the province. If Lorne had really penetrated it without Reivaro catching him, it had almost certainly been a fluke of cleverness and surprise, and it was unlikely that Jin would find a way to duplicate that success.

It tore at her heart to leave her son all alone in enemy territory. But the cold battle logic she'd learned under fire on Qasama told her that for now the most important goal was to make sure Corwin succeeded in his own mission.

So instead of going to Archway, she would go to ground for the night and then, tomorrow, would head to Smith's Forge. Not to Whistling Waller's, of course—there was every chance that, having learned the secret of the Braided Falls cave, Reivaro even now was tracking her or otherwise had her under surveillance.

But she could get *close* to Waller's. Somewhere else in town, somewhere far enough away to divert Dominion attention from the bar but close enough that she could get there to help if Sedgley betrayed them.

And while she did all that, she could only hope that Lorne was still alive and free. And that he wasn't about to do anything that would change that status.

It was strange, Lorne thought as he ambled down the Archway street, not having a chin.

Not that the chin was gone, of course. Far from it. As far as the outside world was concerned, in fact, he actually had more chin than ever. More chin, a bit more nose, a little extra dangle on his earlobes, and noticeably wider cheeks.

But the fact that he couldn't feel the breeze on his real chin, nose, or earlobes made it feel like they weren't there.

All of it courtesy of James Hobwell's chief make-up artist, Jennie Sider, and the magic of modern cinematic prosthetics.

Oddly enough, after doing all that work on his face, Jennie had completely skipped over the chance to make any changes to his hair color. Lorne's assumption, after years of watching dramas and thrillers, was that the first thing any fugitive did was dye his or her hair, usually making it darker but occasionally going full blond. He'd mentioned that to Jennie, who had quite reasonably pointed out that facial-recognition programs like the ones Reivaro's Marines were probably using wouldn't pay even passing attention to hair color.

She had, however, clipped the hair in a few strategic places, which had altered his appearance more than he would ever have expected from such relatively small changes.

The whole process had taken nearly an hour, after which she'd turned him over to Hobwell. Before becoming a producer, it turned out, he'd been a line director, and he'd proceeded to spend another half hour coaching Lorne on how to alter his stance and walk to project an entirely different persona.

The final result was a person Lorne himself barely recognized. Which was exactly what he'd hoped for.

Even more importantly, Reivaro's facial-recognition programs apparently didn't recognize him, either. In the forty-two hours since Lorne had bounced his impromptu way into Archway he'd made three excursions out of Polestar Productions' guest apartment, which Hobwell had lent him, spending a total of four hours out in the open. So far none of the Marines he'd passed had given him a second look.

Maybe they'd concluded he'd gone to ground, either because he was waiting for his mother to join him or because he was trying to recruit assistance from the general populace. Or maybe they decided his flamboyant entry must have left him injured or unnerved.

Certainly their easy and bloody victory on the steps of Yates Fabrications five days ago would have skewed their opinion of Cobra abilities and resolve. Especially given how meekly the rest of the region's Cobras had surrendered after the carnage.

Lorne rather hoped that was what the Marines were thinking. Four hours of wandering the city had given him several targets to choose from, and a rude awakening would do Reivaro some good.

Early on in their take-over of Archway, the Marines had commandeered the former Cobra HQ, a modest two-story building in the west-central part of the city. Lorne had thought that Colonel Reivaro might have reconsidered that decision and moved to some place either more defensible or at least less well-known to his enemies. But Lorne's second reconnoiter had shown that the Dominion still had a presence there, complete with a pair of combat-suited Marines standing guard outside the main entrance.

Even if the circumstances had been normal, with DeVegas province's full Cobra contingent up and running, two Marines would have been a formidable deterrent to attempted entry. The parrot lasers built into their epaulets had an instant and lethal response to anything their inbuilt computer/sensor system recognized as a threat. For anything the computer didn't automatically react to, the Marine could lock and fire the weapons with a flick of his eyelids. On paper, those two Marines standing at rigid attention on either side of the door should be able to hold off an army.

But the system had one crucial weakness: it couldn't target something coming in from directly overhead. Lorne had already used that design flaw against them once.

Time to do it again.

Across the street from the Cobra HQ, facing it from about twenty meters away, was a three-story apartment complex. Lorne ambled toward the Cobra building on the apartment building's side of the street, noting with bitter-edged amusement that all his fellow pedestrians were also avoiding the Marines' side. Vehicular traffic on that particular stretch was also sparse, with most drivers apparently choosing to detour around the block rather than drive past the Dominion stronghold.

Which was just the way Lorne wanted it. The fewer civilians in the area, the less the chance one of them would be injured by his impending attack.

Lorne reached the cross street that passed along the side of the apartment building and turned down it. Just before the edge of the building cut off his view of the two Marines, he looked up into the sky, lifting his hand as if to block off the late-afternoon sunlight. With his hand still up, he threw the Marines a final, furtive look, the kind a nervous citizen might give to his conquerors.

And with that glance he put a target lock on the ground midway between them, a second lock on the pavement five meters upwind of the entrance, and one more on the window of the room Reivaro had been using as his office. He passed out of view of the Marines, took two more steps—

And came to a halt, digging the first of his three grenades from his coat pocket. He hadn't yet tried his new throwing trick with multiple targets, but he knew his nanocomputer could handle sequential attacks with every other weapon in his arsenal, and it was reasonable to assume it could do the same here. Assuming he'd gotten the angle of the arc right when he pretended to shield his eyes—and having paced the attack and distance off earlier he *should* have it right—his nanocomputer ought to have no problem dropping the grenades precisely where Lorne wanted them.

Shifting the first grenade to his right hand and getting the second ready in his left, he looked at the top of the apartment building, leaned back and to his right, and threw.

As it had back at Matavuli's slit trench, he'd barely begun the throw when his nanocomputer sensed the movement, correctly ascertained his intent, and took over control of his servos. A fraction of a second later, Lorne felt the sudden stress on his arm, shoulders, chest, and legs as the strength of the effort was magnified a hundredfold. His arm whipped over his head, and as his hips and legs automatically shifted to correct a brief imbalance he watched with awe as the grenade sailed upward. It missed the edge of the eave by a whisker and disappeared over the roof.

He had the second grenade in the air just as the first sailed out of view, and the third was on its way before the second cleared the eave.

And by the time the first concussive blast shattered the city's tense calm he was on the move again, ambling back the way he'd come, hoping to catch a glimpse of his handiwork.

He got it, but just barely. His second grenade, one of his two remaining smoke bombs, hit the pavement just as he spotted the two Marines lying on the pavement where the concussion blast had sent them sprawling. Even as the third grenade came arcing down toward the window of Reivaro's office, the thick plumes of smoke blanketed the whole area. There was a flash of muted light through the roiling cloud, but

Lorne couldn't tell whether or not the last grenade had broken the window or just expended its energy on the wall beside it.

He would be able to tell once the smoke cleared. But he knew better than to stick around that long. The various pedestrians on the streets around him were on the move now, most of them running away from the sound of the triple blast, while a handful of the courageous, curious, or stupid ran toward the commotion. Lorne joined the former group, catching up to a clump of eight that had happened to form and attaching himself to their perimeter.

It was just as well he hadn't lingered. The mass exodus had made it barely thirty meters before a half dozen Dominion aircars zoomed into view, converging on the area from all directions. Maybe the Marines *hadn't* been caught napping, after all.

Still, Reivaro had definitely missed a bet. From what Lorne could see of the aircar search pattern, it looked as if the Marines were scouring the rooftops, clearly making the assumption that that was where the thrown grenades had come from.

They were still searching the roofs and the nearby alleys when Lorne and the crowd disappeared from their view.

Castenello had warned that the *Dorian*'s delay at the ambush net would cause Commander Ukuthi to give up and move on from his designated rendezvous point. Barrington had insisted that the Troft would instead be patient and wait.

To Barrington's quiet relief, he was right.

"Your arrival, I began to doubt it would occur," the

Troft said after the two ships had established contact. "An interesting saga, I see there must be one."

"An interesting saga, there definitely is," Barrington told him darkly. "We ran into some friends of yours on the way here." He leaned a bit closer to the CoNCH speaker, listening hard for Ukuthi's response.

"Friends of mine?" Ukuthi asked. As best as Barrington could tell—and his best was admittedly not very good—there was genuine puzzlement in the Troft's voice. "Understanding, I do not have it."

"Someone set up a flicker net between here and Aventine," Barrington said. "We figured they were trying to stop the next Dominion ship traveling that route, so we waited around to help out. You're saying those *weren't* your allies?"

"The truth, it is far from that," Ukuthi said, and this time there was a genuine-sounding grimness to his tone. "I believe they were from the unknown demesne I spoke about once before."

"Which demesne was that?"

"The demesne which first contracted with the Tua'lanek'zia demesne to attack Qasama and the Cobra Worlds," Ukuthi said. "The Tua'lanek'zia demesne was the one that then brought the Drim'hco'plai and my own Balin'ekha'spmi in to assist."

"Ah," Barrington said, as if he'd lost track of who was who in this mess. "If I remember right it was the Drim'hco'plai who had you pinned down at the Hoibe'ryi'sarai home world. Is that correct?"

"It is," Ukuthi confirmed. "I had the thought they might seek to intercept a ship of the Dominion of Man."

"And you didn't bother to mention that to me?"

"Your forgiveness, I ask it," Ukuthi said. "In truth,

I expected the attack to occur closer to Qasama. That was why I requested you rendezvous with me here, instead of at Qasama itself, that we might complete the journey in united convoy. I intended to warn you of the possible threat when here we met."

"If you were worried, why didn't you just suggest we fly together from the Hoibie homeworld?" Barrington countered.

"I knew you would wish to deliver a report to your companions at Aventine early in the journey," Ukuthi said. "I therefore gave you a course that would take you within short messaging distance before guiding you here."

"I see," Barrington said. "One moment."

He tapped the mute key and looked at Garrett. "Opinion?"

"It fits the facts as well as any other theory," Garrett said, frowning in concentration. "It *does* rather imply he's been manipulating us from the start, though."

"Which we'd already considered a possibility," Barrington pointed out. Still, the internal consistency of Ukuthi's story meant there was nothing they could definitively hang around his neck as a lie. At least, not yet.

But at this point Ukuthi and his manipulation were only second place on Barrington's priority list. Time to deal with the one in first.

He tapped off the mute. "We'll be discussing this in more depth in the future," he told Ukuthi. "Right now, I have a shipful of injured men who need medical attention that's beyond my ability to provide. I need Qasama's coordinates, and I need them now."

"Of course," Ukuthi said, sounding vaguely surprised

that it was even a question. "The Qasama system is approximately one day's journey along the final vector that brought you here to me. The final coordinates, I am sending them to you now. As I said, my purpose was to bring you here was merely so that we could unite and complete the voyage together."

"Then let us do that," Barrington said, twitching his eye to tap into the data stream. The coordinates Ukuthi had promised were there and had already been coded into the helm. The proper course was laid in, and engineering reported the *Dorian*'s drive was ready to kick them back into hyperspace. "We'll leave as soon as you're ready."

"Readiness, we have it," Ukuthi assured him. "Provide me with a countdown, and we shall drape the cloak of darkness together."

Barrington pursed his lips. *Drape the cloak of darkness.* An interesting turn of phrase. Was that how all Trofts spoke of hyperspace, he wondered, or was it unique to Ukuthi?

Or was Ukuthi simply waxing poetic because he'd heard that humans responded well to poetry? "Thirty-second countdown on its way," Barrington said. "Do you have it?"

"I have it," Ukuthi said. "At Qasama shall we see each other next."

"At Qasama," Barrington confirmed.

Or possibly they would see each other earlier than that, he reminded himself. Possibly at the next trap Ukuthi had set up for them, in fact. Right now, there was still no reason to trust him. Nor was there any specific reason *not* to trust him.

At least, not yet.

CHAPTER SEVENTEEN

The black turned to gray, became wild and discordant colors, then went to black again. Then it did it all again. It was like a carnival ride for the brain, and sometimes Merrick rode it like there was nothing else in the universe that he needed to do.

Other times, he rode it as if letting go would erase all the colors from his mind forever.

He'd lost track of how many times the cycle had repeated itself when, to his weary surprise, he awakened to a world of normal colors and a dazed but more or less normal mind.

And along with the colors and sanity, an incredibly intense thirst.

He blinked his eyes a few times as he looked around. He was in a room in what seemed to be some sort of house, with muted sunlight coming in through small, high windows. Outside the windows seemed to be forest, though the image was obscured by a layer of grime on the glass. The room's furnishings were sparse: the bed he was lying on, a small table at his side, and a single chair. All of the items were dark wood, and all of them looked rough and handmade. In contrast with the almost amateurish furniture, the walls were covered in exquisite, highly detailed tapestries.

"You're awake," an unfamiliar voice came from behind him.

Merrick twisted his head around, a brief stab of dizziness washing over him as he did so, to see a young woman walking toward him from a half-open door. He craned his neck a little more, hoping to get some idea what was on the other side of the door, but all he could see were more tapestries. "Where am I?" he croaked. His voice was startling, far worse than just his massive thirst should have accounted for.

"My home," the woman replied as she came around the side of the bed he was lying on. She was blonde, the typical Muninn coloring, and a bit on the short side. "What do you hear today?"

Merrick frowned. That was an odd comment. "I don't know," he said. "Just you, I guess. Why do you ask?"

She shrugged. "Often during your illness you claimed to hear things that weren't there."

"What sort of things?"

"Sometimes it was the masters' flying boats," she said. "Other times you heard predators on the prowl nearby."

"And you looked and saw that nothing was there?" Merrick asked, suppressing a grimace. He must have been using his audios during one or more of those iridescent nightmares, without enough awareness or self-control to keep from blabbing about what he was hearing.

"*Looked*?" she echoed, her lip twisting. "Certainly we didn't bother to look. Not after the first time you proved to be wrong. My time is too precious to waste on a madman."

"I don't doubt it," Merrick said. Belatedly, he realized part of the reason for his odd-sounding voice: his audios were running at a strange and unbalanced setting, as if a child had gotten into his brain and started throwing switches at random. Carefully, he reset them to proper levels. "I appreciate your hospitality," he added. His voice was still hoarse, but at least it was no longer freaky. "My name is Merrick. May I ask yours?"

"I know who you are, Merrick Hopekeeper." She gave a little snort. "And let me be honest about my hospitality. If your friends hadn't insisted, I would have thrown you out days ago."

"I'm sorry I've been a burden," Merrick said. "It was never my intent."

The woman's face softened, just a little, and clearly grudgingly. "I don't doubt it was not your idea," she conceded. "Though let us be clear that it was your own clumsiness that first occasioned your arrival. I am Alexis Woolmaster."

"I'm honored to meet you," Merrick said, his stomach tightening as something she'd said suddenly penetrated his lingering fogginess. She would have thrown him out *days* ago? How long had he been here, anyway? "May I ask how long it is that I've been imposing on you and your home?" he asked carefully.

"You were brought in the night three days ago." She gave another snort. "You frightened the sheep. For that alone I would have sent you away."

Merrick looked back toward the dim light coming in through the windows. Three days. Three *days*. While Anya and Kjoic did—

Did what? Sat in the forest and waited for him? Or had they given up and set out for Svipall on their own?

Or had one of his captors gone to get them? He had some vague memory of someone talking about that before the kaleidoscope cycles began, but had no idea whether or not it had happened. "You said my friends insisted I be permitted to stay," he said. "Are those friends here now?"

"They are," a new voice came from the doorway.

Again, Merrick turned his head to look, again fighting back the vertigo. This one was a man, older than the young woman facing him, wearing a camouflage sort of outfit of mottled brown, green, and gray. A memory clicked: this was the same middle-aged man who'd been with the group that brought him here after his encounter with the bersark field outside Svipall.

More to the point, it was the man who'd said he was going to find Anya and Kjoic.

"You may leave us, Alexis Tucker," the man said.

For a moment he and the woman locked eyes, and Merrick wondered if she was going to remind him whose house this was. Then, with a slight compression of her lips, she slipped past him and disappeared through the doorway.

The man watched until she was gone, then pulled the chair over beside the bed and sat down. "I am Ludolf Treetapper," he said, his eyes flicking briefly down Merrick's body. "I see your mind has returned to reason."

"Mostly," Merrick confirmed. He still felt weak, and

even the smallest movement of his head seemed to
spark more of the dizziness. Dehydration, probably,
and for a moment he considered asking Ludolf for
water. But there was something about the man that
made him reluctant to ask for favors. "I thought her
name was Alexis Woolmaster."

Ludolf snorted. "So she now calls herself," he said
scornfully. "When I first knew her she barely knew how
to pleat the fabrics created by others. Alexis Tucker
she was then, and Alexis Tucker she will always be."

"Ah," Merrick said noncommittally. Clearly, Ludolf
wasn't a man who bothered with tact and personal
diplomacy. Merrick knew people like that, and they
tended to go through life leaving emotional brush fires
in their wake. "Were you able to find Anya and Kjoic?"

"Eventually," Ludolf said, his eyes steady on Merrick. "You'll see them both later."

"Wait a second," Merrick asked, frowning. He
would see them *both*? "Are you saying you kept *Kjoic*
here, too?"

"Why else would we be in Alexis Tucker's home
instead of our own?" Ludolf countered. "We certainly
couldn't bring a master there."

"But you can't just hold him here against his will,"
Merrick protested. "He's a *master*. They don't take
well to things like that. The minute he's free, they'll
turn the whole area into a burn zone."

"I agree," Ludolf said. "The simplest way to avoid
that would be to simply kill him."

"No," Merrick said firmly, a surge of adrenaline
momentarily mastering the dizziness. Kjoic was his key
to getting into the Troft building at Svipall. The last
thing he wanted was to have some wide-eyed local

drop his body into a river somewhere. He started to sit up, clenching his teeth against the light-headedness—

"Calm yourself, Merrick Hopekeeper," Ludolf soothed, putting a hand on Merrick's chest and easing him back down again. "There will be no need for violence or death. Not yet. Master Kjoic remains in this place of his own free will."

"Does he, now," Merrick growled, sinking back onto the bed. A good, solid shove on Ludolf's chest, he knew, would send the man halfway across the room and maybe teach him not to play games like this.

But that would reveal Merrick's strength. He might have foolishly talked about hearing things during his bouts with brain fever, but he'd recovered enough to remember that all this was supposed to be a deep, dark secret.

"He does," Ludolf assured him. "When he learned that one of his slaves was ill, he insisted on remaining until you were once again ready to travel." His lip twisted. "He also seems to believe that *we* are his slaves now, as well. Tell me, why do you wish to enter the masters' gray building?"

"There are things in there I want to see," Merrick said.

"What things?"

"I won't know until I see them, will I?"

"That's not an answer."

"It's all I have right now," Merrick said. "Maybe later I can do better."

For a moment Ludolf gazed at him in silence. "Who are you?"

"You already know that. I'm Merrick Hopekeeper."

Ludolf waved an impatient hand. "Words," he

scoffed. "A name is not a person, as you well know. I want to know who you *are*. *And* why you've come here to this part of Muninn."

"Why don't you ask Anya?"

Ludolf's lip twisted. "I did," he said sourly. "She would say only that you were once a fellow slave of a distant warrior-master."

"She's right," Merrick agreed. "That's who I am. No more; no less."

"You expect me to believe that?"

"I expect more courtesy between strangers," Merrick said pointedly. "Certainly with regards to each other's privacy."

"Privacy?" Ludolf asked, raising his eyebrows. "This from a man who claims to be a great and powerful warrior himself? A man who has defeated many of the masters in open battle? A man who claims to have torn a jormungand apart with his bare hands?"

Merrick stared, a fresh surge of adrenaline bubbling through him. He'd just about convinced himself that his loose words to Alexis were the biggest mistake he'd made during his drug-induced mania. Apparently, he'd said or done far worse.

But what exactly *had* he said? Did he tell them he was from the Cobra Worlds? Did he tell them he was a Cobra?

Worse, did he *show* them he was a Cobra?

And then, his fogged brain caught up with Ludolf's accusations, and the rising panic abruptly receded again.

Merrick had never torn a jormungand apart. Not with his bare hands. Not even with his lasers or his arcthrower. Not even close.

So where in the Worlds had Ludolf gotten the idea that he had?

Obviously, Anya must have told him more than the simple fact that Merrick was a fellow slave. She must have hinted at what he was capable of, and Ludolf had taken the vague statements and tried to fill in the blanks. Probably hoping to spark a reaction or maybe goad Merrick into filling in some of the blanks himself.

The revelation came as a relief. Still, the relief came tinged with a sense of disappointment. Anya knew how closely they had to guard the secret of who he was. She shouldn't have given out *any* information about him, let alone details or even broad hints about his abilities. Especially not to a total stranger.

Unless Ludolf *wasn't* a total stranger. Unless Ludolf was, in fact...

Merrick felt his eyes narrow as he studied the man's face, noting with distant amusement that Ludolf was simultaneously studying Merrick's. The man's eyes... his mouth... the shape of his cheekbones...

"Sounds like the ravings of a drug-crazed man to me," Merrick said, keying his infrareds to their emotion-reading setting. "I wouldn't believe a word of it if I were you. Tell me, what's it like to finally have your daughter back with you?"

Ludolf was good. His body never twitched, nor were there any sharp intakes of air, and his expression never cracked.

But Merrick's infrareds told a different story. The man's heartbeat leaped, blood suffusing his face with surprise or chagrin at Merrick's unexpected question. The pattern flowed back and forth as Ludolf clearly tried to decide whether to deny it or face the fact that a total stranger had somehow discerned the truth.

It took him nearly five seconds to decide. Merrick waited, content to give him whatever the time he needed.

And then, reluctantly, Ludolf inclined his head. "Anya said you were clever," he said. "More clever, I see, than I realized."

"Thank you," Merrick said. "Then I assume you're glad to see her?"

Ludolf's eyes seemed to go a little flat. "We're glad to see her," he said. "She is not so glad to see us."

"Ah," Merrick said. From the way Anya had talked about them, he wasn't really surprised by that. "Well, then, let's hear your side of it. Tell me about your rebellion against the masters."

"That is the past," Ludolf said flatly. "What matters now are the present and future."

"That's fine," Merrick said. "Assuming you can lock away the past where it can't affect anything else. Personally, I've never found the past to be so accommodating."

"I have no wish to talk about it."

"Then I'll give it a shot," Merrick said. "If I understand correctly, you and your wife—Anya's parents— organized an attack against the Trofts. It failed and you ran off into the forest, leaving her and the rest of Gangari holding the bag. That about right?"

Ludolf's throat worked. "It is not evil to try a great task and fail."

"It is when that failure ends up costing someone half their life in exile," Merrick said. "Especially when that someone is your own daughter."

"The price of freedom is sometimes great," Ludolf said. "And sometimes that price and final victory are widely separated. The war continues, and we *will* regain our world." He tried a smile that didn't quite come off. "And do not worry about Anya. We will willingly accept her back."

Merrick stared at him. "*You'll* accept *her*?" he repeated, wondering if he'd actually heard that right. "Seems to me it's more a question of whether she'll accept *you*."

"Relationships in this part of Muninn are perhaps not the way they are where you come from," Ludolf said stiffly.

"Perhaps," Merrick said. "And perhaps Anya has changed since you let her take the brunt of your punishment. What do you say I go and ask her?" He swung his legs over the end of the bed and sat up.

And fell straight back down again as the world suddenly tilted around him.

"You will see no one until you are fully recovered," Ludolf said severely. "I don't know why you were foolish enough to tread near a bersark field, but you now pay the consequences."

"I'm fine," Merrick insisted, clenching his teeth as he waited for the spinning to stop. "I just need some food and water."

"They will be brought to you," Ludolf said. "And then you will sleep again."

"*After* I see Anya," Merrick said.

"When you are well enough," Ludolf said. "Until then, you will eat, drink and sleep." With a final nod, he stood up and strode out.

A few minutes later Alexis Woolmaster returned,

carrying a tray on which was balanced a mug, a jar of water, and a plate of cold meat and some kind of root vegetables. She helped Merrick up into a sort of half-lying position on the bed and assisted him in eating and drinking. He finished off most of the pitcher before his thirst finally eased, but to his mild surprise discovered he wasn't all that hungry. He ate perhaps a third of what she'd brought and declared himself full.

To his annoyance the water didn't seem to have helped his dizziness. As Alexis left with the tray he lay down again, promising himself that he would rest a few minutes, wait for the water to be fully absorbed into his system, then get up and go find Anya.

Ten minutes later, he was once again fast asleep.

"Coming up on Qasama," the nav officer called. "One minute to break-out."

Barrington nodded silently, rubbing his thumb restlessly along the side of his forefinger as he looked around CoNCH. This was it: the make-or-break moment. If Ukuthi had been telling the truth—if Qasama was indeed waiting when they dropped out of hyperspace—he might yet pull this off. Most of the seriously injured men in sick bay were still clinging to life, and could theoretically yet be saved.

If the Qasamans were willing to help them. Somehow, he had to find a way to make that happen, by pleas, bribes, or even threats. If they refused, this could still crumble in Barrington's hands.

Of course, if Ukuthi had lied, and all that was out there was more empty space, the crumbling would be even more guaranteed.

There was the thud of relays as the *Dorian* once again entered space-normal. Barrington held his breath...

And there, neatly centered in the main display, was a planet. A cloud-mottled mass of green and blue, the kind of planet that humans could thrive on. The tactical display came on as the incoming sensor data was collected, organized and refined; and there, right at the edge of their view, was a distinctive curve of cities, villages, roads, and cleared land. The region the Aventinians had originally dubbed the Fertile Crescent and which the inhabitants themselves called the Great Arc.

They had found Qasama.

"Getting a reading on Commander Ukuthi," Castillo called from his station. "He seems to have come out early. He is directly aft; range, three million klicks."

Barrington frowned as he tapped into the data stream. Ukuthi hadn't said anything about hanging back like this. Was there a problem? "Get a signal to him, Commander," he ordered Garrett. "Ask him what the hell he's doing. Politely, of course."

"We have an incoming signal, Captain," Garrett said. "Commander Ukuthi says he thought having a Troft ship coming close in to Qasama might alarm or prejudice the inhabitants against us. He says, with your permission, he'll hold position in backstop position, in case our mutual enemies decide they want another crack at us."

Barrington scowled. Actually, the other had decent logic on both points. Barrington had been trying to figure out how exactly he was going to explain the presence of a Troft warship at his side; and any ship that tried to come in for a quick attack on the *Dorian* would probably pop in right behind the Dominion ship, a tactic which would end him squarely in the middle of a cross fire.

"Reply, sir?" Garrett asked.

"Acknowledge his message," Barrington said. "But keep an eye on him. Helm, take us in, minimum-time course to orbit. Find the local transmission frequencies and attempt to open communications."

He got acknowledgements, and leaned back in his chair. Nothing to do now but mentally rehearse his speech for whenever someone down there decided they were ready to talk to him.

The first big question was whether they would even know what the Dominion of Man was. They might have records of where their ancestors had originally come from, or someone from the Cobra Worlds might have mentioned their own origin somewhere along the way. Either way, though, there was a good chance he would have to start basically from scratch.

The tricky part would be choosing which elements of Dominion politics and society to emphasize, and which to gloss over. The Cobra Worlds' information about Qasama had indicated that it was organized beneath a strong, centralized government headed by a group called the Shahni, very similar to the Dominion's own Dome-controlled structure. The Moreau data, in particular, had also spoken of a strongly patriarchal society, again an echo of the Dominion. On paper, at least, it should be easy enough to convince the Qasamans that they and the Dominion were kindred spirits.

The catch was that all of that information predated the Troft invasion. It was likely that the Qasaman structure had survived the devastation, but it was hardly guaranteed. There were certainly historical precedents for that type of society undergoing a massive upheaval after a war, and Barrington would have to tread lightly until he figured out their current arrangement.

"Congratulations, sir," Garrett said quietly into his thoughts. "You did it."

"Thank you, Commander," Barrington said. Yes, they'd done it. They'd found Qasama. And, with luck and some careful politics, they'd found healing for Barrington's injured.

And after that, Santores would bring in the *Megalith* and set about building up the battered world hanging in space in front of them. They would create an array of imaginary but convincing defenses and attack capabilities, setting Qasama up as more and more of a potential threat to the Troft territory around it until the Dominion's enemies concluded they had no choice but to attack. Those allied demesnes would assemble a task force, hopefully from the warships currently facing the Dominion, and rush here to neutralize the potential threat to their rear.

And at the height of that slaughter, the *Megalith* and the follow-up task force already on its way would suddenly appear behind them with a devastating counterattack. When the dust of the battle dissipated, the Trofts would find themselves with considerably fewer ships to send back to the Dominion front. A tactical blunder of that magnitude might even crack the enemy alliance, much as the Qasaman victories during the previous invasion had put a strain on their own group of attackers. If even more warriors' luck was with the human side, the *Dorian* and some of the other ships might even make it through without being destroyed.

There would be no such luck for the Qasamans, though. With only the illusion of defenses in place to protect them, they would be destroyed. Completely and utterly destroyed.

But the Dominion would have the victory they needed. To the Dome, that was what mattered. Victory, at any cost.

"Captain, we have an acknowledgement from the planet," the comm officer called.

Barrington nodded, glancing at the range indicator as he keyed his board. At their current separation, there would be a five-second round-trip delay in communication. That could be bit awkward, especially since the Qasamans probably weren't accustomed to dealing with such things. Still, it shouldn't be too bad. "This is Captain Barrington Moreau of the War Cruiser *Dorian*," he called toward the mike. "I bring greetings to Qasama from the government and people of the Dominion of Man. May I ask who I have the honor of addressing?"

Five seconds passed. Then another five, and another. Barrington frowned, wondering if they'd lost the signal. But the readouts confirmed the carrier was still there.

Maybe whoever was manning the system didn't speak Anglic. Some Qasamans did, he remembered from the records, but not very many. His best bet was probably to just keep at it until they could bring in a translator. "Repeating: This is Captain Barrington Moreau of the Dominion of Man—"

"I send greetings to you, Captain Moreau," an old-man-type voice broke in. His Anglic was slightly accented but otherwise flawless. "I am Moffren Omnathi, Shahni of the people of Qasama. Forgive my delay in answering your communication, but your arrival was unexpected."

"I'm certain it was," Barrington said, tapping into the data stream. The Cobra Worlds records included a *lot* of information and history on Omnathi, both before and after the Troft invasion. "I know that under normal circumstances we would want to move this contact along slowly and carefully, with all due and proper respect for our individual nations' diplomatic customs—"

"We have just finished a war, Captain Moreau," Omnathi interrupted. "We have no need nor desire for long discussions. Tell me why you are here."

A man who believed in getting straight to the point. Barrington could appreciate that. "My long-term goal is the opening of diplomatic ties between the people of Qasama and the Dominion of Man," he said. "My short-term goal, however, is more urgent. I have a great need, and must ask you and your people for an equally great favor."

The time lag this time was precisely five seconds. "Speak your request."

Barrington braced himself, painfully aware of the minefield stretched out in front of him. His request for assistance would require him to admit that the *Dorian* had taken a beating from the Trofts at the ambush net. At the same time, he had to maintain the image of a massively powerful Dominion and Dominion Fleet, lest Omnathi balk when Santores arrived later with promises of a new defense grid for the planet. "Three days ago, while en route to your world, we were attacked by a numerically superior force of Troft warships," he said. "While we came away with the victory, many of my crewmen were badly injured in the battle, some of them beyond our ability to heal. According to the Cobra Worlds' records, you have medical techniques and capabilities far beyond ours. I therefore humbly ask if there is a possibility of your world accepting them for treatment. For suitable payment, of course."

Holding his breath, Barrington began to count out the five seconds. From across CoNCH, he could feel Castenello's eyes on him. If Omnathi refused...

"Your request is not a light one," Omnathi said. "We do not accept strangers easily on Qasama. Nor do we offer resources which are in short supply and desperately needed by our own people."

Barrington sent a hooded look at Castenello. The Tactical Officer had predicted this answer, and had strongly suggested that the next step up the ladder would be to threaten the Qasamans with the *Dorian*'s massive firepower.

Which Barrington had no intention of doing. Aside from everything else, threatening a people who'd just thrown off a massive Troft occupation force was just plain ludicrous.

"But your name intrigues me," Omnathi continued. "Tell me, are you related to Jasmine Moreau, known to many as Jin?"

Barrington blinked. And yet, in retrospect, he should have expected this. Commodore Santores had once commented on how often the Moreaus had somehow found themselves at the flashpoint of significant historical events, and nowhere had that been more true than on Qasama. "Yes, I am," he told Omnathi. "My grandfather was brother to Jasmine Moreau's grandfather."

"Indeed," Omnathi said. "In that event, Captain Moreau, we would consider it an honor to treat your wounded."

"Thank you," Barrington said, relief washing through him. "I offer my personal thanks, as well as the gratitude of the Dominion of Man."

"As I say, it will be an honor," Omnathi said. "I will alert my Surgical Master. I trust he may contact your subordinates on this frequency to work out the details?"

"Of course," Barrington said, motioning to Garrett. "Our Chief Medical Officer will await your Surgical Master's call." Out of the corner of his eye he saw Garrett nod and begin speaking softly on the comm. "Once again, I offer my deepest gratitude."

"Your gratitude has already been accepted," Omnathi said, a bit dryly. "There is no need to add more, certainly not until the requested healing has taken place. Understand that I cannot promise any such healing will be successful until we've examined the patients."

"Of course," Barrington assured him. "As I said, these are cases where our own methods have proved inadequate. Where you are unable to save a life, that life was already forfeit."

"We will do all in our power for those lives," Omnathi said. "I must go now, Captain, and see to the necessary preparations. I look forward to speaking further with you in the near future."

"As do I," Barrington said. "Until then, farewell." He keyed off. "Commander?" he asked.

"Doctor Lancaster has begun prepping the patients," Garrett reported. "They should be ready for transport by the time we reach orbit. He's also tied into the frequency Shahni Omnathi was using and will be ready to talk to the Qasamans whenever they get their liaison in place."

"Good." Barrington checked the time. Over an hour yet to orbit.

Still, he'd gotten the injured men this far. It would be the height of unfairness on the part of the universe to allow them to survive all this way only to die on the trip down in a landing shuttle.

No, they'd make it all right. They'd arrive safely, and the Qasamans would heal them.

And the Dominion would express its gratitude by setting up their world for destruction.

"Begin prep on the landing shuttles," he ordered. "I want them ready to fly, with the injured aboard, the minute we make orbit."

He looked over at Castenello, gazing at the man's stiff back. "And begin prepping the *Iris* for flight," he added. "Commodore Santores will want to know that we've located Qasama."

CHAPTER EIGHTEEN

Corwin had assumed Whistling Waller's would be something quiet and dignified. A genteel sort of bar or lounge, like those he'd visited way too often during his time as a Governor in Capitalia.

It wasn't. The place, to put it crudely, was a dive.

The wooden bar was chipped and stained. The table Sedgley had insisted on steering them to was equally battered and badly in need of another coat of paint. The clientele was about as distant from the well-dressed policy-makers in the Capitalia bars as it was possible to get: rough, loud men and women who had put in a hard day's work and were determined to get as much enjoyment out of their limited time and money as they could.

Still, having slept overnight in his clothes and skipped his morning's shave—Sedgley's suggestion on that one—Corwin had to admit that he fit right in.

Maybe that was the point. Maybe Lorne and Matavuli had anticipated the inevitable scruffiness associated with being on the run, and had chosen Waller's to match. Or maybe the point was that the Dominion would assume members of the Moreau and Broom families would be above places like this, and not bother to watch them.

Corwin hoped that *one* of those, at least, was indeed the point.

Sedgley had gone to the bar to get their third round of beers—the mugs were as stained as the furniture, and the beer was obviously an acquired taste—when Corwin heard a soft voice from behind him. "Don't turn around."

Corwin started to jerk, moved quickly to throttle the reaction, and got away with just a small twitch. "Kicker?" he murmured.

"Yes," the voice murmured back. "You have the stuff?"

"It's a suitcase in the trunk of my car. License number—"

"I know which one it is," Kicker interrupted. "We saw you come in. Is Jasmine Broom with you?"

Corwin shook his head fractionally. "No, she went to Archway to help Lorne."

There was a short silence. "Did she, now," Kicker said. "Interesting."

Corwin frowned. "Why is that interesting?"

"Never mind," Kicker said. "Any trick to getting the things in place?"

"I don't know," Corwin said, his mind still on his niece. Did Kicker know something about Jin that he didn't? "Each one comes in two pieces that fit together underneath—"

"Yeah, yeah, I got it," Kicker interrupted again. "Sit tight—we'll get the stuff and go. Your car got a code or a clicker?"

"Both," Corwin said, thinking fast. Talking quietly with the man at the next table wasn't likely to draw unwanted attention. Handing over the clicker for a car, though, definitely would. "The code will probably be easier—six-one-one-five-eight-three. You want me to come with you and give it a test?"

"No, we got it," Kicker said.

"You sure?" Corwin persisted. "I only had a description to work from, and—"

He broke off as a muffled and distant crashing sound momentarily silenced all conversation in the bar. "What was that?" he asked.

There was no answer. He hesitated, then turned around to see why Kicker had gone quiet.

The table behind him was unoccupied. Kicker wasn't there.

What *was* there, all the way across the room by the door, was a curved panel set in the wall.

Corwin turned back around . . . and only now did he finally notice the similar panel behind the bar in line with the table Sedgley had chosen for them.

A cleverly disguised parabolic sound reflector.

Whistling Waller's wasn't just a name. It was, in fact, a description.

He started as Sedgley came up from the side and set his mug on the table in front of him. "You two have a good chat?" he asked.

"I assume so," Corwin said. "It was over pretty fast. Any idea what that noise was a minute ago?"

Sedgley grunted as he took a swallow. "I don't know," he said, his voice muffled by the mug. "But odds are it was your niece."

❖   ❖   ❖

Jin arrived at Smith's Forge just after six, an hour before Sedgley had estimated that he, Corwin, and Kicker Pierce would be able to rendezvous at the bar. She would have preferred getting there earlier, but wasn't sure she could wander around aimlessly longer than that without drawing attention.

As it turned out, even a single hour of anonymity proved to be overoptimistic. She had barely parked the aircar and entered one of the shopping areas when she became aware that she was being watched.

Though not aggressively so, or even very obviously. The watchers—there always seemed to be two at a time—never got in her way, never got in her face, never even approached her. They were just *there*, hovering at the edge of her vision, trying to stay just beyond the corner of her eye. More than once the only time she was able to spot them at all was by using her vision enhancements on window reflections to give her a glimpse of who was behind her.

She puzzled at it for the first few minutes, wondering why they didn't just move in on her. They were in civilian clothing, so her first thought was that perhaps they were Dominion Marines trying to fit in among the locals. Her second thought was more sobering: that they were instead regular civilians whom Reivaro had persuaded to spy for him. Either way, they could be keeping their distance simply because no one who wasn't wearing a Marine combat suit wanted to tangle with a Cobra.

They were ten minutes into the silent game when she suddenly realized what they were *really* up to.

They already had her pegged. What they wanted was a list of her allies, either people she'd come to

Smith's Forge to contact or people she was there to recruit. They wanted to know who else might be ready to fight back against Dominion martial law.

And once she realized that, her response was obvious.

She didn't dare approach any of the actual citizens, of course—the Dominion would snatch them up and have them under interrogation within the hour. But what she *could* do was pretend to leave messages, make vague hand signals to unseen persons, or gaze out into space as if someone was sending signals to her.

She spent the next three-quarters of an hour doing just that. For a while it actually became almost fun, with her gazing into nowhere and watching the reflections of the watchers trying to figure out what she was looking at. She moved back and forth through the shopping district, going into many of the smaller stores to browse and joining the rest of the shoppers walking along the brightly lit pedestrian alleyways. One of the buildings was of particular interest: an abandoned wooden structure at the edge of the main district that had probably been some kind of showroom, its windows fogged by dirt, its sagging roof supported by slender and stress-bowed interior columns. It was slated for demolition and replacement some time in the future—there was an official-looking notice on the door—but for the moment it looked like it would be the ideal spot for a clandestine meeting. Jin took full advantage of that impression, passing by the building three times and pausing to peer through various of its windows twice.

The watchers were pretending not to recognize her, of course. What struck her as odd was that none of the ordinary citizens she passed seemed to recognize

her, either. At first she put it down to her dirty and
rumpled appearance, the result of spending the night
wedged up in the branches of a tall tree outside
town. But after a couple of wide-eyed children were
abruptly shushed and redirected by their parents she
realized that those who *did* recognize her were also
pretending very hard that they didn't.

She hoped that was because they were on her side
and were trying to keep her secret intact. More likely,
though, they simply didn't want to get involved with
her, either for or against.

She'd been playing slow-motion fox to the Dominion's
hounds for nearly an hour when the hounds finally made
a move of their own.

Her first hint was when she noticed that the set
of watchers at the edge of her vision to her right
had suddenly grown from two to four, with a similar
grouping appearing off to her left. Unlike the previous
shadows, these were dressed in bulkier outfits, with
long coats and barrel-like chests.

Which strongly implied that these new watchers
weren't just citizens or civilian-dressed Dominion
folk. These were fully armed, fully armored Marines,
and after watching her in vain for an hour, they were
ready to take her down.

And so, mindful of the meeting between Kicker and
Corwin that was hopefully going on across town, the
meeting she'd come here to distract attention from,
Jin jumped to the top of the nearest building, leaped
across the street straight over the heads of the closest
group of Marines, and headed off across the rooftops
at a dead run.

It was one thing to catch an opponent flat-footed. It

was something quite different to catch him unprepared. Unfortunately, while the Dominion might be the first, it was definitely not the second. Jin had only made it to her second roof when three aircars blazed into view overhead, two of them dropping down to flank her at eye-level, the other swooping ahead in front of her with the apparent goal of forcing her to stop.

Which she did, but only long enough to duck under the aircar to her left and angle off toward that edge of her current rooftop.

She had jumped the street to the next building and had taken a few running steps across it by the time the aircars regrouped and caught up with her. This time, they crowded significantly closer and lower, nearly brushing her elbows and flying low enough that even a champion limbo dancer wouldn't be able to get beneath them.

So, naturally, this time she went up and over, choosing the one to her right, leaping over the vehicle in a pole-vaulter's horizontal roll.

The pilot was quick on the uptake, popping the aircar upward as she flew over him in an attempt to knock her off of her ballistic arc. But the vehicle's inertia made the maneuver a shade too slow, and she escaped with just a slight nudge to her stomach. Again, she headed toward the edge of the roof; again, the aircars changed course and reformed their box around her.

If they kept this up, she knew, sooner or later they would get her. The buildings in this part of town were all one- and two-story structures, low enough for the drivers and pedestrians below to watch the dramatic chase, too low for a proper wall-bounce maneuver. Of course, at this height a simple jump was all she needed to get her safely down to street level, but there was also no chance of her pursuers losing track of her in the process.

Besides, the last thing she wanted to do was try to mix with the people below. If and when the Marines decided there was no longer any point in trying to take her alive, she didn't want innocent civilians caught at the end of a laser barrage.

Fortunately, she still had one move up her sleeve. Just across the street to her right was the abandoned showroom she'd already passed several times before. The one building in the area she knew that she could force the aircars into without damaging useful real estate or risking injury to anyone inside.

The aircars were catching on to her tricks now, and it took some fancy footwork on Jin's part to get away from them the crucial third time. But she made it, and a moment later she was headed straight for the showroom. As the aircars once again reformed, she leaned into her run, putting on a burst of speed that left her pursuers momentarily in her wake. She could hear them revving, adding speed of their own, as she reached the edge of the building and jumped.

Only this time the plan wasn't to simply land on the roof. As she reached the top of her arc, she swung her left leg in a tight circle in front of her, using her antiarmor laser to cut a hole in the dilapidated roofing material and the wood beneath it. She finished the hole just as her arc brought her to that spot, and as the plug fell away and dropped into the building, she dropped in right behind it. Her nanocomputer took over, waggling her arms to readjust her legs into landing position for the extra distance involved in a two-floor drop. She watched the floor coming up at her, her audios cocked for the sound of one or more of the pursuing aircars slamming into the showroom's side.

The hoped-for crash hadn't come by the time she hit the floor. Her knees bent to take the impact, her feet bobbling slightly on some of the debris scattered across the floor before she finalized her balance. She straightened up, looking around.

And froze. Facing her a dozen meters away was a semicircle of five combat-suited Marines.

For a frozen moment no one moved. Jin's eyes flicked across the blank faceplates, her mind as frozen as the tableau. How could they possibly have known she would be coming in here?

The Marine in the center—a sergeant, she noted distantly—stirred. "You people are so stupid," he said, his voice sounding mechanical and inhuman through his helmet's speaker. "Did you really think we hadn't noticed your interest in this place?"

Jin took a deep breath. *Stall*, she reminded herself. *Keep their focus here on me*. "Of course you noticed," she told him. "That was the whole idea."

"Really," the sergeant said, and Jin could imagine a sardonic smile behind the faceplate. "You *wanted* us to anticipate you would come in here trying to escape?" Deliberately, he turned his head to either side, waving a hand that took in the entirety of the empty building. "Yes, I can see all the allies you had waiting for your counterattack."

"You're right, I don't have any allies in here," Jin agreed. "But you should remember that, kilo for kilo, there are a lot more of us on Aventine than there are of you."

"Ah—frontier wit and wisdom," the sergeant said. "Goes well on tombstones. Unfortunately for you, it's not true. For all the show you made over the past hour of pretending to contact fellow malcontents, we have yet to see evidence that you actually talked or sent messages to anyone."

"Maybe you just saw what you wanted to see." There was a sound from above her, and Jin looked up to see one of the aircars that had been pursuing her float lazily over the hole she'd made.

And with her eyes turned upward, she put a quick targeting lock on the centers of each of the four stress-bowed pillars holding up the roof.

"No, I don't think so," the sergeant said. "I think you knew we were on to you. I also think that the real reason you're here is to be a diversion."

Jin's heart froze. If they'd already taken Corwin and Kicker—

"Really was a waste of time," the sergeant continued. "We've got more than enough men to keep an eye on you *and* your son."

The hard band that had wrapped around Jin's chest eased a little. Did that mean they *weren't* on to Corwin and Kicker? "I wouldn't underestimate Lorne if I were you," she said, her eyes dropping from the Marine's faceplate to the deadly epaulets on his shoulders. The little computers operating those lasers were supposed to only go automatic when they sensed an imminent attack. Theoretically, what she was about to do didn't fit that algorithm.

But the Marines could also trigger the lasers manually. The crucial question was whether she could make her move before they had time to react.

There was, unfortunately, only one way to find out.

"I wouldn't underestimate *us* if I were you," the sergeant retorted. "You little dirtwater worlds are all alike—"

Spinning around, Jin turned her back on them and took two quick steps, as if she was trying to make a run for it. On the third step, she threw herself forward at the floor, twisting around in midair to land on her back, her arms and legs flailing as if she'd tripped over something and the fall was an accident.

And as her legs swung upward, moving far out of line with any of the Marines and their counterattack sensors, she triggered her antiarmor laser.

Her nanocomputer took over, lining up her left leg on one of the pillars, firing a bolt into the sagging material, then shifting to the next, firing, and shifting to the next, the whole procedure taking barely half a second. With a multiple splintering *snap*, the pillars shattered, and the air filled with a grinding roar as the roof disintegrated and tumbled toward the humans gathered below.

The Marines were caught flat-footed, with nowhere to go and nothing they could do except drop into low crouches and brace themselves against the avalanche of debris tumbling toward them. Jin, with no helmet or combat suit, couldn't afford to ride it out.

But lying flat on the floor, she had an option the Marines didn't. Quickly bending her left knee upwards, pulling the foot close in toward her body, she fired one final laser shot straight down into the floor, blasting a hole through the tile and wood. Then, bracing her heel on the edge of the hole, she threw power to her servos and convulsively straightened out the knee, sending herself sliding on her back toward the wall behind her.

It almost worked. The wall she had aimed at remained standing, at least at the bottom, and she only bumped her head a little as she slammed into it. But the roof was in worse shape than she'd thought, and when it went, it *all* went. Even as she skidded to a tooth-jarring halt at the wall, a broken section of roof support beam slammed down on her amid a choking cloud of splinters and dust.

Fortunately, the beam landed across her legs, where they could bruise her skin but not threaten any vital organs. Squeezing her eyes shut against the dust, she keyed her opticals, using the enhanced vision to guide her fingertip lasers as she sliced the beam into manageable pieces. Pushing the last piece away, she started to struggle upward—

And jerked in surprise as a pair of hands grabbed her upper arms and hauled her the rest of the way to her feet. "You all right?" a voice wheezed in her ear.

With a supreme effort Jin stifled the reflexive twist-spin-and-fire maneuver she'd been about to execute. The Dominion wouldn't bother to ask how she was. "I'm fine," she said, starting a more reasonable turn. The gripping hands released her, and she finished the turn to find herself looking at an unshaven young man, the red ring of one of the Dominion's so-called insignia neckbands peeking out from his collar. "Are *you* all right?" she asked, frowning at his pinched face.

"It's just the dust," he said. "Nice move, by the way."

"Thanks," she said, looking back over her shoulder. Through the mass of swirling dust the five Marines were barely visible, lying unmoving amid the debris.

They looked dead, but a quick shift to infrared confirmed they were still giving off normal human heat signatures.

"Don't worry, they should be okay," the Cobra assured her darkly. "Not that they deserve it. Not after what they did at Archway."

"Were you there?" Jin asked, turning back to him. "Did you see what happened?"

"No, but I heard all about it afterward."

"So did I," Jin said. "My point is that neither of us knows whether or not any of these Marines were involved. If they weren't, they don't deserve to die." She gave a little shrug. "Maybe the ones who were involved don't, either. That's for a court to decide."

"If we ever get them that far."

"We will," Jin said. "And when we do, we need to make sure we're the ones holding the high moral ground. That means keeping killing to a minimum."

"Yeah, you tell *them* that," the Cobra growled, his eyes flashing hatred toward the unconscious Marines. "Come on, let's get you out of here."

He turned and headed down the street at a brisk walk. The pedestrians and cars, Jin noted as she hurried to catch up, had magically vanished from the area. "My aircar's the other direction," she told him.

"You mean the aircar they already know about?" the Cobra said pointedly. "Lucky for you, we've got another one set up. Brand new—well, brand-new used, anyway—registered to a local woman who looks a lot like you. I'll take you to it, and then you get the hell out of town. In here."

He turned and walked into an open shop door. Jin glanced back at the demolished building as she followed, catching a glimpse of the three Dominion aircars burning belatedly back toward the scene. Apparently, whoever was in charge of air support and the herding of the rogue Cobra Jasmine Moreau had decided his job was finished and headed for home.

His meeting with Colonel Reivaro later tonight, she guessed, would not be a pleasant one.

The car they'd gotten her was an older model, without any bells or whistles, and looked like it was on its last legs. But the engine ran smoothly, the interior was clean, and the face on the registration tag did indeed look like a slightly older version of Jin herself.

Perfect.

"You got somewhere to go?" her guide asked as he opened the garage door for her. "Not that I want to know," he added hastily. "The less I know the better."

"I've got a couple of options," Jin assured him. "Thanks again."

"No problem." He fixed her with a stern look. "You just watch yourself, okay? You and your son are sort of like heroes to everyone out here. Reivaro's going to want to slap you down, and fast."

"I'll be careful," Jin said. "And don't worry. If this works out like we're hoping, the Dominion will soon have a lot more headaches than just Lorne and me."

The Cobra grunted. "We can hope. Good luck."

A minute later Jin was driving down the streets of Smith's Forge, blending in with the rest of the town's vehicular traffic. Ten minutes after that, she had passed through one of the gates in the outer fence and was on the main road to Archway.

Yes, there were several options in front of her. But there was only one that she wanted to take.

Unfortunately, it wasn't the one she knew she *had* to take.

Archway was where her son was, and where he was in danger. She desperately wanted to go to him, to offer her help with whatever scheme he had planned.

But the minute she set foot there, the Dominion would be on to her. Probably even before she arrived—Reivaro was surely smart enough to know that his center of power was her most likely destination and have his men waiting.

And even if she somehow managed to find Lorne without bringing the Marines down on him, how much could she realistically help? Her whole body was aching from the workout she'd just put it through, and with her arthritis and anemia it would take more than a few hours for the pain and weakness to go away. About all she could do for Lorne was to get in his way and slow him down.

So Archway was out. Lorne was out.

But there was one other place she might try. A place where Reivaro might not expect her to go. The place where this whole thing had started.

Capitalia.

That was where Commodore Santores came when he wanted to meet with Chintawa and the rest of the Cobra Worlds leaders. That was where new Dominion edicts and orders were distributed from.

And that was where Paul would be brought if and when Santores and the MindsEye were finished with him. When that happened, Jin intended to be waiting for him.

And he'd better be alive and well. Because if he wasn't, they would be sorry. *Very* sorry.

The *Dorian*'s injured had been transported down to Qasama, along with the cadre of medics and support staff Dr. Lancaster had sent to assist, and against all reasonable odds, every one of the casualties had survived the transfer. The Qasaman doctors and surgeons had begun their work, and Omnathi had contacted Barrington to say he'd been assured that none of the injuries were beyond their skill. Barrington had thanked him and, three hours after the official end of his watch, he'd finally turned CoNCH over to Filho and retired to his cabin for some long overdue sleep.

He'd sent his aide, Lieutenant Cottros Meekan, to get a sandwich from the officers' mess when a specially flagged preliminary report came in.

Five minutes later, Barrington was back in CoNCH.

"We didn't spot it right away," Filho said, gesturing to the sensor records he'd pulled up. "It was only when we got down to a detailed analysis that I noticed it. Even then, as you can see, our first orbital pass wasn't quite on the right angle to get a good view."

"We get anything on subsequent passes?" Barrington asked.

"No, sir," Filho said, bringing up another image alongside the first. "By the time we came back around, it was completely concealed. But that one picture, plus the neutrino emission profile, gives us an eighty-five-percent probability that that is indeed the *Squire*."

Barrington felt his hands curl into fists at his sides. The *Squire*. One of the *Algonquin*'s courier ships, the one Santores had sent to Caelian to bring back Governor Uy.

And which, according to the reports the *Hermes* had brought to him from Aventine, was overdue on its return. At the time the *Hermes* headed out to return to the *Dorian*, in fact, no one knew what was causing the delay.

Apparently, the delay was being caused by the *Squire* no longer being in Cobra Worlds space.

Only how in the name of hell was it *here*?

Barrington's original multi-band broadcast to Qasama on the *Dorian's* arrival had hit all the Dominion's usual frequencies. If Lieutenant Commander Tamu was alive, well, and in command of his ship, he should have heard the hail and responded.

But the other likely scenario—that the *Squire* had somehow been captured—was absurd. How could anyone on Caelian, with even fewer weapons and resources to draw on than the central government on Aventine, have taken down a Dominion of Man courier ship? Subterfuge? Incompetence? Treachery? Treason?

"I had to put it on the data stream," Filho said into Barrington's thoughts. "But I figured no one would really notice it for at least a few more hours."

Barrington nodded. Which was why the weapons officer had flagged it for his captain and not for any of the other officers. He'd wanted to give Barrington some time to draw his conclusions and come up with proposed responses before Castenello got hold of the news.

It was a nice and slightly improper gesture. Only in this case, it was probably wasted.

Because Barrington hadn't the foggiest idea what to do.

Had the *Squire* come here willingly? In that case, why hadn't Tamu signaled him when the *Dorian* first arrived? Had the courier been brought here against Tamu's will? Seizing a Dominion ship was technically an act of war, and Barrington had no doubt that Castenello would see it precisely that way and demand that a military response be launched.

Only what action could Barrington bring with over a hundred of his men currently in Qasaman hands? Even if the Qasamans themselves were too civilized to make war on injured men, the very fact that the men were on the ground made them effectively enemy hostages.

"Captain?"

Barrington turned around. Meekan was standing a few paces behind him, the sandwich container Barrington had sent him for hanging loosely and probably forgotten in his hand. "Yes, Lieutenant?"

"My apologies for the impertinence, sir," Meekan said, his eyes on the images. "I was just wondering if the *Squire* might have run into the same sort of trouble we did on the way here. In that case, perhaps there was no response from Commander Tamu or his men because they're also undergoing medical treatment."

"Then why didn't Omnathi tell us that when we first contacted him?" Filho countered.

"Possibly because I never asked," Barrington said, stroking a finger absently across his lip. The *Squire* couldn't have hit the same net the *Hermes* had, not starting from Caelian. But there was no reason their attackers couldn't have set up a second net on that vector. If the net had included only spider ships and no main-line warships, the courier could conceivably have emerged from the encounter damaged but able to make it to Qasama. If Commander Tamu had obtained the coordinates from Uy or someone else on Caelian, he might well have opted to keep going rather than turn back to Aventine.

In which case, what Filho had spotted down there might have been merely the Qasamans in the process of putting the *Squire* in repair dock, with no deliberate attempt to hide the courier from the *Dorian*'s view.

It was possible. It was also damned unlikely.

But again, even if the Qasamans were pulling a fast one, and he could prove it, what were his options?

"We need more information," he said, tapping briefly into the data stream and confirming that Filho had only uploaded the raw data of the neutrino emissions, not the suggestion that the source of the neutrino emissions might be a Dominion spacecraft. "I want full scans of the planet, concentrating on the area where these emissions are coming from. Until we have at least a ninety-percent ID, you're to hold off on any conclusions as to the nature of the source."

"Understood, sir," Filho said, a bit uncertainly. "Let me remind the captain that it wouldn't take much effort for anyone else to reach the same conclusion I did."

"But only if they notice it," Barrington pointed out. "With all the other Qasaman information in the data stream, there's a good chance no one will, at least for a few more days." He shrugged. "If they do, I'll deal with it then."

"Yes, sir," Filho said, clearly still not happy. Still, the man had been in the service long enough to know how this sort of thing worked. Maybe he was merely surprised at the fact that Barrington, who usually shunned such games, had suddenly decided to set foot in that arena. "One other thing, sir. I've been looking at some of the weapons-lock data from the last engagement, and something odd caught my eye. None of the enemy vessels, neither the spiders nor the bigger warships, had any identification markings."

Barrington frowned. "That has to be wrong," he said. "Troft ships *always* carry ID markings."

"I know," Filho said. "But these didn't."

Barrington looked across at the main display. Troft warships had displayed IDs in every battle the Dominion had fought against them. Troft merchant ships displayed IDs; some of them proudly, others grudgingly, but they always had them. Even Troft ships on missions that could be politically embarrassing or inflammatory—such as the attack against Commander Ukuthi at the Hoibie home world—displayed IDs.

Only these hadn't.

Why hadn't they?

"I'm thinking maybe this is the secret Commander Castenello is sitting on," Filho continued. "His claim that we learned nothing more by entering the battle than we would have if we'd kept our distance."

"Very likely," Barrington agreed. "What Castenello perhaps fails to realize is that sometimes the lack of information is as valuable as any actual information could have been. Regardless, this is an intriguing development."

"Agreed, sir," Filho said. "Any orders?"

"Keep at it," Barrington said. "See what else you can glean." He turned to Meekan. "And while he's trawling for data," he added, "I want you, Lieutenant, to go down to Qasama with the next medical supply transport. Commander Kusari is sedated and undergoing surgery right now, but as soon as wakes up I want you there to have him look at this neutrino profile. He should be able to tell us if the profile shows engine damage and, if so, what kind of damage it might be."

"Yes, sir," Meekan said, his eyes flicking to Filho. "Ah . . . there *are* other men aboard who could tell you that, sir."

"A few, yes," Barrington agreed. "But Kusari came up through the ranks on courier-size engines. There are only two or three others aboard with his same level of experience."

A brief, almost imperceptible glance of understanding flickered between Filho and Meekan. Others might know as much as Kusari, but they were all lower-ranking and couldn't be trusted to keep their mouths shut. "Understood, Captain," Meekan said. Unlike Filho, there was no uncertainty in his voice. "With your permission, I'll return to my quarters and get a shore kit." He looked down at his hand, as if suddenly noticing the sandwich. "Shall I leave your sandwich in your cabin?"

"No, I'll take it now," Barrington said, looking back at the display. "I think I'll stay here a little longer."

He nodded toward the display. "I'm thinking that if the IDs were scraped off or painted over, there's a chance we might be able to pull up at least a partial marking. Commander?"

"Could be, sir," Filho said. "Let's give it a try."

CHAPTER NINETEEN

They could, Paul thought more than once during the journey, have at least given him the dignity of allowing him to walk.

But Captain Lij Tulu was in a hurry, and Paul moved all too slowly these days. And in Lij Tulu's defense, even Paul had to admit that the Dominion warships were *big*.

And so he submitted to the indignity of being wheeled on a medical gurney from the *Algonquin's* sick bay to the lifts, to the hangar bay, into a landing shuttle, across to the *Megalith's* bay, and onto a reverse course that he expected would end him up in the *Megalith's* own sick bay.

Only it didn't. Instead of the warship's sick bay, they ended up on its bridge.

It was a huge place, far bigger than Paul expected, though in hindsight he realized that he should have known that a ship this big would have a bridge of commensurate size. The place was a full two decks high, with control balconies encircling holographic displays, and a bewildering multitude of flat monitors and readout panels on the bulkheads, the whole area crammed with uniformed men and buzzing with the hum of quiet conversation.

On the upper level, on a balcony overlooking the men and stations of the deck below, Commodore Santores was waiting for them.

"Captain," the commodore said gravely, nodding to Lij Tulu as the tech maneuvered Paul's gurney through the floor's outer areas and brought him to a halt at the command station. "Cobra Broom," he added, shifting his gaze down to Paul. "My apologies for disturbing your recovery. But a situation has arisen in which I find myself in need of your assistance."

For a moment Paul considered reminding him that it was the damn MindsEye and Santores himself who had made his recovery necessary in the first place. But there was nothing to gain with recriminations, especially when everyone present already knew about them. "I'm listening," he said instead.

"Nine days ago one of my courier ships, the *Squire*, failed to return from a mission to Caelian," Santores said. "When Governor Uy refused to shed any light on its disappearance, I ordered a complete grid-scan to be made of the planet. The ships tasked with that mission have now returned, bringing with them the information that the *Squire* is no longer on Caelian. At least, not in its original form."

"What makes you think the Caelians had anything to do with it?" Paul asked. "Maybe the ship had an accident en route."

"Oh, the Caelians are involved, all right," Santores said in a voice that sent a shiver up Paul's back. "And

I want to know exactly how. Since courtesy has gained us nothing, I intend to move the conversation to the next level."

"That level being?"

"I'm taking the *Megalith* to Caelian," Santores said. "I will ask Governor Uy—once again, politely—what he's done with the *Squire*. If he continues his refusal to answer, there will be consequences. *Military* consequences."

Paul looked into Santores's eyes, another shiver running through him. At that moment, gazing into those eyes, he had no doubt whatsoever that the commodore meant it. "You said you needed my help," he said, forcing his voice to stay calm.

"You're coming with me," Santores said. "As a friend of Governor Uy, your job will be to make sure he understands fully that I mean what I say."

"If he doesn't believe me?"

Santores smiled, a humorless, dark curve of the lips. "You had better hope that he does," he said. "For his sake. And for the sake of his world."

For a moment the only sound was the murmur of background conversation. Then Santores raised his eyes to Lij Tulu. "Captain, I'm leaving you in command of Aventine," he said. "Keep the work going, especially the transport armor-plating project. We need those ships ready for war as soon as possible."

"Yes, sir," Lij Tulu said. "I assume the work has top priority?"

"Absolutely," Santores confirmed. "And keep a close eye outward. If any Trofts enter the system, I want to know who they are and what they want."

"If they refuse to cooperate?"

Santores looked down at Paul. "I'm tired of not being cooperated with," he said quietly.

"Understood," Lij Tulu said grimly. "I'll make sure they do."

"Good." Santores looked across the bridge. "Return to your ship, Captain. The *Megalith* will be leaving orbit in two hours."

It was another two days' worth of dreams and dizziness before Merrick finally and truly woke up.

This time, along with being thirsty, he was famished.

Though maybe the hunger was just a result of the delectable aromas from the covered dishes on the small table beside his bed. Beside the table, Anya sat quietly in a chair, her eyes closed in thought or meditation or sleep. "Hello," Merrick croaked. His voice sounded just as raspy as it had been two days ago, he noted, but at least there was no longer any fringe of craziness about it.

Anya's eyes opened. "Hello," she said, studying his face. "How do you feel?"

"In my right mind, finally," Merrick said. "I hope you haven't been sitting here this whole time."

She shook her head. "An hour only. I brought food for when you woke up."

"You knew when that would be?"

"We know the effects of bersark poisoning very well," she said gravely. "Though you were slower than most to awaken."

Merrick glanced around. There was no one else in the room. "Off-world biochemistry, probably," he murmured, pushing himself up into a sitting position. "That smells good. I hope you brought some water, too."

"I did," she said, reaching down and producing a bottle that had been sitting on the floor beside her chair. "We've already eaten. This is all for you, if you want it."

It was just as well that Merrick wasn't being asked to share. Over the next quarter hour he proceeded to demolish the entire meat casserole, vegetable mix, and bread that Anya had brought, as well as drinking the entire bottle of water. Apparently, it *hadn't* just been the aroma.

And while he ate, Anya brought him up to date on what had happened over the past six days.

"We were brought here after midnight on the night you left us," she said. "I was afraid Ludolf Treetapper would kill Master Kjoic—"

"You mean your father?" Merrick asked around a mouthful of warm lamb or mutton or something sheepy-tasting. "Ludolf Treetapper, your father?"

Her lip twitched. "My father," she agreed reluctantly. "He told me that you had said not to kill Master Kjoic, so he tried to get him to leave. But he refused, stating that you were also his slave and he would not abandon his property to sickness."

"Interesting point of view," Merrick commented. "Like I said, he must be new to the slave business."

"Perhaps," Anya said. "Ludolf has a base near here, but he could of course not take a master there. He thus persuaded Alexis Woolmaster to allow us to use her home and ranch."

"Your father tells me Kjoic considers them to also be his slaves now," Merrick said, frowning. *Ranch?* He'd been under the impression they were still in the forest. What kind of livestock could Alexis be keeping out here? "Has Ludolf been able to explain otherwise?"

"He hasn't tried." Anya's throat worked. "Ludolf wishes to see what the masters are doing in the building at the edge of Svipall. When he learned that Master Kjoic also wants to see inside, he concluded that might be his best chance of gaining access."

"Which is more or less what I've been assuming," Merrick said grimly. "Only I realize now that it's not going to be that easy. Kjoic's looking for records on whoever might have killed the crew of his crashed ship, which means he's not going to just waltz in there and ask to see their files. Not when the murderer could be standing right there. *Especially* not with a crowd of slaves in tow."

"I don't believe Ludolf planned to be so obvious," Anya said, a little crossly. "I believe he plans to enter the building late at night, when there will be fewer of the masters inside and on guard."

"What makes him think that the place quiets down at night?"

"He has observed vehicles arriving at sunrise and leaving at dusk," Anya said. "They land beyond the fence in the village and go through large doors into the building."

"And what makes him think they're carrying masters and not just supplies?"

"Because—" Anya broke off. "They were of a style that carry passengers," she continued more slowly. "But that doesn't say there were passengers aboard, does it?"

"Not really," Merrick said. "I might also point out that that kind of building is usually for manufacturing, at least the ones I've seen have been. In that case, the aircars might be bringing in raw materials in the morning and taking out finished product at night."

"And not masters at all?"

"There might also be some turnover of staff involved," Merrick conceded. "Though if there are passengers, they might also be of the non-master sort. The Games seem to be a pretty big deal in Svipall—maybe those are new contestants they're flying in."

"They do not hold the Games every day," Anya said, her forehead creased in thought. "Only once in each six. But why would they put a manufacturing plant by a simple Muninn village? Would it not be better in Runatyr or one of the other large cities?"

"There must be some resource nearby they needed," Merrick said, checking his nanocomputer's clock. If there had been a Games session the night he ran into the bersark patch... "That, or they want to keep it quiet and out of the spotlight. You said the Games were held every six days?"

"Yes," Anya said. "There was one the night you were poisoned, and another tonight."

"Well, then, there's our chance," Merrick said, spooning up his final mouthful of casserole. "I go to Svipall tonight, and while everyone's distracted by the Games, I sneak into the building and see what they're up to."

He expected Anya to light up with the straightforward cleverness of the idea. Instead, he got a complete stone face. "What?" he growled. "You don't like it?"

"You tried that plan once already," she reminded him. "You were nearly killed."

"I made a mistake," Merrick said. "I won't make it again."

"And if you make another?"

"Then I'll take another six days to recover and be right on time to try it again."

Her stone face went a little stonier. "That is not funny."

Merrick winced. "Sorry. The point is that this is our best shot. I can sneak in, see what they're doing, and get back out again. And if I'm *really* lucky, along the way I may spot a safe way to get Master Kjoic and your father in later on."

"And if you are captured?"

"I won't be," Merrick said. He peered into the empty casserole dish, decided regretfully that there wasn't anything more he could get out of it, and set it back on the table. "Come on, let's talk to your father." He stood up and took her arm.

To his surprise, she pulled back from his grip. "You go," she said. "I must return the dishes, and help clean them."

"You're kidding," Merrick said, frowning at her as he keyed on his infrareds. Her facial blood flow indicated tension. A *lot* of tension. "Come on, that can wait. I want your advice on whatever plan we come up with."

"I thought you already had a plan."

"I do," Merrick said. "But Ludolf may have modifications to suggest."

"It's your plan," Anya said. "You may simply tell him that."

On in other words, she didn't really want to face her father?

Merrick sighed. But he couldn't say he was all that surprised. Whatever had happened between Anya and her parents over the past six days, reconciliation apparently hadn't been part of it. "Fine," he said, letting his hand drop from her arm. "I'll see you later."

He found Ludolf sitting on a bench by the west wall of the house, gazing out at probably fifty sheep grazing on the grassy plants carpeting the floor between the trees. "Anya had said this was Alexis's ranch," Merrick commented as he came over and stood beside the older man. "I assumed she was mistaken, or using a different meaning of the word."

"Where else did you think Alexis Tucker obtained her wool from?" Ludolf countered.

"I suppose," Merrick conceded, noting again Ludolf's use of Alexis's older and less distinguished name. Clearly, the man hadn't done any polishing of his diplomatic skills over the past couple of days. "So what keeps the forest predators from walking in and eating them? I don't see any fences anywhere."

"You've already seen one example of the fence she uses," Ludolf said. "Bordering Alexis Tucker's land is a thin strip of bersark. Most animals have learned to leave such areas strictly alone."

"Can't say I disagree with them," Merrick said, shivering at the memory. "What about the fafirs? They should be able to just go over the bersark patches."

"They can," Ludolf said. "But sheep are one of the few herbivores that can ingest bersark without being affected by it, but also do not completely break it down. That leaves a slight scent of the poison on their breath, which fafirs and other tree-hunting animals recognize and avoid."

"Nice," Merrick said. "If you could find a way to get the stuff on your own breath without killing yourselves, you'd never have to worry about forest travel again."

"Perhaps." Ludolf peered up at him. "I assume you are finally recovered from your own poisoning?"

"I am," Merrick said. "And I have an idea."

Ludolf favored him with a sort of half-smile. "Tell me," he invited.

Merrick had expected Ludolf to balk at the thought of sending an unknown, untrained, untested spy into the Troft compound. To his surprise, the man loved it.

"An excellent plan," Ludolf said after Merrick had laid it out for him. "Do you intend to enter the village the same way you did the last time?"

"Basically," Merrick said, a sobering thought suddenly occurring to him. He'd assumed Ludolf had pressed him earlier about his capabilities because Anya had given him a few hints, if not told him outright. Now, belatedly, he wondered if it had in fact been that Ludolf had been in the woods the whole time, with a front-row view of Merrick's strength-enhanced entrance and exit from Svipall.

Maybe he could find out. "I'll need to find a replacement vaulting pole, though," he said, keying his infrareds and focusing on Ludolf's face. "I lost my other one on the way out of Svipall."

Ludolf's facial blood flow didn't change. "You had no such assist when we saw you leave the village," he said. "Nor did you need one."

"That's because I had bersark pounding through my muscles on the way out," Merrick reminded him. "I won't have that enhanced strength this time around."

He held his breath, mentally crossing his fingers. If Ludolf had seen him enter Svipall and knew that was a lie . . .

But again, there was no change in the older man's

infrared pattern. Apparently, Ludolf and his team had only caught Merrick's exit, not his entrance. "I can find you a pole," he promised. "What else will you need from us?"

"Nothing," Merrick said. "No—on second thought, I need you to make sure Master Kjoic doesn't know I've recovered."

"Indeed," Ludolf said, nodding. "He's already made it clear that as soon as you are well he means to press on with his journey. I will keep him occupied and unaware." His lip twisted. "It's an odd feeling, being slaves again. But this time, at least, we know there's an end in sight."

"Ah," Merrick said. "I gather you've been out here in the forest ever since your failed revolt twelve years ago?"

Ludolf's face hardened. "The revolt did not fail, Merrick Hopekeeper," he said stiffly. "What failed was merely a single battle of that revolt. We *will* throw off the masters' oppression and regain our freedom."

"I hope so," Merrick said. "Let me go get myself cleaned up and maybe find some fresh clothing. Is there an official starting time for the Games?"

"The masters usually wait until after sundown," Ludolf said. "It will be safest to enter after that."

Merrick wrinkled his nose. Probably true... except that he needed at least enough light in the sky to use his infrared trick for finding the safe path through the bersark. "I think I'd like to get in a little before that," he said. "I want to look over the area before the crowd begins to gather."

Ludolf frowned, but shrugged. "If you think that would be best," he said, standing up. "I'll tell Alexis

Tucker to furnish you with new clothing, and prepare a guide to escort you to Svipall."

Merrick frowned. He'd assumed that with a mission this important Ludolf would want to be there to watch. "You're not leading me yourself?"

"Master Kjoic has become accustomed to his chief slave being available at all times." Ludolf placed a hand on his chest. "For now, I am that slave. As we've already agreed, we do not wish him wondering why the routine has suddenly changed."

"True," Merrick said, focusing again on the other's face. "So you're going to just hang around here playing slave while I go into Svipall?"

"Were you not listening?" Ludolf growled. "I am Master Kjoic's chief slave. I must remain here to serve him."

"Right," Merrick murmured. It was perfectly reasonable, of course.

So why was Ludolf's facial blood flow indicating sudden stress?

"Come," Ludolf said, gesturing to the door. "I'll take you to where you can clean up." He smiled faintly. "I suspect you may also wish another meal soon. While you eat, and while Alexis Tucker prepares your new clothing, I can tell you what I know about Svipall's people, buildings, and terrain."

"It all sounds very good," Merrick agreed. "Especially the eating part. Lead on."

CHAPTER TWENTY

The darkness slowly faded, slowly enough that Jody didn't even notice anything had changed until the light was already pressing against her eyelids.

She'd expected to feel lousy. Tired and sore, or maybe just plain sore. But she felt neither. As far as she could tell without moving or opening her eyes, she was just fine.

There had to be a catch somewhere.

Carefully, suspiciously, she opened her eyes.

To find herself lying flat on her back, the faces of Kemp and Smitty looming over her.

So it had worked. Isis had functioned like it was supposed to, and Jody was now a Cobra. And her friends had come to be with her at her awakening, just as Kemp had said they would.

Only their faces weren't the smiling ones she'd been promised when she last closed her eyes. The two men were talking quietly together, their expressions grim.

She felt her breath catch in her throat. Had something gone wrong?

The twitch in her breathing had evidently been louder than she'd realized. The conversation broke off in mid-murmur and both men looked down at her. "Well, hi there, sleepyhead," Kemp said, his face finally breaking out in a smile. A relieved smile, Jody noted with some relief of her own. Maybe she wasn't in trouble after all.

Smitty was smiling, too. But his smile was token and mechanical. "How are you feeling?" he asked, his voice as perfunctory as his smile.

"Pretty good," Jody said. "No pain, which I understand is always a plus after surgery."

"This was Qasaman surgery," Kemp reminded her. "I'm told it's a bit more pleasant than the Cobra Worlds variety."

"Good to hear," Jody said. "So what's wrong?"

"Nothing to do with you," Kemp assured her. "The doctor says your procedure went fine, and you'll be ready to start your training tomorrow."

"They've got a good crew picked out for you," Smitty added. "Ghofl Khatir will be heading it—"

"Yeah, thanks, I'm looking forward to it," Jody interrupted. "Now quit stalling and tell me what's wrong. Is it Rashida?" she added, suddenly noticing the other woman's absence. "Has something happened to her?"

"No, she's fine," Smitty said. "Omnathi sent her to Sollas right after you went under Isis and she hasn't gotten back yet."

"Is she in trouble?" Jody asked. She'd always had a feeling that Omnathi had never been truly happy with the tasks Rashida had been forced into during the Troft invasion. In a lot of ways, she knew, Qasaman women were second-class citizens, and Omnathi was as old-school as they came.

"Not that I know of," Smitty said. "Omnathi wanted her to report to the rest of the Shahni about Caelian, the Trofts, and Aventine. She knew as much as anyone except possibly Omnathi, and he was too busy to go."

"Ah," Jody said. Though of course that was what Omnathi had told them. Unfortunately, Omnathi wasn't exactly known for telling the whole truth when the whole truth didn't suit him. If he thought Rashida was getting too cozy with the Caelians—especially Smitty—he might have magically found a job that got her away from them for a few days. "Have you heard from her since she left?"

Smitty shook his head. "We haven't talked, but she sent a couple of messages. I gather they're keeping her pretty busy."

"So I'm fine, and Rashida's fine," Jody said. "You going to make me play Twenty Questions, or are you going to tell me what the problem is?"

Kemp and Smitty exchanged looks. "The problem," Kemp said, looking reluctantly back down at her, "is that we've got some unexpected company. Three days ago, out of the blue, the Dominion of Man War Cruiser *Dorian* came to call."

Jody felt her chest tighten. "The Dominion's *here*? They've found us?"

"Well, they've found Qasama, anyway," Kemp said sourly. "The *Dorian*'s up in orbit as we speak, with about a hundred men in hospitals in Azras and Parma. Apparently, they stopped off for a battle on the way here."

"How lovely for them," Jody murmured, a bitter taste in her mouth. After all she and her family had gone through to protect Qasama from the Dominion, and here they were anyway. "What do they want?"

"As far as I know, all they've asked for is medical aid," Kemp said. "Omnathi said yes, and as I say, they sent down a bunch of badly wounded men and another bunch of support personnel."

"You think that was a pretext to sneak in some spies?" Jody asked.

"I suppose that's possible," Smitty said. "Though I can't see what they could learn at ground level that they can't learn from orbit."

"Not necessarily, given that the Trofts found a few surprises when they got down here," Kemp pointed out. "But the big problem isn't the *Dorian*. It's the *Squire*."

The last bit of fog vanished from Jody's brain. "Oh, no," she murmured.

"Oh, yes," Kemp said grimly. "We don't know if they spotted it, but I know Omnathi didn't get it completely concealed until after their first orbital pass."

"Have they asked about it?"

"Not that I know of," Kemp said. "Unfortunately, no questions either means they *didn't* spot it, which we're all hoping, or they *did* spot it and are being privately suspicious about how it got here."

"What's Omnathi planning to do about it?"

Again, Kemp and Smitty exchanged looks. "I don't know," Kemp said. "But apparently his first move is to get you out of here."

Jody felt her eyes widen. "Excuse me?"

"Because in case you'd forgotten," Kemp said,

ignoring the question, "the *Dorian* is commanded by one Captain Barrington Moreau, kinsman to one Jody Moreau Broom. Omnathi doesn't think letting Captain Moreau find you here with his missing courier ship would be a good idea."

"Well, he's wrong," Jody said flatly. "In fact, he's a hundred eighty degrees wrong. I'm probably the only person on Qasama who *can* talk to Captain Moreau about this."

"And tell him what?" Kemp countered. "That we stole the *Squire*, killing a couple of crewmen along the way, and brought it here for the Qasamans to examine?"

"We tell him the truth," Jody said. "We have to. Sooner or later, he's going to find out, and it'll be a lot better if we come clean before he digs out all the pieces himself."

"I see you grew up with the same kind of father I did," Kemp said with a hint of dark humor. "You always got off with less punishment if you told him you broke the window before he found out on his own."

"But there's no guarantee he's like our fathers," Smitty said. "Anyway, it's not our decision to make."

"Maybe it should be," Jody said. "We're the Dominion's long-lost children. The Qasamans aren't. Well, you know, technically they are, but we're the ones the Dominion specifically sent out here. They're bound to go easier on us than they will on the Qasamans."

"I'm not arguing," Kemp said. "I'm just saying that we're out of the loop on this one."

"Are we?" Lifting her head, Jody peered down her body. Everything looked fine, plus there were no straps or restraints holding her to the bed. Time to give these new Cobra implants a test drive. "You have any idea where Omnathi's communicating with the *Dorian* from?" she asked, putting her palms on the sides of the bed and pushing herself carefully into a sitting position.

"Whoa," Kemp said, putting his hands gently but firmly on her shoulders. "You're not going anywhere. Not until you've had a preliminary run-through. Try it and you'll probably fall flat on your face."

"Okay," Jody said, taking his hands and pushing them away. Her arms felt oddly light, her movements strong and fluid and easy. Briefly, she was tempted to try a little strength experiment, just to see what would happen, but decided against it "Go ahead."

"Go ahead what?" Kemp asked, frowning.

"Go ahead and give me the run-through," she said, swiveling her legs off the bed onto the floor.

"We can't—easy," Kemp interrupted himself, this time taking her upper arm as she started to stand up. "Keep it slow. Let the servos take the load."

"Got it," she said, easing herself up. The movement definitely felt different, she noted, rather like trying to move in a lower gravity field. "Is there any trick to walking?"

"All sorts of them," Kemp said, his hand still on her arm. "Just take it slow and easy. Once around the room, and then you sit down again. Okay?"

"Once around if I trip or fall down; twice around if I don't," Jody bargained.

Kemp rolled his eyes. "*Half* around if you fall down."

"And then we do some strength training," Jody added.

"Jody, we can't do this," Smitty insisted. "There's

a whole six-day regimen involved in teaching new Cobras how to use their gear."

"This is Qasama," Jody reminded him. "They have shorter timetables."

"That *is* the Qasaman timetable," Smitty said patiently. "You're just going to have to take a deep breath and accept that this will take some time."

Jody clenched her hand. Unclenched it quickly as the sheer strength behind the grip dug her fingernails painfully against the skin of her palm. Smitty was right, of course. These things took time.

Only she didn't have time. Certainly not six days' worth. The minute Captain Moreau found out about the *Squire*—"You didn't answer my question about Omnathi's transmitter."

"I have no idea where it is," Kemp said.

"And even if we found it, they're not likely to let us in," Smitty added.

"Then we try the back door," Jody said. "You said they've got wounded in the Azras hospitals?"

"Wait a second, hold on," Kemp protested. "What are you going to do, crash the party?"

"Why not?" Jody said, taking a careful step. It felt a lot like walking in the powered Djinn combat suits she and Rashida had used on Caelian. "They must have a way of communicating with their ship."

"They aren't going to let you talk to the captain," Smitty warned. "And Omnathi isn't going to let you talk to *them*."

"Sure," Jody said. "Actually, I wasn't planning to ask either of them."

Out of the corner of her eye, Jody saw the two Cobras again exchange glances. "Yeah, we kind of figured that," Kemp said. "But you still need to take the time to learn about your new equipment."

"Agreed," Jody said. "You've got six hours."

She'd expected at least a little widening of the eyes in response. She got nothing. Apparently, both of them knew her well enough to have already figured out where she was going. "That's not enough," Kemp warned.

"It was enough during the invasion," Jody said. "I heard the Djinn could be trained that fast."

"That's because they were already used to using the combat suits."

"So am I," Jody countered. "Doesn't matter anyway. We've got to get to Captain Moreau before he calls Omnathi on the *Squire* mess. Six hours is what you've got."

Kemp made a face. "Okay, fine," he said. "Six hours of training, and then we'll run you through some exercises. You get through them without damaging anything or anybody, and we'll declare you competent enough for your latest crazy scheme. If not, you go back to real training and Omnathi has to handle the Dominion on his own. Deal?"

Jody took a deep breath. "Deal," she said. "I expect the Qasamans have a training room or two down here. Let's go find one."

Ludolf had said that he would be assigning a team to guide Merrick back to Svipall. In fact, the "team" ended up consisting of a single person: Hanna Herbseeker, Ludolf's female companion the night Merrick was poisoned.

Anya's mother.

There was little conversation during the walk from

Alexis's ranch to Svipall's western edge. Hanna seemed preoccupied and not inclined to talk, while Merrick concentrated on watching for predators, remembering their route, and working on what he was going to do once he was inside the village.

It was nearly sundown, and the sun had disappeared behind the tall forest trees behind them, when they reached the edge of the bersark field.

"There," Hanna said, pointing through the last line of trees toward the well-remembered chain-link fence. "Do you think you can get across safely this time?"

"I'll be fine," Merrick said, suppressing a flicker of irritation at the implied insult. "Go ahead and leave if you need to," he added. "I imagine your husband has a busy night ahead of him, with all he's got planned."

Hanna shook her head. "I can stay," she murmured. "He won't need my help."

Merrick felt his throat tighten. So Ludolf *did* have something in the works tonight besides just playing slave for Kjoic's benefit. "Are you sure?" he probed carefully. "From what I was hearing he sounded like he was going to need all the warm bodies he could get."

Hanna gave a little snort. "You underestimate his strength," she said. "Or you overestimate the scope of his plan. Tonight's beginning will be small."

"What about Anya?" Merrick pressed. Could Ludolf be planning to take his daughter on this unknown mission instead of his wife?

"She understands," Hanna said with a tired-sounding sigh. "She has always understood."

"Understood what?"

"Her proper role." Hanna pointed again. "You'd best go. Good luck."

"Right," Merrick said, getting a grip on the bamboo-like vaulting pole Ludolf had given him. There was something going on here, something he was pretty sure he didn't like, and he was definitely going to track it down as soon as he was back at Alexis's. But right now he needed to get into Svipall, and he needed to get going before the fading light robbed him of the ability to see the safe patches of ground. "Stay back, please. If they spot me, I don't want them spotting you, too."

He passed through the last line of trees and paused at the edge of the field, activating his infrareds. The last time he'd done this, all he'd needed were a series of safe patches that were big enough and close enough for him to jump between. This time, he needed all of that plus a set of smaller patches where he could plant the end of his vaulting pole.

It proved easier than he'd expected. The last time through, he'd been focusing on the larger patches and had therefore ignored anything smaller than a quarter of a square meter. Now that he was looking at all of it, he saw that there were dozens of small spots where the pole would work just fine.

Aside from a few times goofing around with his brother and sister when they were children, he'd never done any real pole-vaulting. Fortunately, he wasn't going to need any such skills here. All he needed to do was *look* like he was using the pole, while he simply used his leg servos to jump as usual. As long as he made sure to keep the end of the pole planted in the dirt, Hanna shouldn't suspect a thing.

Once again, he made sure to wait until the gaps between the nearest houses on the other side of the fence were clear before setting off. With the extra complication of dealing with the pole, the trip took a bit longer than the last time. The question of what to do with the pole solved itself as he neared the village and spotted a long strip of safe plants along his side of the fence. Midway through his final vault, he gave the end of the pole a sideways push, and as he cleared the fence he watched the pole land in the plant clumps, disappearing from view beneath the leaves.

As he had the last time, he spent the first few seconds crouched motionlessly on the ground inside the fence, listening for any sign that his unorthodox entry had been noticed. Once again, it looked like he was in the clear. Now all he had to do was stay out of sight until the villagers began gathering for the Games and hope he could slip in among them without anyone calling him out as a stranger.

First, though, a little long-distance study of the Troft building seemed in order.

Ludolf's briefing on the village had naturally not been laid out with an eye toward Cobra strengths and observational capabilities. But the handmade maps and other raw data had been detailed enough for Merrick to make his own assessments. His best shot, he'd concluded, was the town meeting hall a bit west of the village's center. While the building itself was only two stories tall, it had a pair of corner bell spires that ran another five meters upward. More importantly, the spires had enough room inside for him to climb invisibly right to the top.

Getting his bearings, adding a little light-amp enhancement to compensate for the darkening sky, he headed in.

The streets seemed largely deserted. There were only a few people visible, most of them apparently in a hurry, all of them far enough away that Merrick didn't have to worry about being spotted. Possibly all the rest of the people were indoors, eating or doing whatever preparations they needed for the impending mass gathering. Mindful of the old woman he'd bumped into the last time, he made sure his path would keep him clear of her house. She'd already pegged him as a stranger, and he didn't want her getting another look at him and wondering why he was still around.

He'd changed streets, and could see the twin bell spires over the distant rooftops, when he heard the sound of footsteps coming up behind him.

He'd already set his own stride to match the brisk and slightly nervous pace he'd observed from Svipall's other pedestrians. Now, he picked up that speed a little more, trying not to make it look like he was attempting to get away.

The other footsteps sped up to compensate. They weren't old woman's footsteps, either, Merrick noted with a sinking feeling. Someone else had spotted him, and whether or not that someone had realized he was a stranger, he was clearly trying for a closer look.

Merrick glanced around, keeping his head movements to a minimum. As far as he could tell, he and his pursuer were alone. He might as well deal with this now. Making sure his stunner was ready, he jerked to a halt and spun around.

To find himself facing probably the last person he'd expected.

"I was right," Dyre Woodsplitter growled, coming to a halt two paces away. "It *is* you."

"It's me, all right," Merrick said, his mind freezing as he stared at the other man's face. Dyre Woodsplitter, the man who'd bullied him and otherwise given him a rough time aboard the slave transport that had brought them all to Muninn. Dyre Woodsplitter, who had traveled with their group across the forest to Anya's village of Gangari. Dyre Woodsplitter, whom he and Anya had left in that village when they ran away.

Dyre Woodsplitter, whom Anya had identified as her betrothed.

"You were a fool to come to Svipall," Dyre growled. "Why are you here?"

"I could ask you the same question," Merrick countered. First Leif, Katla, and Gina Streamjumper; and now Dyre Woodsplitter, too. Had the Trofts airlifted in the whole damn village?

"I had little choice," Dyre said bitterly. "All those who have seen your face and Anya's have been brought here."

"Ah," Merrick said, his stomach tightening as it belatedly made sense. Somewhere in the back of his mind he'd assumed the Trofts kept close track of their slaves, with profiles and photos of everyone on file. Apparently, that wasn't the case.

And of course, even if it had been, Merrick wouldn't be in the system and any photo they'd had of Anya would be twelve years out of date. The Trofts could have taken new photos of all the returning slaves, but they clearly hadn't bothered to do so.

"The masters knew you would come to Svipall," Dyre continued. "They've promised safety and reward to whoever finds you."

"And so you have," Merrick said, keying his infrareds.

Dyre was a big man, but he was well within range of Merrick's stunner. If necessary, Merrick could drop him before he could even finish taking a breath to shout with.

The problem was that the stunner was a flash of low-power arcthrower current, and while the resulting flash and thundercrack were small, they weren't negligible. Silencing Dyre wouldn't do much good if Merrick woke up the entire neighborhood in the process. "So now what?" he asked. "You going to cash in on that reward?"

Dyre's eyes were steady on him. "If it were only you, I would already have called to the masters," he said. "But Anya is my betrothed. I will not willingly bring harm to her."

Merrick felt his forehead wrinkle. "Anya's not here," he pointed out.

"That's of no matter," Dyre said. "I don't know how or why, but her fate is somehow tied to yours. Your destruction will also bring suffering to her. To protect her I thus must also save you." The big man took a big breath. "So be it. What do you wish from me?"

On one level, Merrick reflected, Dyre's cooperative attitude was completely unexpected. On another level, it made perfect sense.

More importantly, the infrared analysis of Dyre's face was coming down on the perfect-sense side of the equation. "I need more information on the masters' building," he said. "I'm thinking I should be able to get a good view from one of the bell spires."

Dyre snorted. "You'll see nothing of any use from such a distance. If you wish to see it from close, even from the inside, you must volunteer for the Games."

Merrick felt his mouth drop open. "You're not serious."

"Anya said you'd been trained in your master's version of the Games," Dyre said, looking Merrick up and down. "Did she lie about that?" His lip twisted. "As she lied about your inability to speak?"

Merrick winced. As with Kjoic, surprise at the unexpected company had shocked him out of the role he was supposed to be playing. "I was the one who asked her to lie about that," he said, an obscure impulse pushing him to take the responsibility onto himself instead of admitting that the mute act had been Anya's idea. "I was afraid my accent would draw attention."

"Perhaps," Dyre said. "You didn't answer my question."

"If you mean the Games, yes, I was trained," Merrick said. Being thrown into an arena with a jormungand and a few razorarms *sort* of counted as training, he supposed.

"Then why do you fear them?"

"I don't," Merrick said. "I'm simply thinking that walking into the masters' stronghold might not be the smartest thing I could do today."

"If they knew your face, you would already be in their hands," Dyre said impatiently. "But if you prefer to climb a bell spire, I would not dream of stopping you."

"Okay, okay, relax," Merrick said. He was right, of course. And again, if he wanted to betray Merrick, he could have already done that. "How do I get in there?"

"You walk to the entrance and tell the master that you wish to volunteer," Dyre said with exaggerated patience. "And you need to do so *now*. The hour is already drawing near."

Merrick chewed the inside of his cheek. It was risky. Damn risky.

But if he could pull it off, it would be worth it. After all, there was no safer way of infiltrating an enemy stronghold than to be invited in. "All right, you're on," he said. "Is there any special trick to getting in? Any particular words or phrasing I have to use?"

Dyre rolled his eyes. "I see now why you thought it wise to remain silent. Of course there are words." He huffed out a breath. "The only way this will work is if we go together."

He huffed again. "Follow me."

CHAPTER TWENTY-ONE

He turned and strode off toward the Troft building. Merrick hurried after him, his mind spinning, trying to figure out how to diplomatically tell Dyre to back off, that he didn't need his help.

But all the excuses and soothing diplomacy in the universe couldn't alter one very important fact. Namely, that Merrick *did* need Dyre's help.

He shook his head, feeling the heavy hand of irony. He'd undertaken this whole mission, in large part, because of Anya. Because, looking into her eyes, he'd realized that she and her people needed his help. Now, Dyre was risking his own life and freedom to help a fugitive for the same woman.

Either he and Dyre were both fools of the highest order, or there was something about Anya that both men recognized was worth fighting over. An old saying whispered through Merrick's mind: *For her price is above rubies . . .*

The side of the gray building facing into the village

had two doors: a large, hangar-sized folding door, and a smaller, person-sized door, the latter flanked by two armed Trofts. Stretching out in front of the doors was the open area where Merrick had seen the villagers gathering six nights ago. With the area currently unoccupied, he could see that a twenty-meter-diameter circle had been marked off in the center of the field. That, presumably, was the combat ground. A meter back from the circle and spaced evenly around it were the four pole-mounted floodlights he'd also seen the last time.

The poles were fairly thin, and as they started across the field Merrick keyed his telescopics for closer study. If the poles were made of metal, and if the current going to the floodlights was on the same circuit, a quick burn-and-weld with his fingertip lasers might be able to short out all four of the lights at the same time.

But the poles were just wood. Still, the power lines to the lights were visible, running down along the sides and disappearing underground. It would now take four laser shots, but he *could* shut down the lights if the evening degenerated into last resorts. Hopefully, it wouldn't.

The entrance procedure wasn't nearly as big a deal as Dyre had made it sound. Merrick and Dyre merely walked up to the guards, gave their names—which, for Merrick, was the name Nicolai Hidetanner—and Dyre told them they wished to participate in the Games. The Trofts checked with someone via comm, then opened the door and passed them through.

It was something Merrick could easily have done on his own. Still, he had to admit there was a sense of safety in numbers, even if that number was only two.

He had nurtured a small hope that the building might turn out to be a single large room, and that by simply stepping through the door he could see everything that was going on inside. The Trofts, of course, hadn't been that stupid or careless. The room he and Dyre stepped into was long and narrow, with the front section set up like a waiting room and the rear section looking like a compact hospital diagnostic center. The bench seats in front held six more young men, talking quietly among themselves as they eyed the newcomers. In the rear section, four hospital beds were nestled in the middle of a collection of sensor, monitor, and drug-dispensing equipment. A pair of Trofts in medical smocks looked up from their work as Merrick and Dyre entered, and one of them picked up a shallow, rectangular dish and started toward the newcomers.

"Bersarkis?" Merrick murmured, nodding toward the dish.

"Bersarkis and more," Dyre murmured back. "The Games in Svipall are a test. The potions the masters use are . . . not pleasant."

"Really," Merrick said, hearing his heartbeat speeding up. Dyre hadn't mentioned anything about the Trofts pumping strange chemicals into their slaves' bodies.

In which case, maybe this wasn't about anything nearly so noble as protecting Anya by protecting Merrick. Maybe Dyre's plan was to maneuver Merrick into a medical test program in hopes of taking him out of the picture completely.

If which case, he was in for a surprise. In the far wall, half hidden by the hospital setup, was another door, unguarded and not particularly sturdy-looking.

At the first sign of a hypo, Merrick decided, he would stun everyone in the room with a sonic blast and make for that door. With luck, he could find out what was happening in the rest of the building and get out before they realized what they had on their hands.

Of course, once the Trofts knew there was a Cobra loose on their world, Merrick's life on the run would instantly be a lot harder. But he would deal with that problem when he got there.

The Troft made it through the crush of medical equipment and started across the waiting room. Merrick braced himself...

Dyre took a step forward, pulled up his sleeves, and extended his arms with his palms up. The Troft stopped in front of him and pressed four small tan-colored patches onto the inside of his right forearm, spacing them along the arm from wrist to elbow. A larger, dark-red patch went onto Dyre's left forearm. [These patches, use them at need,] the alien said, pointing to the row on Dyre's right arm. He pointed to the red patch. [This patch, use it only when ordered.]

Dyre bowed. [The order, I obey it.]

Taking the cue, Merrick had already pushed up his sleeves and held out his arms. The Troft gave him a similar set of patches, repeated the same instructions, then returned to the medical area.

Merrick looked down at his arms. The patches were cold, and the adhesive on them made his skin itch. From the top they seemed to be simple pieces of plastic, but now that they were in place he could feel a hard nub in the center of each one pressing into his arms. "What did he mean, at need?" he murmured to Dyre.

"These are bersarkis," Dyre said, wiggling his right

arm slightly. "When you need extra strength you squeeze the center or give it a sharp slap to drive the drug into your blood."

"Ah," Merrick said, a shiver running through him. After his experience with the bersark patch outside Svipall, he had zero interest in dealing with anything even remotely connected to the plant.

Fortunately, he wouldn't have to. Any extra strength he needed tonight would come from his servos, not some marginally refined poison. "What's the other one?"

"The people of Svipall call it simply Red Patch," Dyre said grimly. "No one knows what it is. But you heard the master. When you are ordered, you must inject it into your arm."

"Got it," Merrick said, carefully pushing his sleeves back down over the patches, wondering if there was some way he could surreptitiously remove them now that they were out of sight.

At the very least he should try to get rid of the Red Patch. Bersarkis was bad enough; the idea of putting an unknown chemical from a Troft lab into his body was several orders of magnitude worse.

The problem was that, without knowing what Red Patch did, he had no idea how to fake its effects. He would just have to hope that he wasn't the first one into the Games and could watch whoever went first and try to read from their reactions what the drug was supposed to do.

"You."

Merrick looked up. The six men sitting on the benches were staring at him and Dyre. Their expressions weren't exactly encouraging. "Yes?" Merrick said cautiously.

"You're not from Svipall," one of the men declared. "Where are you from?"

"I grew up in a village on the far side of Runatyr," Merrick said. "But I was taken by the masters when still a teen, and haven't been home in many years."

"Where were you taken?" one of the other men asked.

"To another world," Merrick said. "The masters there spoke differently than I did, as did their slaves. I had to learn how to speak all over again."

A third man snorted. "You had best prepare for a third learning."

"Yes," the first man said dryly. "You sound like a swaddling."

Merrick hunched his shoulders. "Yes," he said, putting some embarrassment into his tone. "I am aware."

One of the others murmured something to his neighbor, and they both laughed.

And with that, to Merrick's relief, they seemed to lose interest in him. Dyre brushed past and went to an empty spot at the end of the left-hand bench. Taking the cue, Merrick walked over and sat down beside him. "Okay, so you don't know what Red is," he murmured. "Do you have any idea what it *does*? Does it make the person stronger, or faster, or what?"

Dyre hunched his shoulders slightly. "I don't know. We'll have to learn together."

Merrick winced. Terrific.

He had run up the level on his audios, trying to see if there was anything he could deduce about the rest of the building from its background noises, when he heard the sound of approaching grav lifts. Apparently, someone elsewhere on the planet had once again sent observers to the Svipall Games.

Five minutes after the aircar's arrival, the two Troft guards came in and ordered the eight men outside.

And naturally, since Merrick desperately wanted to go second or third, the Trofts picked him to go first.

His opponent was the man who'd first challenged him in the waiting room and asked where he was from. Merrick had expected some last-minute instructions, but the two of them were merely called out from the group and pointed toward the open corridor leading through the silent crowd toward the brightly lit combat circle.

"They said your name was Nicolai Hidetanner?" the other man said quietly as they walked side by side toward the circle.

"Yes," Merrick said. "And you are Emil Grain-planter?"

"Yes," Emil said, his voice tight. "I know Svipall is not your village. But our safety depends on how you perform tonight. For our sake, do whatever is necessary to please the masters."

"I understand," Merrick said, wishing he did. "You, too."

"I will," Emil said. "Have you seen these Games before?"

Merrick shook his head. "Not the ones here, no."

"When we reach the circle, you go right and I go left," Emil said. "We stand beneath the lights on either side, facing each other. Stand still until given the order." He touched his right arm. "Do *not* use your bersarkis until then."

Or until never. "Got it," Merrick said aloud. "Good luck."

Emil threw him an odd look. "Thank you," he said,

his voice as odd as his expression. "May we both live to see the dawn. If not, may death come quickly."

Before Merrick could come up with a reply to that, they reached the circle and headed their separate directions. He reached the light, stopped, and turned.

The quiet crowd seemed to grow a little quieter. With the light shining straight down on him, Merrick didn't dare break his stance to look up at the aircar overhead, but from the sound he guessed it was about thirty meters up and ten behind him. Too far away for his fingertip lasers, but certainly within range of his antiarmor.

Whether he could actually take it down, of course, would depend on how heavily it was armored. Again, hopefully, it wouldn't come to that.

[The Games, they now begin,] an amplified Troft voice called across the area. [The combat, you may begin it.]

Across the circle, Emil straightened up, slapped at his right forearm, and charged.

The sheer quickness of it took Merrick completely by surprise. Fortunately, the circle was big enough that he had time to recover and move away from the edge of the crowd before Emil could close the gap. He made a show of slapping at his own arm, making sure his fingers missed all the patches, and braced himself for Emil's attack.

According to Anya, bersarkis was highly efficient at giving its user extra strength and suppressing pain and anything else that might interfere with combat. But the drug apparently did nothing for a fighter's combat tactics. Emil didn't pause to throw a kick or punch, but simply ran full-tilt into Merrick, slamming his right shoulder into Merrick's ribcage and bowling him over.

Or rather, trying to bowl him over. Even as Merrick started to fall backwards his servos took over, twisting his torso to the left and simultaneously jabbing his right palm against his attacker's left shoulder. The move sent Emil flying harmlessly to the side, his momentum carrying him on for another few steps as he fought frantically to keep from falling on his face. Merrick, for his part, got away with just a quick sideways skip before his servos got his own feet back underneath him.

He turned to face Emil as the other struggled his way back to balance, and for a moment the two men faced each other. Merrick had expected to find rage or at least chagrin on Emil's face, but the other simply looked back at him, his expression blank.

Hunching his shoulders, he once again charged.

This time Merrick was better prepared and was able to dodge aside as the other rushed past. But Emil was better prepared, too. Instead of simply rushing helplessly past Merrick after his clean miss, he braked to a halt, spun around, and threw a hard punch squarely into Merrick's side.

Once again Merrick's servos reacted with inhuman speed, throwing him in the direction opposite to the incoming punch so that when Emil's fist actually connected it was with far less force that it would otherwise have been. The remaining impact, powerful though it was, was easily absorbed by Merrick's ceramic-laminated bones.

Fortunately, that wasn't what the crowd and the Trofts would have seen. Even if someone had been quick-eyed enough to notice the start of Merrick's movement, the universal assumption would be that his short arc through the air was due to the strength of Emil's punch.

Still, Merrick was going to have a good-sized bruise where the fist had connected. Worse, sooner or later the man was likely to land a punch somewhere in Merrick's lower torso, an area that wasn't protected by any of his unbreakable bones. At that point, even with his programmed reflexes, Merrick would be at risk of serious organ damage.

The last thing he wanted to do was hurt any of these people. But getting himself killed or maimed wasn't part of the plan, either.

Time to end this thing.

Emil was charging again as Merrick recovered his balance and turned back to the fight. This time, instead of dodging, he braced himself; and as Emil got within range, he threw a hard punch of his own into Emil's lower ribs.

The impact jolted Emil to a halt, his eyes going wide as an agonized explosion of air burst from his mouth. Merrick took a step back, waiting for the man to crumple to the ground.

Only he didn't. Apparently, bersarkis didn't just control pain, but also gave extra endurance. For a few seconds Emil just stood there, rocking back and forth on his heels. Then, shaking himself like a wet dog, he focused again on Merrick. His lips curled back in a death's-head smile, and his left hand slapped the sleeve of his right arm. He shook himself again as his second jolt of bersarkis flowed into his bloodstream. Then, bunching his hands into fists, he once again leaped to the attack.

And now the fight began in earnest.

Merrick had always liked weapon- and martial arts-type movies, holding a special admiration for the high-speed, carefully choreographed fight sequences that were a staple of such dramas. Now, for the first time in his life, he felt as if he had been dropped into the middle of one of those battles.

Except that this one wasn't choreographed. This one was real.

Emil fought like a madman, throwing punches, kicks, and sometimes his entire body at Merrick, with apparently little thought for tactics and no thought at all for self-preservation. Merrick fended him off as best he could, trying to figure out how to take him down without inflicting permanent damage.

Still, sooner or later, the bersarkis in Emil's bloodstream had to run out, and at that point the man would hopefully keel over from either accumulated injuries or sheer fatigue. Merrick just had to hold him off until that happened, and the fight would be over.

He had just deflected the latest punch, and delivered an open-palm jab to Emil's shoulder blade, when the amplified Troft voice gave the order Merrick had been dreading. [The red patch, you will use it now.]

Emil staggered back a few steps, breathing heavily. He glanced at the hovering aircar, then behind him at the Troft building, then finally turned back at Merrick. His throat worked, and with clear reluctance he brought up his left arm and slapped his right palm against it. His back spasmed, jerking him straight up like a puppet on a shortened chain, then sagged him into a sort of standing limpness.

Watching him closely, wondering if the man was

about to have a stroke or heart attack, Merrick tapped
his own left forearm and mimicked Emil's reaction
as best he could. So far all Red Patch seemed to
be doing was calming Emil down. Was it a sort of
anti-bersarkis?

[Your opponent, you will kill him now.]

Merrick felt his mouth drop open. What the *hell*?

Emil shook his head sadly. "I am sorry," he said.

And charged.

Merrick had thought the other man had been fight-
ing all-out before. He'd been wrong. He'd thought
Emil had been more or less a mindless animal before.
He'd been wrong.

He'd thought he'd been fighting for his life before.
Now, suddenly, he was.

It was like battling an invulnerable razorarm, or
trying to stop a runaway car with his bare hands. Emil
had become a wild man, flailing at Merrick with every
single-minded brain cell and every gram of strength.
Thirty seconds into the clash, Merrick knew that there
was no way he could keep himself unharmed long
enough to survive. Not unless he obeyed the Troft's
order and killed Emil first.

Unless . . .

It would be a terrible risk. But it was the only other
choice he had. The only chance for both of them.

Getting his bearings, trusting in his nanocomputer
to block or dodge Emil's attacks, Merrick began to
back slowly toward one of the wooden floodlight
poles. This was going to take timing and luck, and
both required that he first maneuver himself and Emil
into precisely the right spot.

Fortunately, Emil no longer had any brainpower

left to wonder if he was being maneuvered. He simply continued to advance, swinging his fists and feet and head, trying to find an opening for the death blow he'd been ordered by his masters to deliver. Merrick eased them backward until they were only two meters from the pole. A quick glance behind him while dodging a punch confirmed that the spectators in the area had moved elsewhere, leaving him an open path to the pole.

Now, all he had to do was wait for Emil to throw the right kind of punch.

It came three attacks later: a straight-in, right-hand punch toward Merrick's chest. As the fist lanced toward him, Merrick pushed off with his leading foot, falling back from the incoming blow as he'd done so many times in the past few minutes. The fist slammed into his sternum, adding a jolt of extra momentum to Merrick's movement.

Only this time, instead of simply continuing backward, Merrick gave a final shove off the ground, adding a twist to turn him a hundred eighty degrees over. As he slammed chest-first into the wooden pole, his left hand caught the back of the pole at his stomach, his right hand caught the front of the pole at his throat—

And with a pull-shove from his arm servos, he snapped the pole in two.

His momentum faltered slightly with the impact. Giving a last pull on the lower part of the pole with his left hand, he threw himself across the broken part as it toppled toward the ground.

There was no time for him to see whether or not the pole was going to hit any of the crowd back there, nor was there anything he could do about it if it was. The move had been quick enough and subtle enough

that all anyone should have seen was Emil hitting him
so hard that his impact with the pole had been hard
enough to break it.

And even with bersarkis flowing through his blood,
there was no way a human being should be able to
survive such a blow and the accompanying damage to
heart and lungs. Rolling limply off the downed pole,
Merrick flipped over one final time and landed on
his face in the dirt.

Dead.

At least, that was what he hoped they would all
think. Lying motionlessly, keeping his breaths small,
slow, and shallow, he waited tensely. If Emil wasn't
fooled, or if he interpreted his order to mean tear-
ing his opponent's head off to be sure, then Merrick
would have no choice but to kill him.

And then, to his relief, the amplified voice again
filled the silence. [The Game, it has ended,] the Troft
said. [The body, carry it to the analysis area. The
survivor, he will accompany it.]

There was a stirring from the crowd, and Merrick
felt strong hands close around his arms and legs and
lift him gently from the ground. Other arms slid
beneath his legs and back, and he felt himself being
carried across the ground to the Troft building. Beside
him, he could hear heavy, gasping breaths: Emil, no
doubt, with the stress and agony of the battle finally
starting to catch up with him.

Hopefully, they would be taken to different areas
of the building for analysis. Even more hopefully, the
"corpse" would be taken past the outer room, where
Merrick would have a chance of seeing more of the
Trofts' operation.

[Dyre Woodsplitter and Mihlje Dawnhunter, you will enter the circle.]

Merrick suppressed a grimace. No time to mourn the dead, not even a moment of respectful silence. Death and agony were slave things, not something the masters needed to concern themselves with. The masters had work to do and important studies to make.

And above all, the show must go on.

This time it would be Dyre with his life and health on the line for the Trofts' amusement and edification. Merrick could only hope, for his sake, that they wouldn't make this one another battle to the death.

Though if they *did*, and if Dyre lost, the whole complication of Anya already having a betrothed would pretty much disappear.

Merrick felt his face warm with shame. There was absolutely no call for him to even think that way. There was nothing between him and Anya. Not at all. And when looked at it through the cold light of logic, he knew there couldn't be. Their backgrounds, their cultures, their homes—the two of them were just too different. They worked well enough as comrades-in-arms, but there could never be anything more. Never.

The bersarkis had been injected, and the battle in the circle was in progress by the time Merrick's handlers maneuvered him through the door into the preparation room. [That bed, put him on it,] one of the medical Trofts ordered. [That bed, Emil Grainplanter will lie on it.]

[The order, I obey it,] Emil wheezed.

Keeping his eyes closed, Merrick keyed his opticals. Emil was trudging through the medical equipment toward the indicated bed, looking like death hunting for a place to happen. Still, he looked like he would survive.

In the meantime, Merrick had problems of his own. The minute the Trofts hooked him up to any sensors his lack of actual death would come instantly to light. His choices were either to let that happen and pretend he'd simply been knocked unconscious with no deliberate fakery involved, or else to make his move for the rear door before they could get that far.

From the half-open door came the voice of the Troft Gamemaster, ordering Dyre and the other man to use their Red Patches. The people carrying Merrick laid him gently on the examination bed and began to file back through the equipment maze toward the door and the field beyond.

"Masters!" Dyre's voice came faintly across the breeze. "The man who was killed—he wasn't Nicolai Hidetanner. He was Merrick Hopekeeper. He was the slave you've been looking for!"

And with that, Merrick's choices had suddenly boiled down to exactly one.

He shoved himself up off the bed, rolling his legs over the side and hitting the floor running. Someone behind him screamed as the dead man came back to life—

And then he hit the inner door with his shoulder, bouncing it violently open, and charged into the main part of the Troft building.

It was, for the most part, the single large room that he'd originally guessed it might be. The large open floor of the lower level was flanked by rows of office-type doors, the upper area edged with catwalks where armored guards kept watch. The main floor was filled with lab tables, glass-and-steel equipment, and all the vents, burners, filter systems, separators, and analyzers of a modern chemical lab.

And like the catwalks above, the main floor was teeming with Trofts.

There was information to be had in here, Merrick knew. Massive, vitally important stacks of information. The kind of data that he and Ludolf had both hoped to find. The kind of information that Commander Ukuthi had sent Merrick here to find in the first place.

But there was no way Merrick could gather any of it. Not here and now. There were too many Trofts, too many lasers, and not nearly enough time. Right now, his first and only priority was to get out without getting himself killed for real.

And yet, almost paradoxically, this was the first situation he'd encountered since his arrival on Muninn that was in any way familiar.

Because part of his Cobra training had been dedicated to scenarios dealing with enemy-held buildings and landscapes. Typically the goal of those exercises had been to defeat and neutralize, not simply escape. But the basic principles were the same.

And in the next fifteen seconds, Merrick used all of them.

He ran. Full speed, as fast and as hard as his servos and bruised, aching muscles could take him. Not just on the floor, where he had to dodge tables and astonished Trofts, but up onto the tables, over and sometimes through testing equipment, back to the floor, back onto the tables, whichever route let him move the fastest.

He was halfway across the room before the first laser shots started raining down on him from the armed Trofts on the catwalks. But the shots were few, cautious, and inaccurate, as the guards apparently hesitated to risk damaging fragile and expensive equipment. One or two of the techs on the floor seemed inclined to play hero, moving to cut off the intruder's path. Merrick didn't even bother running them over, but simply dodged around or over them.

Anywhere else in the Troft Assemblage, he suspected, his speed and power would have instantly damned him as a Cobra. But here on Muninn, the Trofts' own schemes had worked against them. With Merrick's body assumed to be full of bersarkis, nothing short of firing his lasers or sonics would reveal him for what he really was.

The door at the far end, like the one he'd entered the test area through, was heavy and clearly armored. But such doors were designed to keep intruders out, not to seal occupants in, especially in a chemical lab where a simple dropped beaker could have lethal effects for anyone in the vicinity. Merrick's shoulder against the door popped it open with barely any resistance—

And then he was out, legs pumping even harder as he ran through the cool night air across the uneven ground. A glance over his shoulder showed the Troft aircar was still hovering over the Games area, frozen in midair by the confusion and chaos of Merrick's escape.

A glimpse was all he got before he reached the edge of the forest and plunged in, keying his light-amps as even the dim starlight was cut off by the leafy canopy.

The chaos wouldn't last long, he knew. Another few minutes at the most, and the hunt would be on in earnest. Especially with Dyre's betrayal to spur them on.

Merrick had trusted the man with his life. This was how that trust had been treated.

Anya probably wouldn't believe it. She would probably accuse Merrick of lying, or of misinterpreting whatever Dyre had said. Even if she believed him, she would probably make excuses for her betrothed.

Merrick couldn't make her believe what had happened back there. But he would damn well make sure she knew about it. For her safety, as well as his.

And for no other reason, he told himself firmly. No other reason at all.

CHAPTER TWENTY-TWO

Archway, Lorne thought with grim satisfaction as he gazed across the city, was coming to a boil.

And that was good. Because Reivaro, the Marines, the Dominion of Man itself needed to know that the Cobra Worlds were not to be trifled with, or the wishes of its citizens ignored.

Governor Chintawa had tried diplomacy and civility, only to be ignored. If violence was the only thing the Dominion understood, then violence was what they were going to get.

And if Lorne was the only Cobra in DeVegas still able to deliver such messages, he was more than willing to take on the job.

He smiled. And when, he wondered, had he started thinking to himself in history-book-style quotes? Maybe that kind of mindset came with the territory.

Territory that was turning out to be a full-time occupation. His first attack had been just four days ago, when he'd hit Dominion Marines' headquarters,

knocked over a pair of guards with a concussion grenade, and littered Colonel Reivaro's office with shards
of glass. Reivaro hadn't been there at the time, but
the message had been abundantly clear.

Two days ago Lorne had struck again, slipping into
a section of the city the Marines were busy searching,
and wrecking one of their aircars. That had gotten
him a lot of media exposure, plus a fifteen-minute,
teeth-clenched broadcast statement from Reivaro that
had included a warning about what would happen to
anyone caught in the act of sabotage.

But those attacks, visible though they'd been, had
been merely pinpricks. They'd been designed to get
Reivaro too mad to think straight, and to get the
Marines jumping at their own shadows. It was time
now for Lorne to give Reivaro a solid gut-punch.

In this case, Yates Fabrications.

The factory was a good half-kilometer from the rooftop where Lorne was currently crouched, surrounded
by a swath of open parkland and a couple of dozen
Dominion Marines. Matavuli had said the place had
shut down, but apparently Reivaro had gotten it up
and running again.

Lorne's mother Jin had successfully sabotaged the
plant once. Now, it was Lorne's turn.

He keyed up his telescopics another notch, studying
the guard pattern. The number of men on duty over
there had steadily decreased as Lorne's raids elsewhere
in the city had forced Reivaro to redistribute his forces.
If Lorne was lucky, there might be a gap where he could
slip through without being spotted. Once he was inside—

"There you are," an all-too-familiar voice came from
behind him.

Lorne felt his whole body go rigid. *Reivaro?*

"Don't," Reivaro continued, his voice casual. "Whatever you're thinking about trying, just don't. All possible avenues of escape are covered, and trying to make a fight of it will just get you killed."

Lorne took a deep breath. The man *might* be bluffing. "I suppose I can't complain," he said, keeping his voice light. "I had a good run."

Reivaro snorted. "Hardly. Stand up and turn around. Slowly."

Bracing himself, Lorne obeyed.

Reivaro wasn't bluffing. He was standing in the center of the roof, twenty meters away, a dozen combat-suited Marines spread out at his sides.

"I'm almost sorry you got ambitious," Reivaro continued. "As long as you were running around Archway making noise and not much else, I was more than happy to let you play." He nodded toward the distant factory. "But now you're looking to damage something with real value, and I can't let you do that."

"Nice try," Lorne said, determined not to let the other's jibes get to him. "But I heard your broadcast the other night. You were ready to spit nails."

Reivaro gave another snort. "You don't know the first thing about population-control psychology, do you? Let me give you a short lesson."

"Sir?" one of the Marines murmured. "We really should finish this."

"Relax, Sergeant," Reivaro said. "Cobra Broom's not going anywhere. Lesson one: a population that sees itself as being occupied or oppressed starts getting restless and angry. If you don't do something about that, it tends to erupt in acts of violence."

"And so you work harder to suppress it," Lorne said.

"Or you can be clever," Reivaro said. "Because you see, if there's one lone person making trouble, especially big and flamboyant trouble, it acts as a safety valve for everyone else. The rest of the people will just sit back and let him do it for them."

Lorne stared, his brain suddenly feeling like it was trying to run on ice. "You're bluffing," he insisted. "You're making all that up."

Reivaro shrugged. "You're welcome to believe that if you want. But do you really think that ridiculous disguise actually fooled anyone? No, you didn't register with the city databanks we downloaded; but the fact that you didn't register with *any* database was the most obvious red flag of all."

He shrugged. "Still, I imagine Polestar Productions will get their money's worth out of it. At the very least, you'll probably rate your own mini-series someday. Certainly couldn't be as absurd as that ridiculous Anne Villager program." He gestured. "Hands behind your back, please."

Lorne glanced up, seeing now the distant dots of hovering aircars. Another glance down the side of the building showed a group of ground cars waiting for him to try a wall-bounce.

And meanwhile, a dozen Marines had their epaulet lasers pointed directly at him.

"I *can* kill you," he warned Reivaro, trying one more time. "And killing me will make me a martyr."

"You can *try* to kill me," Reivaro said calmly. "That's not the same thing as actually doing it. And martyrs aren't nearly the powerful rallying cry that most people think. In fact, most martyrs aren't accorded that lofty status until long after the event." He smiled thinly. "And then only if their side wins. Yours hasn't. Nor is it going to."

Lorne stared at him . . . and for the first time in his life he found himself genuinely and passionately hating another human being.

But Reivaro was right. Lorne had lost this one. His only hope was to surrender and hope to fight another day.

The cuffs the Marines had brought included flat pieces that ran along his palms, preventing him from activating his fingertip lasers. Lorne half expected them to put a bag over his head to prevent him from seeing where he was going, but the colonel apparently wasn't worried about that.

Not that Lorne could blame him. With loyalty collars around the neck of every other Cobra in DeVegas, the only other one still free was Lorne's mother Jin.

If she *was*, in fact, still free. For all he knew, Reivaro had taken her, too.

Aventine's Cobra program had always included rigid psychological testing and assessment, with the result that there was seldom any reason why a Cobra had to be locked away for a crime or misbehavior. But such incidents did occasionally happen, and Commandant Ishikuma's response had been to construct a Cobra-proof holding cell in the basement of their HQ building.

With Lorne's hands safely cuffed behind him, Reivaro had relaxed somewhat, and as they reached the building he dismissed all but two of the Marine escort, ordering them to secure Lorne in his new quarters. With one each holding one of Lorne's upper arms, they walked down the stairs toward the building's main storage and sleeping facilities. They reached the bottom of the steps and walked around them toward the cell—

"About time," Badj Werle growled, standing up from one of the two chairs that had been placed along the wall beside the cell door.

"Come on, come on, let's get this over with," Dill de Portola added as he stood up from the other one.

The two Marines holding Lorne's arms came to an abrupt halt. "What are you two doing here?" one of them demanded.

"What do you think?" Werle countered. "Reivaro wanted a couple of Cobras to help secure the prisoner. We're the ones Ishikuma assigned to the job. End of story."

"No, *end of story* is where we get to go to bed," de Portola put in, digging a finger behind the red loyalty collar, half hidden behind his jacket collar, as if trying to relieve some of the pressure on his neck. "So move your butts, will you?"

Neither Marine answered. Lorne looked sideways at the one holding his left arm, wishing he could see the man's expression through his helmet. From the lack of response, he guessed both Marines were accessing the Dominion's information network looking for the orders.

"'Course, if you'd rather do it yourselves, that's fine with us," Werle said into the silence. "Could be really entertaining to watch you try to lock a Cobra into a small room."

"Yeah, some other time," the Marine said. Apparently whatever he'd found had confirmed Werle's statement. Releasing Lorne's arm, he gave him a little shove forward. "Just be sure he's inside before you take off the cuffs."

"Yeah, thanks, we got the procedure memo," Werle said as he and de Portola came forward. "We'll take it from here," he added, stepping up to the Marine still holding Lorne's right arm. As the Marine finally let go of the arm, De Portola walked around Lorne's left side, moving behind him, and both Cobras reached toward the prisoner.

It happened so fast that Lorne almost missed it. Werle's right hand, straying casually toward the Marine's shoulder as he reached for Lorne, suddenly erupted in a flash of light and a muted thunderclap as his arcthrower fired a skin-tingling blast of current into the inner edge of the Marine's left epaulet, frying the laser cluster's sensor and control system. Simultaneously, de Portola's arcthrower fired from behind the Marine into the right-hand epaulet, destroying the control area there. Even as Lorne jerked reflexively away from the twin blasts, de Portola followed up his shot with a hard forearm blow to the back of the Marine's helmet; and as the man dropped limply to the floor, Werle gave Lorne a hard shove to the side and flopped backward onto his back, his leg swinging up to try to bring his antiarmor laser to bear on the second Marine.

But the move was slow, and the Marine was fast, and the shot never came. "*Rache!*" the Marine snapped.

And with a muffled *pop* like the breaking of a pair of bones, the loyalty collars around both Cobras' necks exploded in twin flashes of brilliant yellow fire. Without so much as a yelp of pain, the two men collapsed and lay still.

"Fools," the Marine snarled under his breath, hurrying to Lorne and grabbing his arm. "I thought they might try something stupid like—"

The last word came out in a strangled yelp, and he let go of Lorne's arm and grabbed for the floor as de Portola's limp legs inexplicably came back to life and kicked his feet out from under him. The Marine got one hand beneath him, too late to do anything more than slow his fall slightly and tip him over onto his shoulder. He rolled over onto his stomach—

And was knocked half a meter sideways as the sole of Werle's foot slammed hard against the side of his helmet. He hit the floor again, and this time, didn't get up.

"So the damn things are vocally triggered," de Portola commented as he got back to his feet. "I wondered about that. Come on, Broom—wake up. Show me your hands."

"Yeah," Lorne said mechanically, feeling a little sandbagged as he swiveled his back toward the other. "Did your collars just—?"

"So if we can stuff a sock in their mouths, we can bypass the whole thing?" Werle suggested as he grabbed the two Marines by their ankles and dragged them into the cell.

"I'd hate to count on that," de Portola warned. "They've probably got one or two other triggers set up. *I* sure would." There was a brief sizzle of laser fire against the skin of Lorne's wrists, and suddenly his hands were free.

"And to answer your question, yes, they went boom," Werle said dryly as he emerged from the cell and closed the door behind him. "Very effectively, too. The Dominion sure knows how to keep their slaves in line."

"Luckily, we Cobras have always been a stiff-necked lot," de Portola said, coming around in front of Lorne.

Reaching up, he tapped his neck behind the shredded edges of his jacket collar where the exploding loyalty collar had tried its best to take off his head.

Almost hidden behind the shredded cloth was yet another collar, this one thin and flesh-colored and showing a pattern of spiderweb cracks across its surface. It was pressed up against de Portola's neck, right behind where the loyalty collar had been.

Lorne raised his eyes to de Portola's smile and gave the other a smile of his own.

Great-Uncle Corwin, who'd been forced out of his governorship and had subsequently dedicated his free time to the ridiculous goal of developing better ceramic laminae for some future generation of Cobras, had come through.

"Come on," de Portola said, tapping Lorne on the back. "There should be a car waiting."

"They're going to figure out pretty quickly what happened," Lorne warned as the three of them hurried to the stairs.

"I don't think so," Werle said grimly. "They'd have to have a Cobra to examine first . . . and sometime in the next hour there will cease to be any Cobras in DeVegas province."

Lorne stared at him. "You're kidding. Where are they all going?"

"Underground," de Portola said. "Some literally. Others are heading to Capitalia and other towns and cities."

"But—" Lorne broke off.

"What about the people here?" Werle finished his question. "Yeah, I know, and we don't like it any better than you do. But the Dominion wasn't really letting us do our jobs anyway. As of right now, public safety's the Dominion's problem. Let's see how well they do at it."

"You realize what might happen," Lorne warned. "Not even counting the people who might get hurt while we're gone. This might push the Dominion into open warfare against us."

"If it does, it does," Werle said. "At least then they'd have to give up the pretense that everything they're doing here is for the good of the human race."

"Besides, Santores is smarter than that," de Portola soothed. "He knows he can't take and hold this many planets. Not with the force he's got."

"I hope you're right," Lorne said.

"Of course we're right." Werle grinned suddenly. "We're *always* right. Come on, let's see what kind of fine and elegant transport Ishikuma has laid on for us."

"Right now, I'd settle for a cattle transport," Lorne said.

"Don't say that too loudly," de Portola warned. "You might just get it."

In some ways, Jody thought as she headed through the darkened streets toward Azras's First Hope Hospital, it was rather like the first time she'd tried walking in high heels.

Not that it was hard, or that she felt in danger of falling. Far from it. Not only was walking with Cobra servos quite easy, but there was a sense of balance that she'd never had before.

But that very sense of balance could turn around and bite her. If she let her body fall too far out of vertical, her new nanocomputer might decide she was falling and take over her servos to compensate. She still wasn't familiar enough with her gear to allow it to do so without fighting it, and the resulting minor chaos of muscle versus servo would be awkward, not to mention embarrassing. Worse, if it happened in sight of any of the Dominion Marines guarding the hospital, they might recognize the telltale signs and her advantage would be gone.

But Kemp and Smitty had run her through this part of her training a lot in the past few hours. She would make it through.

The doctors and hospital staff they'd contacted had been unable to offer any information on the Dominion patients, mainly because Captain Moreau had been careful to withhold their names and ranks. But Moreau had also asked Omnathi to allow a few of his Marines to help guard his patients, and Omnathi had agreed, and two of that handful of men were now stationed outside one of the recovery rooms. All logic suggested that an important officer was in there, which was exactly the person Jody needed.

All her enquiries had by necessity had to be quiet and subtle, lest Omnathi hear she was snooping around and wonder why, and one of the questions she hadn't dared ask was whether or not the Marines were wearing combat gear. As she rounded the last corner into the final corridor, she saw to her relief that they were instead in the burgundy-black dress uniforms she'd seen back on Aventine.

Of course, they still had their laser-equipped epaulets, with their lethal sensor-controlled targeting. In contrast, Jody barely knew which end of her own weaponry was which. But she and the two Cobras had worked up a couple of possible strategies for her to use.

She felt her lip twitch as she walked toward the Marines. No: the proper phrase wasn't *Jody and the two Cobras* anymore. It was, instead, *Jody and the* other *two Cobras.*

Because Jody, too, was now a Cobra.

That was the new reality of her life. She still wasn't entirely sure how it made her feel.

But such soul-searching would have to wait. One of the Marines turned his head toward her as she approached, and from the sudden change in his expression she guessed he'd realized who she was. He opened his mouth, presumably to clue in his fellow guard—

"Is he awake?" Jody asked briskly as she came up to them.

That was apparently not a question either of the Marines had been expecting. "Ah—" the first one began hesitantly.

"Never mind," Jody cut him off. "Tell him Jody Moreau Broom is here, and that I need to talk to him." Without waiting for an answer, she started to walk between them.

The Marines might not be very quick with words tonight, but their actions were more than adequate. Even as Jody started toward the door the men moved toward each other, blocking her path. "Not so fast," the first Marine growled.

"Are you deaf?" Jody demanded. "I said I need to talk to him." She put her hands on their chests, as if attempting to push them back out of her way. Not surprisingly, given the difference in relative mass, the push got her nowhere.

"You're not seeing anyone for a while," the first Marine said as he grabbed her wrist. The second Marine did the same, and a second later Jody found herself with her arms upraised as if she was surrendering, her hands locked in their twin grip at the level of their shoulders. "Cuff her," the first Marine added.

The second grunted an acknowledgment and reached around to his back with his free hand.

And with the situation nearly resolved and the two Marines therefore starting to relax, Jody pushed her arms forward and inward, forcing their arms inward as well. Before they could react, she grabbed the sides of their heads and shoved them together.

One of the men had just enough time for his eyes to widen in disbelief. Then their heads slammed together with a wet-melon sound and they dropped to the floor in a tangled heap.

Jody took a deep breath, her arms starting to shake with reaction. It had been a gamble—a horribly dangerous gamble, given the Marines' armament. But it had paid off.

The epaulets were programmed to react to any threat the tiny computers calculated could be potentially damaging, including a rapidly-approaching incoming object. Unfortunately for these particular Marines, and exactly as she'd hoped would be the case, the programmers had written in an exemption when that incoming object was a fellow Marine.

Or, in this case, a fellow Marine's head.

Stepping between the unconscious men, Jody pushed open the door.

It was, as anticipated, a recovery room, its furnishings consisting of an adjustable bed wrapped in an array of monitoring equipment, a rolling food table, and two guest chairs. The man sitting up in the bed was middle-aged, with short white hair and a tired, haggard face. Above the waist he was wearing a loose white hospital tunic; below the waist, his legs were encased in some kind of mechanical cocoon covered with tubes, wires, and monitors. Beside him, another, younger man in a Dominion uniform had pulled up one of the chairs alongside the bed.

Both men looked toward Jody as she walked into the room, and she saw the uniformed man twitch his eyelid. "I apologize for the interruption," Jody said. "My name is Jody Moreau Broom. May I ask whom I have the honor of addressing?"

Slowly, the uniformed man stood up. "Lieutenant Cottros Meekan," he identified himself cautiously. "Aide to Captain Barrington Moreau."

"Lieutenant Commander Eliser Kusari," the man in the bed added. "Second Officer of the Dominion of Man War Cruiser *Dorian*. Forgive our surprise, but you're the last person we expected to walk through that door. Especially a *guarded* door. The guards didn't challenge you?"

"They did," Jody said. "I was more determined to speak with you than they were to stop me. Don't worry—they should be all right in a couple of hours."

"That's good to hear," Kusari said, in a voice that warned there would be serious consequences if they weren't. "You have friends, I gather?"

Jody thought quickly. Until the guards woke up, hers would be the only story about what had happened. Even then, depending on how scrambled their short-term memories were—"Quite a few, yes," she said. "In this case, though, only Caelian friends were involved. Whatever consequences you choose to invoke, there's no reason to invoke them against any of the Qasamans."

"We can discuss that at a future date," Kusari said, eyeing her thoughtfully. "You said you wanted to speak to me. Very well: speak."

"Thank you, sir," Jody said, inclining her head to him. "I presume that by now you've discovered that the *Squire* is here on Qasama."

There might have been a twitch of Meekan's eyebrow. "We have," Kusari confirmed. "Did you come here to explain how that happened?"

"I am," Jody confirmed. "It's a bit more complicated than it appears."

"It generally is," Kusari said. "Is Shahni Omnathi aware that you're here?"

"No," Jody said, feeling her stomach tighten. And he would probably be furious when he found out, too. If she and the others didn't get off Qasama tonight, she was going to be catching serious hell from at least two different directions. "But you deserved to hear the whole story, and I'm one of the few who can tell you."

"Or *would* tell us?" Kusari countered. "Fine. You can tell us your story; and afterwards you can tell us what you want."

Jody frowned. "What I want?"

"I've done some reading on the Moreau family, Ms. Broom," Kusari said. "You have a long history of being involved in Cobra Worlds politics. I don't for a minute believe that you came in here out of a purely altruistic desire to set the record straight."

"You're right, I have a request," Jody said. "But let me first tell you how the *Squire* came to be on Qasama."

For a moment, Kusari and Meekan looked at each other. Then, Kusari gave a small nod. "Very well," he said. "Lieutenant, would you bring over that other chair?" He smiled slightly at Jody. "I have a feeling this is going to take a while. We might as well be comfortable."

CHAPTER TWENTY-THREE

Just to be on the safe side, Merrick took the long way around back to Alexis's forest ranch.

Though it was clear midway through his travels that the extra caution was unnecessary. The aircar that had been watching the Games was slow to take up the chase, and when it did, it headed in the wrong direction entirely. Whereas Merrick had gone east, and Alexis's ranch was to the northwest, the aircar instead headed due north. The two other aircars that subsequently arrived and joined in the hunt didn't do any better.

But Anya would be waiting for him at the ranch, and Merrick had no intention of leading any Trofts there. So he headed east, then south, crossed the river that flowed past Svipall, traveled along it to the west, and finally crossed it again and headed north.

Along the way, he approached as many large nocturnal animals as he could find, especially the larger predators, in hopes of confusing any Troft infrared sensors that were able to penetrate the forest canopy. A few of the predators showed some mild interest in him, but each time a short burst from his sonic was enough to discourage them.

Finally, two hours after his mad dash through the Troft drug lab, he crossed the bersarkis strip at the edge of Alexis's ranch and trudged wearily around the groups of dozing and late-evening-snacking sheep to the house.

There was a figure sitting on the porch, and Merrick's first assumption was that Anya had waited up for him. But as he got within a few meters, he saw to his surprise that it was, instead—

[My remaining slave, he has finally returned,] Kjoic said as Merrick came up to him. The Troft's radiator membranes were fluttering, in anger or frustration or both. [The rest, they have fled from my presence.]

Merrick frowned. The others had *fled*? [Apologies for my disappearance, I offer them,] he said carefully as he bowed. [The other slaves, when did they leave?]

[The older female slave, she returned from a journey,] Kjoic said. [The other slaves, they then gathered together. Their disappearance, a few minutes later I noticed it.]

So Hanna had returned from guiding Merrick to Svipall; and then the whole group had just *left*? Including Anya? [Their destination, did they specify it?]

[Their destination, they did not reveal it,] Kjoic said. His membranes fluttered a little harder. [But other truth, I have been told it. Your identity, it is not as you proclaimed.]

Merrick was trying to figure out what the Troft meant by that when there was a sudden rustling in the trees and bushes behind him. [Movements, you will not make them,] a harsh Troft voice ordered.

Merrick froze, a curse bubbling in his throat. Tired after his long hike, and knowing that the bersarkis barrier protected the ranch from predators, he'd gotten inexcusably sloppy at the very end.

And he was about to pay dearly for his failure to scan the area before entering it.

But recriminations were a waste of effort. The crucial question now was, how deep in trouble was he?

Deep enough. From the sound of the footsteps wading through the grass and leaves, he guessed there were four of them.

Under some circumstances, particularly during Qasaman invasion, that wouldn't have been too bad. Especially given that the Trofts behind him had no idea who and what he was. Even if they were wearing armor, he should be able to take all four of them out before they could return fire.

But if he did that, his secret would be out. Even if he left no survivors, the Trofts who'd fought on Qasama and the Cobra Worlds had had more than enough experience with Cobras to identify the laser frequencies and arcthrower power profiles their weaponry used. A good investigator might even be able to deduce from the target positioning and shot grouping that a Cobra's sensors and nanocomputer had been involved.

[His identity, what is it?] Kjoic asked, his voice trembling a little. [An alien agent, that is what you named him to me earlier. That identity, it is now confirmed?]

[That identity, it is confirmed,] the lead Troft said.

Kjoic's membranes pressed straight out. [Horror, I feel it,] he said. Bounding up from the bench, he hurried away from the house, giving Merrick a wide berth, and disappeared to Merrick's rear and out of his field of view.

[A half-turn, you will make one,] the lead Troft ordered. [Your hands, you will keep them visible.]

The best thing Merrick could do, he knew, was to play along and watch for a chance to escape somewhere down the line. Hopefully without having to reveal who he was. Keeping his arms well away from his sides, his hands open, he slowly turned around.

There were indeed four Trofts back there, all of them armored, all of them holding military-grade laser rifles trained on their prisoner. They stood closer together than good soldiers should, he noted absently, probably preferring the risk of a little extra bunching to the risk of being close enough to the surrounding trees to be targeted by one of Muninn's arboreal predators. Kjoic had skittered around behind them, pressed up close to their line like a frightened child peering over a picket fence. Above the armored shoulders, Merrick could see Kjoic's radiator membranes fluttering even more than they had been earlier.

Apparently, learning that your adopted slave was an enemy agent wasn't in his limited repertoire of experiences.

But Kjoic's sensibilities were far down on Merrick's list of concerns at the moment, If Anya and the others hadn't just left, but had instead been scooped up by the Trofts, he needed to know that. Right now, with his captors feeling pleased and confident at their successful mission, would be the time they were mostly likely to be loose-tongued about such things. [My location, how did you find it?] he asked.

[Your clothing, it was recognized,] the lead Troft said. [Its origin, the humans in the village identified it to us.]

Merrick grimaced. Alexis Turner. Woolmaster, indeed, and obviously well-known among the people of Svipall. That possibility had never even occurred to him.

The question was, why hadn't it occurred to Ludolf? Or had it?

[Questions, it is not your place to ask them,] the Troft continued severely. [Your hands, you will place them on top of your head.]

Let them take you, Merrick reminded himself firmly. *Look for a way out later.* He settled his palms on the top of his head—

And without warning, the Troft who had spoken crumpled to the ground.

He'd barely started to fall when the soldier beside him also began to collapse. The third had just enough time to swivel his head around before his own knees buckled and he dropped. The fourth had enough time to swivel his head and to jerk reflexively to the side.

Which is why only then, with the fourth Troft's movement, did Merrick see a small but brilliant flash of light angle up beneath the back of his head.

A burst from Kjoic's laser.

The last of the soldiers hit the ground, and for a long moment Merrick and Kjoic stared across the bodies at each other. Kjoic broke the silence first. [An enemy agent, you are indeed one,] he said almost conversationally. [That truth, I suspected it from the start. Proof, I did not have it.]

With an effort, Merrick found his own voice. [The masters, what has happened to them?] he asked. If he feigned ignorance and stupidity, maybe Kjoic could be persuaded to rethink the idea that Merrick was more than he seemed.

But no. [A gap, there is one in all Drim'hco'plai demesne battle helmets,] Kjoic said, lifting his laser slightly. [A fatal flaw, it can sometimes be.]

Merrick shook his head, his mind still reeling. So Kjoic was freely and openly admitting that he murdered the soldiers.

But to what end? Was he trying to frame Merrick for the killings? What in the Worlds could that gain him? [Understanding, I do not have it,] he said.

Kjoic's membranes fluttered. "Of course you understand," he said in smooth, flawless Anglic. "You just refuse to believe."

Merrick felt his mouth drop open. [Understanding, I do not have it,] he repeated, just to have something to say.

"It's quite simple," Kjoic said. "You're an enemy agent." He gestured toward himself with his laser. "So am I."

He slid his laser back into its holster. "Come. We must be away from this place."

With an effort, Merrick forced his head to stop spinning. The surprises were coming way too fast. "And once we've done that?" he managed.

Kjoic's arm membranes fluttered. "Then," he said, "you and I shall have a talk."

For a minute after Jody finished her story the room was silent. "Interesting," Meekan said thoughtfully. "Your thoughts, Commander?"

"Tamu's behavior was certainly marginal," Kusari

said. "Whether or not he exceeded his authority or standing orders will be for an Enquiry Board to decide. Of course," he added, fixing Jody with a dark look, "so far we have just her side of the story."

"Agreed," Meekan said. "You said Lieutenant Commander Tamu was still on Caelian?"

"Yes," Jody said. "We do have the two Marines from the gunbays here, though. Now that this is out in the open, I expect Shahni Omnathi will be willing to allow you to speak with them."

"Before or after he flays you alive?" Kusari asked pointedly.

Jody winced. She'd known Omnathi wouldn't be happy with her unilateral action. But up to now she hadn't thought in terms of flaying. Perhaps she ought to. "That depends on you," she said. "Or, rather, on Captain Moreau. You asked earlier what I wanted in exchange for this information."

Meekan gave her a knowing smile. "And that is . . . ?"

Jody braced herself. "At the end of the Troft invasion of Qasama, my brother Merrick disappeared. We believe he was taken by some unknown group of Trofts to an unknown location. I want to take the *Squire* and go find him."

Once again, the two officers exchanged looks. "I presume you're not simply planning to go star to star until the heat death of the universe," Meekan said.

"Not at all, Lieutenant," Kusari said thoughtfully. "You'll note she said *find*, not *look for*. I'd surmise she already knows where he is."

"I do," Jody said. "Or at least, I have a starting point. The Drim ship the Qasamans captured to take us to Caelian had been capturing spine leopards from the Qasaman forest, for purposes we still don't know. That ship had a course history in its computer that gave us its previous location."

"And since you also don't know the purpose of your brother's kidnapping, you're assuming the two are related?" Kusari asked.

Put into words that way, she had to admit, it *did* seem a little far-fetched. "I know it's a long shot," she conceded. "But Merrick's been missing for over a month and a half. If he's still alive—" She broke off. "I know you understand the concept of not leaving a comrade behind," she said, forcing the emotion out of her voice. "If there's even a chance he's still alive, I have to go after him."

"In a Dominion of Man ship," Kusari said.

"Technically, it's a Qasaman ship now," Jody countered. "As such, I don't really need your permission to take it. All I want is some assurance that Captain Moreau won't blow us out of the sky."

"And whether his restraint will depend on whether or not a pair of his officers are aboard?" Meekan asked pointedly.

Jody looked him straight in the eye. "We did in fact have a discussion about whether or not we should consider taking hostages as a last resort," she said. "We decided that wasn't a path we wanted to take. If we don't get the captain's permission, we'll just take the *Squire* and hope we can get out of range before he can shoot us down."

Meekan shook his head. "I'm sorry, Ms. Broom," he said. "But the captain could never and *would* never authorize such a thing. The political ramifications alone would be devastating to him and to his command."

Jody felt her throat tighten. She'd been afraid that that would be their response.

"Which is why," Meekan continued, "I'll have to authorize it instead."

Kusari's mouth dropped open. "*What*?" he demanded.

"The captain can't do this, sir," Meekan told him calmly. "Neither can you, for the same reasons. But I'm not as satisfying a target for anyone's political revenge."

"Never mind the politics," Kusari growled. "What about the military aspects? Turning over Fleet equipment to non-Fleet personnel puts you squarely into court-martial territory."

"As Ms. Broom has already pointed out, the *Squire* is no longer technically Fleet property," Meekan said. "As to the rest, I'm willing to take the risk." He smiled tightly at Jody. "As she said, sir: no one left behind."

His eyes narrowed. "Besides, there's another factor in play here, a factor which has only just come to light. Tell me, Ms. Broom, have you ever heard of a demesne called the Kriel'laa'misar?"

Jody searched her memory. "I don't think so. Where are they located?"

"We don't know," Meekan said. "But a few days ago some of their ships tried very hard to capture both the *Hermes* and the *Dorian.*"

Jody frowned as the key word registered. "*Capture*? Not *destroy*?"

Meekan nodded. "Exactly."

"Wait a minute," Kusari said, frowning. "I thought Filho's report said the ships didn't carry any ID markings."

"They didn't have any *visible* markings," Meekan

said. "But it turns out the markings had simply been covered over. Hastily, too, Filho said, like ships that hadn't originally been intended for such a mission."

"But which had been sent out at the last minute to hunt for Dominion ships when those ships suddenly appeared at Aventine?" Jody suggested.

"Exactly," Meekan said. "We're wondering why they might be looking for humans from the Dominion; and now, you tell us someone has likewise captured a human from the Cobra Worlds. Another coincidence?"

Jody felt a chill run up her back. She'd been trying mightily to figure out who would have taken Merrick, and for what purpose. The possibility that his disappearance might be tied to the Dominion's war with the Trofts had never occurred to her. "So you're thinking that if I find Merrick, we might be able to figure out what else is going on?"

"It's a possibility, anyway." Meekan turned to Kusari. "Sir?"

Kusari huffed out a breath. "I can't condone this," he said, his voice dark. "It's a violation of standing orders, not to mention borderline treason."

"Yes, sir." Meekan seemed to brace himself and twitched his eyelid. "Lieutenant Meekan to Tactical. A spaceship will be leaving Qasama within the next hour. By my authorization, under Captain Moreau's name, the ship will be allowed to depart unhindered."

There was a moment of silence, presumably as he received an acknowledgment, and he again twitched his eyelid. "Ms. Broom, you have one hour to get the *Squire* ready to fly. I hope that will be sufficient."

"It will," Jody assured him, standing up. "Thank you, Lieutenant."

"One more thing," Meekan said. "Obviously, the *Dorian*'s not going anywhere until our injured crewmen are recovered enough to return to the ship. But before you leave Qasama, I want a copy of the course history you mentioned."

"Of course," Jody said. "I don't have it on me, but if you'll give me a data connection I can send you a copy."

"Just make a copy and leave it under my name at the hospital admission desk," Meekan said. "We don't want a data trail that someone might follow later."

Jody winced. "Understood," she said. "Again, thank you."

"Thank us by finding your brother," Kusari said heavily. "And if you have a spare minute or two, see if you can also find out who the Kriel'laa'misar are, where they are, and what the hell they want with our people."

"I will, sir," Jody promised grimly. "All of it."

The aircar the four Trofts had arrived in was tucked away in a small clearing just beyond Alexis's bersarkis border. Kjoic stopped at the vehicle long enough to grab a laser rifle and a pair of survival packs, then led the way back into the forest. The limp the Troft had presented during the last two days of their journey, Merrick noted distantly, was gone without a trace. Apparently, the injury had healed during Merrick's own convalescence.

If, in fact, it had ever been more than a ruse to begin with.

Finally, two kilometers from the ranch, Kjoic called a halt. "I presume you have many questions," he said as he seated himself on a partially decomposed stump. "Those questions, you may ask them."

"Okay," Merrick said, keying his infrareds as he sat down on a log facing the other. Troft facial blood flow didn't reflect emotional changes nearly as much as it did in humans, but the aliens' radiator membranes should more than make up for it. "Let's start with what happened on the crashed ship. You said there was a fight, and that you hid from it. I didn't think about it at the time, but the fact that the locals weren't still hunting for you implied that they thought they'd gotten everyone, which implies in turn that they didn't know you were even there. You were a stowaway, weren't you?"

Kjoic's membranes fluttered, and Merrick's opticals spotted the brief surge of heat flow there. "Very good," the Troft said. "Unfortunately, I was discovered as we approached Muninn."

"And so you killed all of them?"

"Yes," Kjoic said simply. "It was necessary."

Merrick shivered. The very casualness of that admission, combined with the businesslike way he'd dealt with the four back at Alexis's house, clearly showed that he was no stranger to violence. "So who are you? What's on Muninn that's worth killing for?"

Kjoic waved a hand back toward Svipall. "You've already seen it," he said. "The testing and the chemical studies taking place in Svipall could be vital to the fortunes of the war."

"You're a bit behind the times," Merrick said. "The war's over."

"Not the war against the unimportant human worlds at this side of the Assemblage," Kjoic said, a hint of contempt in his voice. "That action was ill-advised and pointless. I speak of the war currently being waged against the Dominion of Man."

Merrick felt his throat tighten. So there *was* a new war on the far side of the Troft Assemblage. He and his mother had speculated about that at the very beginning of the Qasaman invasion, but at the time it had been pure guesswork. Now, it was confirmed. "I don't know anything about that," he said.

"Perhaps," Kjoic said, eyeing him closely, his membranes fluttering a bit more. "Perhaps not. But I will not pry into your origin or the world you call home. What is important is that we both seek information on the chemical that the Drim'hco'plai are creating."

"I don't know anything about that, either," Merrick said.

"You know more than you say," Kjoic countered. "Perhaps more than you realize. Allow me to tell what *I* know. The Drim'hco'plai were one of the demesnes who sought to subdue and conquer the nearby human worlds. They now claim to have created a weapon that will permit final Troft victory in the war against the Dominion. This—" he gestured again toward Svipall "—is where I believe they have created it."

"Did they say how it's supposed to work?"

"They claim it will turn humans against each other," Kjoic said. "Creating treason and betrayal in the very midst of the human forces."

"Very poetic," Merrick said. "Also a little far-fetched."

"I agree," Kjoic agreed. "But the question is not whether the concept seems likely. The question is whether it is, in fact, true."

"Yes," Merrick murmured. On the face of it, the whole thing was ridiculous.

And yet . . .

He'd seen the power of the bersark plant. He'd seen

the strength and near-invulnerability of the jormungand snakes. He'd seen at least one example—bersarkis—of the Muninn natives taking the exotic natural chemicals they were living among and turning them into equally exotic drugs.

And he'd seen Dyre, who'd been fully aware that protecting Merrick was also protecting his betrothed Anya, calmly and loudly betray him to the Trofts.

Was that what Red Patch was? Some sort of loyalty-conditioning drug?

"The razorarms," he murmured.

"Pardon?" Kjoic asked.

"I was just thinking about the razorarms of Qasama," Merrick said slowly, trying to sort out the odd thought that had suddenly jumped across his mind. "Big predators with symbiotic links to birds called mojos. The mojos are mildly telepathic and act as controllers for the razorarms' behavior, guiding them toward prey and away from danger. All through the invasion the Drims were snatching razorarms from the human areas, despite the fact that the Qasamans routinely shot down their collector aircraft. We could never figure out why the Trofts were risking that kind of trouble, especially when the whole planet was full of the things for the taking."

"And you now know the reason?"

"Maybe," Merrick said. "The mojos adjust the razorarms' thinking—what there is of it—as they modify their behavior. Maybe the Drim were taking razorarms from both settled and unsettled regions in hopes of finding differences in their brain chemistry."

"Searching for how and where the conditioning has taken place," Kjoic said thoughtfully. "Interesting.

Such large and dangerous predators, are they also on the human world of Caelian?"

"No razorarms, but lots of other nasties," Merrick said. "Were the Drims taking animals from there, too?"

"That world was certainly invaded," Kjoic said. "Whether they had specific target creatures in mind, or were simply seeking possibilities, I have no knowledge. But this is indeed a promising beginning to our enquiries." He stood up. "Let us add more distance from our common enemy while we decide our next course of action."

"I have a question," Merrick said, not moving from his own seat. "I'm a human. My reason for wanting to stop the Drims is obvious. What about you?"

Kjoic's membranes stretched out for a moment, then sagged again. "I am an agent of the Kriel'laa'misar demesne," he said. "It is my demesne-lord to whom the Drim'hco'plai are endeavoring to sell this weapon."

Merrick blinked. "Wait a minute. They're giving it to *you*? Then why in the Worlds are you even here?"

"Is it not obvious?" Kjoic asked. "The Drim'hco'plai are asking a large sum of money for their weapon. Is it not well worth our time and effort to steal it instead?"

Merrick stared at him. The rivalry between Troft demesnes was legendary; but for one ally in the midst of a war to straight-up steal valuable technology from another was insane.

But at the same time it had the ring of truth to it. "So when you suggest we work together, you mean only until we have the weapon."

The membranes flared. "The truth, you speak it," Kjoic conceded. "But consider that neither of us is likely to achieve the goal alone."

"So we hold off trying to kill each other until we have the drug?"

"It may not come to killing," Kjoic said. "But it will certainly come to victory for one and defeat for the other." He cocked his head in a very human gesture. "Have we an alliance?"

It was crazy, Merrick knew. Crazy, and with a very good chance of getting him killed.

But Kjoic was right. Merrick couldn't do this on his own. He needed allies and assistance, and with Anya and Ludolf vanished into the night, Kjoic was the only ally he had. "Common goal," he said.

"Common goal," Kjoic agreed. "Now, let us be off."

"You have a destination in mind?" Merrick said, standing up.

"I do." The Troft slung the laser rifle over his shoulder, maneuvering it carefully around the radiator membrane there. Then, with only a slight hesitation, he drew his smaller laser from its holster and tossed it, grip-first, to Merrick. "You may need this. Follow, and be silent."

He turned and set off again, heading away from Svipall. Shoving the laser into his belt, Merrick followed.

Victory for one, Kjoic had said. *Defeat for another*.

Kjoic was a special agent, probably trained in espionage, certainly trained in violence. Merrick wasn't trained in either.

But he was a Cobra.

Only Kjoic didn't know that.

Victory for one. Defeat for another.

This was, Merrick had already realized, going to be dangerous.

It was also going to be very interesting.

CHAPTER TWENTY-FOUR

Kemp and Smitty were waiting at the *Squire* when Jody arrived. So, to Jody's surprise, was Rashida Vil.

"What are you doing here?" she asked, giving the woman a quick hug. "Not that I'm not delighted to see you. But Smitty said you were in Sollas."

"You didn't think I would drop all other matters and rush to my friends at their need?" Rashida asked with a tight smile. "Smitty called and said we would be leaving tonight." She looked at him. "And though I believe him completely capable of flying this craft, it is always wise to have a second pilot."

"Absolutely," Smitty agreed. "Just so long as it's clear that *I'm* the second pilot and *you're* the first. I'm more worried about you getting flak from Omnathi or the other Shahni for cutting out on them."

"There is no such danger," Rashida assured him. "My task was complete. And remember, Shahni Omnathi has already given us permission to take the *Squire* and leave."

"Let's hope the *Dorian* is also still on board with that," Kemp said grimly. "I presume we're not going to be overly blatant about our departure?"

"We're going to be blatant like field mice are blatant," Jody confirmed. "We'll wait until the *Dorian* is over the horizon, then scurry out along a course that keeps us out of their sight as long as possible." She looked at Rashida. "I presume you can set up something like that."

Rashida nodded. "Of course."

"Then let's do it," Kemp said. "Smitty's got the systems up and running. Time to blow this fruit stand."

"Right," Jody said.

And hope that Captain Moreau hadn't spotted Lieutenant Meekan's authorization and rescinded it. If he had, this was going to be a very short and very unpleasant flight.

"There," Garrett said, pointing at the display.

"I see it," Barrington said, gazing at the departing *Squire* with a mix of anticipation, sadness, and guilt.

Jody Broom wasn't going to find her brother. That much he was certain of. The odds were overwhelming that Merrick Broom had died on Qasama, probably out in the forest where no one would likely ever find his body. For Jody, this was a fool's errand, with nothing but heartache and loss waiting at the end.

And, if she lived through it, probably the feeling that came of deliberately been used.

Meekan had played his hand perfectly. He had pretended to take the decision out of Barrington's hands in the midst of Kusari's disapproval, even as Barrington and Garrett monitored and guided the entire conversation through the data stream. So caught up in her victory had Jody been, in fact, that she'd never even wondered why no backups had charged in on them after she and her Cobra friends had neutralized Kusari's guard.

And now, there they were. Heading off as quickly and unobtrusively as they could, no doubt half expecting the *Dorian* to open fire and blow them out of the sky.

No, they wouldn't find Jody's brother. What they *would* do was bring a sudden and unexpected Dominion presence to the attention of a brand-new group of Trofts. Possibly this mysterious Kriel'laa'misar demesne; possibly someone else entirely.

But who exactly they found didn't really matter. Commodore Santores's orders were to draw out the Trofts currently at war with the Dominion, to make noise and fury and to lure them into an ambush, either at the Cobra Worlds or at Qasama. Jody and her friends were simply doing their part toward that end.

Barrington hoped she would survive the trials ahead. He really did. She was much too young to die such a bitter death, especially when she wouldn't even know how her death would serve all of humanity.

But whether she lived or died wasn't in his power to decide. Until his men were all healed and safely back aboard, the *Dorian* would be unable to follow to the coordinates she'd given them.

Maybe not even then. Barrington had other responsibilities, not the least of which was to persuade the Qasamans to let Santores make them into the lure that he needed.

And if that task proved easier than expected, there was still Aventine to worry about. Things back there hadn't been going very smoothly when the *Dorian* left, and the more recent news that the *Hermes* had brought had been even less encouraging. Once Barrington got things rolling on Qasama, he should probably take the *Dorian* and head back to the Cobra Worlds.

Still, while Aventine was a concern, it was probably not a genuine worry. Santores was in command there, and the commodore was quite capable of diplomacy and the soothing of ruffled feathers. There was nothing the Cobra Worlds could throw at him that he couldn't handle.

Paul looked across the command station at Commodore Santores. Commodore Santores looked back, and for a long moment the two men held that pose. Then, slowly, Santores seemed to come back to life. "Would you please repeat that, Governor Uy?" he said toward his microphone.

"If you feel it necessary," Uy's voice came from the station's speaker. Not the entire speaker system, Paul noted absently, where his words would be out the open for the entire CoNCH to hear. Santores had opened this communication with Caelian with the intention of keeping the discussion private, at least in the initial stages.

He was, Paul thought, probably very glad he had.

"And I quote," Uy said. "After due consideration of the proper direction of Caelian's future, taking into account the actions of Lieutenant Commander Tamu and the crew of the *Squire*, and further taking into account the attitude of other world governments toward us—" he paused, possibly for dramatic purposes, more likely for a breath "—the government of Caelian has voted unanimously to terminate our ties to the Cobra

Worlds and the Dominion of Man and to unite instead with the people and government of Qasama. Will you require a third reading, Commodore Santores?"

"No, thank you," Santores said, his face rigid, his eyes starting to flash fire. "I must inform you, Governor, that your words and declaration amount to treason against the Dominion of Man. In such cases, there are specific protocols that must be followed."

"I'm sure you'll do whatever your orders require," Uy said. "Just be certain that they're *only* what your orders require."

"That sounds rather like a threat, Governor."

"If you think a planet of five thousand people can be a serious threat, Commodore, the Dominion is in worse shape than I thought," Uy said, a bit dryly. "Regardless, there's no need to respond now. I can wait to hear your comments once you've had time to examine your orders and protocols. And as I stated earlier, you're more than welcome to come down in person for a face-to-face discussion."

"Thank you, Governor," Santores said stiffly. "I'll consider it. *Megalith* out." He jabbed a finger at the control, and the indicator light went out.

For a long moment he stared at the main display across the room. Then, abruptly, he turned to Paul. "Well?" he demanded.

"Well, what?" Paul said. "The Caelians have always been a stubborn lot. They've also always felt that they were ignored, disliked, or marginalized. Obviously, something has pushed them past the breaking point."

"But *Qasama*?"

Paul shrugged, a slightly awkward gesture now that his servos no longer functioned. "A small group of

Qasamans came to their aid during the Troft invasion. Uy returned the favor by sending Isis to Qasama, which ultimately brought the war to an end. I'd say both worlds have finally found the respect and under- standing that neither of them has ever had before."

Santores snorted. "He can't possibly believe this will work."

"I'd say that depends largely on you," Paul said. "What *are* you going to say to him?"

Santores scowled back at the display. "I don't know," he said, the fire fading from his eyes. "I told him there were protocols for this. In fact, there aren't. Nothing I've ever read, nothing I've ever explored in a war-game session, has ever touched even remotely on this situation. I'm going to have to research my options. Carefully, and *very* thoroughly."

"And until you have a plan?" Paul asked. "Do we return to Aventine?"

"No," Santores said flatly. "The Dominion needs to maintain a presence here. If we're lucky, Uy and his people will realize they can't possibly win and take a long step backward."

Paul nodded. He could hope that, too. But he didn't expect it to happen. He didn't know the Caelians all that well; but from what he *had* seen, he knew they didn't draw lines in the sand casually. "What about Aventine?" he asked.

"What about it?"

"It's having some serious drama of its own," Paul reminded him. "I'd feel better if you checked back on it while you sort out the Dominion response to Caelian. It's not like Uy or those five thousand people are going anywhere."

"We stay," Santores said firmly. "And don't worry about Aventine. Captain Lij Tulu is more than capable of handling matters there."

The news report came in while Lorne, Werle, and de Portola were still driving toward Capitalia. "As of oh-one-hundred-hours this morning," the emotionless voice came over the car's speakers, "the planet of Aventine is hereby declared to be under martial law. Dominion forces under the direction of Captain Lij Tulu are moving to secure all government offices, strongpoints, and vital services. Citizens are instructed to remain calm and listen for official news and information. Questions by government officials should be directed to the Dome in Capitalia."

Werle turned off the radio and turned to Lorne. "Well," he said. "What do you think of that?"

Lorne took a deep breath. "I think," he said, "that the war has now begun.

"I also think the Dominion is going to be very, *very* sorry they started it."

IF YOU LIKE...
YOU SHOULD TRY...

DAVID DRAKE
David Weber
Tony Daniel
John Lambshead

DAVID WEBER
John Ringo
Timothy Zahn
Linda Evans
Jane Lindskold
Sarah A. Hoyt

JOHN RINGO
Michael Z. Williamson
Tom Kratman
Larry Correia
Mike Kupari

ANNE MCCAFFREY
Mercedes Lackey
Lois McMaster Bujold
Liaden Universe® by Sharon Lee & Steve Miller
Sarah A. Hoyt
Mike Kupari

MERCEDES LACKEY
Wen Spencer
Andre Norton
James H. Schmitz

LARRY NIVEN
Tony Daniel
James P. Hogan
Travis S. Taylor
Brad Torgersen

ROBERT A. HEINLEIN
Jerry Pournelle
Lois McMaster Bujold
Michael Z. Williamson

HEINLEIN'S "JUVENILES"
Rats, Bats & Vats series by Eric Flint & Dave Freer
Brendan DuBois' *Dark Victory*
David Weber & Jane Lindskold's Star Kingdom
Series
Dean Ing's *It's Up to Charlie Hardin*
David Drake & Jim Kjelgaard's *The Hunter Returns*

HORATIO HORNBLOWER OR PATRICK O'BRIAN
David Weber's Honor Harrington series
David Drake's RCN series
Alex Stewart's *Shooting the Rift*

HARRY POTTER
Mercedes Lackey's Urban Fantasy series

JIM BUTCHER
Larry Correia's The Grimnoir Chronicles
John Lambshead's *Wolf in Shadow*

TECHNOTHRILLERS
Larry Correia & Mike Kupari's Dead Six Series
Robert Conroy's *Stormfront*
Eric Stone's *Unforgettable*
Tom Kratman's Countdown Series

THE LORD OF THE RINGS
Elizabeth Moon's *The Deed of Paksenarrion*
Shattered Shields ed. by Schmidt and Brozek
P.C. Hodgell
Ryk E. Spoor's Phoenix Rising series

A GAME OF THRONES
Larry Correia's *Son of the Black Sword*
David Weber's fantasy novels
Sonia Orin Lyris' *The Seer*

H.P. LOVECRAFT
Larry Correia's Monster Hunter series
P.C. Hodgell's Kencyrath series
John Ringo's Special Circumstances Series

ZOMBIES
John Ringo's Black Tide Rising Series
Wm. Mark Simmons

GEORGETTE HEYER
Lois McMaster Bujold
Catherine Asaro
Liaden Universe® by Sharon Lee & Steve Miller
Dave Freer

DOCTOR WHO
Steve White's TRA Series
Michael Z. Williamson's *A Long Time Until Now*

HARD SCIENCE FICTION
Ben Bova
Les Johnson
Charles E. Gannon
Eric Flint & Ryk E. Spoor's Boundary Series
Mission: Tomorrow ed. by Bryan Thomas Schmidt

GREEK MYTHOLOGY
Pyramid Scheme by Eric Flint & Dave Freer
Forge of the Titans by Steve White
Blood of the Heroes by Steve White

NORSE MYTHOLOGY
Northworld Trilogy by David Drake
Pyramid Power by Eric Flint & Dave Freer

URBAN FANTASY
Mercedes Lackey's SERRAted Edge Series
Larry Correia's Monster Hunter International
Series
Sarah A. Hoyt's Shifter Series
Sharon Lee's Carousel Series
David B. Coe's Case Files of Justis Fearsson
The Wild Side ed. by Mark L. Van Name

DINOSAURS
David Drake's *Dinosaurs & a Dirigible*
David Drake & Tony Daniel's *The Heretic* and *The
Savior*

HISTORY AND ALTERNATE HISTORY
Eric Flint's Ring of Fire Series
David Drake & Eric Flint's Belisarius Series
Robert Conroy
Harry Turtledove

HUMOR
Esther Friesner's *Chicks 'n Chaimail*
Rick Cook
Spider Robinson
Wm. Mark Simmons
Jody Lynn Nye

VAMPIRES & WEREWOLVES
Larry Correia
Wm. Mark Simmons
Ryk E. Spoor's *Paradigm's Lost*

WEBCOMICS
Sluggy Freelance... John Ringo's Posleen War Series
Schlock Mercenary...John Ringo's Troy Rising Series

NONFICTION
Hank Reinhardt
The Science Behind The Secret *by Travis Taylor*
Alien Invasion by Travis Taylor & Bob Boan
Going Interstellar ed. By Les Johnson